The Blood Countess

The Blood Countess

Annouchka Bayley

Copyright © 2024 Annouchka Bayley

The moral right of the author has been asserted.

Apart from any fair dealing for the purposes of research or private study, or criticism or review, as permitted under the Copyright, Designs and Patents Act 1988, this publication may only be reproduced, stored or transmitted, in any form or by any means, with the prior permission in writing of the publishers, or in the case of reprographic reproduction in accordance with the terms of licences issued by the Copyright Licensing Agency. Enquiries concerning reproduction outside those terms should be sent to the publishers.

This is a work of fiction. Names, characters, businesses, places, events and incidents are either the products of the author's imagination or used in a fictitious manner. Any resemblance to actual persons, living or dead, or actual events is purely coincidental.

Troubador
Unit E2 Airfield Business Park,
Harrison Road, Market Harborough,
Leicestershire. LE16 7UL
Tel: 0116 2792299
Email: books@troubador.co.uk
Web: www.troubador.co.uk

ISBN 9781805142102

British Library Cataloguing in Publication Data.
A catalogue record for this book is available from the British Library.

Printed and bound in Great Britain by 4edge Limited
Typeset in 11pt Minion Pro by Troubador Publishing Ltd, Leicester, UK

Matador is an imprint of Troubador Publishing Ltd

For all the Januses in all the worlds...

Cast of Characters

Renaissance

Elizabet Bathory: Countess of Hungary. Married to Francis Nadasdy. *A photon (particle)**

Francis Nadasdy: Count of Hungary. Married to Elizabet Bathory. Also known as the Black Bey. *A virtual particle**. Sometimes: *Hawking Radiation**

George Thurzo: Count of Hungary. Married to Elizabet Thurzo. *Matter**

Elizabet Thurzo: Countess of Hungary. Married to George Thurzo. *Dark matter**

Janus: a Turkish janissary (real name unknown)

Erzi: peasant witch at Cachtice

Ursula Nadasdy: Francis Nadasdy's mother

John (also known as Stephen Ironhead): adopted son of Elizabet Bathory and Francis Nadasdy

Anna Darvulia: servant to Elizabet Bathory

Dorothea: servant to Francis Nadasdy

Michael: son of Elizabet Bathory and George Thurzo (surname unknown)

Anastasia Nadasdy: Elizabet Bathory and Francis Nadasdy's daughter

Paul Nadasdy: Elizabet Bathory and Francis Nadasdy's daughter

Beata: servant of Emperor Rudolph II. *Reflection**

Emperor Rudolph II: Emperor of the Western World

Maria Christina: niece of Rudolph II

Giorgio Basta: Count of Huszt, general and diplomat of the Holy Roman Empire

Khunrath: Esoteric scholar, servant to Emperor Rudolph II

Stephen Bocksai: Prince of Erdely, cousin of Elizabet Bathory

Andrew Bathory: cousin of Elizabet Bathory, short-lived king of Erdely

Sigismund Bathory: cousin of Elizabet Bathory, short-lived king of Erdely

Balthazar Bathory: cousin of Elizabet Bathory

Stephen Bathory, king of Poland: uncle of Elizabet Bathory

Pastor Megyery: Priest at Cachtice Castle

Ursula: Szekely girl (from a deposed noble family)

Marta: Szekely girl (from a deposed noble family)

Fabbri Brothers: Italian 'journeymen' printers. Jewish conversos.

Present Day

Vera: writer of Bathory's story, scholar. *Photon (wave)**. Sometimes, *Three Body Problem**

Lucretia: scholar, friend of Vera, Pandora

Mark: scholar, Vera's lover. *Three Body Problem**

Laura: student, Mark's lover. *Three Body Problem**

The professor: scholar, Vera's boss. Sometimes: *matter**

Rachel: scholar, the professor's wife. Sometimes: *dark matter**

Ollie: scholar, friend of the professor (surname unknown)

* Indicates scientific principles upon which the characters are loosely based. Therefore, you can watch how the characters with these associated principles move, act and interact with each other from both human and nonhuman perspectives.

Prologue

And the lady has committed a terrible crime against the female blood. Those who stand accused of complicity have confirmed their statements and even now have added darker details of the terrible crimes committed by her ladyship, the widow Nadasdy, born Erzabet Bathory, proving beyond doubt the guilt of all the accused, which surpasses the imagination in the many murders, slaughter and tortures undertaken by the Countess Bathory. Be assured that Erzabet Bathory has engaged in cruelty of all kinds. She is nothing short of Evil itself. And as these most serious crimes should be matched by the severest punishments, we have decreed she be walled up forever in her castle to be forgotten by history...

(Translation of the original letter sent from the Lord Palatine, 7th January 1611)

They called me the hand of the devil. Scourge. Straight out of the thin fold that keeps hell and earth apart. Part woman, part monster. A descendant of the Son of the Dragon, Vlad, the Prince of Darkness, who drank human blood and defied the pull of the earth so he could spit into God's own heaven. They told stories of my depravity. How I lured young women to me, promising them my protection, my favour, a safe place behind my castle walls, whilst Turks, Tartars and Hadjuks ran across Hungary, wild as winter wolves, watching, waiting for human blood.

In my own time, they stripped me of my lands, my influence, my power, and lined their pockets with my wealth – *my* fortune. In your time, they brought out books and moving images about me that describe the horrors I am meant to have inflicted on these innocents, these unprotected girls; calling me all sorts of strange and damnable titles; Elizabet Bathory: torturer, killer, psychopath. Elizabet Bathory: the Blood Countess.

But this isn't their story. It's mine.

Chapter One

What struck me most wasn't the shouting and hissing that filled the courtyard. It was the moment a young woman reached down to cover her daughter's eyes with her hand as I was led past, as if to erase me. 'Led' isn't the right word. Led is the word I use to remember it. It lessens the wound. It makes it all easier. I had been bound around my waist and was being dragged by a group of blacksmiths to my trial. The rope they'd used to bind me with was fraying and smelt like ashes and dust.

The men pulled at it, making my body jerk and twist involuntarily as if I were possessed under the ice sky. A crowd had gathered in the square. They cursed and heaved and hissed together; one stone mouth that vibrated with damnation to hell. "Blood Countess!" The murderer who bathed in the blood of her victims to keep herself looking so young. "Bathory the Monster!" "Bathory the witch!"

Witch and monster were words I had become used to a long time ago. They were words simpler to shout across a courtyard than 'revolutionary' or 'radical'. After all, a woman could be neither of those. Not in my time. And certainly not in the Eastern

Empire. I would never be known for what I really was. Today, I would die – not as a woman but as a creature; a thing that was no longer human and that had certainly never been divine.

I was being sentenced by the noblemen who ruled Hungary at the command of our new Holy Roman Emperor. A smudge. A flick. And ink on the page spelled out my demise. I would be walled up in my tower. What's done is done. They were eager to get it all over with so they could start spending my money, their fragile temperaments torn about by our northern winds, all squinting eyes and gooseflesh.

And the lady's lands and wealth shall be forfeit.

I'd seen many things in my lifetime, but nothing could have prepared me for what had happened outside my window those past few weeks. All the blood. All the pleas for mercy that were abandoned when the tongues, hands and fingers of my serving women had been severed from their bodies. Then they had come up to my tower and tied my wrists in front of me as I lay frozen and compliant by the sight of all the blood. Such human acts of violence are hard to rub out. They stick fast as flies in honey. They stick like blood. I blink. *Stay with it all. Don't slide away into nothing.* I say this to myself, but I soon realise I'm saying it to you. I'm saying it to you, dear reader, because you are the only one who can listen. In the pages; inside the ink. Your memory. Your beating heart. *You.*

If they heard me talking to you, they would say I was in communion with the devil, and you would be the thing cast out – flung far from here and sent back to where you hailed from. So, I cast this so-called spell quietly. I didn't even move my lips. My fingertips touched each other, pointing downwards towards the ground in the reverse of prayer. If you had been able to look at my shadow, it would appear black and long and more than human. But if you dared to look at my body, the real one, the one that first took shape in the world in the year of our Lord 1560, you would simply see an old woman, hair greying, tied up and silent.

I'd always seen my end and I knew it would come violently. The future lived close inside my bones. It was tightly packed inside my body. Dormant. Even as a child, I knew it would uncoil its stories as soon as I learnt how to listen to it. Even you, your world, the way you angle your head now to read, your life would move and ripple out through mine – through my story, and even though we would never meet, we would *hear* each other echoing in all the overlooked places that make up a life.

Standing in the square, I thought back to when I first arrived here as a child. I saw the smaller, less nimble hand that still lived inside the one before me here, now. *One day, I'll hear all the stories that have made up my body, all the stories past and all the stories to come, the secrets of all my mothers since the beginning of time.* And as I grew older, I did indeed start to hear them. I honed this talent, learning to hear not only stories past but the speeds and sounds of the future, *'travelling'* between worlds.

And yet so very little of this future was actually much different from my own reality. We still lived the same stories over and over. Bound and powerless, just as I was now. Only your ropes would be made out of time, wrapping round you again and again, and I would still be Bathory the Monster until you heard my story through yours and found it sounded just a tiny bit *different this time*.

I slowed my breathing just enough to hear my heart beat out its rhythms. I matched each one with a silent prayer: *let me glimpse, just one last time, the secret world that lives inside ours.* The courtyard fell away. I slid between its vibrations into a different kind of waking, leaving the dark and violent dream that was unfolding before me. The courtyard filled up with golden light and the braying of otherworldly horses – half here, half vanished, their hooves falling in and out of time, stepping between here and *elsewhere*. I climbed on one of their backs, even though my body remained bound in the square, and rode fast until I saw us both flatten and lengthen, becoming thin as watery ink spilling on the page of time. *Dear reader, do not believe everything they tell you about history.*

The gang of blacksmiths that had been instructed by our new Lord Palatine to drag me to the square noticed my reverie, and one didn't slap but punched me hard in the face whilst invoking the name of God, calling me away from my 'devil'. The punch brought me back to the world of men – to *this world*, the one I was soon to exit forever. I was brought to a sudden stop, relieved that I was no longer being tugged about like a fallen doll in the mouths of dogs. The man with the eager fist roared triumphantly and the gang shouted and whinnied in response. They were more animals than men, though they paraded around like small gods today.

The surface of the square shimmered for a moment in a burst of sun, and the crowd fell quiet as the shadow of a man emerged. He didn't push or even brush a soul out of the way; not a single one of them. They moved around *him*, closing the gaps he made as quickly as he passed. He paused before sitting down on a wooden chair that had been brought out for this strange and very public sentencing, surveying us all. He was dressed in a black tunic that held waves of pearls that fell about its surface. They were foam on a nighttime sea, throwing patterns rhythmically across the shifts of his body. Hypnotic. Dark. And I, his captured prize – Elizabet Bathory, *the Blood Countess.*

It's one thing to know you're going to die. It's another to actually walk towards it. To see it all around you. The blood. The bitterness. I'd have never died peacefully in my sleep. But to see death in the eye of another – in the kind of look I was seeing *right now* in his eyes, dear reader – that's something very different. And although the inevitability of it had passed from God's hands to a man's, still, it lost none of its power.

"...And the lady's crimes are many, too many and too horrible to doubt."

I steadied myself. *Here we go.*

Three women were brought to stand in front of me, called upon to point and accuse me – *monster!* – in the name of the Holy Roman Emperor. Their clothes were covered in blood from slow wounds. The stains emerged from the inside out like secrets that have tried so hard to remain hidden. Anna, my oldest and most trusted friend, stood directly opposite me. I remembered the first time she had called me a *talto*, which she said meant 'traveller to other worlds', teasing and laughing at me for my odd little ways. This was before I had been married. Once I was, we no longer spoke openly of such things. It was too dangerous.

It made me smile now to think of her gruff teasing. In a way, she was right, and *taltos* could travel to other worlds to see the future. Just not in the way people thought. We travelled without moving anywhere. We travelled by *listening* to what was right in front of us, collapsing the thin veils that held time together. *Taltos* listened in the same way a mushroom listens to every one of its fibrous parts, even as they scatter underneath the soil, inside the trees, and all the way to China. But now, after everything that had happened, this kind of talk all seemed so foolish and superstitious.

Anna could barely stand. She'd been brought out to accuse me. She swayed, opening and closing her broken mouth a few times even though no sound emerged. I imagined her speaking to the winds, the trees, the sky; to all the things unintelligible to the human world, making her peace and preparing to dissolve back into the great river of sounds and lights forever. I knew the moment she passed out, she wouldn't return.

Anna sought my eyes with hers and I smiled at her against my terror. I smiled *for* her, to tell her that I saw who she was, that I knew her and that I still loved her. I smiled to tell her that I stood *with her* and that all the violence in the world couldn't take that away from us. The nobles and peasants trembled and gasped when they saw it. The Blood Countess smiling at her own trial! Horror! Some crossed themselves, and I could make out others muttering the Lord's Prayer. Others still touched wooden amulets around their necks; secret little pagan carvings that no one cared to admonish them for, now that the devil's own lover was standing before them. Although *he* just kept looking at me from across his sea of pearls and black velvet.

He. Like a blade; my endless pursuer. I even thought he smiled a little, eager to catch my eye and transmit that secret bond that the victor always has with his final object. He cleared his throat to silence the hisses of those closest to him. Then appeared sober. The very picture of concern.

"The lady is forbidden to speak. If she speaks, she may cast spells or invoke devils. If she speaks, she is to be put to death immediately. We do not seek to put her witchcraft on trial. But be assured, the lady is damnable, as we shall prove."

It was only then that I looked right at him. Rage flew around inside my body like a broken bird, its wings pulsing inside me, erratic. I strained against my own silence until I became exhausted. *Stay alive! Stay for awhile longer.* In a way, I think, like everyone else in that crowd, I wanted to see what would happen next. To see *how* they would rub me out.

My body was so pale and thin that I looked almost translucent. I hadn't eaten for days, or even a week. I glanced down quickly at my hands to check that life still flowed in my body; to reassure myself that I hadn't already been turned into a ghost. After all, I was silent – *silenced.* I could only watch future histories get made in the present at my own trial – watch how my bones would be emptied of their stories to make new futures. Isn't that what it is to be a ghost?

I looked up. My accuser's eyes hadn't changed in all the years we had known one another. They were still the same cold blue. They were still ice inside the sea. My silence would echo through time, made clear by its own absence, like so many other stories of witches and demons and fallen angels hushed and shamed, a zero on the inside of history, a gaping hole. But the thing about holes is that they only ever lead elsewhere. And in that doorway to elsewhere, something new would emerge, something I had seeded quietly, deep in the past. A different story that lived *inside* the main one – the one that these men told over and over to bind reality up under their feet, in the same way you might trample over a silent earth, making it quiet.

In my time, like the earth, a woman lives only through the hands and words of men. She isn't her own kind of species – not yet – but a creature made by *man*. Some languages have been given too much power; the power over life and death and everything else that matters. In the silence *right here, right now*, in your silence, dear reader – the silence that a book effects on the one who reads it – I'll tell my side of it all. I'll start as a girl, the first moment I arrived at Cachtice in my carriage. I'll tell my story to fold time; to be here *and* elsewhere, as if no time existed in between. I'll tell the story that lives inside what history has made of me. Maybe that's the power of a *talto*.

*

The clatter of the carriage comes up behind me. Louder, then louder! Its wheels split the ground, shedding splinters and stones. Origin sounds. Like the rumblings of thunder that shake the ground awake with hands that you can't see but that you can feel all around you. From beneath the earth these surface tremors sound slight, no more than the scratchings of children, but to me, the child standing above ground, trembling and afraid, they herald the first profound fissure that will haunt my life forever. *Don't take me away! I don't want to be married!* I squeeze my eyes shut to make it all disappear.

Flashes of warm sunlight still linger in me, printing the world I'm about to leave on the reverse side of my eyelids. Then these too fade down and everything becomes dark. When I open my eyes again, I see only the inside of the carriage. Its flimsy walls are lined in blue silk. My mother, my castle, my home – they're all gone. I am a bride now with nothing but that to hold me to the earth.

The rough roads of Hungary toss me around. I feel as if I'm inside the sea, being thrown about inside its blue immensities. I steady my body, grabbing onto the edge of the seat, the sides of the walls, anything I might hold onto. But everything is moving. The whole world is movement. My mother, well aware of my fondness for painting, has stashed a wooden chest filled with pots of pigments and parchments. Bran, who had been sat on top of it before we set off, topples to the ground – my soft grey teddy bear, the size of two hands. He's filled with horsehair and has become misshapen over the years I've dragged him along with me. I grab him, pressing him to my face to remember his softness. But he's become so cold from the icy chill in the air. To me, however, in my barely-still-child state, this brittle iciness means something much more. It's like his spirit has left. Or more precisely, like it's stayed behind at home whilst I'm being driven far away, leaving only a grey husk.

I open the chest and take out a pot of yellow pigment. I spit into my hand and mix some of the gaudy colour into it until I have the smallest amount of paste. It's not quite the gold I have in mind, but it will do. I colour over Bran's eyes. Now he'll always see the light of heaven. He'll always be in paradise and every time I look at him, I'll be reminded of my true home. The one beyond boxes and bones. The one in the sky, beyond the reach of *people*.

It's several days before we arrive at Cachtice, a place I'll come to call home for the rest of my life. The textures of the land are similar to those I grew up in, but something's different. Perhaps it's just the light. And the trees here are thicker than they are at home, and full of colour. I step out of the carriage, helped by a man, who utters odd sounds, and immediately I throw up. Two older ladies, waiting at the steps of the castle in fine dresses, flutter like paper butterflies, laughing, but a third, a younger one, comes over to me.

"Elizabet, I am Anna. I shall be your lady's maid. Here, let me help you." Her voice is raspy in my language, but I understand her and there's something kind, or at least soft in its toning. Anna takes my hand, rubbing it a little to restore its warmth, and starts to lead me away.

"Wait!" I yell, running back to the carriage. I scramble up to the door and climb inside, dragging my chest of paints and poor misshapen Bran behind me. Anna comes to help me. The others simply stare and laugh a bit more.

"Leave these for the servants to bring, my lady!" She makes to put her hand around Bran's body. "Is that a toy? You'll have little need for that after you're married. Let me take it and put it away."

I shake my head in a ferocious 'no', wresting him away from her. No one will touch him but me. These people with their strange sounds and odd light – what if when their different hands touch Bran he should disappear? What if I should disappear?

"This is your new home now, Elizabet", she says, leading me away into the quiet rock of the castle that closes around us. "We hope you'll be very happy here and fulfil your role with grace."

Everything feels so formal, so starched and bitter. We make our way towards a tower that pierces the very sky with its height, moving up a spiralling set of steps until we reach a large wooden door at the top. Anna struggles to open it, but eventually its weight gives way to her bony shoulder. There's a bed, a table, a sewing chair and box, a tapestry on the wall depicting a glorious battlefield, a wardrobe and a copper bath filled to the brim with hot water. I try to hide my tears as the ladies undress me and eventually scoop me into it.

"Fetch the Countess her new clothes," says Anna, and immediately turns to one of the entourage of servants she's brought. "Take these to the courtyard and burn them."

And there they go, the last vestiges of my old life, to the pyre. The soulless frames of witches, all made of cotton and silk.

She stays to wash me and, I feel, also to inspect me surreptitiously. My body looks like it glows, the candlelight catching the sheen of the copper bath and the still-hot swishing water that seems to have known when I would arrive. I am becoming *golden*.

"Such a strong body and a strong-willed mind, too, I imagine. You'll need it here, my dear Countess. Cachtice is a magical place, but we're a people of the borderlands. There are those who hate us; dark people with dark skin, dark eyes and wicked ways. Do you know their name, child?"

I shake my head, suddenly afraid again, although I'm not quite sure yet of what.

"They're called 'Turks'. Can you say 'Turk'?" I shake my head again before staring at her in total stillness. Her language feels abrasive and scatters like iron fillings yet to magnetise around my ears. "Ottomans," she says in explanation.

Now this word I know.

I repeat it in her – my – new language: "Tu-r-k." It feels strange on my tongue. The door opens as one of the older ladies goes out to burn my clothes. It shuts hard and fast, and I am left alone in the glowing water as the others turn down the bed and start, one by one, to blow the candles out.

When I climb into bed I pull the blankets over my head, creating a little cocoon around me with my arms oustretched. When I grow tired, I rest my arms, which I've been holding the blankets above me with and sit up straight, like a veiled woman, safe in my woollen world.

"Don't worry, Bran. It'll be all right," I whisper.

His golden eyes look a little sinister in the half-dark now. But I know he loves me, and I love him. I know he can hear me, somehow. I just know it.

I slip off into sleep, but the edges of my awareness tell me that I'm not lying down anymore but standing up. I've moved across from the bed to stare at the wall on the other side of the room, although I don't remember being anywhere in between. *That's strange.* It's as if I've been pulled, magnetised even, by something stronger than I but that doesn't belong here. The lines between the bricks start to hum and buzz like bells slowly vibrating in one low, furious note. The vibrations hit my belly fast and uncautiously. *I will not be afraid!*

I reach out my index finger and trace the stone lines in front of me. Soon, the hum rises. It becomes deafening to me. I press my hands to my ears, but it feels useless, as if the source of the sound isn't outside but is coming from somewhere within me, impossible to stopper up. The lines and cracks start to pour out a golden kind of light; their edges are airborne, particles that move about me, rising in the room, hanging in the space around me. *But I'm not afraid.* I'm curious.

The bricks start to fade away, overtaken by the brightness and the noise, defying the solid grasp of materiality. The light takes on the quality of wax, fixing the fluidity of time into a block that will one day print out history anew. Then, without warning, a face emerges, staring back from inside the wall. I can see it clearly. As if the wall has become a moving target and she the bullseye, taking shape *right now* in front of me.

She's a girl, younger than I for sure, but at the same time older – far, far older. She clutches a bear that looks just like my own Bran. She's trapped inside the wall, like the spirits of old I heard about in my first home who appear to young girls, or so they say. Only she isn't some wrathful demon or evil creature come to tempt me to my darknesses. She's quiet, staring, ancient. "What are you?" The blood rushes to my head. I start, flinging arms and legs and chest until I realise I'm still in bed, startled and abruptly awake.

My breathing is racing. The sun is rising, invading the room like a glory of crusaders flooding and falling about. For a moment, I fear that the dense morning sun will kill me – will whip around my body and tear me apart with its own strong and wild horses. But it doesn't. It simply gives new shape and definition to all the things I had seen in the room in the night. This is what my life has come to look like. This is who I am now. Elizabet Bathory. Elizabet Nadasdy. Elizabet the eternal youth. Years later, this tower itself will be my captor. The bricks will come alive and crush me into history and you will know me by another name.

But the girl in the wall will know me differently. She will know me as I really am.

*

In the morning, I went outside. The rocks and stones were a dull grey, and there was that strange light in the sky again. I remembered my home before this one. Its people were far more *alive*; the colours they wore, and the bright sounds of their squabbles and little victories. I couldn't remember any of these now even though they had seemed so important then. Here, in a strange reversal, the rocks, the trees, the stones and *that light* were more alive, as if people were no more than ghostly furniture and land the real ruler, the real lifeblood of the place.

A quick jolt came to my right arm, making me cry out fast. I looked up sharply. An immense man had grabbed me above the elbow and was turning me around so that I ended up being led-almost-dragged in the opposite direction. I looked up at him, helpless and full of anger. His clothes were covered in black soot and his hands were bloody. He gnashed a strange-sounding word at me. I looked blankly back at him.

"Away," he repeated but this time in a broken form of my language that all but boxed my ears. He pulled me up with one arm until the muscles along the side of my body stretched and stung, and my feet nearly left the ground. The only person to have ever spoken to me like that before was my mother back in my first home. I felt the wind of pride hit my chest and silence me. Over the shock, for just a moment, I heard a clanging noise. Metal striking metal over and over. Patient. Rhythmic. Regular. Material meeting material. He dropped my arm and continued walking away from noise as if I hadn't even been there in the first place. I tripped and fell to the ground like a sack of grain, but I spilled nothing of myself. No tears. No blood. Only shame.

For a moment, I stared at him as he went towards the storehouse, my tower room looming over him, casting a shadow across his clothes like an afterthought that he moved in and out of carelessly. Was I the ghost here? Was I even real? I started to feel the rising fizz of anger pour through my veins. My heart started to beat faster. Faster! Faster!

The rhythmic sound a little aways from me picked up again. *Clang! Clang!* I got up, turned on my heel and walked straight back to where I had been looking, almost daring him to see me again. I took a few extra steps forward and peered over the edge of a low wall. It was then I saw something that made me go very cold, freezing my veins. I felt that I was remembering something, but it wasn't from my little lifetime. I felt like it came from a time before mine, and it filled me with dread.

On the grass, there was an unfinished metal chair that aped a throne. It was being roughly beaten by two men with large hammers, who then picked it up and moved it into a low outbuilding. The men weren't just silent as they raised and struck with their hammers. They were *silenced*.

The outbuilding glowed a warm red from inside. A woman was circling it. Her hair was white and black and stood away from her head in some kind of monstrous parody that later in life, when I knew her as Erzi the wild one, would make me smile, before trailing down along her body. She was waving a kind of rattle fashioned with small bells that clattered and jangled at the building. She looked completely mad. I couldn't tell if she felt reverence towards the building, or if she was consumed with rage. Maybe both.

She suddenly glanced up at me. I gasped and for some unexplainable reason hit the ground in terror, hiding as best I could, face in the dust, behind the low wall. There was something about her. Something beyond her flesh that made her seem dangerous to me. More dangerous than the giant man. More dangerous than anything human. I stayed there, laid out flat and breathing in the ancient powdery dirt of Cachtice for a long time.

When Anna found me there, she seemed to fill with relief but quickly pulled a long strand of my hair with such force that it made me tear up. "*You* gave me a fright," she said, pulling the strand down on the *you*. "What are you doing out here? You should be in your rooms, readying yourself." I wasn't sure what I should be readying myself for. This place seemed too secret and too urgent all at once. But I said nothing. I simply pointed to the house where they had put that metal chair.

"What's that building?"

"That's where the blacksmiths work."

She gestured to it and then paused. Lines began to emerge, crossing from the centre of her forehead. The frown became so deep that for a moment I imagined her growing with ivy, overrun by the wildness of the place. Of course, I'd seen blacksmiths in my own country, but at home no one had even noticed them. Here, they exerted a kind of power I hadn't come across before, an eerie and magnetic halo that repelled everything that came close, as if a thousand tiny spirits surrounded them when they walked, edging out people, animals, even the dust. I looked up to my tower. The sun was higher overhead now and I blinked, scattering it from my small upward-turning eyes. It felt, as I did so, that the light was cut into hundreds of pieces.

Anna, still silent, deposited me back in my room and only spoke to order me to 'stay and get ready'. So I did so, until a whole day and night had passed, although I still had no idea what to be 'ready' for. No one tells an unmarried girl anything. It's an eternal frustration that I'd learnt to live with long ago. I slept, prayed, and eventually, afraid that the numb boredom might move from my body into my soul, began to chart the sky, copying what I saw in paint on the stone floor, with only Bran for company. When night eventually fell, I fell asleep, my body fanning out across the wet colours. I woke up as dawn was drafting its brilliant orange into the clouds. As I sat up, I noticed the paint had imprinted itself on my dress and I put my arms around myself, as if to hug the sky.

Anna finally came up the eternally winding staircase and into my room again. She sat on the edge of my enormous wooden bed, taking my hand in one of hers and holding the curve of my chin and cheek in her other. "Elizabet, you mustn't disturb the blacksmiths when they are…" she paused "…working. Do you understand me? It's not safe. Leave them to their world and they'll leave us to ours."

"Yes," I responded dutifully. I'd already shifted my attentions from the blacksmiths to the sky during my long day and night of isolation. But hearing about them again sparked a tiny new flame of curiosity in me. "I will, I promise, but, Anna, what do they do? Please tell me."

At first, she glared at me, but when she noticed my paint-covered dress and floor, something in her softened. She said nothing about either. She simply took my hand in hers again and then drew a little circle on my palm, tracing it faster and faster as she spoke, taking on the air of a master storyteller.

"They dig into the ground and then heat what they find until it's hotter than hot, so that it loses its shape and becomes like a liquid fire. Then, as it cools down, they beat it into swords, or tools – all sorts of things."

My eyes widened and she let go of my palm suddenly, smoothing her own dress out.

"Some people say that's the reason that they're so close to the gods inside the earth."

"Is it true?" I asked, enchanted and a little afraid.

She sighed and turned her head away. When she looked back at me, her face had hardened a little again.

"No. Of course not. They're simply a group of men who work hard and dream, like all men do, of having more power. The power they have – they have had – is gone for good. It's no bad thing. You can't upturn the order of things. At least you *shouldn't*."

She wiped her face in a sweeping motion, purging some kind of long-held grief from herself, and then bit her lips together into a thin fold.

I hadn't considered the 'order of things' before. I preferred her first description about being close to the gods in the earth. The second one felt too close to something I was on the edge of: the world of men. I had been raised almost exclusively by women. My father had been a distant figure, an outline inside which occasional memories flashed up but which were ultimately thin and insubstantial, a painted impression without fixed form in my life. My cousins, Sigismund, Andrew and Balthasar, were just children. They were brats to me and though my uncle was the king of Poland and my family all powerful lords and princes forever at war, they were kept far from me and my world. To hear about the world of men and the way they went about running things was strange and exotic information.

When Anna left, shutting the door behind her with a strong warning that I'd better stay out of sight for now, I grew bored and began playing with my nearly exhausted paints again, daubing and mixing until even my skin was festooned with colour. It was at my most tattooed moment that the door was unexpectedly opened again, and Anna emerged, this time in a flurry.

"What kind of mess are you?" she barked. "Count Thurzo is here. He's finally come to inspect you – to meet you – and you're not ready! What is wrong with you, child?"

"Who is he?" I asked.

Anna shook her head furiously as if she hadn't time to explain.

"He's *important*. Now hurry up!"

Through the now wide-open door more and more serving women started pouring in, disrupting the thick silence that had lain about the room for days. Anna spoke a few words to them that I didn't understand, and they swarmed about me, lifting me up with a few well-placed tugs before pulling me about like a rag doll. Anna had already disappeared.

My black hair was combed straight until I felt the skin of my scalp in ways I had never done before. There was no time for washing, so the paint blotches were scratched off my arms. A chest that I could have sworn hadn't been in the room before was opened, and out of it a kind of second skin emerged. A dress so tight in some places and so billowing in others was hurried over my head and under my feet in a few moments. Its corset, however, was the worst of these pains. I was no stranger to finery, but this bejewelled cage was as tight around me as rope around a thief.

Still the women kept on pulling and pulling on its cords and ribbons until it felt like I wore my ribs on the outside. And then it was over. One serving maid held my hand so I didn't collapse, and we wound down the stairway to the courtyard and over to the main building. The sky was greyer and darker, and sitting right there on the low wall was the crazy dancing woman, rattle in hand, but now silent and still as a cat caught in the hunt. She stared at me like I brought nothing less than the plague with me.

I was hurried into a large reception hall, which we reached by walking along several passageways. I peered at the regular rectangular openings in the stone that chopped the sky into portraits of twilight. I was becoming light-headed on account of the corset that trapped me like a delicate spider inside my own web. As I was rushed along, I felt the presence of the girl I had seen in the wall the night before. She was running just ahead of me in the bricks, sliding through the stones and between the casements. My eyes started to blink rapidly, and I felt I couldn't breathe at all. I turned to the wall and shut them for a moment to stop all the blinking, which was making me dizzy. She appeared right in front of me as I opened my eyes, slipping momentarily to the floor, and stood over me like a ferocious being, half remembered.

"Don't take it! Don't take the ring!" The last word fell about me, echoing like an angry ghost: *danger.*

I hadn't heard these words with my ears. I just knew they were hanging there somewhere in a subtler space that defied the ear and spoke straight to the mind. A thick hand pressed salts to my nose and I came to. I was hoisted to my feet like a sack of barley. The next thing I knew, I had been deposited on the inside of a door, which was quickly shut behind me. And again, I was alone. Almost alone. Because by the fire, standing straight and stiff as an oil painting, was Count Thurzo.

The first thing I noticed was the stillness. If he hadn't turned fractionally to take me in, I would have thought him one of the undead. His face was a mass of vectors, its bones razor sharp, all angles from the side, but when he turned, its shape was the oval sliver of an unfulfilled moon. He wore light felt gloves, long boots and a large crucifix that fell in and out of the folds of his tunic. The newly lit fire raged in the grate. We stared at each other for a long time, his eyes flickering alive like a great insect's, before he snapped to see me full face, saying simply, "Where are my manners?" He then gestured to an ornate pair of chairs at the other side of the room and moved easily and gracefully towards them.

Unable to take half a step without fearing another swoon and still light-headed and confused, I replied with only a muffled, singular cry. He had already sat down and watched me as each step I took brought forth another quiet and painful cry and then another. I started flushing, not for shame, but simply because there was little air in my lungs and my heart was pounding fast and furious. I made it to the chair in what seemed like the longest walk of my life and sat down. He smiled momentarily. "Those dresses really are a waste of time, aren't they?"

I blacked out then.

The next thing I remembered was a serving woman slapping me in the face. She curtseyed, muttered some foreign sounds that sounded apologetic and raced out of the room. Thurzo was still sitting opposite. After a moment, he spoke.

"Elizabet, I'm sure I speak for everyone when I say we are happy you've arrived at Cachtice." He smiled almost paternally. "I make a point of meeting all the newcomers to our land, but with you..." he paused and raised his eyebrows whilst exhaling "...you, I have been told, are something else."

I detected a note of sarcasm, but I wasn't sure. His accent was refined but I still had to concentrate to understand him.

"Tell me, why have you come here? Why marry Nadasdy? After all, he is... less *impressive* than you are."

I stared at him, this strange, elegant man of whom I knew nothing, and then remembered my own manners.

"My parents wished it and I'm ready to fulfil my duty."

I cast my eyes down, but then felt compelled to look straight back up at his face again. The flames from the grate had given him the look of a shadow play. I'd been prepared since I had been a lot younger than I was now to be polite, to receive and be received by noblemen and women, and this meeting was not unlike any other I had grown up with as part of my every day. Except it was entirely unlike any other I'd had. I was so very alone. I breathed in deeply and winced a little. He moved over to me very slowly and deliberately and then held both his hands, palms out, towards me to show me he meant no harm.

"Let me loosen the back lacings an inch."

He paced around me until I couldn't see him anymore but could only feel his breath on my neck. The sensation was strange. It felt I was in the presence of an enormous creature, a bat or a snake, something that would push its teeth into me if I moved even an inch. Instead, he awkwardly fumbled with the back of the corset to give me a hair's breadth more breathing space. When he returned immediately to his chair, he looked so very uncomfortable, as if he'd have rather been anywhere else but here. He adjusted his own clothing a little, sighed quickly like a parent too preoccupied to want to attend to a sobbing child, but in finding he must, simply gets down to it, and then looked at me again. I, who had never experienced anything like what had just happened, simply gawped. He laughed and repositioned himself more jovially on the armchair.

"Now, tell me, your uncle, Stephen, is he not in Poland?"
"Yes."
"And is he ruling... well?" He repressed a small smile.

I had never been asked about politics before. I didn't reply. Too much was new. I felt like a pearl, loosened from a broken string and falling fast into the dirt below.

"Very good, then. Well, I trust you'll find yourself plenty of things to occupy your days with. I hear you can read and speak in several languages. We must arrange some kind of tutor for you, so you can continue in this unusual pursuit. Nadasdy will be along to make you his wife before the year is out. He's fighting the Ottomans." That exasperated half-sigh and the look of bored annoyance returned. "He always returns and, of course, we always fight." He went quiet and sucked his cheeks in as he swallowed. I wasn't sure if he was suggesting that he always fought Nadasdy or the Ottomans. But then, I wasn't sure of anything anymore.

"I like painting," I suddenly blurted out.
"What?"
"I like to paint."

"I see."

He got up and went to the door. I had stood and curtseyed and felt relieved to be rid of this strange, still man, when he stopped. He turned back and crossed the hall in brisk, equally measured paces.

"I almost forgot, here is Nadasdy's family crest. You should wear it on your finger or around your neck, or whatever the fashion for young brides is. God knows if I know."

And he dropped a heavy kind of signet ring into my palm. My blood started rising and beating in my ears and I went quickly to return it to him, but he was already out the door, his equal steps sounding metallic, like the beating of the blacksmith's hammer earlier in the day. Those rhythmic, even-paced steps would be a sound I would hear across my life, even when he was no longer there.

I held up the ring he had given me and went over to the fire to inspect it more closely. It was heavy in my hand and showed a huge dragon curling its ancient tongue. I glanced over my shoulder to make sure no one had quietly come in and then immediately looked between the gaps in the flames to see if the vanishing girl would emerge. There was nothing but heat, smoke and that insubstantial wobble of air that always moves around a fire. The certainty of these qualities allowed a shiver of relief to edge across my back and shoulders, pulling at the still-tight ribbing and creaking of my costume. Fire was fire, in all the worlds. "If you're there, I just want you to know that I didn't take it. It was given to me. What should I do with it?"

But there was no response, so I turned on my heel, moved the heavy object from hand to hand as if passing it like a hot coal between myself and someone else who didn't want the thing either, and eventually ran out of the hall to find someone, anyone, who would break the thick silence that had set around me.

Chapter Two

The towering walls and smooth arches of the hall make the plasterboard podium I'm standing at seem a bit pathetic. A microphone, balanced in front of me, connects remotely to a small black box that spills out wires like an electronic Medusa, blinking its green eyes at me. For a moment, my arrival to this particular point in time disturbs the currents that work deep inside the cables. A high screech deafens the room.

Everybody else will call it 'feedback', but I know that it's the sound of time haunting my waking world, throwing me about from point to point across the trajectory of my life without having been anywhere in between. Howling like the wind does against a flat window. Howling like gods trying to break down the doors between worlds.

I look around me and instantly know where I am, and which point in my life I've come to. I'm already a historian working on uncovering the secret history of the *Blood Countess*. I know this because I recognise the hall I'm standing in. It lies deep inside the labyrinthine heart of all the lecture rooms that dot and snake around the university, so I must already be teaching here, which would place me somewhere in my thirties. Time has returned me to the moment I start to speak of her – the Countess Erzabet Bathori – in a way that gets noticed.

I grip the podium I'm standing at tightly to steady myself. It feels like the whole world is moving around me. Time often brings me back here. I've been to this moment before. Before and before and before.

Bathory wasn't what they said she was. Behind the story of the monster there's a woman, a radical, a revolutionary! But blood sells better than truth. It always has, no matter what histories might come to light. And it's more useful if you want to make a point about something. Beware, Bathory the Monster!

I've made a lot of enemies uncovering Bathory's secret history. Unravelling the woman for who she really was rather than simply giving more evidence in service of the story history has told us about her *over and over* again. If history is the ultimate trial of our tiny lives on this planet, then few people have been tried *over and over* again more than Elizabet Bathory. Every time you open a book, or watch a series or film, there she is, bathing in blood. Her very name seems to contain an echo, a whisper: *Monster!* It hides behind her more innocent syllables, promising dark and seductive acts of violence.

People love their monsters, especially when those monsters are supposed to be serial killers or vampiresses and all the things history accuses Bathory of being. The monsters that humans make out of our darker desires: power and fame and wealth and sex. What could a powerful woman be other than a monster? Take away the monster and – *oh horror!* – you upturn the order of things because stories are spells. They create worlds.

I squeeze the podium even tighter, feeling my flesh and the reassuring touch of its material meet halfway. *Okay. Good.* Now I'm ready to start. A sea of expectant faces seated in rows of auditorium-style chairs that fold at their mechanical waists stare back at me with anticipation. The hall is full of people, the gleam of notepads and lit screens, a few students in their early twenties whispering, and at the front, a group of four older men, legs crossed, eyes fixed on me, waiting for my next move with the kind of predatory aloofness that only years of academia can cement inside a person's bones. They hover like vultures or bats, waiting for me to make the slightest error. Waiting for me to try to undo the most powerful spell of them all: a spell called history.

I've lived all these moments so many times before, moving endlessly between worlds, time writing and rewriting itself in the infinite set of falling pages that bind us all briefly to life. I live out my own life as a kind of time traveller with no fixed point. The North Star of *history* flips between poles, and I track and trace its fits and starts because I remember everything. As a historian, I speak about war and murder all the time – all the murders Bathory is meant to have committed in her lust for power.

But what no one in this hall knows is that my own disruption in time, my own ability, or rather my curse, to understand the world in the way I do, was itself born out of murder. A splash of blood in the snow. A heavy kind of winter silence. And a last breath. I was only a child when it happened. I died for just a moment, probably only a handful of minutes or so in your account of the world, but for just long enough to bring back a glitch in time with me when I unexpectedly returned. A glitch that I live inside of every day.

The thing is, whilst that last breath should have heralded the end of my time on earth, it didn't. Death itself was snatched away from me as fast as the life that had been. And so I belonged to neither one – neither to life nor to death. Instead, I inherited this strange and exhausting relationship with time. Instead of time flowing forward, evenly separated by minutes and hours and years, it flowed in multiple directions at once. It threw me about like a paper doll across a life that should have ended only once and long ago.

All the moments that grew like winter crocuses from after that day in the snow should have been erased from the book of stories – things like the rest of my childhood, adulthood, my old age. These should never have seen the light of day. I haunted a future life that should never have happened, and it spun time out and around me in disordered sequences, flashes of memories that should never have been but that I hovered inside of, like a shadow that breathes. Like a ghost.

It all came with a price, though, because in this pocket of borrowed time, I could never make anything *new*. I couldn't intervene or change any of the events that time threw me in and out of. I knew everything that had happened to me and would happen again, but I was powerless to do anything about any of it. History has the same kind of cruelty. It operates with the same logic.

We watch as stories get fashioned for us *again and again*. The moment when I came back to life, that otherworldly glitch brought something back with it; a seed inside the shell of *me* and *my* tiny life. A glimpse of a woman in a tower that came like a flash across my skin. A woman who had been wronged by history. An origin story. A wound inside the body of time itself. A wound that wouldn't be done with me until I could close it up once and for all. I carried it inside my body until I discovered it had a name: *Bathory*. How many Bathorys have lived only to be erased from history? Women rubbed out from the book of stories until only a wound remained, a grand zero, empty of the double pulse of life.

Now, in the huge hall inside the university, I squeeze the podium so hard that I think it might snap. I release my hands and start to read from the pages I now see I'm holding out in front of me. Each curl and dot on the page brings forth *her*. The wound. The Countess Elizabet Bathory. Not Bathory the Monster, locked up in her tower like some ancient fairy tale. Not the serial killer, the witch, the vampire. But Bathory the woman.

When I say the word 'woman' *here, now*, in this hall, I let the word float up as if it is something harder to imagine than all those other more damnable words. I glance at the sea of faces, lowering the tone and rhythm of my voice. I wet my lips with my tongue and start to speak quietly, but with a rhythm, beating Bathory back into life:

"What happens when a woman becomes bigger than the forces around her? What happens when she cannot be tamed, coerced, or threatened? What stories does she search for in the memory banks of her life to pave the road that she's already walking? And what does history decide to make out of her...?"

The men in the front row cross and uncross their folded legs. At first, they're charmed. One even blushes a little when I look towards him, and flutters his eyelids at me bashfully. But it's not long before it all gives way to something more sinister.

"How does history write a woman out of her life?"

The granite jaw of the man in the middle hardens, giving his oval face a sudden angle, a point that will grow into an animal constellation in time, crossing all my horizons. He grabs his bag and walks out. It's a simple thing to do, but I know what it spells because I know what has come before and what will come after this moment. I remember shaking a little when, not so long ago in the course of linear time, he had grabbed me by the elbow, angled his lips to my ear and said, *I'm going to teach you a lesson about power you'll never forget.* When you live outside time, there's no such thing as human battles. Not in the same way at least because cause and effect mean very little without the straight arrow of time. But this is the closest I'll ever come to one, and it haunts me over and over. *Just like it haunted her*, I think to myself.

All these stories, pasts and presents, merge into one, the origin story that I seem to cycle around. Whichever thread I pull across time, a face like this one emerges. If not his then another's, a refrain in the flow of events. This refrain is dark and difficult. It's hard to swallow. It's about the kind of rage that seeks to bite into the spirit of a woman until nothing is left. Until her spirit flees the earth, erased from time itself. We've all bought into one story or another. History makes us look for causes and effects, for monsters and witches. But time tells it all very differently. I blink a few times to scatter the memories and continue.

"What if Bathory wasn't a monster, but a revolutionary who momentarily broke the chains a world that was not ready for her had bound her with? What if Bathory was not a monster, but for a time a woman who stood up for all the silent women around her, bringing them into being, into consequence? What if her journey towards imprisonment and death was paved not in blood, but in ink...?"

*

Anna is teaching me a few words in her language. It's similar to mine, a dialect from the south. Or maybe mine's the dialect and hers is the original. It's hard to tell. After meeting Count Thurzo, I realised that I did have a gift. I had a gift with words, and whilst I had thought this entirely normal in my birth home, here it was a skill that was received with amazement. It was as if I possessed some kind of uncanny power. Inside, this made me glow with pride. I could speak and, what's more, I could lift the spell of speech from out of marks on a page. My power was almost fully realised in this area. I could even write down my own stories and add to the voice of the world.

It seemed to make people uncomfortable. Except for one, who smiled rather than frowned each time he saw me perched outside with a heavy book in my hands, muttering to myself as I wrote things down in the margins. Instead of tutting a barely audible 'devil' or 'witch' like the rest, he tried to catch my eye rather than evade it. He was a newcomer like me, an outsider.

But, unlike me, he had come to Cachtice from across the Ottoman border. And, unlike me again, he was a servant.

He wore his clothing roughly, as if someone had squeezed him into a shape in which his body didn't quite fit. Despite this awkwardness, he walked with ferocious power. He was almost always silent – in fact, I caught myself wondering if he had any voice at all, or if his Ottoman ruler had ripped out the basis of speech from somewhere beyond his tongue. He became the subject of my unwavering fascination. The serving women always scattered when he passed by. They muttered to themselves darkly about him too. It felt good to know I wasn't the only one they felt this way about.

"Anna, why do they hate that coal carrier so much?" I asked her one day.

"Because he's an Ottoman *kutya* who has killed their husbands," she replied with sharp acridity, stabbing her needle through the cloth on the word *kutya*, which meant *dog*.

"He killed their husbands?" I asked, my eyes widening.

"Not theirs, but others."

"So, he hasn't *actually* killed their husbands," I stated flatly.

I was growing bold and complacent these days. Perhaps it was my impending marriage that brought it out of me. Anna constantly reminded me of this. She warned me over and over, even twice daily sometimes, that I mustn't continue in this vein when Francis Nadasdy, my husband-to-be, returned, for fear of heavy-handed consequences.

"Anna," I persisted, "what are the Ottomans? I mean, really? Are they men or not? If they're no more than 'dogs', how can it be taking so long for Nadasdy to defeat them?"

"There are worse things than men, Countess, than monsters of men, even than monsters of earth. The devil, he's our greatest monster."

"Are the Ottomans monsters, then?" I said, my eyes growing wide.

"Yes – no. Not quite. They're just men. They shed the blood of the body, whilst the devil," and she wagged her finger at me, "sheds the blood of the soul."

"Anna, tell me more about the coal carrier. *Please*. Why is he here?"

She exhaled sharply and when she finally spoke, it was all in a rush.

"He's a janissary – who are a group of soldiers, prized so highly by the Ottoman Emperor that his enslavement at Cachtice is the jewel in the crown of Nadasdy's rule."

Her eyes narrowed as she whispered, "Cold-blooded killer. A devil amongst men," and for a moment I wasn't sure who she was talking about.

The coal carrier was built like a wooden printing block and at Anna's words I imagined him pressing himself into history until it ran not with ink but with blood. It was strange to reconcile this idea with him carrying his basket and running errands around here.

"How could Nadasdy enslave a *devil*?" I asked, suddenly thinking that my husband-to-be must be something stronger than a devil – an angel perhaps?

Anna put her endless embroidery on the bed, stroked my forehead and then took my hand, which was becoming slenderer as each day passed. She traced the length of each of my fingers with her own.

"The devil is in all of us, and we beat him out daily with prayer."

'Then that Ottoman servant, he doesn't do the same?"

Anna became exasperated again, dropped my hand and picked up the needlepoint.

"His prayers are sent to the wrong place. Now stop, Elizabet. Just stop."

I preferred to rest in her odd but warm company, so I did stop. But the next day, I determined to seek out the silent

Turkish man. He had his back to the stone wall of my tower, one foot pressed flat against the brick so that his thigh, knee and leg formed a triangular shape. He smiled broadly, and I noticed he was missing one tooth. His lips were chapped, and I felt as if he might be also missing a long beard. He waved his hand in a circular motion towards his chest and back out again, and for a moment, I wasn't sure who had sought out whom. I was being beckoned! I looked around me and then away haughtily. But when I finally looked back, he did it again. What servant beckons a countess? He was *fascinating*.

I rose and padded over to him cautiously. Then, to my astonishment, he spoke clearly and precisely in my own mother tongue, his emphasis and accent transporting me home.

"Little Wing, how are you today?" He looked me over as he spoke in the way a physician might check a patient before pronouncing on ailments and cures. He was my enemy, my servant and, according to Anna, likely to have been my husband-to-be's killer if fate had left him in the Sultan's hand. But he spoke my language, *my* language, *my mother's own dialect*, and in this moment, I felt he became closer to me than anyone else at Cachtice. I felt it in my stomach.

"Why do you call me 'Little Wing'?"

"Because you're part angel."

"What?" I thought he must be either mad or toying with me. He simply stared right back, mirroring my incredulity, and then suddenly bowed his head as if he had been beaten by some unseen inner master, all at once remembering his place in this world.

I took a step forward, attempting to press him. But he didn't move. He just kept his head bowed towards the dust, one hand over his chest and the other in a loose fist, hanging towards the ground. I suddenly felt very young and very alone, not at all a countess, but a naïve child who might be able to read and write but in truth knew nothing of the world. I noticed a stray feather on the ground by my feet. It gave me the sense that I'd been here before. Not in the past or even the future, but in a place that haunted from a world that was far, far away and not entirely at one with ours.

The Ottoman lifted his head partially so I could only see the briefest slope of his eyes under his furrowed brow. I took in a sharp gasp of cold air as his eyes pierced into me. It was as if he too had seen what I had sensed. His eyes were like two stars that had come far closer to the earth than is normal. They were dancing.

I was overcome. Then I ran.

From that moment on, the Ottoman became my sole preoccupation. Of course, I couldn't tell anyone about it, not least because of who he was, which only served to interest me further, but mainly because my pursuits were meant to be solitary: painting, weaving, reading. When I saw him carrying coal from one entrance to another, emerging each time blacker in body, as if he'd entirely consumed the quarry he carried through the skin, I followed him. I followed him right down into the circular belly of my tower's basement.

Peering around the last wall he had stopped at, I saw him stoking the hearth with a few of the sooty black circles that he removed from the top of his coal basket. Then he sat down, curling his legs underneath his body in a way I hadn't seen before. The light illuminated the sparse room, and I saw stacks of books and papers strewn about, scrawled with the curls and dots of the Ottoman language along their spines and faces. He didn't move a muscle but unexpectedly called out to me.

"Little Wing? Is that you? Come and sit by the fire."

I bit my lip and imagined myself running away in the opposite direction, escaping to the fresh air and strange light of Cachtice above ground. But then I did something I did not entirely expect of myself. I came out shyly from the shadows and moved towards him.

"Come and sit down," he commanded, again, without moving. I knelt slowly to his right side, the fire dying down on my left as if the three of us – Ottoman, girl and fire – formed all but one of the four sides of an invisible square in an otherwise blind expanse.

"Good. Little Wing, have you ever been in love?"

What? The question was so bizarre in this strange nowhere kind of place filled with coal and books, that it took me by surprise.

"What? No," I retorted cynically. I was disappointed in him. *That's it? That's what this Ottoman is going to talk about?* I wanted him to tell me about his war, of why he hated my kind. Of justice or his own religion. Instead, he sat there, looking into the fire. *Love.*

"Pity. You see, if you don't know what love is," and he frowned slightly, "very little of what I tell you will make sense to you." My heart started beating. What if he tried to force himself on me, or if he'd lured me down here with his dancing eyes to kill me in cold blood in revenge for his capture by my husband-to-be? But then I stopped. He was staring into the fire and whispering something in another language, transported, as if I didn't even exist. Then he smiled at *nothing*, turned to me, snorted once as if anticipating my fears, and resumed his enchantment with the flames.

No one at Cachtice spoke of anything to me, least of all of something like love – not even Anna when she prattled on about my marriage. It was a word that didn't seem to exist here. I looked at his softly drawn face. He was static now, as if frozen over in time – with time. He was a puzzle, of that I was absolutely certain. *All right*, I thought to myself. *All right, janissary. Love, then.*

"I want to know what you know," I said flatly in retort. "You can tell me anything and I'll listen. But if you try to kill me, even if you *do* kill me, my husband, Nadasdy, will tear you apart and hang your body in the square."

He raised his eyebrows, shook his head and laughed a little through his nose. It made me feel very young. Then he fixed me with a stare that was at the same time menacing and as if sharing the wildest joke he knew.

"In my country, we're told that love holds the worlds together like an invisible magnet at the centre of the skies."

He pointed towards my chest, as if for a moment he had confused the heavens with the body. But I kept on listening all the same.

"But then, they also tell us to fight and kill – all in the name of love, Little Wing. Love of God, or love of Sultan. Love of land. Don't they say the same here, Countess? Isn't your husband, even right now, killing my people in the name of love of your 'Holy Roman Empire'? Strange that we're all prepared to die for a thing that we don't know anything about. Don't you think, Little Wing?" And he fixed me with that stare. It was like he was looking into my bones.

I didn't have an answer. I was still stuck on his previous gesture, drifting somewhere between the heavens and my own body, so I simply repeated the only words I had available on the subject, sounding more like Anna than myself: "But monsters only shed blood. It is the devil who sheds the blood of the soul."

He turned his head to meet my gaze at this. He laughed quietly again.

"Little Wing, do you already know everything?"

I began to panic all over, feeling caught again in that wild stare he fixed me with. It was astral, as if it came *through* him from somewhere else. Perhaps I didn't really want to know what he had to say. I was afraid of it. My thoughts started to tumble around inside me: my new husband-to-be, whose face I had never seen; Anna and her stories of the blacksmiths seeking more power, losing their connection to the gods inside the earth; the janissaries who were meant to be 'devils, not men'.

"I think I want to go upstairs now," I replied calmly, in total contradiction to the thudding that was going on inside my heart.

He simply shut his eyes and started half singing, half mouthing something I couldn't make out. It sounded like some kind of prayer. I got up, brushed myself down and walked as bravely out of the dark basement as I could. I didn't dare once look over my shoulder. Later that night, I dreamt the Ottoman stuck a jewelled dagger into my chest. The jewel was set inside the eye of Nadasdy's crest.

I tried to ignore him after that. When I saw his oddly shaped outline on the horizon, I walked in the opposite direction, or reversed my steps brusquely; half in anger, half in terror. After a time, he stopped watching me and I felt better for it. But I found I had begun to miss his strange company. Anna was endlessly busy and everyone else was either too polite or too afraid of me to speak to me. A few weeks of rereading an old Latin Bible, hand-transcribed with ornate lettering that clutched to its margins as if for dear life, had left me so bored that I soon sought out the companionship of my strange, captivating enemy. I craved stories, and whilst I was fairly certain he was no biblical reading made flesh, he was undeniably the most curious person I had met – save for Count Thurzo, of course, whose still, oval face hovered almost continually at the edges of my awareness like a conflicted angel. Or demon.

"Little Wing," the Ottoman said when I found him delivering coal again to the blacksmiths' building, hauling the heavy sack up and down the textured terrains of Cachtice as if were merely a half-empty sack of flour. "What brings you to find me," he paused and looked up towards the roof of the building, "in this *loveless* place?"

*

I know what it feels like to die. There's a shake in the body as an incredible pressure gathers. It starts inside the bones and moves all the way up to the surface of your skin. Then your blood rises to meet it, raging and whispering, startled out of its usual course. Atomic pulses seek each other out. Their secret, intimate doubles call for one other desperately but are never able to collide. Then they shake deep inside the body; a thousand tiny radial planets, pouring out majesty and fire in fits and starts that shudder inside the nape of time. And finally, there's peace. An incredible silence and you feel grown, airy – a large house in the summer with the breeze racing through it, whipping curtains and cobwebs into momentary and lateral frenzies.

When I feel death seize me, I look down at my eight-year-old body encased in a neon snowsuit. There aren't any cars around, or even any passers-by. Just me, alone in the blank whiteness. I see that my hair is still pulled back into two long braids falling on either side of my head; small puddles of black ink that are now running down towards the snow, writing me into the shape of an ending. The white line marking the parting of my hair is *so* white and *so* long; it looks for all the world like a mountain range that's been split in two by a crease on a map. Whiter than the sky in winter. *Whiter than snow.* It goes on forever and as I follow it, I lose the ability to distinguish between space and time.

Looking at myself lying there in the snow is like looking at an image on tracing paper. Each sheet, its own original. I'm outside of time, peering through a thin, papery nothingness that keeps me at an impenetrable distance from my own body. Then a web of dust and stars, pulsing with life, creeps across me with a final shiver – with what *should be* a final shiver. I don't breathe, not with my lungs anyway, but I think *breath* and become entangled in all these shining fibres.

A woman appears from inside the paperiness of the world I'm leaving behind. She's covered in scales and feathers and colours. She smells *new* – like dew and soil after a storm that comes from inside the sea. When she moves, she judders and starts, electromagnetic, approaching me from point to point, trace to trace, without seeming to have been anywhere in between. In this ghostly moment between life and death, she looks like me, like a mirror image that's grown older, more ancient than the thing it tries to copy.

Her palm opens in front of me, and I see hundreds of different doorways flash up inside it. Each one is a story, netting its particular universe into the curve of her fingers. My own surfaces are becoming blurred, like tiny particles of dust waiting to be reshaped inside the otherworldly palm she offers out to me.

"Where would you like to go, Little Wing?"

"Home."

She glances at her hand. "You can make any of these places your home. There are so many stories, Little Wing. So many destinies folded in time. Choose one."

I look back to the place where I had left my body bleeding into the snow. Now I see the empty indentations of large boots that have walked away from the silent reddening crescent I've made with my blood. I see a little body dying right there, all her future stories freezing in time and then shattering like a great sheet of ice. A silence emerging in future time, where once a woman might have been.

A child that was me.

I look back to the feathered and scaled woman. *Azrael, the Angel of Death.* She hushes me and continues to show me the worlds circling in her palm. *Don't look there,* she says, pointing to the blood on the snow, *look here, now.* One of the worlds stays long enough within her lineless hand for me to make out its colours and shapes. As I slow my thoughts down to focus on it, so does it, as if the worlds in her hand and my own racing and dying mind are intimately connected. I feel myself pulled in as the image breaks the borders of her palm and fixes itself around me.

Its skies are yellow and blue and grey. Dark treetops puncture the clouds. The air is cool and crisp and full of the smell of green things growing thick. Below, I can see a tower, a window cut into the rock, and at the window, a woman, trapped inside her room. I see her, filled with *life*, and she pauses and looks directly at me. She leans on the sill without moving, as if she's seen me before and knows I'm no daydream but an otherworldly force come to linger at her window. She's like a quiet storm that comes to scatter the shells of foamy creatures on the seafloor, to push them from out of her psychic body so that they might one day walk out and create the shelf of life.

I know instantly that we're linked, like two sides of the same coin. I see her winding her way backwards from the moment of her death to her first breath, as if the umbilical cord that connected her to her mother's womb was her final destination, and not the other way around. And I know this means I can go to her, *as her*. My own story – the story of the child murdered in the snow – will dissolve into hers. Disappear into this origin source. Strong as a tide that lives only through the traces it makes. A story about women *who, this time, will survive*.

My attention ignites, becoming an incredible magnet that pulls the blood which is now spilling out into the snow below in a torrent from the side of my head, towards the tower window, creeping across an unseen mass of otherworldly veins that link me to her. To my eyes, in this deathly state, her window cut into the rock appears to be etched in golden threads of light. Its lintel is a lattice of white and red tremors – the inside of a body, pulsing cellular. I am moving towards it! Towards her!

"That one. That's the one," I say to the Angel.

"Then, Little Wing, you must go."

My Angel of Death suddenly reaches out and snatches me up with her strong and vicious arms. She presses her lips to my ear.

"This story is full of death and violence. It is an origin story, and you will rewrite it. You will experience the order of time differently than those around you to do this. Make no mistake,

Little Wing, it will be painful, but *you will pass through it*. And all your labour will be a gift – the gift you will give in exchange for your return to me. All life has a price, and all stories are about how one pays that price over time. Yours will be about how these stories come to be written into time."

I pull back.

"If it's an origin story, does that mean it comes *before* time? How can I tell a story that exists *outside* of time?"

She smiles and looks at me as if she's known me for thousands of years.

"Time lives inside you."

Her otherworldly fingers reach across my body and then around my face, as if fixing me back into form, and I start to feel heavy. I start to feel gravity again. I pull back to look at her, standing in front of me like a terrible and beautiful goddess with thousands of faces. I want to print her onto my mind, but I know I'll forget her the moment I open my eyes and am born in this new world. When she speaks next, it feels as if her words are writing themselves into my atoms.

Time lives inside you.

I feel an unexpected thud ricochet through my chest and inside my ears. Then there's an immense rushing, as if I were falling from a great height. I see myself – the life I'm dying away from in the snow for a moment. And then I see the life I'm moving towards, the woman inside the tower, living so many years in the past, her story, about to unfold again in time through me, through my living of it. For a moment, I pause. It makes me sad to see myself die as a little girl, covered in blood in the snow, even from this immense height. I see the white pathway return, the parting that split my hair into two distinct sections on either side of my head. *No. Let me live!*

And then, without warning, I sit up. I simply sit right up in the very same place I had fallen down only moments before. I have interrupted death and returned to the same spot. And it's strange because everything feels different. From the moment I open my eyes, I know I'm two in one. Not possessed. Not that. Just that I will hover between two lives, knowing both. An ancient knowing that will play out through my flesh. My life. My *lives*.

The Angel of Death is right. Time starts to run differently from that moment on. Instead of moving in neat, even tempos across a steady rhythm, it trembles, stumbles, hovers and whispers; a great ghost, moving like a hurricane across the sky, taking everything with it, pressing the world into new, temporary shapes. When I sit up in the snow, I see the pool of blood still arcing out around my body. Three of my teeth have been dislodged. I remember that it had been snowing again before my momentary exit from the world. Now the new white flakes around me are reddening with blood. A sharp breeze picks up and sends some of the flakes flying upwards in a dance. It makes me smile, and I think: *I have become snow. My blood is in each flake's tiny rotational symmetry and how it dances upward, defying gravity!*

It's quiet and nobody's around. So, I go into the new, settling snow like a little burrowing mole. I wash myself with its whiteness. Then I start to panic because I feel the cold like I never have before. *What happened? What happened to me?* My little lungs are throbbing with frozen air and shock. I think of the woman who passed through the fibres – the Angel whose palm had held all my destinies, the 'her' that was 'me' and who was at the same time ancient and young and somehow out of time. I hear her voice vibrating across the different breezes that come as the wind changes course around me: "*Time lives inside you.*" I smile as I feel a thousand wings beating around me.

I clean and scrub the blood out of my hair and off my skin with new snow, using my fingertips. My clothes will have to wait. I go to the doorway of the refugee block, my grandmother's doorway. Before I walk through its gaping mouth, I touch the door frame all around the opening. I'm too small to reach the top of the frame, so I just hold my palms upwards and flat above me, as if feeling its surface, tracing its length, although a good two feet remain between us. Then I run them down the other side. I don't know why I do this odd little ritual, but I know it's important. I know I need to rebirth myself, and this door – the doorway which I had fallen and died at – was the womb I needed to come through in order to live in the world again. I finish tracing the surfaces, breathe in, and walk back inside.

It's only later on that I remember anything of how I had come to die. Violence is slow to the mind and fast to the body. It doesn't have a language, only sensations that play across the skin like shadows you can never get rid of. Language comes later.

Chapter Three

"Why do you Turks hate us so much?"

"I don't hate you, Little Wing. Come, you mustn't be seen talking to me here."

"Why not? It's my castle after all. I can talk to whomever I like!"

"Very well, but don't lose your head," and he flicked his hand to his left temple. It was such an odd gesture, and it was accompanied with his wild kind of smile.

I laughed out loud for the very first time since I'd come to Cachtice.

We walked quickly out of sight of the blacksmiths' furnace house together. I led him, as I didn't like to be in the unnatural aura of that building for one bit longer than necessary. But he soon trailed behind, humming occasionally and stopping to pick at a random daisy, as if he were merely summering here and not a slave-Turk following after the mistress of the region.

Once inside the main building of Cachtice, we walked into the basement of my tower together and he sat down with his legs under him again.

"What do you want from me, Little Wing? What can I give you to lighten your little growing heart?"

It was a strange way of talking, but I ignored that.

"I want to know everything you know. I want to know about the Ottomans, about the Sultan, about why you're here. I want to know about power, about the gods in the earth, about love. I want to know how you can be a slave and yet seem so –" I didn't quite know what he was, so I just gestured, opening my palms to admit that both my words and hands failed to capture anything of him. If he hadn't been a slave, I would have said, "so free of *everything*?" But the heavy stoop of his shoulders from all the coal carrying made that feel wrong too.

He laughed, slowing my barrage of questions by raising his hand. He looked at me with a kind of fondness that at once seemed warm and safe, and yet in the same moment threatened to topple me from a great height. He was like a lion or a wolf that had been turned out of his forest and yet had lost none of his power.

"All right then, Little Wing. I'll tell you everything I know." He turned his back momentarily and selected a book and a few handwritten pages that he pulled from out of a pile stacked up in the corner.

"You can start with these." He held some papers handwritten in Hungarian out to me, but when I went to take them, he retracted his hand momentarily, smiling a little and fixing me with his astral gaze.

"But it's important you read these slowly, Little Wing. *Slowly.*"

*

Whenever you hear stories about time travel, the stakes are always so high. *Kill the bad guy! Find the hidden treasure! Save the hero!* But in truth it's not like that at all. Every time I find myself else*when*, the only rule is this: survive it. Get through it.

Here, now, something rectangular is taking shape around me as I emerge in time, drawn a little more into being, even as I become aware of it. My elbows are resting on it so I must be sitting down. I'm at a long dining table. It's littered with tall bottles and long-stemmed glasses. Other now-absent vessels have left half-circles in wine on the white tablecloth, which map the passage of hours and minutes. I must have been here all night. It's a college party in a dark wood-panelled dining room, although it's hard to tell which one or exactly when this is. They all blur into each other at some point.

These are the kind of parties you get invited to when you work at a university. 'Fun' is not something you have at them. Fun is something you pursue; the thrill of the chase – of an idea, a grant, or a promotion. Or a person. Everyone always lives in the future in academia. *And I'm the one who's meant to be the time traveller!* Everyone always wants more because whatever is *here, now,* is never enough.

"Dopamine-chasers," I mutter to myself just as I fully emerge in this pocket of time.

Before I say any more, I must tell you that when I travel across time, I don't emerge into an empty space, shocking everyone with the strange magicks that make me appear or disappear at the drop of a hat, *hey presto!* Time doesn't work like that. It never has. You don't emerge *in* time. Time puts you in a position as if you had been there all along. You join a timeline that everyone assumes is the only one in the world. Everyone else just gets on with their day, whilst you, the time traveller, inevitably end up feeling *scattered,* remembering the in-between world that no one else does, the moments when all the flights of time congeal and re-emerge.

When people say 'shaken to my bones', that's the feeling, and I imagine this means that the universe is made up of multiple timelines – infinite ones, in fact, that we're not meant to remember but that, for some reason, I did each time I emerged.

Maybe this is the real shock of untimely death, the shock of seeing behind the rafters of temporality. You just feel awkward and out of place the whole time. But I can't think about such immensities right now. Right now, all my concentration is bent on working out exactly where I am, so I don't slip up and reveal myself a time traveller. So that I can *survive*.

It takes a lot of effort to live like this, and it gets difficult when I arrive in moments when I'm a child – four, five, or six years old – because even though I'm an adult woman, ancient even, a child's brain doesn't have the same filters an adult's does. The body and the mind entangle, and I hear myself saying things like, *Mummy, when I was forty, I went out by myself all the time. Why can't I go now?* and other things that everybody else describes as 'quaint' but that are, in truth, signs that a little time traveller is standing right in front of them. Unnoticed.

It's a lonely business and after a while it makes small parts of you grow hard and cynical, cementing an exhausted sense of defeat inside your bones. No one believes a word you say thereafter, if you've said even once that you travel across time, with no coherence, with no rhyme or reason to your flights away. What kind of life can withstand the teeth of timelessness in the long run?

I search for my phone, noticing my fingernails as I do. At this point in linear time, I'm far too 'old' to be wearing chipped black nail polish, and yet, there it is. Staring me in the face.

Date, time, position? 2012 approx.

Okay.

I glance around me and raise my eyebrows. Wood panels. Oil paintings. Port and cheese. I'm completing my PhD. I still haven't published on Bathory yet. But I will. So I can relax a little in the full knowledge of what will happen. Of what has already happened a hundred times over in the future.

Nowhere else in the world could brand this level of superiority and bottle it as well as they do in a university like this. But I'm definitely the wrong colour to take full advantage of it. My skin is olive, and my eyes are dark, and nobody can quite place me. They try not to ask, but inevitably do. You don't have to be a time traveller to feel the permanent awkwardness of being mixed heritage in a sea of nervous whiteness.

The other thing about this place is it's full of endless secrets. Secret alliances. Secret funds. Secret infedelious touches. These are the hunting grounds scholars live in. A world of if-onlys that takes shape inside every careful invitation to 'dinner and drinks'. A university is one big predator. Everyone knows everyone else's business. Their lives depend on it. Position, place, time. Without these, the gods of academe would fall. The structures would crumble down in a mess of uncertainty. You must be discernible, fixable, readable. If not, you might find yourself on the wrong side of *history. Exorcised from the institution like an unruly spirit who has never – and should never – belong.* I smile to myself. I've been there! *Over and over again.*

My eyes *here, no*w, fix on a man close by. He's about forty. His green eyes and long limbs make him impossible to miss. His name is Mark and we're lovers, although this is a generous word for it. We've both hypnotised each other into believing that neither one of us is who we really are. I'm *not* a traveller in time. I'm not at the mercy of the temporal forces that live inside me but that are at the same time beyond me – forces that will remove me at any moment like a careless smudge on a page. I am a woman that will do anything for his love. He is a man who cannot. Will not. No matter how hard he tries. No matter how hard he strains against his own narration.

And narration is something he does *all* the time. Even when we're in bed together, like a child who speaks rapidly about what's going on even as he builds and destroys his own tower of brightly coloured bricks. He narrates me into mother, sister, friend. He falls silent when it comes to 'lover', and I often wonder if there's no vocabulary for this inside him. The blank sheets on the bed terrify him. When I whisper into his naked ear, he grabs my hands gently at the wrists. "Shh." Then he bites. Then and only then, does he speak the word *lover*.

I look at him from across the table. He's talking to a young graduate student called Laura. She's loud, drunk and totally in love with him.

"…But I think that it's more than that! I think that *history* was a concept that was invented, even in the Renaissance. Even as late as that! The way we understand history anyway."

Passionate. Young. And she clearly believes in cause and effect. Something buzzes against the walls of my pocket. I discreetly pull out my phone again, but the screen is a mess of lines, as if it's just been dropped in water *or has moved across time. That figures,* I think to myself. I look back to Mark and Laura. These are faces I'd rather forget.

If I look too hard at her now, I'll see her face turning into its future, and I can't bear to see that just now. To see the trees and sky that lie above her grave. I blink. I can almost hear her as she leans towards Mark in the dining room. Not her thoughts but her desires, the way she imagines her future will be. *If only I can make him like me, then he'll see my worth. He'll see my work is worth funding, and when I'm hired, he'll see me as an equal. He'll see me and we'll be together.* The predatory doors of the university close around her.

"Nonsense." And he laughs gently, warmly, at her, whilst fixing her with his gaze. She moves to disagree, but he lifts his finger.

"Laura, now you're going to say that there are many histories, many *historical distributions*. History experienced horizontally rather than in a ladder of past, present and future. It could well be, but what do you hope to achieve with that? People are starving and dying because of *history*. Would you deny them the opportunity of justice? It's poorly conceived. It doesn't *do* anything. Nothing meaningful in the world at any rate."

He looks at her over the top of his round glasses that house a mild prescription. He hardly ever wears them at home. She catches her breath, about to retaliate, but then thinks better of it. He has a point after all. Our sense of justice depends on linear time. She falls silent, a little sad even, and is lost for words. He puts his hand out, palm upwards, flat, and horizontal before her. Inviting.

"Care to get a refill, instead?"

She nods. He leads her to where a decanter of ruby red wine sits on a small table, as the hum of chatter in the dining room picks up. He puts his hand at the small of her back as she pours. And *bang!* I see a hypnosis fall over her like an invisible veil. For a moment, the scene playing out in front of me reminds me of something. But it's not my memory. It's definitely not a memory from out of my own disordered lifetime. It comes from the wound. It comes from Bathory. It's as if I've momentarily been transported into a decadent court. Instead of nylon dresses and sheer tights, the women around me are all fluttering in ancient gowns. And instead of Mark's green eyes flashing under the lights, I see a tall man, deep in the past, dressed in black. His eyes are blue and cold, and his tunic is covered in white pearls that glint and wink like lights on a dark sea. I blink a few times to scatter the image. *Don't come for me now, Bathory. I've only just emerged in my own timeline and I'm feeling a little nauseous. Just let me be.*

A woman with long black hair that wraps around her shoulders like an animal shawl taps my arm. She's a fair bit older than I am and holds herself haughtily, her chin raised just enough to show she's not to be trifled with. Her accent is Italian, rolling and falling, a deep cascade of clouds in autumn. She doesn't know it right now, but I know her like I know the lines on my own hand. And that's because we haven't even met just yet, well, not in her sense of time. But at another point in her life, she'll leave me notes in a small panelled hole in the wall in the library so I can find her, and we'll work together to break each other out of the wounds we carry and that have changed our lives so deeply. *Slowly. Slowly.*

"I hate it here," she says to me.

I try not to laugh. This is so her. This is how Lucretia would introduce herself to someone she thought she was meeting for the first time. She too had experienced a short untimely death, and that's why eventually she'll be able to see me. *Really see me,* as I emerge and vanish across timelines. What is it about having lived and died once already that makes one so cynical? I think to myself as she eyes me. Maybe it's because if you've lived and died before, you know something about how crazy the world is. How wild it is to believe in the permanence of *anything.* I simply nod in assent and look away.

Lucretia takes a sip of wine and jerks her head towards Mark, who is now whispering in the young girl's ear. The girl looks panic-stricken, as if she's about to be eaten up, but rather than move away, she places a hand on his arm in a manner that only she must believe is discreet. She smiles and looks up at him for reassurance, as if he might protect her from himself.

"Universities are hard."

"How so?" I ask, feigning distractedness to resist throwing my arms around her and saying, *Lucretia, it's me! Let's go and sit on the roof at your place, drink wine and share everything about what it is to have already died once in the world until it all hurts a little less.*

"We wear all the sins under our skin. Look at these panelled walls, so full of dark secrets. You have to look at the *body* if you want to get the truth," and she brushes her arms with her fingertips as she speaks, displacing the light hairs first one way, then the other, before dismissing all the people in the room with a dramatic flick of both wrists. Her way of speaking has an odd kind of poetry to it.

"Look at *him*. And her. Dancing the dance of power. Both of them." She makes a small retching sound. "It'll end badly."

I always remember this moment in time. Not because of what happens here but because of what *will happen next* now that Mark has placed his hand on the small of Laura's back. Who could know that one little touch could be so instrumental in a young woman's life? Who could know that it would spell her death?

Lucretia's waiting for my response. She appears to me now like a goddess ruined by knowledge; a man's version of Lillith inside our strange ivory-towered world. I can almost hear her heart beating out a tide of old memories as she speaks.

"What are you working on?" I ask her, to change the subject, as if I don't already know and haven't read every last word she's ever written and will write in now's future. She's like a dark star sitting quietly inside a constellation. Waiting for something quietly to pass her by before drawing it to her. She rolls her black eyes ever so slightly and speaks flatly, bored with my question.

"Alexandria. The lost library." They were two empty bullet points. "But at the end of the day, who gives a shit? We lost it all anyway. All that knowledge. All that wisdom. Gone." And she snaps her fingers.

Yes. This is Lucretia. Still living out her own death in life, although right now she doesn't know that I know. Lucretia the dreamwalker. A visionary trapped in the body of a slightly bored professor.

I resist the urge to disagree with her right now. After all, knowledge appears everywhere, stretching out in more than just libraries and texts. Shivering inside the body. She's the one who teaches me that. Teaches me how to *hear it* like some kind of shamaness or ancient witch. But I hesitate. What good does all the knowledge in the world do if you can't act on it? And nothing I do can change the events I live over and over even though I've tried a thousand times. A grand zero sucks me inside it and spins me round and round in new configurations that have become predictable by now and which I have no clue how to escape. The grand zero of history. *There has to be a way out!*

"What about you?" she finally asks. "What do *you* do?" Her brooding momentarily lifts.

"The Countess Bathory. The famous *Blood Countess.*" As soon as I speak her name out loud, I can feel her – *Bathory,* as if she had been summoned to peer through my veins, my hair, my bones; waiting for me to discover her, just as she was discovering me. I see her, as I saw her when I first died, leaning on her window sill, locked in her tower. Her lips move and tremble. They form words I can almost hear: *write me well...*

"Heroes and antiheroes, they come and go," I say, "but Bathory is more than that. She's like a cautionary tale. *Beware you don't come across Bathory the Monster!* Even today. Still, it's all so empty of evidence. Her very public trial. Her accusers. There's nothing except the word of the few men that went on to pocket all her money – and it was *a lot* by the way. Trillions by today's standards." I trace a round red ring on the tablecloth with my finger. Little marks that indicate where something once stood. Marks that can be washed out if you have the right kind of detergent and try hard enough.

"I think history and silence work together. They work deep inside us all. So, to rewrite Bathory, I'll need to rewrite nothing less than the idea of history. What it *does* to people – to women." I pick up the glass in front of me and look through it. "I mean, rewrite the way history is really *lived*."

Lucretia looks at me like I've read her mind. I haven't, of course. We've discussed this all before on the top of her roof, looking through her kid's telescope at the net of heaven above us.

"Be careful." She says it slowly, eyeing me.

"Why?"

"The spirit of a silenced ghost is hard to manage. In both worlds. Leave the workings of time be."

I laugh in agreement. Then I pause and look at her and I can't help it. I reach out my arms and hug her. My friend. My partner in crime. The only person in the whole world, it seems, who understands my deathly state – or will do soon.

She bristles, confused as to why a near stranger would be so affectionate.

"But what if it's time that won't leave *me* be?" I say. She disentangles herself, not unkindly, more out of perplexity.

"Then I'd say get ready. Not just libraries but people, they have been burnt for less."

Chapter Four

Erzi's rattle was still ringing and jangling when I ran outside. Racing down my spiralling tower had made me a little dizzy. Dozens of people crowded the vestibule, huddling away from the rain. I shoved and pushed and slipped through their wet limbs until I could see the outline of the doorway ahead. The sun, behind the greyness of the sky, had lit up its corners, promising that heaven was contained, *here, now,* just beyond reach. *Safety.* I ran towards it in zigzags until at last I made it through and out to the courtyard and the low wall, the vast distance between Cachtice and the mountains unravelling ahead. I was afraid and wanted to keep running and not stop until I reached my mother's arms again. I was afraid of Nadasdy – even though I still hadn't met him.

Erzi stood like a shadow from the future, her rough and crackling hair standing about her head like her very own witch's familiar as I ran out. She smelt of the forest and carried all the unpredictable rage of the wind, waving her rattle in my face and glaring at me, almost yellow with rage.

"Go, evil sister. Go!"

Her anger was palpable, pouring through her in haptic arcs that reached out to grab at me even though her fingers were far away. She muttered something, shaking the rattle again, narrowing the gap between us with surprising agility. As she bore down upon me, I lifted myself up to my full height and screamed right at her in a single cry, lobbing a ghostly ball of fire out of my mouth.

She looked stunned. Such a sound shouldn't be inside the body of a young woman. But then she dismissed it – nothing more than further proof of my own evil otherworldliness. I continued running. There was a rough dirt path that fell at a disturbingly abrupt angle on the other side of the boundary wall. It led directly downwards to the blacksmiths' angry little building – the one that boomed all day as if a terrible giant were trapped inside it. I hesitated for a moment. Anna emerged from out of nowhere, shouting, "Found you! Come back here this instant." I jumped over the low wall away from her and went tumbling down the elbow of the hillside path. I sent dust and stones and blades of dry grass into spirals of motion after me and might have even raised the dead and buried with the force and spectacle of my descent.

I had raced away because Nadasdy had returned, and he hadn't wanted to meet me or even see my face.

"He preferred that you were kept away at Sarvar Castle instead of waiting here for him at Cachtice. I suppose that's my error, though. *I should have thought of that,*" Anna had said.

I felt as if I had been punched hard in the belly.

"Elizabet, make sure you're quiet as a mouse and out of sight this week. In fact, perhaps you should stay in your tower rooms unless he sends for you. When a man returns from war, he can be a little – strange, at first. Why don't you resume your painting, or try a new image to weave?"

My entire life had been organised around waiting and preparing myself to receive my husband-to-be's approval. My own thoughts and desires were things to be kept out of sight and so I had built a thriving world away from everyone in secret. Now, he didn't even want me to exist in the same space as him at all.

I regained my footing at last and kept on running away from Cachtice, from Nadasdy, from Anna and all her strange, controlling comfort. On the horizon, the blacksmiths' furnace house came up to meet me, its two wooden columns open-mouthed, looking for all the world like splintering jaw bones that held the house in a permanent expression of terror. I felt the thud of fear split my belly, but I wanted only to escape from Anna, who would no doubt lock me back in my room to wait for when – for *if* – my husband ever wanted to meet me. So, I ignored the fear. I ran to the other side of the building and stopped to catch my breath. Blood trickled all the way down my legs. My monthly cycle was upon me, and the fall had disrupted the cloths I used. Still, I didn't care. I just wanted to escape. At all costs.

Who or what was Nadasdy? Why did war make him so strange that I had to be hidden from him – to be erased – lest I disturb him like sand in an hourglass, before the right time? A few tears fell down my face. I was trapped between too many fears. I sat against the smithy wall and tried to calm my breathing. After a moment, an arm grabbed me and stood me up.

"Away." It was the huge man I had encountered on my first day in Cachtice.

"No! No! No!" I panicked, the word tumbling out of me again and again until I had no more breath or will or even sense of its purpose anymore. The blood drained out of my face, and I simply stared up at him. He let me go, grunting a few words. I now spoke enough of his language to understand, "It was worse at Mohacs."

I knew a little by now of what he meant. Mohacs was a battle so bloody that it had passed, almost immediately, into myth. Every story was told through it. It haunted all the unspoken things. *Mohacs* was everywhere. When the Turks come, they come hard, *always*, and once all the soldiers were dead, the peasants had been armed with nothing but crude swords, knives, even household iron. Their bodies had been torn to pieces. In the custom of the time – both Hungarian and Ottoman – our peasant armies had their vanquished heads spiked on crude wooden poles on the field, and the ground had been full of nothing but flesh and teeth for months.

Whilst every battle in our violent time was bloody, no battle was quite like this one. It should have been the end of violence. It should have been the war to end all wars. Somehow, it was the very opposite. Every tapestry in Cachtice was emblazoned with it, the corridors no more than ghostly architectures of flesh, living out their dreams in the woven wool fibres that covered Nadasdy's home in too many stories. *It was worse at Mohacs* had a double use. It was both used to stop children from whining about silly things and to make all the spoken words of the adult world sober with the eternal memory of blood. How blood ran in everything here! In the tapestries, in the stories and in the strangeness of my husband-to-be's sudden return; a man who had been at the head of each battle since he could use a sword. What kind of violence was in him?

I got up and crept around the side of the smithy wall and looked in at the open doorway. In the corner, the metal chair that had been hammered outside months before sat square and upright. In the half-light, it no longer looked like a throne. It looked like a shadow had crumpled together and gained form. I wanted to touch it, almost imagining it might disappear into ashes the moment I made contact with its surfaces. Nothing that sat in that chair could feel regal. It could only feel cold and small and lost, abandoned in a blacksmiths' forge to rule over nothing but hammers and iron things yet to be made.

The giant blacksmith saw me staring again. This time, I had trespassed right into his domain. He watched, shaking with some darkness I didn't understand, then nodded his head, and another man in a black leather apron picked me up with both his hands. The men hammering in the house stopped what they were doing and stared, unmoving and unmoved at the sight of me. I was flailing in a strange silence. The huge one looked directly at me. I could almost feel him flood with memory. His eyes were no longer here. But I knew where they had fled to: Mohacs...

"You want this throne, *too*? It's yours, Bathory-witch!" and I was sat down on it so hard that my bones jolted and for a moment I felt my whole body turn to lightning. The men started to jeer and whistle. The air fizzed with a dark excitement. One picked up a hollow metal circle and threw it to the man holding me down. "Crown her. Crown the Bathory-witch."

And he did. I didn't understand what was happening to me. Blood was beginning to splutter out from under my dress and I could feel it seeping onto the chair. I was in terror. I couldn't move. I began to feel lightheaded. No one was coming down here. I would have to get out by myself.

"Stop!" But they just kept laughing.

One man ran his fingers across his throat. "If you speak of this, you'll be next, *Countess* Bathory." I could feel the pulsing of hatred in his sounding of each syllable of my name. I put them together then, my name and Mohacs, and saw myself emerging through the patterns they made, as if I were running with ink. We were all linked. I just didn't know how. *Bathory-bitch. Bathory-witch.* I covered my ears with my hands, but I could still see them all crowding around me. Hate. Bitter, rageful hate. The kind of hate that creates death in an eyeblink.

All at once, my ear began to bleed. I heard a ringing noise and felt myself loosening from the bonds of this world. "Please, God, save me!" I whispered to myself as I felt my chest tighten, spasms of pain running through me in cold lattices. But neither God nor any human soul came, so I squeezed my eyes shut and left my body behind.

*

Why am I in the snow? It's not winter. In fact, it's the end of spring. Why am I lying here? This isn't Cachtice. I'm in the wrong place. I feel my cheeks. Cold. And my hair, it's tied strangely in two knotting lengths down each side of my head. Blood is everywhere in the snow. I'm in strange garments. What's happening to me? I must get back to Cachtice. I must get back to Cachtice!

*

I woke up in the metal chair. The blacksmiths were still there but had continued with their work once I had… once whatever had taken me momentarily had done so. I touched my face again, just to reassure myself that I was still alive and in control of my limbs. I turned my head to the doorway to see if I could make a quick escape through its open arch. Outside, sitting with legs crossed beneath him, was the Ottoman. He was looking right at me. As soon as he saw me moving in the chair, he jumped up and came in through the doorway. The men stopped what they were doing and hissed. One grabbed a large poker and ran his hands suggestively down it before stabbing at the air towards him. I ran out as fast as I could. The Ottoman ran after me.

As soon as we were away from the building, I fell into his arms. I couldn't sob; it was as if the heat coming off the blacksmiths in all their rage had dried up any water in my body. He held me very close to him, cradling my head like a baby's. Then, after a moment, "Little Wing, can you walk just for a bit? Let's get you somewhere safe." I nodded. I put my hands up to my forehead. Something felt cold and heavy. He helped me slip the metal crown off my head. He spat at it three times to ward off the devil and sent it rolling away. He took my hand, and we ran fast, first towards the castle.

"No! Not back there!"

He nodded his head in assent and soon we were careening away from its gate and in the direction of the woods.

The trees opened, and we ran between their bellies. When I lurched ahead, the Ottoman would reach out and grab my hand, tentacular, as if his arms had the capacity to stretch and grow and seek me out. Then he would lead me to the left, to the right, to the left, and so on until I felt that we had reached the forest's own beating heart, far away from Cachtice and the terrors of its strange inhabitants. Breathing hard, his off-white tunic and trousers were now stained green around the legs, as if he were slowly becoming part-forest himself. Then, abruptly, he let me go.

"Little Wing, we're *far* away now. Stop and catch your breath."

My back had given up and I collapsed into the soft grasses between the trees. I was immensely thirsty, but I could hear no stream around, so I sucked at my own tongue, which only made me cough. The Ottoman rested his elbows on his knees, inspecting leaves and moss, before looking up and around. He ripped a bit of dewy moss from the foot of a large tree.

"Here. Don't eat it, just suck the water off." I frowned but took it from him all the same. "Calm yourself, Little Wing. We'll find some water in a bit. He ripped off some for himself, looked at me as if daring me to join him, and placed the whole lot of it in his mouth. He then quickly spat it out.

"Don't forget to brush off any insects first."

I nearly dropped it. He laughed, stretched and sat down beside me.

"I've spent a lot of time in forests."

He shut his eyes, but I still felt him somehow watching me. How many states could this Ottoman be in at once?

Silence fell between us, but the forest hummed and sang, alive with a thousand creatures whose eyes, feelers and antlers vibrated with the knowledge of our arrival and our inevitable departure. All the terror suddenly moved through my body, escaping in tears. The Ottoman sat up and held his palms out to reassure me that he would make no attempt at me, then took both my hands in his. I allowed him to hold them and realised that this was the second time a strange man had done this bizarre ritual of palms.

I thought of the Count. Would I have allowed him to hold my hands? To be fair, unlacing my corset was probably more intimate, but this touch, this contact, was altogether different. I flushed, reminded myself of my rank and title and wound my relaxing jaw back into an aristocratic kind of granite. But I kept holding onto his hands, nonetheless.

He smiled at me.

"Little Wing, friendship is the greatest of all loves."

"Then you have it," I replied.

"And you mine." He curled my right hand in his and held it to his heart. "I will always be looking after you."

Silence fell again. I cried a little more. Then, together, we listened to birds and beasts and odd winged creatures who clicked and buzzed and disappeared into the leaves and branches, becoming one with the surfaces on which they sat. "Look," said the Ottoman, pointing to a small clump of white crocuses. "Watch how, year after year, they grow back. *That's* power! And you have that power too, Little Wing."

He smiled and pointed towards my heart.

"Except your heart is even stronger." He lay back again, pulling some more moss off the tree and offering me half, which I promptly refused. "Nadasdy will eat the Ottomans, limb by limb. But Bathory will save us, Mohammedans, Christians and Jews, all alike."

He chewed at the moss a little and I watched to see if his lips would go green as they merged with it or if he would, in fact, remain entirely human, unaffected by what he consumed.

"I can't save anyone. Not even myself," I said eventually.

"No, you can't. Now you are the one who needs saving. But you will. And you will not. The world is perfect as it is."

"The world is full of evil. I'll die of fright over and over just thinking of – that metal – thing." I didn't say this in retort, merely in the sad way of a girl who had all but skipped childhood and knew too much already.

"Yes. Do you know why the blacksmiths put you in that chair?"

I was too afraid to ask. The fear stunned me into silence. Instead, I looked up at the light streaming down from in between the tops of the trees. The rays illuminated particles of pollen and dust, as if heaven was letting a sprinkling of itself fall in tiny orbs and wisps, for no other reason than simply to prove its continuing existence.

"Little Wing, you really should know why. You need to understand the people which you will come to rule, no matter how frightening they appear and no matter how they threaten you."

I momentarily closed my eyes and sighed. In the moment before opening them, I felt myself ageing rapidly on the inside, though my skin remained fresh and full of spring. I looked at him and nodded, chin first, jabbing it silently in assent as the corners of my mouth turned downwards in a new expression that would eventually score my face with burden.

"A long time ago, before you were born, the peasants rose up against their masters here at Cachtice – all over this country. They were starved and sometimes tortured – often for sport – and then they were turned out to fight. To fight us at Mohacs. And by God did we slaughter them. I mean, they were only peasants. They might as well have been armed with spoons." He looked directly at me, putting his hand towards his heart again.

"And I am a janissary. I am and always will be, even here. Even now. Even without a sultan. My sultan is in my heart and my mind, not in Turkey, not anymore.

"My family were born not so far from here. Do you understand me, Little Wing? My grandfather was a Christian, so poor he couldn't even buy bread. We were taken by the Sultan's army, my sister and me. My sister is…" he paused, reaching for a word that eluded him, finally settling on a simpler one unable to contain his meaning "…*gone*." He looked down. It was the first time I'd ever seen him look sorrowful. "But they took me with them. I was no more than a boy. They trained me to fight my own people. And I loved it! I loved serving my lord. They didn't just teach me fighting, you know."

Here, his sorrow broke, and he looked at me out of the corner of his eye as if weighing up whether to let me into a deep secret. He had started to sparkle again.

"My teacher was taught by the descendants, they said, of Haji Bektash himself – the great, ancient father who knows all the mysteries of the human heart and is the singular direction, the inner compass, for all janissaries like me. We were sent out. We raced through the battlefields until our faces, fingers, even the hair on our heads dripped with blood." He paused in his moment of seeming reverie, sucking at the moss again.

"These poor Christian peasants." He snorted, as if they had been no more than flies hovering in his way. "They were sent out to fight *us*. Their masters returned, the few who survived, to the whip, and to starvation." He shook his head at the ground, as if the earth itself was ready to commiserate with him.

"One peasant rose up and created an army out of the few that remained. Power abhors an empty throne, but for peasants to claim their own throne – well, that just upturns the whole world, doesn't it?" He smiled at me warmly – again, another secret in his eyes. "The nobles were outraged. Your own father was amongst them, Little Wing. They rounded them all up, found their leader – a blacksmith called Dosza – and told his followers to make a metal chair and a crown of iron." He looked at me again, grabbing my hand, which was starting to involuntarily shake with fear.

"They then bade them heat both until they glowed in the fire. They sat the peasant king upon it and crowned him until his body," he paused, "*melted*." They tortured and killed all the rest who had followed him, and the roads were lined with their bodies – in the Ottoman way. In *our* way."

"Stop!" I pleaded, covering my head with my white arms. He caught himself and looked a little remorseful.

"There's no stopping violence, Little Wing. If not Turkish, then Hungarian, then some other country. We're all demons of blood. This is what it is to be human. We repeat our violences over and over." He circled his hand at the wrist like a sundial speeding through time.

"Then I no longer want to be human."

"Everything eats, Little Wing. This is the realm we're living in. The Sultan will bite at Nadasdy, Nadasdy will bite at the Turks, the peasants will bite both the Turks and Nadasdy, and the Lord Palatine-to-be, Thurzo, he will bite, piece by piece, at the flesh of the land. And so it goes, round and round. And they call *me* a mercenary!"

"Thurzo?" I asked, surprised. "What do you know of Count Thurzo, janissary?"

"It's my business to know everything." He paused, as if regaining himself, and smiled at some inner joke. He jabbed a stick into the ground, absent-mindedly.

"I am nothing now," he said, though his eyes were dancing again. "My own sultan will condemn me if I return, for having been captured. And here, I'm powerless. I'm only a trinket of Nadasdy's victory. I can't bite anyone."

His stories of violence and the wild reverie he had slipped into frightened me. I realised then that I didn't trust a soul on earth, not even him. I pulled myself up quickly, looking for the best way to run again.

"Except me," I said, as my eyes darted around. "That's why you rescued me from the blacksmiths just now, so you could bite the 'Bathory-witch.'"

"Believe what you like, Little Wing. But there are greater things at stake than the bloodlust of nations." He seemed calm, not at all offended, as if he already knew all about my fears and terrors; all about me.

"Like what? What could possibly be at greater stake?" I asked.

"The soul, Little Wing. The soul itself." He muttered a few words that I didn't understand, an invocation to his god, perhaps. They sounded soft and full of breath, even though they were pronounced only in the back of his throat.

"With so much eating, how can we stop our innermost selves from becoming sick?"

My body calmed its wild heartbeat at this. I went very quiet. He had a way of speaking that shook me awake, and yet it was antiquated and odd, like a lullaby that was somehow out of time. I looked him directly in his green and hazel eyes.

"You've never once told me your name, janissary. Sometimes, I think I don't even know if… if you're even real. Sometimes, you speak to me in ways I don't understand!"

"You still don't trust me, do you, Little Wing?" He said it more like it was an interesting conundrum to solve rather than a slight against him. We both fell quiet for a moment. Then I broke the silence, surveying him with my eyes, which were fast growing into a woman's.

"I think I'll call you Janus," I said. "Janus was a Roman god who had two faces; one good, one evil. It will remind me, every time I speak with you, not to fall too completely under your spell."

"Sounds like a good plan." He lay back and closed his eyes

again. Then without opening them, he smiled to himself as much as to me and concluded, "*my lady.*"

*

A tiny trickle of blood emerges from my right ear. I put my small child-sized index finger to it, catching a drop. The rest falls on the shag carpet. I have a strange sense that it's not my blood but that it belongs to someone deep in the past, long dead, in fact. A girl, maybe thirteen or fourteen, sitting terrified in a strange metal chair. I'm only four years old at this moment in time, and all I want is to run to my mother and get her to get the bleeding girl in the metal chair away from me. But my mother's in the room with the disco music. She and my father's friends are dressed in sharp business suits, but their ties and shirts are all a bit sweaty and askew now. I can hear the clinking of ice cubes in crystal glasses.

Instead of racing to the sounds, the people, to my mother for help, I cross the hall and go to my parents' bedroom. It's quiet in there with the door shut, and my ear starts to settle down. The tactile wallpaper is covered in a delicate palm tree mural, an outline, all modern and sketched like an unfinished thought, a holiday to a warmer, calmer place that we'll never visit. The sound starts up again. It's like a screech and a rumble at the same time. I press my hands back to my ear. *Shh!*

I climb inside the wardrobe to hide from the noise and am embraced by the thick, furry arms of my mother's coats. The sound dies down, as if we were playing a game of hide and seek. I breathe in slowly to steady myself. The child I am thinks it's the sound of monsters rolling past as they search me out. But the woman in me – the woman who has been circling through moments of shattered time – knows what it is. It's the sound of time breaking into pieces.

I press my nose to the fur and smell the rich, musky tones of my mother's perfume. It's the small things – the smell of perfume, the taste of bread, the sensation of sun on the skin – that anchor you to the world when you've returned from death, finding yourself adrift in time. These sensations grow inside you, telling half-finished tales of what it is to be human, waiting for you to order them and tell new stories through their shapes.

It's late and I'm still hiding in my mother's closet. Even at this age, I feel silly. I want to join them upstairs – but how will they *see* me? A four-year-old who needs to be sent back to bed and scolded? Because who would believe that though I was a four-year-old, I was at the same moment *older* than them all – a storehouse of memories deep in my bones? 'Uncanny' was the word most people who sensed this used to describe me. But perhaps that's true of all girl-children, not just those who live differently in time.

I can't reach high enough to put the coats back on the hangers. I cry a little. Then I pull myself together. I go to the armchair in the corner and try to drag it to the closet so I can climb up its arms and tidy the mess I've made of the furs. But it's too heavy. I sink to the floor, giving up. Space and weight always defeat you when you're a child. The sound of time starts again, and I blink. Everything changes around me. I'm hovering by my mother many years in the future. Now she's the one who's reduced in size, but her changes are the effect of time's definite weathering. Now space and weight defeat her. She pats my hand and I lean closer into her as she smiles weakly and full of love.

"My darling, have you come to make me feel better?"

"Yes, Mummy."

It's the wrong word. I don't call her that anymore. I've moved so quickly through the years that language hasn't caught up with me yet.

I blink again. Time reorders around me and I'm back on the floor by the armchair with the party raging upstairs, drowning out the sound of those clinking ice cubes. I go to the cupboard and climb into one of the coats. It trails on the floor behind me like a litter of cubs at my heels. I reach up to the dressing table and grab a cylinder of lipstick. I unwind the tube with my childish fist and smear its warm pigments all over my face, imprinting a tangle of red over my lips, cheeks and nose. I can't control the movements, though this is something I've done so often in bathroom mirrors, car windows and in the reflection of my phone screen as an adult, years in the future.

I head upstairs to the party and enter like the last, unannounced guest at a ball, covered in the sticky red paste.

"When I lived at the court in Hungary, I used to wear capes like this all the time!" I say, my four-year-old tongue clacking and lisping through the words.

The adults laugh. "Wherever did you get that idea from?" My mother and father walk over to me and smile. I spend the last few minutes of the night wrapped in their tendernesses and giggles. One of the guests offers to help me wash my face and take me back to bed.

"You're so sweet," he says. "I wish I had a daughter like you. I just love the colour of your skin and your dark eyes. So *cute!* Shh now."

I lie very still. I'm alone in bed. I have a stack of brightly coloured, softly woven felt turtles, a child's toy, all sitting on top of each other in the corner of the room, just in eyeshot. There are four of them. I count them to remind myself what age I am, and how many family members I have right now. I keep on counting. Counting. The universe holds still. The turtles are stacked up like an indelible spine holding up the world. Later, I would read Indian myths about stacks of turtles holding up not just the earth but the whole cosmos. I would pause and think how it seemed like a really good idea. Time is a spine holding bodies together in space. But there are other ways to organise it all. To live in and out of time without disintegrating.

The sound begins again. It pulls me from right to left under the blanket. On my left is the wall my bed is pushed up against.

On my right, the man from before blocks my escape and a tall, dark woman stands in the doorway. She looks at me. I stare at her own perfect red lipstick, which I can make out, only just, in the shadowy landscape of the room, although at first, in this nighttime light, it looks almost black. It lies over her lips like a promise, an introduction to the darker parts of the world and all its secrets.

"Let's teach her fucking parents a lesson. Hold her down."

I make to scream but the man holds his huge hand over my mouth.

I gasp for air over and over. In linear time, this is the first moment I learn about how we inherit violences that have nothing to do with us. This is the first moment I learn how close we all are to death at any moment. The snow will come later to remind me, and it will rip a hole in time when it does.

The room starts to fall away, becoming first a mass of vectors and points, beginning to become somewhere else. I can't see the bedroom doorway for the woman with the black lips *advancing, advancing*, so a different one emerges this time. It opens up around me, crumpling the edges of the bedroom, the man, the woman, and my own flesh. And everything dissolves and is rebuilt.

I find myself at once tapping a microphone with a perfectly manicured fingertip. There are at least two video cameras on me. The third camera belongs to the funding body. In its placement directly in front of me, it watches me more keenly than the others, taking in my expressions. I smile because I know that the one thing it won't have captured is my abrupt emergence into this slice of time. *Because time lives inside you.*

I clear my throat. *Let's begin*, I think to myself.

Today, I want to talk about time. I want to talk about what it really means to travel in time, without spaceships and technologies, but with the body. I want to invite you to come with me on a journey into the world of 'what-if' to unravel 'what-is'. So, take a breath, suspend your will to order time into neat packets of meaning, close your eyes if you must and one-two-three jump...!

*

When I finally left the forest, I went back to my tower. The rain and the wind and the darkness had ceased, but I wore them all on my skin. The blood had destroyed my dress beyond all washing. Anna was nowhere to be found, which filled me with a strange mix of relief and perplexed worry. Without her scolding to habituate the situation, everything felt a little out of place. Also, I had no way to wash as the servants still all scurried away from me on sight and there was no hot water without them.

I took the sheet off the bed, went to the pitcher, which was on the nightstand, and dipped the corners into it. I wiped as much of the mud and blood off me as I could and then rolled around inside the sheet, like an Egyptian refusing to be buried. I drank the rest of the water, lit more candles and lay naked on the floor. I wanted to feel the stones beneath me for a moment – feel the certainty of their silent and ancient bodies come to meet me.

I sat down on the floor, attempting to fold my legs under me in the same way Janus did. I breathed out, relaxing my bruised body. It felt so peaceful, just sitting. At first, I listened out for the sounds of the castle at night. There were so many! So many creatures outside the windows, so many small moths, tiny spiders and sighing cobwebs waiting in the unseen parts of the room, as if my stillness had always been the invitation they had written to me, and all I had ever needed to do was show up.

Eventually, I stopped listening out for them and allowed their sounds to enter my ears on their own, vibrating and whispering in their peculiar rhythmic tongues. A moth appeared and zigzagged across the vectors of light thrown about by the candle, orbiting its flame like a tiny moon that waned away a little more with each crossing. Eventually, it fell down, dead at my feet.

"Little wing," I said tenderly, "perhaps we're both little wings."

I didn't want to get any residual mud or blood on the bed, so I looked around the room for something to cover myself with as I slept. There was one of Nadasdy's interminably violent tapestries on the wall, depicting yet another battle. It seemed apt that the mud from the forest and the blood from my own body might mingle with the battlefield scenes stitched out in such detail. I took the small sewing chair from the corner of the room and stood on it to unhook the tapestry. It came down easily enough and I wrapped myself up in it. It scratched my skin a little, but I relaxed myself into its grip.

"This feels strangely like my wedding night," I whispered to Bran, who still sat on the bed by the plumped-up cushions. I fell asleep almost immediately, embraced by my husband's rich history stamped out in woollen fibres.

Nadasdy had asked to meet me the following week but had then been called away urgently by Thurzo before we could conduct the formal arrangement. It no longer bothered me, as now I was busying myself in my tower sitting cross-legged in the way Janus had shown me, trying to talk to moths. It was a better pastime than any 'husband's approval'.

"What are you doing in there?" Anna would call through the thick door, which I had made shut under the iron handle with the sewing chair, claiming my own space for the first time. Most times, I wouldn't answer, and eventually she would get exasperated, turn about and leave. Sometimes, I would shout back, "Nothing! I'm naked. Leave me alone," and then try to settle back into receiving all those creaturely sounds.

"Elizabet, this is important," came Anna's loud voice through the thickset door. "Nadasdy can't meet you. He has to go with Thurzo. Be ready for next time."

"I shall," I shouted, hoping that she would go so I could get back to listening closely to the tiny world.

"Elizabet?" she repeated. "It's not good for a girl of your age to spend so much time alone and unsupervised. People will say you're a *talto*."

I laughed to myself at this. Now being out of sight had suddenly become as prohibited as being seen. There was no way to be a young woman in this world.

Talto. In my language, it meant shaman. Not 'witch'. Not anything so dark or devilish. Not anything so criminal. A *talto*, according to anyone you asked, was a person who lived sometimes in another world. But it also meant a person who was, to all intents and purposes, a dreamer and an outsider. I wasn't so sure what it meant at Cachtice, but from the tone of Anna's voice and the memory of the blacksmiths' *Bathory-witch!*, I deduced I might not want to find out. She waited a moment for a response, but I offered none and soon felt the air pressure change as she took herself off down the winding stairs.

I got up from the stone floor and hovered by the window. The Cachtice sky was a mess of colours. I wondered if the colours themselves had their own kind of language, their stories ricocheting across lands, waters and bones in words unfamiliar to human ears. I looked down at my hand, glowing gold and pink in the approaching sunset as I leant out. I was becoming part of the sky's phantom speech, my body a droplet of blood racing around it, an entangled part of its own divinely embodied lightshow.

I caught myself in my reverie. A little aways, below my tower, Nadasdy was talking to Anna. It could only have been Nadasdy on account of the fabulous crest and clothing he wore. But I couldn't see his face. He pressed some gold into Anna's palm before walking off to the stables. He was in no way impressive like Thurzo. In fact, he looked more like a lithe, pale weed. And he didn't stride like Thurzo did but was awkward, like his feet didn't quite know what to do with the earth below him, and the earth, in turn, had decided to make a game out of it.

Suddenly he stopped dead in his tracks, and I could have sworn he felt me watching him, just as I had once felt Erzi the wild one watching me. Then he walked on, shielding his eyes from the brilliance of the light, and possibly also from me, so that I wouldn't see his face before my appointed time. I could make out Thurzo in the distance and took an instinctive step back. I felt all of a sudden that his fate was woven into mine, perhaps even more so than Nadasdy's would be. And in all this, where was I? Was my fate never going to be my own?

I sat back down on the floor and dug my palms beneath me so that they would press as hard as possible against the cool greyness of the rocky material that made up my chamber. The sensations I had been trying to call up flooded in at once. The stones began to pulse in rhythmic symmetry with my own heartbeat. They filled up with light again and this time I didn't flinch or gasp. I simply waited. I waited until the entire room became gold. And then I stood. I stood up in the shimmering womb that closed around me and waited to receive whatever the light inside the stones wanted to tell me.

At first, I didn't hear anything at all. I only saw a large circle orbited by four smaller ones in my mind's eye. They were bonded together, holding fast to each other like a family of atoms held in an embrace, the mother in the middle and her four children standing around her. I felt she wouldn't move until hellfire itself arrived to scatter them all, alchemically, into something else. This was some tiny world writing itself large. This was the story that stones tell each other – their origin story that binds them together on a tinier plane. And I could *hear* them.

The circles soon faded and, once more, it was just me and the golden light filling the room. I called for the girl in the wall, the one who lived across time, but she still didn't come. Instead, I felt myself all at once drawn upwards. The golden light had now rolled into the shape of a horse that bore me on its back and threw me about like a feather entangled inside its rearing mane.

We were rushing somehow. Simply rushing, not through space but through some other force that altered my sense of *here, now.*

*

There are so many downsides to travelling in time. But perhaps the hardest thing to bear is the crushing loneliness. *Timewalking* makes it impossible to build those deep, loving connections over many years, the ones that unfold gently, cautiously, and which require linearity and consequence to function, cornerstones without which the architecture of human trust cannot exist in the world. But, on the other hand, I never felt the sensation of loss. I always knew that whatever happened, time would return me to those who would otherwise have been lost to linearity at some point through death, change, or any kind of schism that weathers and breaks togetherness. Everything that happened had done so over and over and, in a sense, I never lost anyone. I simply haunted events. A ghost made out of matter. A ghost in the endless machine we call life.

I wondered if my cells were constantly reproducing a temporary flatline, and I was in a never-ending cycle of waking up from it – over and over. Buying milk. Brushing my hair. Boarding a bus. Embracing a friend. Laughing out loud. These required an infinite and ultimately exhausting relationship with electricity; the endless energy to animate the pathways of the body through sheer will of the soul. Was it really Time with a capital 'T' that was in charge, animating me and my world, living through me, *as* me? Or was it the electricity that I made with my body that brought time to me in glitches and shudders? I concluded that there was no answer to this. There can't be an answer to it, because how can we imagine peering behind the veil of time, if our lives are the very thing we're trying to look beyond? They say too much knowledge makes you lonely. Travelling in time takes that knowledge and uses it to crush you with. To crush your sense of separate self.

So when Lucretia and I met for the 'first' time, it would have been 2017 in your reckoning of time, even though time would throw me back years and moments to when we had crossed paths prior to that, she unaware that these random encounters would one day lead to deep and indivisible connection. I knew how our friendship blossomed. She didn't. It's just the way things work in crumpled time. But, this time, she stopped me dead in my tracks because *she saw me emerge from the in-between world.*

Lucretia was always beautiful, not in any traditional sense, though. Her thick black hair was wrestled into a curly bun, shots of grey running through it, haunting as seal song. Her beauty was crow-like. She stared into you, seeing everything, and it was utterly alarming. But something was different *here, now,* because for the first time, she actually *saw* my arrival in the green-carpeted corridors of the library. And this was the single most important event that happened to me since the day of my rebirth into untimeliness in the snow. No one had ever seen me emerge. To do that, they would have to see not just me, but be able to peer into time itself, the great architecture of momentum that vibrated inside all things. And that was impossible. Until now, it seemed.

I'd walked this particular library corridor a hundred times before. Visited this very moment in time more times than I could count on fingers and toes. Metal bookstacks, green carpets, panelled wood. An incredible repetition of space, whose only marked difference could be found in the books that circulated around the stacks like blood cells inside a giant body. Each one holding a different world in between its leaves. So, the fact she saw me emerge meant something different must have happened to *her perception of the world.* Somehow, Lucretia had become able to see time itself rather than its effects on things. I knew from all the years we had spent together in the future that she had always been a little 'witchy', studying occult and mystic practices, Silk Route secrets on scraps of paper or old crumbling books. But all these things belonged to the great wheel of mortal time. Seeing time itself spit me out into form like an invisible whale at sea; this was *new*.

Her mouth fell ever so slightly slack. She was clutching a huge tome of what I could just make out was Latin poetry. For a long while, we just looked into each other's eyes under the dim yellow lights overhead that caught us in a stream of photons like two flies preserved in amber. When she finally spoke, her voice was rough and croaky, the kind of voice that when you hear it, instantly reveals to you that the owner has had one hell of a hard life.

"I… remember you." It was all she said to me, those dark eyes fixing on me. But it was enough.

Later, we sat on a low wall by the weir. The water moved in slow, steady planes before falling from one ledge to another like large sheets of paper, carrying blueprints of the life of each wave to a new horizon. Lucretia was remembering it all, our entire friendship unfolding in rapid slices of time. Her eyes were round and wide and dry. Each blink contained the small unnoticed experiences of seeing me in corridors, pannelled rooms and places on the street. Smiling at her as if I were a guardian angel or in possession of knowledge that she didn't have and that she had never before noticed. These memories were rewiring her from the inside out. Eventually, she broke with remembering and looked directly at me in the present.

"I *know* you. You're the one who has been following me. I thought you were a premonition but you're not. You're a *timewalker*."

My heart was racing. *This is new.* Knowing her and being known by her for what I was. This was *different*. Lucretia suddenly smiled at me.

"And you know me."

"Yes. I know you. I know you hate liquorice. I know you do needlepoint. I know you hate your job, but you love poetry. I know that you too died once as a child. And I know you're the best friend I've ever had."

"I was a small child, and I had a fever that wouldn't stop. I was ill. There were so many nurses holding me down and injecting me with something or other. But they couldn't help. Not at first. I was out of my body. I looked down and saw them all shaking their heads; the nurses, the doctor and my parents outside. I saw a doorway in front of me. It opened like a giant's mouth, and a narrow bridge rose out of it.

"I put one foot in front of the other, thinking I might fall into the void that surrounded me. And then I saw myself, like I had been duplicated. I met *myself* on the bridge. I was a small child, but *she* – *I* – was a grown woman. It looked like she had been through a fire. Half woman, half flame, but calm, and I thought, *That fire must be coming from within her. It must be part of her, burning away everything human.* Then she laughed at me, tenderly, not cruel. And she told me two words. Two words I will never forget: '*Not yet*'."

Lucretia puffed her cheeks out and then looked at me again.

"And you..." Her eyes glazed a little and I could see she was flipping through a new archive in her mind, one she had only just acquired *here, now*.

"I died... in the snow."

I felt a single tear well up in the corner of my right eye. I was about to sob with a strange mix of relief at the emergence of something new, and the slipping away of years of compacted solitude cycling round and round my hollow bones. If I started to cry, I wasn't sure I would be able to stop. I bit down and my jaw shook a little. *Someone has seen me. Someone else who can see the workings of time.*

"Hey – It's okay," she said, and she took my hand. I grasped it in the same way you might grasp a raft in the sea, the straight edges of a shared linearity, a shared moment in time. Now a thought struck me. I looked up at her, still in possession of her hand.

"Lucretia, how come you can *see* me?"

She told me quickly. Her voice was fast and low and for a moment it merged with the rushing sounds of water falling from the edge of the weir. She told me about her *dreamwalking*. That when she fell asleep, she visited the rooms of the sick, the dead, the dying. She held their hands in her own dreamly ones and watched them pass over bridges and into mouths and fires and things that weren't too dissimilar from her own brief journey to death.

To hear her tell it again was wonderful. But I knew this part. I already knew all about her *dreamwalking*. We would talk about it many times in the future, sat on her roof, her moving through people's dreams, speaking with them like some kind of guardian angel or supernatural crow, come to sit with them in their moment of need. *There must be something new here*, I thought. A small seed of a new experience that would hold the key to how and why she could actually see my out-of-time-ness *here, now*, creating new patterns of difference in an otherwise endless cycling.

And soon we found it. The key. The moment that Lucretia had gone from seeing linear time to seeing time's deep multitudes. In one dream, one that had come about a year before this moment, *here, now*, a sick old man had appeared to her in a hospital bed.

"He had seemed sick and frail, but when I looked more closely, I saw his eyes were – well, they were shining. They were like two stars that had come too close to the earth."

The man in her dream had looked up at her with his diamond eyes, grasped her hand, pulled her towards him. Then he had struck her gently on the collarbone. From that moment on, the dreamworld she walked in was never the same. Now it shone. Always. He'd told her to breathe in *slowly, slowly,* and her dreaming body had done so, drawing all the shining particles of the slumbering world deep into her chest.

"And when I breathed out, I became part of the universe. I haven't stopped. I've been doing it every moment, even now in my dreams. Then, today, I saw you *appear* in the library. It's as if I've created new pathways inside my brain and these help me *see* the world differently. I never saw the man with astral eyes again. But in a way he's always with me." She fell silent and we stayed like that together for a while. Two twice-born women, silently making sense of this thing we call the 'world'.

I'd always wondered what my flights in time looked like. I'd only ever *felt* what it was to emerge in a new moment, the rushing, the sensation of being scattered and remade in a moment that my atoms never quite fit in.

"What did it look like, when you saw me emerge in time?"

She dragged the final moments of her cigarette, then flicked the end of it into the river.

"It was like a cloud passing that suddenly decides to rain." Then she raised her eyes to the heavens cynically, undercutting all the poetry that had just come pouring out of her only seconds before.

I snorted. We looked at each other there and then, first smiling, then laughing in complicity. And even though it must have been the hundredth time we'd met, in some deeper, unknown way, it was the first.

*

The golden horse that had emerged in the thick walls of my tower room in Cachtice to carry me away stopped its wild flight, and I found myself standing inside a wall. It wasn't like the heavyset stone of Cachtice. It felt flimsy. Like the ghost of stone, and I became a little afraid. I had wanted to bring the girl I'd seen in the wall back to me, but instead, it seemed, I had travelled to her. Now I was the one standing inside a wall this time, peering into the other world.

In front of me now, there were two women sitting on the floor with their legs crossed under them. One of the women was older, her black hair scraped into a bun, and the other was younger, messier, with olive skin. I instantly recognised her as the one who had visited me when I first arrived at Cachtice. I craned my neck to get a better look. They were sitting about a foot apart, breathing slowly in unison. I had heard of things like this. Janus had told me about groups of men or women that sat together, breathed together, and crossed the barriers of time and space with one clear thought together. He called them the 'Sons and Daughters of Bektash', but I never understood what he meant by that.

"Never reveal what you do to anyone. They'll call you a witch. Of course, that's not the case, but people believe the simplest things. And there's no word in the West for what you are. Not yet anyway."

I had nodded solemnly.

"Now sit opposite me and let's breathe together. Slow the world down one breath at a time and listen to it. Ready?"

Here, now, on the other side of the flimsy wall, it was nighttime, although a small beam of light that was shockingly luminous, almost white, came from out of a bulbous shape that held no fire. I'd never seen anything like it before and it hurt my eyes to look at it. I looked back to the girl with olive skin, my otherworldly visitor from my first night at Cachtice. Looking at her was strange. It was like looking into a mirror that bent the light; that bent time. I felt my skin burn and itch a little and looked down at my forearms. The word 'Vera' appeared like a tattoo from the inside out, before lifting up into the air around me and disappearing.

Vera. It must be her name, the name of the girl who had appeared to me in the wall at Cachtice. But it had come out of me in this strange in-between place – out of my own body. A word from the future hidden inside my skin in the present, in the year of our Lord 1575. Was she a part of me thrown into another world? A part of me in the future that I was already written into, like a story yet to come?

The two women started to chant together. I couldn't make out the words. Perhaps they were not meant for my ears. Janus had said as much – that there were some words that were secret and that it was wrong to listen to them.

"These are the words that open the doors to the heart. Each one is like a key fashioned for its own particular door. Don't snoop at anyone else's door. It's not right and it'll do you no good in the long run."

The older woman suddenly seemed to slump a little, as if she had fallen asleep or into such a deep trance that her body took on the appearance of sleep. I felt a strange sensation, like somebody was breathing next to me, and I nearly died of fright because at the same time as she was lying there on the other side of the wall, she also emerged beside me inside the wall. She looked right at me and then gestured for me to follow her to where Vera was sitting. My heart was beating incredibly fast. I slowed my breathing in the way Janus had been teaching me. Then I shut my eyes, lifted my foot and followed her. I stepped out of the wall and into the other world – their world. I crossed over, and in that moment, I felt myself truly became a *talto*.

She gestured to sit with them both, all three of us together, separated only by the great veil that hangs between all things creating time and difference. Vera opened her eyes and gasped. Then she shut her eyes again quickly and I could tell she was frightened.

"Oh my god. You're not real." She kept repeating it, opening her eyes and then squeezing them shut again, as if such an act might rid me of her altogether.

But I am! I am real!

Janus had taught me that there are many worlds that interpenetrate ours and that the way to communicate with those who lived in them was never to do so by directly speaking out loud, but by placing the words in the space around them until they entered, subtly, into the ear through the fibres that vibrate in between the worlds. He said the words would hang like ghosts, haunting inside the tiny world – the world of atoms – until they found their intended location, humming and buzzing when they did so, moving like lightning that finally finds its companion charge, its singular target across time and space.

So I stood up and 'wrote' in the space around her with my fingertip. And somewhere in this future pocket of time, the word shivered and moved and became sound.

Hello.

"Holy Christ," the woman gasped.

I wrote again. *Elizabet Bathory.*

She gulped, just as I had. Slowed her breathing, just as I had. Felt terror at something so uncanny, just as I had. And then wrote, 'Vera', in the air back to me in response.

I know. I knew it in my body.

The dreaming body of the older woman, however, spoke to me directly. She did not need, it seemed, to write in the air at all and I was utterly confused by this. I looked over to her slumbering limbs that lay by the opposite wall and then back to the part of her that stood beside me. It was as if she had managed to cut a thin line in the border between waking and sleeping, and in that cut, she could be in both places at once, my world and hers. I heard her plain as day. I heard her like you hear people speaking when you dream; faint and watery but audible.

"Come here and sit with us both. We need to ask you something. We need to know how to break the spell of time. You can speak to me directly. I can hear you when I *dreamwalk*. How can we send Vera back to before she got stuck? Back to normal time."

"What do you mean?" I asked.

"She's outside of time, or maybe she's lost inside it. She's been glimpsing you since it all started. Your story. Your world. You. That's why we've brought you *here, now,* to us. We've brought you here to help. Can you help us?"

"Me?"

She nodded.

"But I'm looking for a way out too! Things that I don't understand. I see things – like you and her. I can see the stories that make up stones, and fire and the lights that compose the sky, but I'm powerless, it seems, to change *anything*. My life has been written for me. I travel inside the sky, the stars, the earth, but nothing in the outside world is ever any... *different* when I return." I thought of Nadasdy, my husband-to-be; I thought of blacksmiths; of Mohacs; and of Janus, who smiled though the world kept trying to tear him apart with its monstrous teeth as if it were nothing.

My answer seemed to disturb the dreamwalking woman, and Vera put her head in her hands in despair for a moment. Then she looked up at me in the way one might look at oneself in a glass, touching her face, her cheeks, her lips. I lifted my hand towards her, and she went to meet it with her own. A magnetic force charged the space between us and everything around us started to fold in on itself, changing around the girl from the wall – around Vera. *This must be what the older woman means. This must be Vera moving around outside time. And she's taking me with her!*

If I made it out of this strange *talto* walk across worlds, I would run to Janus and beg him to explain it all to me. *What had I stumbled upon with all this deep listening of his?* No doubt his eyes would shine in that astral way they had, and he would only explain half of it to me, promising me I would discover the rest by myself. One day.

Everything started to stretch as if the world had become a large bed sheet that folded all the tiny worlds between Vera and me together, uniting here's and now's from across all its sides. Anna's warning came back to me: "*Be careful that people don't call you a talto!*" But it was too late for all that now. *Taltos*. The word rang in my ear and became deafening. Anna had said we could summon up invisible winds and ride through them to the other world on the back of a golden horse. At first, I'd thought she was teasing me, tempting my belief. But she was quite serious.

Taltos always brought back some information, some wisdom from the other place that would work out whatever trouble they – whatever trouble *we* – had in our own lives. Sometimes, she said, *taltos* would tell of great battles fought with strange creatures, clearing curses put on family and livestock that had been written down in the other world and could only be unwritten by going there in person; by *travelling*.

But looking at this strange and desperate woman, wanting my help as much as I could have wanted hers as her world stretched and started and turned upside down, I couldn't believe this was the case. If anything, perhaps it was the other way around. If there was any kind of curse, perhaps it had been written here, somewhere in my time, and it was *she* who needed to unwrite it – to unwrite me so we could both live more freely, unbound to my stories and all the human darknesses they contained. I had no answers. I had no special knowledge. I might have become a *talto*, eternally trapped in that tower room of mine, but I was also simply a girl, a bride-to-be, a countess. I too was only trying to survive the great spell God had cast over us all. The spell of history.

The rushing started up and I was tossed on the golden skeins of light once more. I smashed back into my body with a gasp that was more like a calling-out, a cry for help as I entered the material world of Cachtice again. I tried to stand up and promptly passed out.

*

"Janus?" I asked, as we sat together in the safety of the forest at our usual meeting place under the silver birches, "do you think I've entered another world? What was this strange vision? Am I a witch or a *talto*?"

He nodded his head, not in assent but to signal he was thinking about it, sucking his cheeks in a little. After a while, he said, "I think you've peered behind a veil of knowledge and seen part of our skeleton story."

"Is this vision from God or the devil?"

He shrugged. "The devil is like God's shadow," and he started muttering his Turkish prayers. I sighed. He was so unsatisfactory in his answers sometimes.

Chapter Five

Mark's father had died, about six months before Mark got his first job at the university. His father would never know that he would have to shake off his mortal coil to open up a position for his son at the faculty. Mark had inherited the family house too, and when he moved in not long after the funeral, he'd simply added his own things to it without removing anything of his father's. He called the house his *archive*. He had two desks now. His father's – untouched – was pushed up against the wall, and his own was placed in front of it, as if the old man's botanical drawings, still scattered across it, might creep over to meet his son's photographs and be remade in their image, the charcoal turning shiny and colourful and all the more *unreal* for the bright way they captured reality. We all have ways of trying to freeze time.

    I had materialised in Mark's arms right at the moment that Laura was running out of his house and into the street. She'd run when she saw me. After all, she was a student, hypnotised ever since he had placed his hand at the small of her back when she'd poured him wine at that party, as if he had found the secret location of all her devotion hiding inside the walls of her spine. She turned as she ran and out of nowhere shouted to me, "*I'll never be as good as you are, will I?*" ending with a final shriek, "*Bitch!*" Mark had been seeing her on the side, loving us both, spinning tales about each of us in turn. I imagined he had wanted to embed us inside one another to make one superwoman. A woman that possessed all the qualities he loved inside *one body* instead of two, forever split apart.

So, he sent each one of us crashing through the other's life in chaotic, unresolved patterns. Together, we were not one or two but three bodies, an endless problem moving through the horizon, working out which one would need to be erased to make the sky right again. It chilled me to the bone that I'd felt the same thing she did: that I'd never be as good as *her*. That he'd love her more. That he'd chosen her, not me. But I know how this story goes and I still haven't found a way to intervene in it. The thing about normal time is that it's entirely made up of cause and effect. If the arrow of time moves in any other way, justice vanishes.

Lucretia had told me: *stay away from this idiot. He's a danger to anyone he notices. You need to become invisible to him. Otherwise, he'll erase you.* And haven't you had enough of that by now? *That's how these guys work. Damned if you do, damned if you don't.*

In the year or so that I'd known Laura, Mark had become both father and mother to her, although she'd never, *technically*, been his student. Even so, they were joined by an invisible umbilical cord that bonded them together and ensnared everyone else that came in between. The cord pulsed, giving every room they were in a kind of electric quality you could almost see with the naked eye. They fed off each other like savage symbionts; sharing shame and anger across hallways, doorways and in one another's beds.

I kept telling him that his relationship with her was a disaster waiting to happen. That she was, after all, a student and was so very fragile, so constantly lost for words, so porcelain in her responses. He reminded me that she wasn't *his* student, so it should all be just fine. He told me everything about her. How she had several lovers on campus. How he really wanted only me, but I had always been too difficult, too stubborn, too removed. How he'd got *sidetracked* by her and was in too deep. That he was finding a way to break it off without causing any ripple effects in the department. Then he'd try to kiss me, and I'd turn my cheek, so that he landed awkwardly, each time, in my hair.

"See," he said once. "There's too much fight in you."

Of course, all of his stories were untrue. Standing there in the living room together – all three of us – he couldn't deny it. Her presence made it impossible for him to lie about her, about them. He just smiled at us both. It was calm and deeply sinister at the same time. He smiled to say he'd won. He'd tempted our disbelief that he could be a lover to one and a friend to the other. We could take our pick as to who fulfilled which role at any one time. Three bodies that could swap roles at any moment, though he held to his own with a controlled kind of desperation which he kept in place by managing ours.

"*But you loved me.*"

"*No, I loved her.*"

His white angel and his dark rose.

For a second, standing there in the living room, I imagined that we had always been one woman, not two, and he was the origin story that spun us into distinct and separable parts. She ran out of the house and towards the train platform in despair over and over. And he held me back and stopped me from going after her. Over and over. Sun, moon, earth rising and falling. Rising and falling.

Each time I heard how she'd died, I held onto my own body to make sure it was me who had survived the jump onto the tracks. To make sure I was still in one piece. This is how a man erases a woman. One way, at least. This is how he stops her stories. He makes her part of his own flesh in a strange reversal of maternity. When he cuts the cord, she falls. If she has flown too high with him, the damage is terminal.

He rang to let me know. He wanted to be the first to tell me. "*You always were the strong one. I knew one of you was going to die, I just didn't know which one.*" I hung up the phone. But I didn't go to the funeral, just in case the moment I blinked, I discovered that she and I had exchanged places. Her, upright, with him to comfort her – *such an awful way to die* – and I horizontal. Cold. Hidden from the sun. My soul scratching at the wooden box they buried me in, until it found a way out.

What happens when a woman dies? Where do all her stories go? I'd died myself, all those years ago in the snow. Now I hovered around my histories. They made me into part of a story I was long exhausted by – an old story time threw me into, demanding I repeat it over and over and over. I knew that I needed to find new stories. Stories that lived inside the old ones but that were never spoken out loud. Stories simply known. Simply felt. Inside the intelligent spaces *between* my atoms.

I couldn't save Laura from her fate on the train tracks. Even though I lived this moment inside the silent loop time had made out of my life. But I could write about her. I could tell the story that hid inside the one told more often about her – that she had simply been mad and he the victim of an unfortunate circumstance. Case closed. I could spin a net made out of ink that would catch her as she leapt out in front of that train. She'd land instead inside the crosses and dots that spanned the page, peering out from behind the letters with those large grey-green eyes of hers, long after her broken body had vanished from the pages of earth and soil. *My name is Laura and this is my story. I wanted to be birthed out anew by love. I wanted him to be my mother.*

I wrote this all down in my tiny office, long after everyone else had left for the night to be with their families. I wrote her down. Hoping that some record might be made of her life before she was squashed into the sad story of a confused young woman who just shouldn't have come off her medication early. Just another mark on the mental health provision list kept in the office next to the students' union.

"Time," I whispered to myself. "Don't remove me before I finish writing this down. Let me scribble inside your margins some small trace of her."

But time doesn't care for such tiny reclamations. They say time eats us all, but I experienced it differently. Time devours *stories* and so we reproduce them. It's not quite the same thing.

The erasures started around me again, and a new moment emerged, etching itself into being. But this *time,* for some reason, tired of revisiting this particular death, I shouted back, or perhaps it was closer to the truth to say that a deep part within me shouted *inside* time. Rather than the erasures happening *around me,* my bones cut into them with the force of my cry. Ferocious. They cut the endless flow both into me and away from me at the same moment. Now this time I really did feel like I was falling. I saw the pulsing window I'd glimpsed when I first died, arterial – not with blood but with *time.* I wasn't travelling through my own life stories anymore. I was travelling back to the in-between world of the Angel of Death – the scaled and feathered woman I saw when I first died. I made a little rip, a little cut, in all my stories, and like peering beyond a veil of knowledge, I saw *her,* the real subject of all my writings, the origin story. Elizabet Bathory inside her tower again. Her presence felt warm, lively – alive. She reached out her arms and I felt strangely present, alive in the *here,* in the *now.*

So, *here, now,* I go to her. She's writing something down on a torn page. She's using ink she's mixed with water, and I know in my bones that it's because she has no more ink left to use. I know she's trapped. Locked away. But still living – and so alive! Her hair has grown white and wild, and her clothes are fraying. She senses me and invites me over to her. "*For my daughter,*" she whispers. "*I'm telling her not to give up. I'm telling her a different kind of story. Look...*" And before I can read it, the image collapses away and all I can hear are rushing sounds. I'm afraid that time is about to send me into a different part of my own life again. Then I remember all the moments Lucretia taught me to slow down my breathing and *just listen* to the slight movements of the world.

But something's different now. I'm starting to remember things that never happened, tiny things – so small they might go unnoticed – that take place after that fateful moment when Lucretia first saw me emerge in time. *Here, now,* as time shifts and transforms around me, I hear something, though perhaps hearing isn't quite the right word. It's more like a small seed of awareness; a slow, quiet noticing. It slows down the erasures that are taking place even as time aims to snatch me away. In the stillness, I travel further into the threshold between lives, where living and dying fold into one another. I do it by listening. Listening to the dance of time.

The sound of it is deafening. It's as if a giant god has emptied out a storm into the sky and, with one sweep, now collects it all back up into a single, silent point. Tidying it all away. A white expanse pulses once, momentary, electric, and then the blackness rolls in again, penetrating inwards, until even the atoms themselves slow down their dancing. All the lights in the world turn out in an afterthought. Then there's nothing left but hush and dark.

Slowly, a pinprick of light starts to pulse anew, breaking up the void. Sounding now gently before me in the blackness is the unmistakable voice of my Angel of Death. "Little Wing. I'm here." She lights up brighter, going from pinpoint to beacon, marking out a strange pathway towards herself. I run to her, the only form that exists in this tiny world, and she opens up her arms, at once feathered and scaly, folding me into her until we become as close as one person, close as one mind whose separate thoughts are the only thing that mark us into bodies.

"It's all right, Little Wing. Everything is unfolding as it should."

"Nothing makes sense," I plead desperately, begging for any kind of answer that will help me make sense of my world once and for all. "What happened – what *happened* to me?"

Her eyes seem brown, like mine, but when I squint and peer into them more closely, I can see them whirling like tiny clouds of heat and light heading out towards the dusty edges of gods.

"No. It wouldn't make sense," she says. "Not in the human world." She looks at me with such kindness. "Do you want to return to me yet, Little Wing?"

"I want to live."

"Am I not alive?"

I stare up at her, trying to see her through every pore of my body.

"Little Wing, you are haunted by so many things. That's what it is to die and return from death at the same time. You live between worlds. So many tiny universes unravelling inside one human heart."

She taps me gently on the breastbone, in exactly the same manner Lucretia had described the old man in the hospital to have done, and I sense the vastness that encompasses us both echoing in each tap, my ribs becoming part of the fabric of the earth, whilst the space between them draws the heavens inside me.

"Time congeals, Little Wing. It contracts like a pumping heart into life and then expands out to become space." And she holds up her hand, curling it into a fist as she speaks.

"Time is memory and memory becomes form. Your body is just a system of memories breathing the world into its future shapes."

The Angel of Death kisses my lips ferociously. As she kisses me, I feel a tiny ball of golden light glowing warm in her. It flashes momentarily, becoming a network moving throughout her body, its points illuminating a pattern I can't make out. It grows in size, now becoming like a sun, white and yellow, flooding the black emptiness with its gold. I become a node alongside her, nothing but heat and light. A thunderclap comes from inside my blood, so full of force that it throws me back into my separate self. Then rushing sounds, fast and strong enough to tear me into tiny pieces, and that phrase again, rising out from the cacophony, distinguishable, human: *Time lives inside you. Rewrite it. Rewrite your origin story. Then you can return to me.*

The sounds inscribe the words into me in a language that exists in the atomic structure of life itself. Then, everything resumes. I open my eyes and think of all the women who have died inside a monster tale. The violence of an erasure that isn't satisfied with death but seeks to enslave life itself. It must stop *here, now.* It must stop inside the spell of ink.

Chapter Six

My lessons with Janus were different now. Since I had learnt about the way thoughts and feelings were threaded into space across time from my otherworldly wander into the future, he was no longer teaching me how to slow my perception of the worlds down. Now I was learning how to move *through* them.

He taught me that breath and time both travel in the body in the same way, folding the inner and outer worlds like two halves of the same parchment. He taught me that the heart is an organ that absorbs things larger than its own weight, things that go on to thunder and tremor in the sky far beyond that which astrolabes and other gadgets can know. He said that the deep blackness between the planets was littered with giants that sucked in all the light and dust and displaced them elsewhere beyond the known worlds in exactly the same way a person does when they speak, when they feel. He spoke of four doorways threaded through time like stitches inside a tapestry. He taught me that the moon was full of virgins waiting for fallen heroes and described some of the strange, otherworldly and erotic rituals he had been promised by the Sultan if he had died in battle. Then he smiled, called me a child and laughed at me, telling me I shouldn't believe everything that came out of the mouths of men.

But today he was more serious, more focused on the world of Cachtice and its inhabitants. And on my marriage to come.

"Little Wing, I can't advise you on what to do with Nadasdy, save this: whenever he says something stupid, make him feel like he has touched you with his brilliance. When he says something smart, do the exact reverse."

"Are you crazy? I won't escape a beating on any day of the week if I follow your advice."

"On the contrary, Countess. And more, you will show him an ultimate kindness." He paused and shook his head. "And Nadasdy needs kindness. He needs it like fish need the rivers to flow strong and warm under the ice that hardens over them in winter. Nadasdy is a fish clutching to life. His winter is war, and it is a Turkish solstice he winds towards."

I felt suddenly afraid that Janus would disappear very soon. It was a premonition that ran down my spine. "Do you promise to stay here forever?"

He laughed. "No, Little Wing. No. I can't promise that. But I can tell you this: Nadasdy is little more than a boy, but he's seen enough horror – trust me, I and my kind have given him plenty to remember, and he has returned the favour. If you want him to love you, you need to be like salve to his eyes. You must make him feel that where he fails in the outer world, he has succeeded in the walls of his castle, in the walls of your heart." He paced up and down a bit, as if he was about to win some long drawn-out game any moment now. He looked at me strangely then quickly came over to me, grabbing my hand and standing so close that I could almost hear his heart beating in his chest. "We're so close, Little Wing. So close."

I felt betrayed. This was the very opposite of the closeness I craved from him. He was a man who was dishevelled and eternally blackened with coal. He'd been born a peasant and become a janissary, an Ottoman, a *traitor*. But he was the first man I loved – maybe would ever truly love. I smiled as if complicit with his machinations. Then I slapped him with all my might in the face. He was utterly dumbfounded. He rubbed his cheek and stared into me in confusion.

"You can't call me to you like a hunting dog, hoping I will bring you Nadasdy's head in my paws," I growled.

"Ah," he said, his expression moving from confusion to an awful kind of pity that stung me like an agitated bee. "Elizabet still doesn't understand love."

"My heart has absorbed everything Janus has taught it. I have merely 'displaced the same elsewhere'. You want me to control Nadasdy and bring him down? Destroy him, so you can bring him to your *Turk* sultan? Are you mad?"

"No." He said it calmly, gently. Then, "You've missed the point, Little Wing. Who wouldn't lose their head for love – real love? Nadasdy is a powerful boy. Without love, he'll become something more sinister. That's all I'm saying, Little Wing."

The rage in me turned almost directly into silent tears. Why was everything so full of politics, as if all the worlds were threaded through with the wars of men? Why did no one ever ask me what I wanted, what I feared, who I loved? I looked down at the silky surface of my dress. Each stitch vibrated with it – with the politics of toiling, as if I could momentarily feel the very worms who had been put to work to produce such finery, crawling and thrashing about across my skin.

"Your words are for kings and counts or for women who have learnt to speak in the language of court. You're speaking to me now from your second face, *Janus*."

Perhaps these words themselves had been spoken through me, through the silk that lay over my skin, embedded with the lives of thousands of small and industrious creatures who knew better than I about all this wrangling.

"Elizabet, I daren't speak from any other. Not to you."

"Then Janus does not love."

He breathed in but couldn't look at me. He seemed sad. "No." And with this, he looked right into me. Right through me.

I felt something in me crack and harden like bittering fruit still clinging to the tree. I felt afraid and ashamed. I ran away from him like a wild animal – fast. Then faster! Faster!

Three days later, a storm would rage over Cachtice that had been brewing in the same instant, travelling across the Empire, making castles and livestock drip and quake, quietening the clang-clang of the furnace houses, even if only for a brief moment. Janus had taught me all about such storms. He called them the storms of lost stories that were brewed up by hungry ghosts.

*

"Where can she be?" I could hear Thurzo shout out loudly as I burst through the door, my hair dishevelled from running and no servants trailing behind me. The room smelled of wine. Another three months of waiting had passed and Nadasdy was finally ready to meet me. I had still been recovering from my first heartbreak and was spending increased hours each day in the woods without a word to anyone, circling the silver birches and listening to the rustle of the turning leaves. Having grown exasperated of waiting for a full two hours, they had both turned to wine, and now Nadasdy was asleep on one of the armchairs. Thurzo was staring deeply into the fire. He rose quickly when he saw me, tugged his rumpled tunic straight in a short and definitive gesture and tipped his head ever so slightly towards me, whilst widening his eyes a little in reproach. Before I could even make to apologise for my tardiness, he waved his hand saying, "It is a lady's prerogative."

It was the first time I'd seen Nadasdy's face fully. I stared at him, mapping its contours, lines and shallows. He did indeed seem no more than a boy, older than I, for sure, but still soft-cheeked and youthful. All my fears vanished. He was as lost as I was in this world, perhaps twice so. Thurzo came over to stand beside me as I surveyed my husband.

"Amazing, isn't it, my lady, that one might be such a harbinger of death on the battlefield and yet sleep so peacefully inside a castle."

I looked at Thurzo, wondering what similar contradictions might lie in him.

"How are your studies progressing?" he continued.

I thought of the moths and stones, the light in the sky, the girl in the wall, the Bible with its cascading lettering, of the metal crown and the blacksmiths, of the forest and then, of Janus. I nearly laughed out loud at this question but managed to catch myself and nod my head soberly. Thurzo, it seemed, wasn't fooled.

"Cachtice benefits from a rich community, richer and more lapsed perhaps than that of the more fashionable court of Sarvar. A happy accident you ended up here, and so close to my estate." He surveyed me intently. "I hope *we* shall become friends, my lady."

"So do I," I responded. "I should like to hear more of the Ottomans."

He balked. "Such tales might turn your stomach, my lady. They may wear gold and make fine music, but don't be fooled. Were a Turk in your presence, he would slit your belly to gullet in the blink of an eye." He had extended his index finger and was motioning it upwards towards my throat whilst speaking. I would have found this horrifying previously, but Janus' words came back to me and I simply thought: *he is displacing the same elsewhere, he is moving stories he has heard from the battlefield into stories he tells brashly by the hearth. Now he looks to trace his dark imaginings across my body.*

I smiled, replying, "This is my hearth now, my lord. Surely stories of their gold and music will suffice. I can always ask my husband about the blood."

This stopped Thurzo in his tracks. He laughed heartily out loud, all the angles of his face moving upwards towards his lightly wrinkled eyes. Nadasdy shifted and came around for a moment. Thurzo was still laughing.

"Francis, your wife has just beaten me down in the blink of an eye! Francis – Francis! If you play your cards right, I believe you might just be the luckier man. Either that, or you shan't survive your wedding night."

Nadasdy took on the appearance of someone swimming, confused, before settling back down into the silty bedrock of the embroidered armchair, fast asleep once more.

"Enchanting, my lady. Simply enchanting. Perhaps you and I should both take our leave of your sleeping fiancé and retire to another hall." He had not asked but had directed me, putting his arm out for me to hold and patting it a couple of times with his other hand. I took a few steps, holding onto it. I felt I was also swimming now, adrift in the sensations that accompanied becoming the lady of Cachtice and uncertain of when to stand my ground and when to give in.

*

The wind was still running random and chaotic through the cracks in the walls of Cachtice, even though the hungry storms that had been raging on and off since that day Janus and I had fought had, for the most part, passed. I had wanted to go mushroom picking, and Anna had suggested some places famous for fashioning the squat, aromatic delicacies that sat shyly inside the long grasses like budding maids. I had seen Janus' square block-like body moving around parts of the castle, engaged in this or that task, and had wanted to find an excuse to get her to include him as part of the retinue. No doubt afterwards, he would whisper strange things of mushroom-lives to me. I imagined him spinning a yarn about how the tiny fungus was immortal, growing from stars to sky to earth in a network of hidden veins that encircled the planets. Or perhaps that would be the story I would tell him, and he would nod and say that God had favoured me, or God was displeased, or that God felt something or other inside His singular and omnipotent mind.

I felt so utterly rejected, so utterly used by him, and yet I still caught myself wanting to be around him, to hear his stories, to sit with my legs under me in the way he did and learn all I could about breath and time. But not love. I couldn't hear him use that word anymore. It struck me like a dagger in the chest, breaking my heart into new expanded spaces inside my rib cage. When Anna came up to my tower, however, all talk of mushrooms was off.

"You'll be happy to know that we're now preparing your wedding day!"

So it was here. Finally. I would walk along the church steps and up to my husband.

"At last, you will become Countess Nadasdy in the eyes of our Lord." Was the eye of God not larger than us all, its own immortal mushroom, webbing itself into everything, a sonorous and mycelial knowing?

"At last," was all I said. And I took her hand because I knew she wanted me to, although I couldn't help but look away. Anna interpreted this as shyness and took it upon herself to start talking about my wedding night. She reeled off a bizarre and awkwardly formal set of things she called my 'duties', half whispering these in my ear. From what I had heard of the virgins waiting for Janus inside the moon, things could probably benefit from getting a lot more vivid and informal than she described, but I listened and made a mental list of what was expected of me. Later, however, I shuddered a bit. Poor Nadasdy, I thought.

No doubt he has loved another. Can he, in marrying me, divorce his body from his truer desires?

I realised I had no idea how men functioned. And yet I lived inside a world made largely from their imaginings, some of the time at least. What would my own world look like? Later in my life I would find this out. And as fast as I created it, Thurzo would remould it over and over, until it would look only like blood.

It no longer hurts when the serving women scrape at my scalp and knot my breathing with golden ribbons, reed and whalebone. Anna had decided I should be dressed in the Italian style. I found it was all the more tight and elaborate. I loved the colours and the sparkling stitching on the skirt, whose lines, flourishes and folds gave me the appearance of a gnarled oak tree floating above the soil, gliding without roots. The rest of it was torturous. Could we not just return the corset bones to the sea in the hope that the churning waves would spin their forms back into a living, breathing whale again, reversing the course of time in the belly of their unfathomably deep currents?

History will say we were married at Varanno Castle, but the truth of the matter is that Nadasdy was still recovering from his last clash with the Ottomans and so, though we threw a lavish banquet at Varanno later the following year, our actual marriage took place at Cachtice. It seemed in accordance with Nadasdy's shy and reserved personality that he would have his real wedding in a small castle on a hill, and his public wedding in a grand court to which he was less attached.

Anna used the wedding as an opportunity to complete my training in what it was to be a wife and run a castle. She made sure I kept myself up to date with all the foodstuffs, flagons and silver that came into the castle on something called an 'inventory'.

"Put all that writing skill to use," she advised.

I hardly rested, only occasionally catching snatches of sleep across the day or night, soon walking like the undead, never really asleep, but never really awake either. In the hush of a sunrise, quiet to humans but full of incredible noise for everybody else, I woke up. I could see *her*. She had come to visit me in the wall as if she knew that the precipice at which I had been standing was now long gone, and I was already halfway down the mountainside of my own destiny.

She held her fingers out, like she was trying to touch me, and I pressed my own into a rough correspondence on the stone surface. I felt how alone she was. I could almost hear her reply in my mind: "*Your wedding is always happening, every moment in time.*" I didn't quite understand, but it felt comforting to know that somewhere, deep in the other world, my story was being written. If it all went wrong, perhaps I could ask her to erase it, to wipe out the curse like *taltos* before me had done. I thought then that she and I were one in the same person, separated only by the fragments that history had made out of us. I wanted to find out more about what she meant. She placed an image in the space around me: a feathered and scaled woman somewhere in a borderland. The woman spoke a single phrase, but it felt like it set off a chain reaction inside my body: *Times lives inside you.*

I came about in a hurry. Anna was banging on the door telling me that the time had come. And I didn't think of the girl for several years after that. Nadasdy would soon take up every last moment of my mind's cunning. I would learn only to survive.

*

The wedding was full of colours and odours and people all tumbling before me like a ferocious storm that had got itself knotted up inside the laundry. I was fastened into my dress and led down the endless halls towards the apparently 'small' ceremony. My father had passed a few years before and my mother had taken to her bed. My cousins, Sigismund, Andrew and Balthasar, would join us at the more public wedding at

Varanno later that year. I must confess that it felt better this way. How could I become Nadasdy if surrounded by Bathorys? Waiting at the edge of the doorway, in full formal dress, Thurzo stood in his habitual straight and unbending posture.

"Countess, I am happy to play the role of Father, if you'll have me." He bent his arm out for me to hold in the same formal manner he had the last time I'd seen him. Thurzo and I intrigued each other. I knew he didn't approve of my marriage to Nadasdy. He thought Nadasdy too young and too rough, and whilst I was still a youth myself, he believed me a more useful asset at Court than locked up tending to the local matters of Cachtice. But, in an odd way, I was growing to love this place. That strange light fell again from out of the many windows surrounding us. It made Thurzo appear pale yellow, whilst picking out the gold threads of my dress, throwing bursts of illusory warmth around me.

"I would be honoured, Count." He smiled, entangling me around his arm. How lovely he looks when he smiles, I thought to myself. So rich and full of enigma and so unlike the cold block of ice and granite of his usual demeanour. He leant down a little, his lips hovering over my earlobe.

"Let's get this over and done with, shall we?"

My sight narrowed around the shape of Nadasdy standing by the altar. Each step towards him seemed to take years. I saw nothing but his soft, nervous face ahead of me, and was bolstered only by Thurzo's rhythmic pace. By the time I reached the altar, I felt a hundred years old, and when Thurzo suddenly dropped my arm, it was as if all my haggard bones were about to fall down in a heap, throwing up nothing but dust inside the layers of silks that hooked me into the shape of a woman. The priest spoke in clunky Latin. I stared into Nadasdy's eyes. They were grey. And he looked right back. I suddenly had the sensation we were rushing to make cartographies of each other before either one finished the same strange and urgent task, running some race that pitted us as direct rivals.

When it came time to exchange rings, I noticed something rather unusual about mine. It wasn't gold, like the fashion of the time. It was made of solid silver and had the symbol of an upturned moon and a many-rayed sun etched on the inside, a furtive and small image that vanished from sight as Nadasdy slipped it onto my finger. He didn't smile, just continued to look intensely into me, until I became uncomfortable and lowered my eyes. The priest finished the ritual, and we exited the long hallway swiftly, Nadasdy's arm uncomfortably hinging around my waist in a display of intimacy that was entirely undermined by how awkwardly he carried it out.

We feasted for hours on an uncanny variety of meats, and I watched as Nadasdy fought off a number of lewd remarks from his high-ranking soldiers, more grunts and hand gestures that made my nose wrinkle up in nothing short of the most profound disdain. As the night wore on, I fidgeted uncomfortably in my tapestried chair, trying wine after wine until my body began to feel like a wineskin itself. I imagined that if you punctured me with a nail or the sharp end of a dagger, I would erupt not in blood but in wine.

In one of the few moments when Nadasdy wasn't being pestered by soldiers, nobles or Thurzo, I grabbed him coarsely on the forearm.

"What's the moon with the sun?" I asked, holding up my hand and pointing to my wedding ring.

He looked worried and confused, grabbed the ring and pulled it from my finger to inspect it. His brow furrowed, but he said nothing except, "Let's go to bed now." He suddenly pushed his chair back, grabbed me by the waist and carried me across his back in the manner of someone spiriting a dead body off the field. The company cheered.

When we reached his – our – bedchamber, he led me to the door, cursed a few times whilst trying to open it and pulled me inside. Suddenly he became boyish. He sat on the edge of the bed and patted it a few times. I sat next to him. He laid himself back with what would have been a thud had we not been on a mattress, and sighed. He grabbed my hand and put it between his legs. Then, almost immediately, he fell fast asleep.

I poured out some water and washed my face. The coolness revived me a little. I went back to the bedside and hovered over my new husband. I suddenly realised that at this point, I had spent more time with Nadasdy whilst he slept than whilst he was awake. Was this what marriage was? I found myself feeling quite tender towards him. I undressed him, which was no easy task – how different male clothing was to female clothing! I tried to drag him up towards the pillows but found him a deadweight, so instead, I brought the pillows down to him and wrapped the blankets around his body by folding the one half over the half that he slept on, leaving him flat and passed out on the inside like something one might find in the kitchen, baking in one of the cooks' ovens.

I lit several candles and noticed a polished glass coated with mercury in the Venetian style standing in a corner of the room. I walked over to it and stared at myself in my wedding dress. It seemed odd. Beautiful, but too complicated, its hooks and lacings a puzzle that induced more exhaustion than pleasure in me. How was I going to get out of it? I thought of calling for help, but I really didn't want to see anyone. Inside the pile of Nadasdy's clothes lay his ornate, ceremonial dagger – a thing worn at the waist and so bejewelled that it almost glowed, as if producing its own light. I turned around and craned my neck so I could just make out where some of the lacings of the corset were before hacking and hacking away at the dress' vulnerable points so that I could rip and wriggle my way out of it.

When I got down to almost nothing, I turned to the heap of Nadasdy's garments that I had left on the floor. Hesitantly, I slipped on his trousers and tunic, belt, everything. He was certainly broader than I, but I was still tall for a woman and I somehow managed to stay inside the bizarre costume without it falling around me. I looked at myself in the glass in amazement.

"Pretty."

I swung around. Nadasdy had turned his head to see me from inside his encasement. He smiled and fell back to sleep again.

The next morning, I woke to him stroking my face. I looked into those deep, strange grey eyes of his. The mapping and rushing sensation was gone.

"I like you," was all he said.

He sat up, rubbed his face, exhaled, and stared at me, as if steadying himself in front of a great foe. I moved to take his clothes from off my body – the ones I was still wearing from the night before.

"No, just leave it all," he said, looking over my arms, my chest and legs in his attire. He barely removed anything from himself or from me except what was necessary. It was a task. Nothing more. He went about it fast and then faster and faster, smiling a bit when I cried out, not in pleasure but in pain. Otherwise, his expression remained blank, and his eyes shut. I had never felt his skin, although I was already carrying his child.

*

The walls of Cachtice hummed each time I ran my hand along them, speaking of those that had come before and those that would come after in this very space. Only they knew I was with child – I hadn't dare to tell anyone else and was only now whispering it into the creviced ears of the stones that made the upper gallery. The sound of our newly shared secret was torn about by Thurzo and my husband striding into the hall in all their noise and bluster.

"It's as I was telling you, George, actually standing right there in my clothes on our wedding night!"

"Sounds like you might have to beat all that out of her," Thurzo replied absently.

"No, it's... she's..." Nadasdy fumbled around for words. "It's not like that with her," he finally settled on. He sat down in his gilded chair, took a long draught of whatever he was holding, and looked at the floor.

"I like her, George. That's all."

Thurzo smiled, moved over to him, took off one of his gloves as he walked and placed a bare hand on Nadasdy's shoulder.

"I think that's wonderful, Francis. A man should come home to something he likes, and I'll grant you, she is a little different. I like her too."

Nadasdy looked up. "I didn't ask your permission, George."

"No, but you as good as asked my counsel. And unlike the asking of permission, the asking of counsel is a much more solicitous affair. A simple 'yes', 'no', 'good', 'bad' would be far easier for me to give than *counsel*," he laughed.

"You're such a bastard. You're a smug bastard."

"A bastard?" he replied, raising his eyebrows patiently. "No, but I take your meaning. Now, what to do about our Emperor's request?"

"The treasury? How can the Holy Roman Emperor be short of funds? He has claimed *all* the ransom paid to me by the Ottoman lords *I* defeated and now he has the gall to ask for another loan. His Catholic tastes are getting too much for me."

"Francis, watch yourself. You, of course, are protected, and more than most. Nonetheless, remember that even you have limits."

Nadasdy surveyed Thurzo with a quiet rage brewing. Thurzo looked away, giving Nadasdy a polite moment to regain himself before continuing.

"So, we agree that we could all do with a bit more caution. Even now our noble Count Illeshazy is on the run to keep his little Protestant head attached to his even smaller Protestant body. I swear that man is a walking defect in all the ways that matter."

Nadasdy jumped up from his chair, drew his dagger and held it straight to Thurzo's neck.

"Watch yourself, Count. It's not so long ago I picked up the heads of my enemies on the battlefield and threw them one by one to my soldiers. This was after the battle. After *I* won it. Do you know what they did? They invited me to play polo. An Ottoman head for an Ottoman game. We did. It was fun. Don't try me, Thurzo. You have all the words in the world, but I will tear *your* head from your body if you come after me for my religion."

Thurzo swallowed imperceptibly, then pushed Nadasdy's hand aside.

"The 'Black Bey' of the battlefield."

Nadasdy dropped his dagger to his side, but he didn't move an inch.

"Send the money then. But if the Hapsburg touches Illeshazy, I'll march down to Vienna myself."

"Much good may that do you, Francis."

"So be it. Then this 'Black Bey' will step aside and let the Turks do the marching for him."

Thurzo shot Nadasdy a look. It was the same kind of look I'd seen on the paintings of hell that came out from the Flemish courts. Dull and terrifying at the same time. Paintings that emerged on the walls of castles and estates like warnings: this is hell, pray you stay where you are and do not move.

Thurzo turned on his heel and walked out, that unmistakeable *clang! clang!* of his pace becoming quieter and quieter as he put distance between himself and his fury. Nadasdy saw me looking down at him from the upper gallery that framed the room.

"Elizabet!"

"I'm sorry, I didn't know what to do, Francis. You both came storming in here and I was…" I searched for words "…in the middle of doing something – with the wall."

He shook his head and waved his hand over his shoulder to suggest it was nothing to worry about and there was no need for me to explain my weird wanderings.

"Elizabet, I'm only going to say this once, because in truth I fear saying it out loud. That man will be the death of us."

I wanted to tell him. I knew I had to tell him, but I was unsure of how to speak to my husband in a way that he might understand me. We had only spent that one night – one morning, to be precise – in one another's arms. He had been so awkward and seemed to want to get it over with, and although we had begun to speak of all sorts of things by now, speaking about sex was still as taboo as its doing. I faltered, but when he looked at me inquisitively, I steadied myself and simply said, "My lord, I think – though it's hard to believe – I think I might already have become pregnant."

He stared at me. "That's wonderful news. My mother will be ecstatic." He sat back in his chair, his eyes darting from place to place like a startled grey hare.

Then he looked at me. He held his hand out to me and I took it. He kissed mine gently, almost friendly, and smiled at me. "My fertile wife! Let's hope it's a boy, it'll make everything easier on both of us." He rubbed my palm then, and a slow and genuine kindness filled the space between us for a moment. "As for Thurzo," a quick look of victory flashed across him, "this will hit him like an arrow between the eyes." First, he snorted at his own remark. Then he looked nothing short of thrilled.

"Thurzo's only ever been kind to me. And between us, we hold more land, estates and wealth than he could possibly muster. Surely that's enough to secure us some small peace of mind." And I looked down at my belly, filled with sudden apprehension.

"Oh, Elizabet, that's the first time you've said something really stupid."

I thought about it and then blushed, the last vestiges of

childhood rising to my face before vanishing into ivory, perhaps forever.

"We need allies if we're going to keep our lands safe from the likes of *Count* Thurzo. Even now, I've sent our priest, Pastor Magyery, to speak with the blacksmiths here and make sure that in Cachtice, at least, we'll always have a ready army at hand. These Szekely peasants will do anything for a bit of coin and our pastor is well liked. God knows he speaks better than I do. He'll remind them that they owe me allegiance. It's been so forever, even before Mohacs."

The room went dark for a moment, as if the sun had slowed its pace in the sky. All I could see in my mind's eye was the square shadow of the metal throne and the imagined cries of the Szekely blacksmiths as our fathers and uncles had rounded them up in the terrible ways that Janus had described, melting their would-be king on an iron throne of his own. How could Nadasdy hope that these men would rise to protect *us* after all that had happened? I had started shaking, my body speeding up, in the same way a mechanical toy expels all its motion fast before hitting an abrupt paralysis.

"What is it?" Nadasdy asked, a warning slipping now into his voice as if to say *what have you done?* I went over to him and knelt by his chair, placing my hand on his shoulder in an attempt to keep this warlord of a husband that I had acquired calm before telling him the entire story of my treatment at the hands of the blacksmiths, omitting, of course, the part where I ran away to the woods with Janus, hoping he would take me far, far away forever.

"We must be careful. They're still angry with us. They still mourn…" I stopped myself short of using the name of their peasant king, the one that had been melted down into nothing by Bathorys and Nadasdys and Thurzos before us.

Nadasdy said nothing. He simply stood up, grabbed my hand, and exited the room, silently moving down the labyrinth of corridors until the light of Cachtice fell unhindered upon our skin. He dragged me down towards the smithy. When I turned about, I saw we had gathered quite the crowd of onlookers. Dread hit the pit of my stomach, turning it hard as iron. Nadasdy marched into the smithy and the clang-clanging ceased. The light outside was so bright and the smithy so dark that my eyes could just make out the silhouettes through the open doorway.

I saw my husband grab a double-headed axe from a heap of newly made weapons, swing it with force over and over and behead a good half of the blacksmiths within. I saw him filled with a power I could have never imagined. It was as if some part of the ground had opened up and traded him for something that had lain quiet, waiting for any opportunity to be unleashed from its underworld prison.

Everybody ran out, fleeing towards the woods in a strange mirroring of my own pathway the year before. The huge blacksmith who had tormented me from the moment of my arrival at Cachtice staggered outside. He was wounded and fell directly to his knees, panting and spilling black blood as if a dark chalice somewhere in the centre of him had shattered into pieces. Nadasdy grabbed a still-burning length of metal, the embryo of a huge sword-to-be, from inside the smithy. He then returned to the man as calmly as if he had simply forgotten some domestic item – a key, or a handkerchief – held his head up by the hair and drove the burning iron into his mouth and all the way through him, right into the ground below.

I stood rooted, stock-still, as if denying the eternal movement of flesh. Nadasdy turned to the horrified crowd.

"Never threaten my wife." He came to me, kissed my forehead and on seeing me as if my soul had departed from my body, turned back to the crowd. Through the glaze that fell over me, I picked out the shape of Janus amongst the peasants, but he, like every other form on the horizon, now seemed only vanishing to me, as all the light in the world was being replaced with nothing but rolling greyness.

Nadasdy raised his voice, loud and clear as a Sunday bell.

"Remember your Count. Remember your Countess. But if you remember neither then remember this: It was worse at Mohacs. I am the only thing standing between you."

*

The musty smell and textures of the cloth-bound books lining the walls in the university library poured into my senses as the half-finished forms of the world etched themselves into my awareness. I looked around. A student in wire- rimmed round glasses and black lipstick sat at the huge, dark wooden desk. He was flipping through a heavy pile of books – something on particle physics. His particular brand of 'emo' scientist gave me all the clues I needed to work out *when* I had arrived at. He noticed me looking at him as I aimed to orient myself in time, stuck his middle finger up and pushed his glasses higher up his nose. I fished around inside my pocket and found my phone. I'd gone upmarket with my tech at this point. It was trying to report the date, spluttering a 2 then a 7 then a 1 then a 0. After a minute or two, it settled down. 18-03-*2017*.

Since being able to see me in time and remember everything henceforth, Lucretia had invented an ingenious way for us to communicate despite my disappearances, creating a strange kind of DIY orbit through which we could find each other whenever I emerged at a point in our shared history together. At first, she had suggested that every day she text my phone with a precise location so I could find her if I happened to emerge somewhere close. I was quick to tell her that all this jumping in time disturbed the workings of technology, often scrambling my screen, and so relying on the delivery of digital messages would be patchy at best. Electronics and *timewalking* do not mix.

"I have an idea!" she said. "There's a panel loose on the first floor of the library. Whenever you emerge *here*, go to it. I'll leave you a note with my location, date and time."

I nodded and shrugged, uncertain at first that paper and ink might survive the workings of time.

"It's worth a shot."

2017. The library. Here, now.

Okay.

So she'll have left a note with her location and a time inside the panelled wall. I spun on my heel and walked down to the North Wing corridor to the place she'd shown me, edging towards the wood panels carefully. I looked over my shoulder to make sure no one was watching. Only a few energy-saving lights were on in the corridor, their flickering dying down as time and space grew accustomed to my arrival. I traced each panel with my fingertip until I felt two lines scored in the shape of an 'L'. Lucretia's sign. I laughed to myself about this. If we kept this up, one day the library would be festooned in these little etchings.

The panel made a high-pitched squeak as I tried to open it. I looked around again. A woman passed me by. She was blonde and had a silk scarf tossed over her shoulder. *Very debonair.* When she saw me staring blankly at the empty wall, she asked, "Are you okay? Do you need something?"

She asked it slowly and loudly in case English might not be my first language.

"Doing all right," I responded, two fingers at my forehead in a mock salute. "Don't mind me."

She smiled and laughed a little nervously before moving on. I breathed out heavily with relief, swivelling back to the panel so I could prize it ajar with my fingernails. There was a little folded paper note in the empty space.

4th floor, North Wing, end of stacks. 2-4pm. Wednesday, 18th October 2017

I looked around. There was a clock on the wall that read 15.50. For the first time in a long while, time seemed to have done me a favour and sent me at just the right moment to find her. *Sometimes, the universe is friendly.* I made my way as fast as I could to the fourth floor, my black cowboy boots and skinny jeans clicking and stretching as I climbed the stairs two at a time. I made it, breathless, just as Lucretia was packing up. She smiled. It was like watching a large crow open its beak without cawing.

"Good."

"How long have you been waiting?"

"Four months. Every day. Same time."

"What?"

"Yes. But I dreamt you too. Except you weren't you exactly. I was watching 'you' inside a story. You were in a fabulous dress – I would imagine it was about five hundred years ago, maybe more. And there was a marriage. You were talking with a man. He had those big blue 'bedroom eyes.'"

Bathory and Thurzo! Lucretia had seen them in her dream. A dream she dreamt of me and my world.

"Come on, let's go. If Bathory can't help us directly, let's see if we can cure you of this time problem ourselves."

She moved to leave but I reached out my hand to grab one of her arms.

"Wait. Lucretia, there's something I want to ask you. Maybe I've always wanted to know it." I fixed my gaze on her, on her beautiful face. "Why are you helping me?"

She surveyed me, tutted, and did not once take her stare from mine. "Do you understand nothing about friendship, Vera? My teacher taught me how to slow down the world and peer behind the veils – some of the veils at any rate, the one I told you about, the one dying in the hospital bed in my dreams. With the astral eyes?"

I nodded.

"You think I'm just going to sit around and say, 'Thank you very much'? We pass our knowledge on. We all do. You will too, in your own way. Neither you nor I are crazy, Vera. We know that the world is made up of many worlds. It's just you and I, we *see* what others *feel*, what they have a slight premonition of as they're falling asleep, or as they glance at the clock to see that hours have passed when it felt only like a few seconds. Don't you get tired of doing it alone?"

"Doing what?"

"Being the product of *all this history*!" She laughed hard, unfolding her other arm out to all the books on the shelves, though her eyes never once moved from mine.

"Yeah. Yeah, I suppose I do."

"Well then." She shovelled her remaining books into her bag. "This is what it is to peer behind the veil."

*

At *my house. From 1pm. 29th November 2022*

I put the page back in the panel, adding a little smiley face to Lucretia's scrawl. I was about to leave when I turned back, took it out again and drew a comedy piece of the male anatomy on the page where she had written the number '1'. It would make Lucretia smile when she found it tomorrow, even though she would call me childish. Within ten minutes, I was at her house. It was filled with brightly coloured cushions that she had hand-stitched with curses and expletives in and amongst curling flowers and clouds. Soon, we were both sitting on the floor in the study, which was filled with books and yellowing papers. Over the years, once every conceivable space for books in her house had become full, tomes and manuscripts of long-finished projects she'd written lay on the floor, creating small rivulets of paper and cardboard across the house.

The windows let in green light on account of the vast number of plants and pots that cast the living room in their vibrant hue. For a second, I wondered if Lucretia herself ran not on food but on photosynthesis alone. If I could see beyond her skin, would I find that she was really made out of vines and leaves and green things? I'd never actually seen her eat in all the time we'd known each other. But she could never be described as vampiric, even though her black clothes and tall cheekbones made her almost a parody of such a creature. Lucretia was far too alive to be one of the undead. She was like the earth. Ancient, and tired, and eternally on the brink of losing her patience with *people*. I rose and picked up a nearby cushion, noting it read *Fuck the Patriarchy* in little pink floral letters. It made me smile wryly.

"Okay, so shut your eyes and just listen. Listen to as many of the sounds that come into your ears as you can. If you listen closely enough, eventually you should hear the way sound *moves* inside the simplest of noises. It's just about slowing everything right down. Slowing down time. Just go *slowly, slowly*."

So I breathed and breathed and breathed until I heard my own heartbeat, first raging, then quietening. And after some while, *I heard it – something else, as if I were hearing the heartbeat of the world. Sound, sight – all the senses – they did more than just report our world back to us. They captured the tiny worlds that moved inside all of the things in the room, each one stamped in its own unique way. At the centre of the universe lay all the tiny movements that built up worlds. Worlds that slotted inside one another in an infinite jigsaw and which made up the everyday that we all take for granted.*

"Everything moves in tiny spirals!" I suddenly exclaimed, jolting Lucretia from her position with my sudden revelation. "And each material, each noise, has its own strange signature."

"Yes!" she responded happily, and rather like she was speaking to a child who had just taken their first step on two upright legs. She was always so patient with me and my 'discoveries'.

"What do you hear?"

She closed her black eyes. "For me, it's a little different. It's like dreaming whilst you're still half-awake. I don't see the movements, it's more like... like I hear a story unfolding. See these stones in the jar?" and she opened her eyes and pointed to a little collection of pebbles inside a glass jar on the table under the green window. "Inside one, I hear a mother and her children crowding around her. They buzz and shift and move – you know, like children when they are hungry or want something. It goes on forever. It's their atomic signature and it never dies. It simply reorganises. Like their DNA, in a way. But you – you also *see* the movements. That's not my way."

I got up, removed two cigarettes from the pack next to the stones, put both in my mouth and lit them, handing her one.

"Maybe we're just both on the spectrum. In a *big* way," I said.

"Maybe. But really, Vera, what is it with your obsession with diagnoses? No wonder you hop around in time whenever you get too close to understanding anything."

I laughed, picked up my wine glass that lay beside me and clinked it to hers.

"Are you sure you still want to get out of here – out of your time problem?"

"Yeah." I turned around and looked through the green leaves onto the street below. "Yeah, I really do." I felt tired. Exhausted by the ghostliness of living outside of the straight line of history.

"Okay then. Put your inner prescription pad away and focus. Lean into the fire of time."

Later, we climbed up on her roof. She had a child's science-kit telescope, and we took turns looking at the worlds far, far away from ours. Eventually, Lucretia spoke up.

"Vera, it's good you're here. Good you're here with me." She patted my foot whilst still looking through the long glass eyes of the telescope. "Every time I go to sleep, each dream I have, it leads to illness and death." She spoke soberly and quickly, although she never once looked directly at me. Only to the stars.

"But it's not just a dream. It's like I hear people's futures. People coming to terms with their end. You know, I worked for a long time at a hospice. What am I saying? You *know* everything. More than I do about my own… future. But the hospice, it helped me to make my inner world and the outer world make a little more sense. I closed the gap between waking and sleeping. In both worlds, I simply helped people cross over. But that was a long time ago, before I fell in love with poetry and ended up here. In academia. For my sins. Having you here with me, wrapped in your own strange puzzle, it makes it easier *for me*. See, this is why I'm helping you. I'm *selfish*."

"Then stay selfish!" I reassured, putting my head on her shoulder.

She dragged deeply on her cigarette and thought about it.

"You know, I think I fell in love with poetry *because* I worked in the hospice. It taught me to respect death rather than fear it. I started to see the world pulsing with life rather than death. The flowers and the trees, all humming with something spectacular – the sound of the universe pulsing inside each tiny creature. You and I, we're twice born."

I thought back to the moment I had died and how I had touched the edges of the doorway to the apartment block I'd fallen outside of, creating an opening – a womb – back into life, and I understood her more deeply.

"I never thought of my experience as a superpower."

"It's not. It's simply deep, slow listening. Hearing all the tiny worlds that spin together to create ours. Most people don't see the inner workings of the world. Or maybe you're right and we are just – how did you say it – spectrum kids?" And she mimed taking out a notepad and flicking its imaginary pages over one by one, as if I had racked up quite the range of diagnoses myself.

I laughed and pushed her until she rolled a little on the floor of the roof. It was the first time I'd laughed so freely and so from the heart since I could remember. For a moment, I really didn't care what time did to me next. I had a friend. What could time do to that?

*

In the weeks that followed the moment outside the smithy, the world had faded to grey, and I wondered around in a trance that was not at all like the different *talto* trances I had fallen into. Time had frozen, and even when my eyes were open, I could see nothing except the cold, blank face of my husband as he drove that sword so torturously into the blacksmith that day. I lay in my tower, sick with pregnancy and nightmares.

After several weeks, I rose, determined to find Janus, but he was gone. More than gone, almost all trace of him had vanished as if he'd never existed in the first place. I went down to the room that housed the furnace at the bottom of my tower. To Janus' room. The books and papers were also gone, leaving a trail of ash outside the hearth. I ran my fingers across the stones. They were still warm, and I smiled a little for the first time in a long time, imagining Janus saying something like, *Yes! I've warmed them with the heat of my prayer for you, Little Wing. Just for you.*

I stopped abruptly. One of the stones was loose and I prized it out. There was a single page inside the hole it left. The page was warm too, neither burned nor singed, only warm. I held it close to the crude fire that must have been lit by someone earlier in the morning. On one side of the paper, in Janus' unmistakable hand, were the words: *For Little Wing*. I flipped it over. It was a poem written not in Turkish but from a land even further away – a poem that had found its way from the courts of Persia to the Ottomans. Janus had once made me read it several times over, helping me translate it and saying it contained a secret that I would understand later, when the world had marked my body enough for its meaning to become real. I read it slowly now, remembering each word as he had spoken it to me.

"'Die, die in this love. Die to the din and the noise of the world. In the silence of love, you will find a spark of life.'"

His love wasn't for me, I knew that. I had understood it, and mourned it, and got on with my lessons. It was for his god, who he saw inside me, inside the rocks and the waters – more an expanding rush of intensities than a god in the sky or a god that presided *over and above* the world. I so badly wanted to love in the way he did, not just to preserve what was left of my heart in this grey and violent world, but to feel it fill up. Grow bigger and burn brighter. He'd started me on this strange journey and now he was gone at the very moment I needed him most – when all the love in the world was vanishing into darkness. I would have to walk my own way. His words came back to now:

All right, Little Wing, but slowly. Slowly.

Since that day outside the smithy, Nadasdy's violence had also become more noticeable to me. At first, it wasn't directed towards me, but to the walls and windows around me. He would rage and fit and then run away, disappearing for days. The first time he struck me was upon return from a skirmish against the Turks.

"Why are the tapestries full of dust? Is this a household or a madhouse? Why do you wander about when you should be doing your duty? How am I supposed to want to share your bed when you do nothing all day but read Ottoman heresy?"

The blow across the cheek was so vicious that I flew a few steps back. When he saw me clutch my nearly spent belly in terror, he ran out of the room and hid from me for several days afterwards, like a boy who feels remorse at pulling the translucent wings off a fly and vows, unsuccessfully, never to do it again.

"Anna, where is my husband?" I eventually asked, amazed that a man might hide from his wife like a child.

"He's in his quarters. Don't disturb him, my lady. He shouldn't be disturbed. It's best you don't." She shook a little and instinctively clutched to her waist, where a large bunch of household keys dangled. I walked up to her, demanded them from her and held them up. Each one glistened like a shard of a magic mirror in the strange light of Cachtice. When I turned on my heel to march in the other direction, she did something very strange. She hurled herself at me, catching me quite off guard. I nearly tripped to the ground but steadied myself against the wall. Anna fell to my feet, holding me by the ankles and begging me not to go. I became full of shock and rage and viciously pushed myself away from her. She covered her face with her hands. When she looked up, her eyes were glistening with tears.

"Please, my lady. Please don't go to him."

I chased the very air away with the speed at which I ran towards Nadasdy's locked rooms. Outside his door, I fumbled with the keys, trying several unsuccessfully until one finally turned. As the door creaked open, I could hear muffled sounds that gave way to shapes. I could see the back of Nadasdy's head through some twenty candles lit around him. His hands were heavily gloved even though we were indoors. When he turned around to see who had dared enter, he had blood on his face. It was then I noticed the serving girl on the floor. She was wounded badly and white with terror. There were small ring-sized burn marks across her back, where a shirt had been ripped to expose the symmetry of her delicate spine, layered over with fresh red lines. Otherwise, she was fully clothed. I grabbed the door frame and froze, stock-still. Memories of my wedding night slid around the edges of my awareness. She was dressed as a boy.

Chapter Seven

Ink. Thick, luscious, sensual. Ink, keeper of time. As it dries, it cradles meaning into shapes, becoming one with your thoughts. It dresses the world of bare life in architectures of intelligence – intelligent biologies that make and remake themselves into new forms. Ink knows what it is to grow life from inside its black belly. Our stories live and die on its back.

To make ink, first you take a bone and char it, burning out all the inner matter. It's important not to allow too much air into the burning because at these temperatures the bone will simply burn away to nothing. Then, you turn the blackened pieces into powder, grinding for hours until your wrists become sore and your fingers are covered in calluses. After this, you mix the fine powder with varnish *very carefully*. The varnish will likely ignite and explode. It might even take down the whole building if you're not careful. At the end of it all, you need to dip your finger into the ink and taste the smallest amount. If you feel nothing on your tongue, no grain, no powdery traces, then this is good ink.

Nadasdy, along with several other nobles, generals and clerics, had been summoned to Venice to discuss the Ottoman problem, and now that our child was three years old, playing clumsily with dolls and puppets of her own, I insisted on going with him to explore the city that I had heard so much about in books – a Venice of colours and shapes, costumes and fabrics. I didn't expect that it would be two small, bald craftsmen that would capture all my interest when I finally arrived, or that meeting them would change my future forever.

On meeting the printer Fabbri and his typesetter brother, I exchanged all the colours and intrigues of the Venetian streets for the dusty inside of a workshop. The Fabbri brothers would teach me everything I needed to know about how to make ink. A little premonition is an odd and dangerous thing. I knew that the hours spent inside their printshop were in some way going to write my future, not only mine, but the future of an entire nation, a technology that would sweep away the old world and bring in the new. I just had no idea how dangerous it would all get.

Fabbri the elder's fingers were stained almost permanently black, but Fabbri the younger was meticulously clean, perhaps even to the point of a feverish obsession. He also had other strange habits. I could often hear him count to ten over and over, and sometimes he would stutter a little. It was barely noticeable and only happened once or twice in the workshop whilst I worked beside him, but enough nonetheless to surmise that some nightmare had once befallen him that now arrested the free-flow of his speech.

"We were journeymen," said the elder Fabbri one day, whilst all three of us stood grinding the ink, despite their pleas for me to keep my hands clean and not tell a soul that I was *labouring*.

"What's that?" I asked. The word sounded almost mythological.

"We were apprentices in print houses across Europe. We've worked in Lyon—"

"Yes, Lyon!" interrupted Fabbri the younger.

"Antwerp, Bohemia – your part of the world, no?"

"Yes, B-Bohemia!"

"Oh, I'm far from Bohemia –" I sighed, thinking how locked away I was at Cachtice and how much a part of the castle even my bones were becoming. "But I didn't know we had presses there."

"Countess, the world of printing is everywhere now," continued Fabbri the younger, "and not all Bibles and psalters. Come, I will print you anything. I will print you a page, yes? A page of anything for you to take back to Hungary with you. I'll design a special type for you. And I will make it so very beautiful." He went bashful all of a sudden, and his brother hit him on the head, leaving little black smudge marks there that made me laugh quietly to myself later.

"Eventually," Fabbri the elder continued, "we returned to Venice, working all over before finding ourselves here. Our own little printshop. We do colour as well, see?" And he held up a sheet for me to inspect. "But in the end, you get tired, no? You are young and a countess." He bowed his head a fraction to show proper deference before continuing. "But if you had been less fortunate in life, perhaps you would have bound your body, worn a hat and a set of whiskers." he smiled and tugged at his own, giving himself permission to poke fun at me, "and become a journeyman yourself. They say there are some that managed it, you know, some women." He paused and suddenly looked very sad and very young at the same time, as if he had lost something a long time ago which occasionally collapsed the passage of time whenever he thought about it.

"I would rather be fortunate in that life," I half whispered, shuddering at the thought of Nadasdy's violence, of the blacksmith and the serving girl and countless other deeds that I could only half imagine as he raced across the battlefield, tearing Turks to pieces from his saddle. It was neither these nor the sight of Nadasdy's absent eyes that chilled my heart.

Those dead grey eyes. The eyes of a man who has taken leave of himself and entered into a mythic space, becoming neither man nor soldier but violence itself. The only thing I could see – the only thing I could ever see when I thought of him – was the image of him driving the burning half-made sword through the blacksmith's mouth at the furnace house. Time and distance followed me there, freezing everything to a halt. It poured into my remembering flesh like a ghostly river, hardening my insides into sheets of ice as we made ink in the workshop.

I blinked and returned to my senses.

"Don't be ridiculous, my lady. You are most fortunate," continued Fabbri the elder. "And we are fortunate that you take an interest in our tiny lives." The brothers both bowed, and we continued to grind the charred bones into powder in silence. Soon, I would ask them again about the life of a journeyman. I would get more than just an answer. I would inherit a boy.

We all worked together until it got late. The sky was letting long ribbons of cloud slip down into the thick blue lines that lay just above the horizon. They vanished as fast as they came, as if they'd never been part of the sky at all. Or perhaps I'd become so absorbed in the press that I hadn't noticed time change around us. Nadasdy had insisted I bring at least one serving maid from Cachtice when I'd dismissed their retinue. He had chosen Dorothea, who accompanied us. She dogged my steps, making it hard for me to spend as much time as I'd have liked with the Fabbris. Anna had also remained at Cachtice to take care of our daughter. I'd named her Anna too, but we all called her Anastasia to mark the difference. When she'd been born, Nadasdy had at first seemed disappointed. His heart had been set on a boy but within a few moments of holding her in his hands, he'd softened. He looked at me as if I had revealed myself to be made of magic, then kissed her on her tiny forehead with complete tenderness.

I realised that I missed both my Annas – Anna Darvulia, my closest ally, and Anastasia, my dearest child – even though

Venice had brought me a wonderment I'd not thought possible in the world. The wonder of ink. On the other hand, I had to battle Dorothea constantly. She was a strange, quiet woman, constantly at prayer, as if she carried the very soul of Hungary on her shoulders. She barely spoke but always watched me. Her white pallor, high cheekbones, combined with the fact that she never walked more than one pace behind me, made it seem as if she had been released not from Cachtice, but from one of the armies of the undead to stalk my waking and even my dreaming hours.

Escaping her withering eye to slip off unnoticed to the printshop wasn't easy. The following day, I asked her to visit an apothecary and have some sleeping roots ground up for me.

"This city is so full of excitement that I feel I become overwhelmed by it and can't for the life of me get to sleep."

"Italians make people restless," was all she said. She muttered some prayers and stared at my body in a way that made me feel a little self-conscious.

"What on earth do you mean?"

"Where is your husband these nights? Perhaps you might visit him and take your rest under his protection. Give him the heir he needs."

The statement was so outlandish from a serving woman, no matter how highly regarded her services, that I laughed out loud despite myself.

"Get me my herbs and I'll send you to him at night so I might sleep undisturbed!" I yelled at her, playing the part of the angry wife rather than the furtive printer. As soon as she returned, I put a few pinches into her goblet the moment she was at prayer and then told the cook to heavily salt our lunch.

I didn't stay to watch her fall asleep. I took her large cloak and ran as quickly as I could over to the Fabbri workshop. The younger Fabbri opened the door at the side of the shop and let me into the workspace. A boy was waiting for me, no more than eight years old, possibly even younger.

"Countess. You honour us beyond what we deserve," said Fabbri the elder, who was standing behind the boy, one concerned hand on his shoulder. "This is my son, my adopted son, John."

John bowed very deeply, staring at me with his small rabbit-like eyes.

"John knows everything that we do about printing. His tiny hands have worked alongside ours for thousands of hours in Spain. We were all delivered by God from the reach of the pretender's Inquisition, the one who calls himself 'Pope' and ruler of the Church, but who sells indulgences. We printed Luther's words and we *survived,* and it must have been for a reason. Countess, you come to us like an angel from the court of Luther himself. It's no accident the Lord brought us together. You have the mark of a printer, the curiosity. Take the boy and do good works in your home. Print. Print anything you wish, but let the whole world know that the devil continues to reside not in hell but in Rome!" He bowed so low that I thought the ground might swallow him up and deliver him straight back to the very Spanish chamber he had apparently escaped from.

Silence fell thickly. I had no idea what to do. Whilst it was true that I had wanted to set up a small press at Cachtice, and whilst I served a Protestant Lord, taking on the Pope himself was something entirely different. Fabbri the younger was the one who eventually spoke. His voice came quietly, but as he talked it began to fill the room, clear as a bell and full of pride – and sadness.

"We worked for the survivors of Carranza. But soon the Inquisition came. They couldn't find us, so instead they made effigies of us, and they burnt them after we escaped, saying that in the eyes of God the wood and straw was as good as our flesh."

"Of course, we were not called 'Fabbri' then!" laughed the elder, disturbing the spell that the younger had woven with his words. "And God must love us because here we are, and here you are. Please, Countess, take John away from this place. He has been printing with us since he could hold a block." He tousled the boy's hair.

"And he's very good at squeezing into small hiding places, quiet as a mouse, and leaves no trace. A useful asset. Print, my lady. Print all the good words and send them across the world."

I shivered with a prescient knowing. But before answering, I walked over to the press. The wooden blocks full of iron type lay flat on the opposite wall. There were shelves of different fonts and I picked one of the many letters up. It felt heavy in my hand. I held it, face up, allowing it to stare back up at me and read me as directly as I read it. My palm vibrated a little as the blood rushed under my skin, making contact with destiny in this unlikely place. As I stared at it, I felt its power. The heavily clad 'A' began to shine and stretch beyond its own borders, but just as the golden horse appeared again, ready to take me up and move me through the worlds, the sound of the main door to the printshop being thrown aside echoed throughout the building.

Fabbri the younger leapt up and slammed the inner door shut behind him as he went. Fabbri the elder and John both grabbed me and threw me to the floor, rolling me under the print table, which they then covered with a huge rectangle of leather. I could hear muffled voices and shouts. Dorothea had woken up out of her deathlike sleep and was searching for the Countess Nadasdy with an armed accompaniment. I squeezed my hand around the iron letter 'A' that had fallen to the floor with me, jolted out of my strange reverie and back into the large and dangerous world of the printshop.

It had been so long since I'd felt the presence of the girl in the wall or seen the strange world of the future that she seemed to belong to. Perhaps it was in printing that she would make herself known to me again. After all, what else was printing other than bones, trees, words and thoughts all coming together for a moment in time to write out our futures and capture our histories? Print and time weren't that different. They both marked the world.

I could hear Dorothea and the guards threatening to break things upstairs, demanding that the Countess be returned to them. It made me furious to feel that the small, bright edges of my freedom were being snuffed out.

"Her husband, Count Francis Nadasdy, insists on her return. *Immediately.*" I heard her say this clearly, as if she was speaking directly to me, knowing I was somewhere listening. Then I heard her assemble the guards and leave the shop, no doubt to spare me the humiliation of being found hiding under a table.

When silence finally fell, I whispered to Fabbri the elder, "I will arrange it. The boy will come with me to Cachtice, and we will start up the press."

Fabbri just nodded. John grabbed the hem of my skirt and kissed it. Then he stared first at the letter in my hand and then at me in wonder, as if he were witnessing a powerful ghost rip at the fabric of death and fall into form. The boy had *seen* me about to exit this world momentarily by the touch of type. Of that, I was sure.

The following evening, my husband sent for me to join him and would not be put off by my various excuses.

"Elizabet, I'm troubled to hear you're spending time with craftspeople. It doesn't look good for us, and Thurzo is hunting for any excuse to blacken our name at the Hapsburg court. I have, of course, taken the matter in hand. They'll no longer *distract* you. Not now and not ever again." His eyes surveyed mine. They were grey. Dead.

I went cold. But I had learnt how to regain myself in the face of his murderessness. It was the only way I would survive him.

"I don't think the Emperor would have given a thought to what your wife amused herself with when travelling abroad."

The words fell smoothly out of my mouth. It was as if they were spoken by a wiser, cleverer person than I. I stared at him, daring him to contradict me, willing him to take me on with words. He paused and surveyed me. Then after a moment he looked uncontrollably sad, as if he were a very young child.

"Not when the game is a Protestant one, my love."

The 'my love' made me flinch.

"I care nothing for religion! As far as I'm concerned, all these religious fights are just excuses, so that men like you can do what you want to each other – to anyone. Even the Turks, aren't they just the same as we are, spilling blood as if they were searching for God inside it? And these Catholics, they even drink it!"

Nadasdy jumped up like a scalded cat. If I hadn't been habituated to it, I would have thought the side of my head had momentarily exploded into pieces, hit by a Turkish cannonball on the field. The man was made of iron.

"Shut your mouth, Elizabet! You'll get us all killed. Do you want that? Do you want to die? Do you want to add your name to the list of witches and Jews that the Inquisition has burnt across the southern parts of our, beloved, Holy Roman Empire?"

He almost spat the word 'beloved', and I knew this was his attempt at bonding us again, finding something we could each focus our hatred on in complicity together.

"The printing presses are too dangerous. I would smuggle a thousand of Luther's books right into the Emperor's court if I thought we could get away with it, but, Elizabet, we can't. We're too much in the public eye. We're indulged in our faith at home with a shaky peace between us all, but if we are seen to ally ourselves too closely with reformist forces, they will have us condemned. And Thurzo *will* take our lands. Everywhere I look, always Thurzo! I bet if I strip the Emperor down one day, I'll see Thurzo's face smiling at me from out of his backside."

I could see he was trying to make things seem normal. The blow was just part of the dialogue. The sending of Dorothea, the armed retinue, the capture of the Fabbris was simply a normal spat between a husband and wife positioned at the centre of a shrinking Empire, but suddenly my head throbbed, and the room swung around, like a fluttering candle flame. I fell abruptly down to the ground. All I could hear was Nadasdy sighing exasperatedly and calling for the servant to bring salts.

"Elizabet," he whispered as he knelt down beside me, "trouble me no more. I love you."

*

I had sent word to John to be on the street alone and dressed as a beggar on the day when the Nadasdy retinue were returning to Hungary.

"Oh," I exclaimed, "what a beautiful little child. Dorothea, take him and clothe him and let him follow us back to Hungary. He can wash my horses." I turned to Nadasdy. "I want him. Might we not bring him back with us?"

Nadasdy simply lifted his gloved hand at the wrist in Dorothea's direction, flexing his fingers in a sign of assent, and John became one of us. It was as simple as that. So I had rescued John from capture and fire, but the blood of his two fathers was ultimately on my hands.

Had we been at home, Nadasdy informed me as we rode back to Hungary, he would have put the brothers to death and left their bodies hung up to serve as a warning to anyone who might, in his words, 'endanger' his wife. "But as we are in Venice, however, I simply returned them to the Catholics," he said. That numb greyness returned. It absorbed me again. His ghostly eyes. The sound of iron and blood. The smithy. And now the smiling, teasing faces of the Fabbri brothers oozing down into fire. Vanishing into Nadasdy's world; into the world we had all made and that I would never stop trying to unmake.

Nadasdy made sure he told Thurzo all about his deliverance of the brothers to the Inquisition on our return. In fact, our feet barely touched the soil of Cachtice before we rode off to Thurzo's castle.

"My wife is so frivolous in her interests," Nadasdy reasoned away, "I would prefer she devote herself fully to me, but such is the price one pays for a jewel of a woman," and he kissed the inside of my wrist as we sat together at Thurzo's table.

"Francis, Elizabet lends you her charm, wit and grace. The least you can do is protect her from the usury and false witness of a pair of Italian Jews." Thurzo looked at me whilst Nadasdy squeezed my hand hard in anticipation of having to silence me.

"Conversos. Didn't you know? Jews who converted. And – I suspect they are not brothers." He snorted a little at this. "You do like to collect strange ornaments, don't you, Countess?" Thurzo laughed softly and then took a dainty sip of wine without taking his eyes off me for a moment.

As usual, Nadasdy drank too much and Thurzo too little for my liking. When Thurzo's servants packed Nadasdy off to sleep, he insisted I stay up with him in the anterior drawing room.

"Do you consider yourself a Protestant, my lady?" he asked.

"I could barely be a devoted wife if I didn't," I responded quickly.

"But in your heart. If you listen to it beyond the yoke of your vows and the treaties of peace between us all, what does it tell you?"

I paused. Thurzo would not be shaken off lightly, and in truth, I didn't really know what I'd call myself. I had learnt more from the Ottoman mysticisms than from the teachings of Lutherans, Calvinists or Catholics. The Fabbris had snuck a copy of the Jewish book into my possession before the damnable day of their capture, and one from the famous Spanish nun and her interior castle. I said my prayers and breached no commandments without guilt. But I didn't buy my way out of sin. Perhaps that's what, in the end, defined me as Protestant.

"My heart tells me that none of these wars – Christian or Turkish – are soon to be over. My lord, do you think we live at the end of days?"

"My lady, I have never seen Francis this enthralled. You care well for him."

"What has that got to do with religion?"

"In this case, everything. I'm just curious as to where your convictions lie." He paused and ran his hand along the front of the ornate hearth that rose and fell in swirls and rosettes, as if testing out its limits. Then he turned towards me. He took the whole of me in in one long look, marking out the terrain of my presence as if I took up more space than I occupied with my body.

"I wish my wife were more like you. Perhaps you would teach her how to appear at court."

He moved over to me, circling around the room so that when he came to a standstill, he was behind me. I could feel his breath on my ear as he spoke.

"She is a sweet and innocent thing who craves my affection."

He began biting my ear gently at first, then became more impassioned. I had refused Nadasdy's bed ever since I had found out his dark secrets. It was no great loss for either of us. He had always been so uncomfortable with me, most often undesiring, preferring that I caress his brow until he fell asleep holding me like a child's blanket in his arms. I knew now this was in part because he was trying to keep the terrible storm of his violence away from our intimacy, holding me up as proof to God that he was capable of something other than pain.

I pulled myself away, taking a step forward.

"Do you really intend to seduce me by talking about your wife?"

"Yes. I want you to know that you and I are cut from the same material. Doting and loving are not our ways. We like to fuck with power."

He became a little out of breath at this, charming himself with his own passion. He grabbed my arms, threw me to the floor and started ripping at my clothes with his hands.

"Do you remember when I loosened your corset when you were just a girl? It feels like yesterday. I wanted you even then, but now over these years, you've become something irresistible to me."

He tore, loosened and kissed rapidly and with precision, gazing into my eyes as if I possessed some kind of secret. I had never known such urgency, such sensual intent from someone. I had always thought Thurzo curious in his coldness, in his constant calculation of nobility, always squaring away the things that offended him into hidden places, just out of sight. Half-naked in his arms now, I found him entirely different as a lover.

Desire hit me. It was a thunderstorm that wasn't close by, but lived right in the fibres of my skin, my flesh, my bones. I kissed him hard on his unforgiving mouth. Janus suddenly came to my mind's eye, the moment I had slapped him for playing politics with my gentle heart – a heart that felt already so old, so abandoned by God that it was all but closed, even to itself. I wrenched myself back from Thurzo.

"You're toying with me. You want to use me as a weapon to strike at Nadasdy."

Thurzo smiled, breathed in the closest part of my body to him and brought me back into his grip.

"Exciting, isn't it?"

*

"To hold a manuscript in your hand is to find yourself momentarily in communion with those who are absent. Like making love to history," Lucretia was saying to me one evening in the college dining hall as we were served an array of plates of elegant food by servers who remained as out of sight as possible. Her eye make-up was running just enough to make her look deeply set, ghostly even, in the candlelight. At once, time displaces me again and I'm brushing my hands along ancient papers in the manuscript room at the library. I imagine the printers that made them, their atomic traces still part of the same pages I'm touching now. I wonder if somewhere deep in the past one of them can feel me brushing my hands along his skin. I wonder if he'd blush a little, all the way in the past.

I turn my head and when I look back, everything is changing again. The library desks and lights fade and fold into new walls and a cold sensation is below me. Lucretia is sipping wine, the little telescope in her hand. It's snowing slightly and the roof of her tiny house is dusted with it like sugar on a cake. She pauses and snaps her fingers right in my face.

"Hey – where did you just go!"

"To the manuscript room. It felt like I could *feel* history in my hands. My body wasn't separate from it. It *was* history. Living, breathing history."

"Have you ever asked yourself why you want time to go back to being linear so badly? Why can't you be content with letting time do what it wants? Don't mistake me, I still get scared. I know each night I'll travel in my dreams and see who will become sick, how they'll die and how I can help them find the hope they need to cross over. And each morning I'll wake up to this world and see the same kind of thing unfolding here, in this version of the world.

"Over the years, I think I've learnt how to accept it. Accept the horror of living and dying and stay with it. Just stay with it. And just because it seems no one else around me experiences the world this way, it doesn't mean mine is wrong. I mean, fuck them. We are *here, now* and we have each other. What I'm saying, Vera, is that you and I see the worlds differently. What if we just went along with the ride? What if you stayed with your time problem like it was… an old friend. You know, difficult and cantankerous, but a part of your life. Would it be so bad?"

She was right, of course. In the grand scheme of things, why should we hold onto one flow of time so desperately? For me, a whole lifetime of experience was based on a sense of time that was so entirely different from what the clocks and datebooks told me. But then I felt it. I felt all the violences. All the murder. I saw Laura's face. I saw other faces I've yet to describe to you – you who are following me like a silent witness in the pages and lines, *here, now*. I saw my own childlike face. I saw Bathory.

"It's the injustice of it. The injustice of all the violence. Of murder. And the erasure of everything that follows. I can't live with it." I nodded to myself, feeling an icy spectre shut around me like a bear trap in the forest of time. "I can't live without *it*. Without justice, I mean."

I'd never said it out loud. I'd never thought about it quite like this. *Here, now,* a different thought emerging and on account of Lucretia. On account of somebody with a whole different way of living in the world, who had come through a little rip in perception, into mine. Lucretia nestled lazily on one of her embroidered cushions. Calling me to account for my desire to live in linear time *at all costs.*

"So the problem is with your *story*. Okay, so we rewrite it. We find new justices inside the old ones that tear them in two, like a seed does to its own shell, *slowly, slowly*. But there's something more here, Vera. Something you haven't thought of. Just think, you're in a unique position to understand history. Think about those manuscripts all collecting dust in our beloved library. We don't have that chance so often – the chance to hold a piece of history in our hands. I wonder, was this what it was like for Pozzio when he held the last Lucretian manuscript in his hands all the way back in the 1500s – the famous lost book from a time more ancient than his? When a history has been silenced for so long, how do we need to change the way we listen to make sense of it? It belongs to another world, no? To another *universe* almost. It seems absent from the present. How can we understand something that has been missing for *so long*? Maybe that's what *you* get. You know, how you can make friends with the world."

I nervously looked away from her black vortex eyes, shuffled some things around in my bag and pulled out my notebook.

"You keep telling me to rewrite my origin story, Lucretia. But – hey – what about you? What about yours?"

"But mine is different to yours."

"Yes, but what is it?"

"I'll show you if you like. The next time you fall asleep."

After we drank a bit more wine and discussed the latest pranks and horrors of the university – *Did you know they were sleeping together? Did you know so-and-so took credit for her work? Did you know that they threatened his promotion if he didn't comply?* – we moved inside. I started feeling sleepy and lay down on the couch in the living room. The plants had turned their heads downwards in a nighttime droop, and the only thing to be seen was the hypnotic rise and descent of car headlights going up and down the road. I drifted off, feeling Lucretia's hand on mine. And instantly I was with her. Except it wasn't quite her. She was larger than life – a goddess from an ancient part of history. She sat at a beautiful arched window, her dark hair flowing slowly, each strand moving in a gentle wave, as if she were under water.

"Here. Look." And she pointed to something in front of her.

At first, I was scared, but I approached, nonetheless. When I looked to what lay on the ornate table in front of her, I saw it was just a simple wooden box.

"Look more closely," she repeated.

She lifted the lid – same old inquisitive Lucretia, same old expression on her face – and suddenly I felt as if a thousand despairing moments, a thousand hospital beds, a thousand bloating or shrivelling bodies moved around me. *Terror. Pure terror.* Then silence. A small blue butterfly flapped its wings. Each time it did, tiny ripples moved in the air around it. *Time was slower here.*

"Its name is Love," she said.

"I thought Pandora's butterfly was called Hope."

"At some point, all these things fall into the same name. What is hope but the promise of love? Love. Amore. Eros. Desire."

The floating room disappeared. Lucretia had snapped her fingers close in my face, and my eyes had responded by flying open. I sat up on her sofa, rubbing my head.

"Whoa, everything feels really fast here, like I'm on about twenty espresso shots."

"That's *dreamwalking*. The world of dreams is slower than the waking world."

"You were – *Pandora?*"

She laughed.

"How come you get to be a goddess? Why can't I be a goddess? Why do I have to be some serial-killing countess?"

She tutted at me. When I looked at her now, she seemed larger and older, as if animated by another world as well as this one.

"Complaining about your origin story? How many veils do we need to look behind until you see? Forwards, backwards, sideways – however we move with time, we *are* our origin stories, and they are us. I mean, how do you think Bathory feels being *you*? You are her. Her origin-future."

"I imagine she would be none too pleased. Like I had wasted so much of my life going round and round at the mercy of *everything*."

"That is a very good point. Another piece in the puzzle, dear Vera."

As I walked home in the dead of night, I took out my notebook. A few flakes of snow fell on the pages as I walked and wrote. I wrote it all down. Lucretia, Pandora, Bathory, me.

How many other names do we go by? How many Pandoras and Bathorys have invaded our waking hours? How many different histories have fallen silent and been scattered by the wind? How many of their silences have become trapped in flesh – coursing through our arms, our legs, our feet, our bones? What kind of exorcism is 'history'? How do we get rid of the ghosts that make us?

*

The first girl turned up dead not long after I had had my affair with Thurzo. Nadasdy had disappeared for a few days and a strange silence had fallen around Cachtice. I had been busying myself for a time trying to find a suitably unseen place to build the press. It was an exercise in deception since Dorothea's ascension to the role of household spy. Every move I made had to be accounted for. I had wandered around the side of Cachtice beyond the main gate, weaving between the tall, bare trees below, and been confronted with the sight of an unusual mound in the snow. The light of Cachtice fell upon it, giving it the uncanny glow I'd become so accustomed to. I knelt beside it and brushed it down. Slowly, a bluish hand gave way to a naked blue breast. The rest of the body emerged as I furiously dug, terrified at what I might exhume. At first, I thought it a horrible accident. A young girl, running away and lost overnight, unable to scream loud enough in the winter winds to attract anyone's attention. I thought she'd been attacked by some wild and ferocious animal. Then I saw the brands.

Their discovery brought a deep silence in me. The snow was falling heavily, but in that moment, it became slow, as if the winds had all at once dropped out of their orbits. All I could hear was this young girl haunting my senses with her cries and the smell of her flesh. I thought about our daughter, Anastasia. Nadasdy had only ever been sweetness and softness with her, with all his tales of her glorious heritage mixed in with the myths and histories of the vengeful gods that littered the pre-Christian world. He saw an indelible dividing line between her and any other girl who might wander about Cachtice, whereas the forest, the light, the stones and the words Janus had had me read and memorise by heart had taught me to understand the world differently. I vowed then and there to get Anastasia as far away from Cachtice and its brutal madness as I could. It would be a theme that recurred across my life in different forms. It would never end.

Nadasdy will pay for this. He will pay! I took my wedding ring and threw it at the castle walls, offering it back to Cachtice forever. I will be the one to make him pay! At Cachtice, somebody is always watching. This time, it wasn't Dorothea.

*

To kill a woman is no easy thing. Nadasdy must have had some mettle in him to do what he did. The crying, the pleading, the calls to absent mothers and fathers must have echoed around his head. Perhaps these only served to drown out the sounds of the real battlefield. Or perhaps it made no difference in the world to him whether it was an enemy Turk or a maid from his own home. Blood is blood, in all the worlds except for his own family. We were somehow exempt. The spectre of war is not easily sated when it exists everywhere else you look. With each brand he pushed into the skin, Nadasdy conquered more land, more flesh, more souls.

When we were first married, he had told me that his mother often visited the field of Mohacs. She had originally gone to bury the dead, wrapping and rolling broken bodies alongside her sisters, servants and peasants. I'd found this hard to believe, Ursula Nadadsy communing with commoners to clean up the field of the dead? At any other moment, I imagined she would have found this an almost unholy betrayal of the noble lifeblood that flowed in her. But perhaps Mohacs had done that – had become a story that undermined the certainty of selfhood, re-inscribing what it was to be human, to be alive after the silence of the war in each one of us. When Nadasdy first learnt to walk, she would take him with her once a year to the site. She would spill a small bowl of blood on the ground and say prayers, lest anyone ever forget what had happened.

"When I grew up, my first battle, my first clash with the Ottomans, I cut my own fingers and drew lines down my face, repeating, 'I am Mohacs, I am Mohacs' as I kicked my horse into the fray."

Anna told me that these stories were just excuses. Nadadsy was simply wrong on the inside, his soul bent all out of shape, and it was my job as his loving wife to make him better. This was not only my duty as a servant of the true God, but as someone who had undergone the sacrament of marriage. If I didn't, the blood of our women would be on my hands too.

"Do whatever is necessary. He's only getting worse."

At first, I thought about going to Thurzo but knew that he would only use such information to his own advantage. Thurzo would enter the stage and find a way to strip Nadasdy of his lands with the kind of urgent excitement that only a man hungry for power can muster. What's more, I would likely end up shamed, fit only to be Thurzo's spoil, trapped within the walls of what was once my castle. If anyone was going to stop him, it would have to be me. Anna's words came from a place of cowardice brought on by years of unquestioning service to the Nadasdy clan, but in the end, our reasonings led to the same destination.

"I'll do it. I'll stop him."

I just didn't quite know how yet.

*

"You need to have a son."

I nearly spat my herbs back into the cup. "Pardon me?" It had been several years since our return from Venice. The thought of Nadasdy coming anywhere near me filled me with distaste and terror.

"It's quite simple, Elizabet. We brought you for our Francis to make sons. Instead, you two have a daughter in the north. It's a good betrothal, I grant you. When Anastasia comes of age, it will make a fantastic alliance." She nodded at me, the only sign of approval she'd ever deigned to give.

How I missed my daughter! We wrote often; each letter she sent pulsed in my hands as if I could hear her writing it, folding the gap between us along the creased line of the paper itself inside the envelope. I raised my child through words on a page. Through the gossip and stories through which I copied a happier version of Cachtice to her. I could never tell her the truth. I couldn't bear to break her growing heart. Anastasia's distance kept her safe from her father's hell, from the hell he brought into Cachtice every time he returned from war. But it also kept her far from me. She responded to each letter I sent, strengthening our bond in the still-childish crosses and dots on the page. They were like little stand-ins for the kisses and squeezes that we would never have, all made out of ink.

I blinked this thought away and returned to the reception hall. To the frosty company of my husband's mother.

"A Bathory-Nadasdy son will become the most powerful man in Hungary. Maybe even in Europe. I'm surprised no one else has told you, but this is your purpose." She rolled her mouth into a small unbroken line, and in this I could see the home from which all Nadasdy's expressions had grown. I knew this look. It was the shape that a threat takes when applied to a face.

"But from what I hear, you prefer gallivanting around with tradesmen than attending to your husband."

"Madam, I wasn't aware that any person alive could be so fortunate as to have a sole purpose."

"Well, now you are. Make me a grandson. The laws of marriage demand it."

"Francis does not love me like that."

"Why, what's wrong with you?" She surveyed me with a slanted expression, her chin raised up so I could see her delicately wrinkled neck.

"It's what's wrong with him that concerns me, madam."

She rose quickly in a manner which suggested that all feigned complicity between us had been cancelled.

"I can see that recent news of you is correct. You think you are a man, or that you can behave like one at any rate. This will only make you suffer. What Francis does with his own property is entirely his own affair. You should mind that too. I'm leaving now. The least you can do is stand when your better exits the room."

"I'm a Bathory, madam. You can't play that sequence with me."

"A son, Bathory, before I lose my patience with you."

Nadasdy came to my room that night. He knocked gently, like a child does at his mother's door. I opened it but didn't easily let him in.

"Elizabet, you know why I'm here."

"Yes, I do."

"Then stop this pretence and let me in."

I moved aside, but as he strode in, I quickly took the key from out of the open door. It was a paltry weapon, but if he turned on me, perhaps I could use it to gauge out an eye or cut his cheeks before he could do me wrong. Instead, he sat wearily on the sewing chair, glancing at my fist clutching the key and snorting as if to say, *You'll need more than that.*

"Whilst you hate me, Elizabet, I love you. You've brought meaning into my life. I'm not a man who understands how to love, or what it even is. But the moments you've held me close are the moments I'm likely to remember when I finally die on the field. I'm not a monster."

"Francis, what you do, it's evil."

"Don't let my strangeness break your heart, my love. I'd never hurt you."

"Break my heart? Is this some bizarre declaration of love?" I was shaking from my very atoms. "You're a murderer!"

"I'm a soldier and a sovereign! I keep you safe with *my* blood. With the blood of *my* company."

"What!" I spat. "No woman is safe here whilst you stay under this roof." I let it hang in the air. *And so our daughter is sent far, far from you.*

"Elizabet, stop." He seemed exasperated, like I was throwing a tantrum and he the patient husband living amidst some kind of irrational chaos.

"They're dying… they're dying to satisfy your bloodlust. What is it you like the most?" I was growling and shrieking now, every limb trembling like a system of leaves on a branch in the wind. "Their blood or their cries? Shame on you, you devil!"

I started beating him with my fists. He did nothing but flinch occasionally. Then eventually he grabbed my hands with his and held me to the floor as if I weighed no more than one of his writing quills. I was caught in some kind of devilish grip inside which I couldn't move, only be manoeuvred. Nadasdy paused for a moment, watching me struggle, and then suddenly let me go.

"No!" He put his hand up to cover his eyes, shielding his head with his arm as if I wielded some kind of angelic fire. "Not you, Elizabet." He stormed out of my room, and I could hear his feet thudding down the winding steps.

Later, when Anna came to my room to serve upon my request, she patted my hand, like she used to before I was married. Then she quietly stroked my hair and said softly, "My darling child, could it actually be that he's as frightened of you as we are of him?" She crossed herself and looked to the ceiling. Her gaze could have pierced right into the heavens themselves with all her wishing. I didn't have the heart to tell her that it wasn't me he was afraid of, but himself. Perhaps this was his real weakness.

Nadasdy had become a Protestant in a grand refusal of the buying and selling of godly forgiveness so favoured by the Catholics. Perhaps it was his wish to be found out and brought to some divine justice to come, and it happened that, for whatever reason, I held the thin sliver of his fading conscience between my fingers. I swallowed heavily. If that were true, then no doubt, in his, he held up the growing shards of my anger that longed to become their terrifying and united whole. I blinked away the image. Countess Nadasdy, scourge of a dying empire. Murderess – of her own husband!

Eventually, I slipped off into sleep. At some point in the night, I found myself standing up, tracing the wall again in the same way I had the first night I had arrived at Cachtice. It felt like a lifetime ago. The buzzing and pouring of light returned. I felt the room stretch and bend in the gold. I looked down at my hands, feeling more present, more alive than I had for years – since before the Fabbris, before Nadasdy, before I had lost Janus.

Janus, where are you? And, without any warning, there I am in the in-between world. The walls let me inside their stone belly that stretches and moves about me. I don't fall or fly or rush. I simply walk in the vast blackness that opens up, even though there's no floor beneath my feet. Instead, I feel the ground below coming from within me, from within my belly, as if the act of walking requires nothing more of physics than concentration and a body.

Ahead, clear and precise as the four walls of a lantern in the night, I can see a figure radiating light. The closer I get, the more clearly I can see her. She's scaled and feathered at the same time, fixed into form before deciding whether she would be a creation of the sky or sea and so appearing to me now as both. As I approach her, I notice that she looks like me, only older – far older. It's an unnatural ageing, like staring into the empty, ancient face of the sky, knowing that it's seen all things that have come to pass with only the thinnest trace of time lining its surface.

I walk towards her. Her eyes are closed. When she opens them, I feel arcs of light cascading around me, making me the temporary eye of their storm.

"Little Wing, you have come back to me again. You have found me through a different door, *this time*." As the light settles around me, I realise what she means. Bodies are doors in her world. A *'different door'; a different body*. I am inside the invisible corridor between worlds. It's not that I look out onto other, separate worlds – worlds made real by some external force that travels through time. It is my own body that makes them and brings them into being, *here, now*. *This is what you meant, Janus. These are your 'giants in the sky'. This is the shape of your 'heart that absorbs all things'*.

I look beyond her. A rectangular doorway made up of wisps and skeins of gold emerges. It opens and I see the face of a small child. Vera. It feels like I'm staring into a polished glass, but instead of seeing myself reflected back in the dim curve of its frame, another time now passes across its face, mercurial and alive. Vera and I stare at each other, astonished. We must have reached the end of clock time, with no voices or desires to spin new worlds into form with all their stories. And so, whilst we might think we lived separately and differently in our own slices of time, *here, now,* we saw how profoundly entangled we really were.

Then, the scaled and winged woman speaks out loud. The sound ricochets through my very bones, crushing everything – every thought – into insignificance. "Little Wing, there is only *you* here."

"But I see you. *You* are here, standing between Vera and me in the doorway." Immediately, all these things disappear in a painful and disquieting response, leaving me alone in this strange space that isn't a space – this strange time that isn't a time.

I look down at myself, holding my bare arms in front of me. My flesh starts to hum and buzz. I feel as though I can see marks emerging once more, crawling from out of my bones to the surface of my skin. I can't make out the phrases written when I look, but I can hear them spoken from a place that exists outside of sound.

"*I am the past, present and future. I am history repeating both forwards and backwards. My body is the doorway between all these worlds.*"

I feel that I'm listening more deeply than I ever have to the material density that gives me my own shape, my name and form in the world. I'd listened this deeply before – to the moths, to the stones, even to the light in the sky that fell around Cachtice in its ever-changing frequencies. I'd listened to Vera and to her friend. And, above all, I'd listened to Janus, to the words he spoke or didn't speak but which I sensed so loudly, sounding all around him. But I had never listened to the sound of myself. *I am my own future and my own past, writing, writing, writing all the possible trajectories; a forest whose passages go neither 'forward' nor 'backward' but which are simply pathways inside its ever-changing boughs. I am my own book made into the form of a woman in the world. And I have the power to write myself anew.* I squeeze my palm into a fist and open it flat again. I see hundreds of small doorways flash up fast upon it, reeling, rotating and changing.

"There are so many doorways, so many destinies, Little Wing. Choose one."

Then sounds of a winter's night. My bedroom in the tower. The wall. The blue-blackness of Cachtice past midnight. And I, standing straight. The Countess Bathory. Alone in the dark.

Chapter Eight

I check the time on my phone. 3.15am. I sigh, drop it back down onto the bed and turn on my side. The dark shapes in the room give me nothing to anchor myself with. I have no idea where or when I am. Sleeplessness is always the same – whatever age you are. I surrender myself to night. I pray to just fall asleep. When I finally start to drift off, I feel the hot breath of someone hovering right over me. Not in body, but somehow in mind. And I know it's *her*, my origin story, waiting at the edges of my consciousness. I slide my fingers under my pillow and feel something cool and round, a silver wedding ring with a strange etching on it that disappears even as I touch it. The breath meets my ear as she starts to whisper: *You need to rewrite me. You need to write me out of my marriage.*

I whisper back, half conscious now: *I'll do it. I promise. I'll write you as you are.* I open my eyes and for a split second I see her; Bathory…

She presses a finger to my lips even as she floats away. *It's you who will be saved. I'm already long dead.*

She was right. I needed to animate myself differently inside the small footnote I continued to make with my life. I needed to tear down the story that was written for me but never by me, consigning me to haunt around the margins of my own life. And if I was coming to know that in this moment, then in the same moment, somewhere in time, Bathory was coming to know it too.

There are so many ways to kill a woman. But what they did to Bathory – to her revolution – was so much more than death. They *erased* all trace of it – scratching her story from out of the atomic universe, unless you slowed down long enough to hear the world she made and still makes, in the quiet spaces in between all the noise. I pick up my pencil again and write in my notebook. I don't do it to tell – not just yet. I write to listen, as if the pencil itself has become a subtle ear, hearing the world as it arcs and scribbles in my hands.

'What if?' is a powerful thing. Who needs cosmic intelligences, when the mind itself is enough to tear apart the known world with its infinite new discoveries? These discoveries – these mental apparitions – become world-making devices in their own right, apparatuses of creation and destruction and everything in between. So it was with all my travelling in time. The solidity of a past leading to a future has never been the guiding principle of my life. Instead, it's as if the rest of the world were drawn on graph paper, moving through the thinly marked squares of events laid out in complex systems and codes, following beginnings and ends, causes and effects. Whether clear or buried, these always exist across the red thread of coherence. At some point along the line, my paper got crumpled and all the codes of cause and effect were lost. If I had been made of another material, I might have lived in a kind of mechanical relationship to right and wrong, to the ethics of a life without any real consequence. But this isn't quite the measure of it. Time itself is the marker of bodies, and so it is more imbued with justice than any other phenomenon.

Time is a tiger inside a forest of lives, wielding stripes of causation on its back. It is a terrible and beautiful body of sinews and colours that rush through thought. Time that structures, in the blink of an eye, any normal day as you walk down the street, work through the morning, or lie down at night. Time. Always time, clothing itself in the fabric of memory, a road of remembrances whose only constant is change. It whispers in the bones and in the stones: nothing is ever as it seems. All you need to do is listen.

Aren't all heroes made out of time? Built and unbuilt on the elegant human skeleton of cause and effect. They require its unbending arc to shoot straight, to become histories. For me, the pain of living responsible to everyone, but outside of time's heroic line, had become too much and I worked to block out my attachment to it – to the idea of time itself. It's strange that it took me so long to realise that my problem wasn't with the lack of justice in the world, or with the memories that I lived over and over in different iterations – memories that had marked my tiny body as a child, as a woman, as an ancient kind of time traveller. My problem wasn't even necessarily with time, but with time's immense scales.

'What if?' is a serious thing. It gives birth to the world. We need new stories. We need to re-story the world.

*

Cachtice had surrendered itself to night. I lit the candles one by one in my tower room. *Slowly. Slowly.* The air was still, as if the lungs of winter had frozen over, leaving everything preserved in a prescient pause. I undressed myself, which took half an age as I had dismissed the servants to be alone, and wrapped myself up in wool sleeping garments, so white and so roughly woven that I could have been mistaken for a sheep somewhere on a hillside.

I felt calm and light after my strange wander into the in-between world, as if nothing would shake my resolve, as if I had arrived somewhere new. It was a moment I would have stretched out forever. I lay down, pushing my cold hands under the pillow, and felt something hard and even colder. I closed my fingers around it, removing it from its hiding place. As soon as I saw the round object, I gasped out loud in a panic, letting it fall onto my palm, my eyes wide open. Flat and unscathed, lying in my hands was my wedding ring, retrieved from the snow where I had found the first frozen girl, blue and dead.

Francis! Just let me go.

The ring had been polished, and the moon and many-rayed sun had been re-etched where signs of wear had once been. I held it up to the candle in disbelief. This can't have been Nadasdy. It was too subtle an action, too full of meaning, leaving too much to be deciphered. Francis would simply have torn the door down and forced the ring onto my finger. No. This was the work of someone yet to declare themselves. I would have to wait to find out who.

*

Thurzo and I were lovers again. It had happened seemingly out of nowhere, but I was glad of it as his passion for me helped me to forget momentarily the shape of my life as Countess Nadasdy. His wild touch provided no moment for drifting, even if it was not the love I so wished to experience. We met in secret in the woods. In the spring, there was a particular clearing at the woodland's heart that for a week or two would bloom in the most incredible blue flowers. Thurzo would wrestle me down to their gentler embrace, pulling and snatching and biting at me as if his life depended on it. Once, when he allowed it, I rolled him onto his back and sat up, looking at him surrounded by them as if he were somehow magically afloat, atop the deepest, bluest sea.

"You're looking at me," he said, uncharacteristically pausing his passions.

"Yes."

"What do you see?"

I considered this for a few moments. The flowers were bent and twisted where his body had disturbed them with mine, but straight and vibrant where he had not. This gave the impression of a swirl of forces and currents that he somehow effected about himself, as if he were an indomitable ship, harnessing nothing less than the gods of the wind on his own divine and ominous journey. He was gazing at me, waiting intently to hear my response.

"I see you lying atop an incredible wave."

He smiled at me suddenly and took my hand like somebody in love might. He kissed my wrist and sucked on my finger. It was odd for him to be so soft, almost carefree for a moment.

"Elizabet, my dear storm. You know how to make a man happy, don't you?"

It took me by surprise. My inner mechanics slowed down from the turbulent whir they were habituated to. He saw my surprise and quiet confusion turn to softness, my eyes growing languid, and he laughed, raising his hand to his forehead and tilting his head to the side.

"I see," he said after a moment. "You want me to be in love with you."

I got off him, stung, turning my back and walking away. After five or six paces, my legs were seized by a kind of fatigue of the mind. I sat back down on the ground, my back to him, aware that he had sat up and was now the one looking at me. Our bodies were two separate points in space along a direct line, an arrow shooting through the blue towards some invisible target. I folded my legs under me like Janus had taught me to and stared across the field's horizon. The colour rose to meet me, vibrant and alive as an alchemical being that dances in currents without human shape. I can't say how long it was, seconds or minutes, but soon I felt Thurzo's hand on my naked shoulder. "Come. I'll take you back to your home."

We didn't speak. I was still rapt in the blue world of spring and didn't want to be parted from it, to be returned to *here, now*. We dressed stiffly, like English marionettes, and made the journey back in silence. When we were close enough to Cachtice, Thurzo lifted me down from my horse like a precious bundle. He kissed my hand. He seemed thoughtful and solemn, but I could hear his mind buzzing, calculating all the possible permutations of our new revelation. We didn't see each other for several weeks.

Anna had told me that Nadasdy was away, on a tour of his smithies, inspecting weapons and arranging stockpiles of supplies. He had become concerned that the Ottomans might stage a new raid and spoke of another enemy coming across the way through Erdely from the Crimea. Thurzo seized the opportunity to come and visit me to discuss a local dispute about some unoccupied castle that he suggested we bring back into the Bathory fold. When we were alone, he said firmly, "Take me to Nadasdy's quarters."

When I questioned him, he put his finger to his lips, took my hand again in the same manner he had before in the bluebells and led me out, his unwavering gaze clasped to me, walking towards the door behind him like he knew every stone in the castle and so could navigate it backwards, forwards or blindfolded.

When we arrived outside Nadasdy's quarters, I asked him again why he wanted to see the bare, uninteresting room my husband slept in. He still didn't answer. He turned the handle and walked inside, surveying the furniture, walls, ceiling, washstand and mercury polished mirror. At first, I thought he had heard the rumours that were circulating the neighbouring castles and was looking for traces of Nadasdy's murderous deeds. But instead, he stood by the mirror and beckoned me.

"Elizabet, come here," he said authoritatively.

I assented warily, shuddering a little, as I didn't like being in this room for a moment longer than I needed to.

He positioned me in front of him so we could both see him rest his head on my shoulder in the mirror's dim reflective surface. He kissed my neck a few times like one of those mechanical birds the Ottomans sometimes brought to court as gifts when negotiations were in play.

"I'm so lucky. I'm so lucky." He kept repeating this and I knew it was more than some new erotic game he had decided to play.

"I could love you, Elizabet. Never in the way you desire, but in my own way. You could become Thurzo."

I spun around, caught entirely off guard.

"Why don't we send your wife to Nadasdy, then you might get your wish!"

He smarted and grabbed my hands.

"What on earth do you mean?" When I didn't respond, he continued, "But I would exchange my Elizabet for this Elizabet. It can be done – quietly. It can all be done quietly."

"How dare you even think such thoughts?"

"I've been widowed once before, Elizabet. One grieves and then one realises that one has to continue living. What a life we would have together. Think of all that power without the barbarism of Francis to contend with, not least in here," and he pointed to my empty marriage bed that lay reflected darkly like a coffin in the night.

I turned around and rested my eyes on the interminably violent tapestry that hung on the opposite wall. My ears started to ring and shake from the inside, but it wasn't the same ringing and shaking that I could remember from the day I had been forced onto the pretend-throne by the blacksmiths, finding myself in a memory that was entirely *other*, in the snow of the other world. It was more like an echo of a nameless fear, a trace of something deeply and disturbingly human that had come to find me from within the walls of this room; from all they had witnessed. I gasped and held onto the side of the bed for fear of falling. It was then I realised that there was no escape. Not with Thurzo, not with Janus. Not even with the bluebells, light or stones, nor the raging falling that I experienced when I disappeared into the other world.

Thurzo put his arms around my waist and spun me back towards the mirror. "Look at yourself. So much power and you don't know what you might do with it, what you might achieve. I know it. I will achieve it." His breathing quickened again. He started grabbing my hair with one hand and lifting my skirts with the other, pushing my head down with the heel of his hand. But this was not for pleasure. There was a darkness growing inside him. He had become one with his surroundings, reconstituted in something more honest in him, more terrifying to me.

"What are you doing?" I shrieked.

"I'm making you mine."

"Stop it, George. Stop it!"

I lifted my head. He was looking at himself in the mirror. He pulled my resistant body upwards sharply and started biting again as if he wanted to consume me, until I was bonded to his very being. He sank his teeth into the top of my ear, and I felt him break the skin. Small drops of blood fell and bounced off the stone.

I kicked his shin, drawing the back of my booted heel down his leg. It caught him off guard and sent him back a few paces. He laughed loudly, pulling off his tunic and shirt remarkably quickly, and then howled excitedly, like a dog. I was terrified. I ran to the door, and he matched my step. He pinned me against it. "You've given yourself to me. You can't take that back. Who'd have thought it, Bathory loves Thurzo!"

"I do not love you!"

"Yes! Protest to me, Elizabet. Then we'll fuck in Francis' bed, and I will be Bathory's lord!"

I raised hell with my voice. I shrieked and cursed and kicked like a banshee. But I knew that no one ever came to this part of the castle. Nadasdy had seen to that. It was his secret domain, an entire corridor of rooms at the heart of the wing where he came to retreat. I steeled myself, gathering an internal momentum that I would use to tear him to pieces. I knew I had it in me. And if I were unlucky and he won, then at least I would have fought all the way to death. To my utter shock, despite the silence that had lain like iron over the whole corridor, the door was thrown open like a thin piece of paper, sending both Thurzo and I across the room. My jaw fell open. Nadasdy stood in the doorway.

He picked up Thurzo and threw him against the wall. Now he was the pinned one.

"You like this?" Nadasdy growled in a voice that sounded like it came not from the throat but from hell's domain. He punched Thurzo's face again and again and again. When Thurzo slid to the ground, Nadasdy straddled him, sitting high on his chest and punching with both white-knuckled fists, each blow sounding like the snap of wood on the cutter's block.

"Stop it, Francis, you'll kill him!"

Nadasdy let out a roar and jumped off him. He then punched me in the face just as hard. He roamed around like an animal inside a cage, tore his own hair and hit his chest. When his eyes fell on the tapestry, he ripped it from the wall. It got tangled up in his feet, though, and he fell over it as if it had pulled him down. Then he started sobbing.

I went over to him on the floor, crying myself. He reached his hands out to me despite my instinctual flinch. I was shuddering and shaking at the thought of his hands on my face. He looked at me pleadingly as if my refusal would lead him to throw himself from the window and consign himself to yet another hell.

Trembling like a leaf, I leant towards him so that he would be able to stroke my cheeks with his fingers in the way he had always done in the days before I had become aware of his nature. I cautiously extended my hands and stroked his face in return. I thought I might burn in the moment I touched him, that the angry ghost of the woman who lay dead in the snow – of all the women he had brought here never to return the same – would rise up against me to shame me. But no burning came. No ghost rose from the dead to punish or condemn.

We strangely mirrored each other in our mutual, delicate touch, as if we ourselves had become a glass that did not reflect what was, but displaced things anew. We stayed like this, half fallen on the floor, forgotten dolls blown about by history, looking deeply into each other's eyes for a long time. Eventually, Nadasdy turned and leant his back up against the bedframe, laying his legs out flat on the stone. He stared at them for a while, then at the door frame, before turning his head back towards me.

"He's your lover," he said flatly, his ivory skin moving in contours as a series of contrasting expressions rose and fell across his face.

I nodded, but in a way that signalled my own awareness at the ridiculousness of it.

"You love him?"

"No."

"What could he possibly give you?"

I paused and found myself saying, "He wanted me."

Nadasdy's face streamed with silent boyish tears. I could feel his broken heart wind back time and break all over again. Eventually, he breathed in and sighed. Then he laughed a little. "I bet you thought I'd be the last person to save you."

I looked at him differently then. I saw how much he needed to be a hero. I saw a warrior boy, made momentarily gentle by his own desperation, who by admitting to the evil in himself had unexpectedly brought himself the smallest experience of peace, the smallest sense of his own fractured goodness. And he would not let that go – just as he wouldn't let go of the hope of earning salvation in the final reckoning. He looked at Thurzo, knocked out and bleeding on the floor.

"Will you take me to your tower? I can sleep on the floor. Please?" His voice was so weak, diminishing as he spoke, listless as a pile of ash.

I rose and extended my hand.

"Come on."

We walked in silence all the way down to the night air of early summer, before entering the tower and ascending again, up, up, up, winding like the heretical Ottoman dances that I had read about somewhere in a book. I opened the door. Nadasdy sat himself on the floor and removed his boots wearily before lying down by the wall. I went to the opposite corner and carefully undressed before sliding into my bed. We didn't once look at each other. But that didn't mean we weren't with each other, suspending, for a moment, all right and wrong, all cruelty. In this quiet moment, we were just two people, neither enemies nor friends, nor husband and wife. Just two people who occupied the same space at the same time, our raging stories dimmed to no more than tiny whispers that made even the rock of Cachtice seem temporarily flimsy and finite; a half-finished thought stripped back to its internal beams and rafters.

I lay still, bending my body and holding my knees with my hands under the blanket. "Why do you do it?" I said, exhausted and quiet.

"Because I can't stop."

*

"I've heard good things about your research, but what do you want to do here, I mean, really? Talk to me."

He says it to me in a way that is meant to invite trust. But I know him. His oval face has been dogging my footsteps across time. There are two instances when I've been in this particular office, with its drab white walls and thick glass windows which refuse to open. I can't quite work out which moment this one is.

I reach for my phone so that the moment time unscrambles and returns its digital workings to the right date and location, I might glance down at it. But he gives me a glare as if to say, *Don't you dare, Millennial.* I sit back, feeling trapped. I can't bear being this close to him.

Whenever I try to re-story Bathory in the public eye, there he is, like so many others, trying to hold her in place. Trying to hold all women in their place. In academia, knowledge is male and it is most certainly white. It had moved from the Vatican to the courts of Europe, becoming enshrined now in the hallowed halls of the university across time. You could move anywhere and any way you liked inside those categories, making your thoughts and your deeds fit as much as possible, but ultimately, whatever was not that, *did not matter.* It was cut from you like a limb deemed 'unnecessary'.

Lucretia never once referred to the man sat across from me using his actual name lest she accidentally summon him or any of his simpering minions with her utterance. She simply used the following: 'Fuckwit'. 'The Biggest Arsehole in the Universe'. Or simply 'Professor Needless'. She always required I did the same.

I shift in my chair, crossing my legs one way and then the other. I try not to make too much eye contact lest I scream. Because I know all about something even he doesn't know he's done yet, though even *here, now,* the edges of it are clearly taking shape in his mind. The wall of windows behind me looks out across a well-manicured square, bursting with geraniums. I look back to the professor. He touches his fingertips together in a tall steeple of gooseflesh and peers at me over its apex.

"I'm curious about the role Elizabet Bathory might have played in the life of the early printing," I say.

"Elizabet Bathory? The 'vampire'? The one who bathed in blood?" and he emphasises the word *bathed*, his nearly lipless mouth bending ever so slightly into a smirk. "What on earth do you want to get mixed up in that nonsense for?"

The phrase is so dismissive. To those who hold power, a monster is nothing but a childish bedtime story that the adults don't believe in. Somewhere between dismissing monsters and fearing them, there's another option: *listen to their stories. They contain secrets.*

"She had a press, you know. And if you follow the patterns of her family history, the Bathory line was clearly being erased by the Emperor Rudolph the Second as they were the biggest threat to his rule in the Eastern Empire. Their connection to revolutionary Transylvania, just across the border from Hungary, was… problematic. She wasn't a vampire or a crazed aristocratic killer with too much time on her hands. She was a printer during a time when people were burned for nothing less than a single scrap of the wrong kind of text. She was Hungary's counter-culture; Hungary's revolution."

He snorts, folding the fingertip steeple away, and looks at me like I'm a silly child who needs to be scolded and sent to bed without her supper. Then he takes in a sharp breath.

"What else have you got for me?"

Now he flips a silver pen between his fingers, eyeing me carefully. Before I have a chance to respond, he continues with, "Did you know that I'm famous?"

I suppress a snort of my own. I'm not really sure how to respond to that. Instead, I look away, to the windows that hang like portals to other worlds and that remain forever shut in this office. Worlds that are inaccessible. The subtext thickens between us like flour in water. It's unspoken. I feel him hanging it in the air around us. I run through options.

No, I've never heard of you before. (Truth) Or, *Yes, I've heard you're amazing.* (Lie) I can't decide so I just remain silent. He continues.

"Your last research project caught quite some attention here. I note you even got a write-up in the national papers. Was that one we funded, then?"

"No, but it was a fun project, and there's so much we could do. I'm looking forward to working with you." (Wrong answer)

"I'm glad you think so." (Lie)

"I'd be very appreciative of this opportunity." (Placation)

"How appreciative?" (Leading)

"Very" (Uncertain)

He juts his chin towards the couch behind me. I roll my eyes openly.

"Interesting." (Challenge) "Elizabet Bathory then."

He extends the silver pen unexpectedly towards me across the desk, pushing a contract forward with his other hand. My expression must show that I'm confused by this sudden turnaround, although the time traveller in me knows exactly what he has in mind. I take it from his hand and try to sign my name. No ink flows. On his left, propped up on top of printed copies of unmarked manuscripts, is a mug with the word 'Professor' scrawled over it in cursive script under the glaze. Inside the mug are a bunch of pens and rubber bands and screwed-up pieces of paper.

"May I?" I ask, and reach for a plastic pen.

He juts his chin again and I sign.

"You're quite self-sufficient, aren't you?" (Rage)

*

"Where is your husband?" John asked.

"At war," I responded.

John's direct, plain speaking with his countess was something that startled others. But I quite appreciated it. All the bowing and soft-voiced obsequiousness of the nobles irritated me. There was none of that with John. He would become a young man whose skill at printing would surpass half of Europe's with its speed and accuracy. He loved the mechanics of the press. He'd barge into a room unannounced to say things like: "We need to get hold of that new type from Italy. There's something I want to try." Or, "We need an extra hand in our service, and not these clumsy old men. They keep ruining the pages."

Once, he'd accidently blown up a pot of ink by a side wall of Sarvar, close to where Nadasdy had arranged a press to be set up for me for all the world to see. The sudden blast of fire when the sulphur, bone and oil had combined together charred and blackened the stone and sent a momentary rain of ink, as if God were writing directly from the sky.

My thoughts drifted from John to Nadasdy.

"What do you want, my love? What can I give you?" Nadasdy had asked. I knew he meant something deeper, something strangely personal, given our crumbled marriage.

"I want to set up a press. I want to print." And so, it went from an unutterable and dangerous thing to one that was almost instantly done.

Sarvar lacked the rugged impenetrability of Cachtice. It was a courtly castle, flat and many sided. An impression pushed down in wax and lifted out, placed on the straightest surface of Hungarian earth for miles. Its wide paths leading in and away from the main buildings seemed built to expose whispers, assignations and deadly murmurs. It dissuaded any casualness of thought or carelessness of pursuit. I hated it. But if we were to have a press, it could not seem in any way clandestine. We would print openly, all the usual texts.

Nadasdy and I had gone to Sarvar together to open it, having sent John months ahead to supervise its construction. The servants had balked at taking orders from a boy, but I'd pressed a handwritten communication in his hand ahead of this: *Take his word in all matters as if it were mine.* John, being shrewder than all of us that year, kept hold of the letter. Nadasdy and I had taken separate carriages. After that night in the tower, he'd promised me that he would never again allow himself the excitements of blood. I was convinced this would turn out to be a lie, even if it had been true when uttered. I found it hard to be near him. He carried too many ghosts.

"I'll take what I can get, my love. Will you at least dine with me once before I return to the field?" I smiled politely but didn't give any answer. When his carriage arrived at the gates of Sarvar, he leapt out of it as if pursued by a wild animal and rushed in ahead, leaving me in the dust.

The press was a thing of beauty. John had outdone himself. The room was full of straight, intersecting lines holding shelf upon shelf of different type, a sacramental altar made out of the vivid pulse of form and lettering. But the iron handles, curvatures and finishes on the stable parts of the press' machinery were of the most intricate and ornate spirals, a dance captured and made solid in space. I asked where he had visioned these astonishing shapes and he responded, "The book from Fano." When I asked him to explain what he meant, he extended his index finger and swooped curling imaginary lines in the air that lay between us. "The writing. In the book. It's curly."

I went cold, remembering the curled and dotted pages I'd read with Janus in the belly of my stone tower at Cachtice. Now I was running my fingers along the machinery of John's most perfect press and for an all-too-brief second, the two moments folded together, as if no time existed between them at all.

Nadasdy had come to inspect what I'd commissioned. When he opened the door, he gasped.

"It's a thing of absolute beauty. Can it really print?"

He held up the frames, weighed some of the individual type in his hands and ran his fingers along the spiralling legs of the table. John didn't speak, merely rounded up a few of his assistants and put them to work. Nadasdy and I watched in utter amazement as before our eyes a frame was assembled, a huge container of already made-up bone-black ink was opened, its contents daubed over and over the iron type, and the press put to use; its heavy rolling machinery groaning until the wet page emerged.

Nadasdy ran over to it faster than I, and I almost laughed as we bumped shoulders in our anticipation of the words having just come to life in the world:

You shall have the power to denigrate into the lower forms of life and you shall have the power, out of your soul's judgement, to be reborn into higher forms, which are divine.

The ink was still drying. Nadasdy looked long and hard at the boy. I held my breath. John had gone too far, I thought to myself. Now all is lost. But Nadasdy smiled broadly and clapped him on the shoulder. He then put his arm around him like a father.

"You do us proud, boy. When it's ready, send the page to my quarters so I can look upon it every day."

Then he caught my eye across the printing table. It was a wild kind of look, but not unkind. He drew his right arm across his body and tipped his head slightly. "My lady." And then he left to attend to God knows what business.

"John, what were you thinking?"

"I think I thought right, madam."

"What is this text?"

"Pico, madam. My father knew it by heart. He taught me. I hope it helps."

I didn't quite know what to make of him after that.

*

Winter approached. I had been tending to the affairs of our estates whilst Nadasdy was fulfilling his destiny as the Holy Roman Emperor's greatest weapon against the Ottomans. His talents had become sharpened. The Emperor showered him with honours and titles until the sound of his name vibrated with gold and favour. Meanwhile, our estates were going to rot. So, it wasn't long before I was summoned to Prague to present news of our castles, pay taxes and update our treaties with the

Emperor on my husband's behalf. I left John at Sarvar; Dorothea, or 'the Spy' as I now called her, at Cachtice and brought Anna with me. She was uncertain as to whether Dorothea could be trusted to run Cachtice, but I assured her that if she wasn't loyal to Bathory, she was loyal at least to Nadasdy.

Since the first day at the press at Sarvar, John had spent a lot of time serving Nadasdy directly, fetching and carrying, sometimes waiting by his door for hours for a task. He also brought Nadasdy armfuls of freshly printed texts. I never demanded he show them to me, but occasionally I would catch a glimpse of one lying out in the workshop, waiting for the pages to be bundled together before binding. The texts were more than just Protestant missives. Nadasdy was reading the classics too; Lucretius, Aquinas, even to my utter surprise a furtive page of something I was certain had come from the Ottomans, a text I'd never forgotten but that was always whirring silently inside me since Janus had first urged me to commit it to memory:

Die, die in this love. Die to the din and the noise of the world. In the silence of love, you will find a spark of life.

It would be in keeping with John's childlike desire for the return of his fathers that he might try to save the soul of the man responsible for their deaths, as if restoring Nadasdy would cause some kind of exhumation and the Fabbris might reclaim their flesh through him and walk out into the sunlight.

I reminded John that his principal duty was to the press, not to serving my husband with his every breath, but it seemed unnecessary. He somehow managed to get it all done, and I wondered if he had given up on sleep in favour of service. With Nadasdy gone, John could at least take some time to be a boy. "Go outside. Feel the light and the wind on your skin," I advised. I knew he wouldn't listen. There was precious little out there for him. He would give his bones to the press and to the hope of the Reformation.

Chapter Nine

Prague. The air was crisp and cold and tasted metallic on my tongue. Its winding river, a watery and indelible spine that curved and curled like a long, shining snake crossing the land. The river threw its golden rays upwards into the sky as if it were in charge of providing the light, unreliant on heaven to pour down its glow upon us all. Proud and bold. When I reached the arched entrance to the palace, I was spellbound. You didn't arrive at the court at Prague; you were absorbed by it. It drew me into its fold, and I felt I would have to secure its permission if I wanted to be let out again. So, this must be what it feels like at the fulcrum of power. To be *originary*. At the centre of all things.

The memory of the iron throne in the shade of the smithy at Cachtice flashed inside my eyes, providing temporary respite from the bitter, brazen light of Prague. *There's no escape from this either*, I thought. Power is threaded through everything. Power is the pulse that animates life. What men use it for – what these men have used it for – has built the architecture of the world. Even the light on the water and the light in the sky have become part of the pact. Or perhaps I had it the wrong way around. Maybe we were all complicit in the movements of light, subverting it through our tiny wars that we dreamt were big but were in fact so very small.

In the same way, perhaps Nadasdy's violence had grown from more than the memory of Mohacs and the wars with the Turks. Perhaps it had grown from the earth itself. I imagined him running around his mother's legs as a child, spilling the propitiatory remembrance on the field of the dead. Had the soil he groped around in slipped somehow through his fingers and into his soul, burying him forever slowly, from the inside out?

I was shown directly to my quarters. An army of servants was sent to bring my bags and belongings to the rooms. My retinue followed me up the steps; Anna was right by my side all the way.

*

The Emperor was a collector of rare creatures, but instead of inspiring wonder and excitement in me, their prowling self-display felt syphilitic and more than once I shut my eyes and leant on Anna's arm as we walked through the open zoo of the court's interior. Nadasdy had told me about him, *Emperor Rudolph II*, who preferred apparently to skulk in the corners and hidden parts of his grand palaces with his birds and beasts. I imagined he approved more of their languid, colourful company than the seething ambition that threaded through all the court's human visitors. But I was soon proved wrong.

When I entered the main hall, I saw hundreds of people milling about its glowing interior. Sound had no direction. It moved as a ball thrown about by the guests, each toss a display of unanticipated trajectories and attentions vibrating throughout the room. I was announced. Several gold- and silver-laced, sparrow-like girls, overpainted and dripping in heavy jewels and trinkets around their dainty necks, watched me with their slow tiger-eyes. They weren't used to seeing a woman enter the room alone.

I wore an emerald dress with traces of gold and brown around the hem, appearing like an ancient tree, slow and knowing and not in a hurry to be uprooted. I too wore jewels, but they were smaller and more plentiful in number; sapphires, rubies, diamonds and small circles of amber. They fell about me like dew, and I had arranged my black hair up with curls cascading down my shoulders.

I walked in an arc around the hall, surveying everyone and everything. Behind all the people, in tiny places on the walls, or carved surreptitiously into pieces of decadent furniture, I saw the same symbol over and over again: a strange figure with one dot inside what must have been its 'head' and an upturned crescent that crowned it. It made me shiver and I promised myself I wouldn't let this symbol stay buried inside my mind for too long lest it wreak a quiet, unnoticed havoc on my thoughts. I had my own enigma of symbology to deal with, my own graven moon and sun scored deep into my wedding ring. Across the hall, in his habitual black, surrounded by courtly noblemen just as eager and ruthless as he, was Thurzo.

Ambition can be an unpredictable thing. I imagined that the humiliation of being thwarted in his last plan might be tearing up his inner landscape. On the other hand, it could be entirely possible that having hit an impasse with his sexual strategy, he might just as simply and coldly try another. Dispassionate in his means as water that easily finds the most viable path in its endless pursuit of the sea. I was grateful for having seen him in his most honest state at Cachtice. It made me realise that I did not want to want again. It wasn't that my heart was broken. I hadn't loved him. It was that the girlish part of me no longer needed to be loved. I just needed to make it through as the woman I had become.

All second guesses at his intentions faded away in the instant we locked eyes. I had always imagined hell hot and full of fire.

But in that moment, I knew hell was cold. It was ice and snow. It was an empty, frozen field in which a young girl might stumble, fall and bleed all the way to death. Hell wasn't in the story books. Neither did it lie under the earth, guarded over by strange denizens, tribes of bitter and horned devils. Hell was human. Nothing other than human. It was in the small, thin vein on the side of Thurzo's skull, throbbing vengeful. It was in the kind of rage that grows an angry blue ghost in the head, always hungry, always waiting. What had I done! Why had I thought it would all be all right? In that moment, I knew I would have to prepare myself because Thurzo was coming for me, and this time no screaming defence or strong-armed husband would put him off. He would have nothing less than my blood. And he would use the strength of an Empire to exact it.

"The Countess Nadasdy!" a man exclaimed loudly from across the hall next to where Thurzo and the small group of nobles stood. "Countess, do come here." He beckoned me, all warm in his gestures. "Come! Come! Yes." I glided over to them, my heart beating so wildly in my chest as I approached Thurzo that I was reminded of the moment I first met him, when I had been no more than a girl and he had unlaced my dress to allow me to breathe. I didn't know the man calling out to me. He was bald and smaller than I, but stout. He wasn't fat. In fact, I imagined that his generous chest and sturdy thighs were made of sheer muscle and battle prowess. He had an eagerness to him, like a wild animal, but not in the way of Thurzo. He was a field animal, a mouse or a rabbit or a vole, nervous and quick and full of energy. But I could also imagine him at the same time being the trapper of such beasts, snapping his jaws shut just at the moment that his next meal answered his call. I kept a good distance between us as I approached.

"I am Basta, Count of Huszt. But please, Countess, you must just call me Giorgio. You're a beautiful woman and I prefer you to be relaxed and informal with me."

I nodded my head slightly towards him.

"Count Basta."

Basta giggled a little.

"So, I hear correctly that you are a formidable ice-woman. I shan't force you to call me Giorgio. Does she call you Giorgio, my Lord Thurzo?" The men all laughed. Thurzo remained silent, angling his head to the side and looking down. It appeared his entire jaw was suppressing an ungodly rage. I felt that he knew that if he looked at me right now, he wouldn't be able to stop short of some kind of brutality, regardless of court, emperor or reputation.

"The only person I refer to by first name is my husband," I lied, "and his name is Francis Nadasdy. Shall I remember you to him, my Lord Basta?"

Basta raised his eyebrow, pursed his lips and made a slight 'oh' sound. The sound dripped with cynicism.

"Countess, there's no need to be so defensive. This is the Holy Roman court. If you're not sleeping with somebody, you're not invited, are you?" And he looked around at his collection of acolytes, who all either nodded, laughed or grunted in amused assent. Thurzo straightened his gait.

"Now that is certainly true. If you'll excuse me, gentlemen, I'm wanted by the Emperor."

"No doubt," said Basta, lasciviously looking Thurzo up and down. "You always were his favourite, *Palatine*."

"Ah, not just yet, Basta. Not yet."

"Soon." He pursed his lips as he spoke, kissing the word even as it left his mouth.

Basta turned back to me as Thurzo walked away, those slow rhythmic steps affecting a forgotten hypnosis over my senses. Basta broke the silence again.

"Now, my dear 'innocent' Countess, I believe your cousin Sigismund is here."

"Sigismund? Here?" I recalled hours of racing around with

him when I was a young child and he a handful of years older than me. When Andrew and Balthasar, our other cousins, had been small, Sigismund and Balthasar had picked on Andrew, circling him and shouting "Holier-than-thou, holier-than-thou," and miming Catholic prayers and gestures. Andrew was always a little different. He loved God, perhaps because he thought that God would be more eternal and long lasting than his own father, who, like Him, had only ever been present in his life in the foreboding stares of the large immortal paintings that hung around the house. Thus, Andrew had two fathers in heaven, and cousins who beat him for being so very Catholic in his ways.

I realised that I had not seen any of the Bathorys for such a long, long time. Andrew, the devout victim; Balthasar, the brute; and Sigismund, who was a strange mix of bully and debonair. I had heard nothing of him since except that he had displeased the Emperor by breaking his marriage to the Emperor's niece. Like most of my family, Sigismund had become entangled in the web of Erdely's politics, Hungary's neighbour to the East. The Emperor used both lands as buffers to kept the Turks at bay. We knew little other than war and blood. We were the gateway to the West.

When Nadasdy and I were first married, he had returned once from a short stay in the region.

"If they ever offer me the throne of Erdely, Elizabet, and if I seem tempted, kick me hard until I am reminded of my senses. That throne is a death sentence. I would rather die in battle than by the hand of some politicking pretender."

"They're my family," I had half whispered.

"Oh, Elizabet. That they are. That they are." He had stroked my cheek and held me close to him under one arm. "You're my sweet and strange one. You're my wife. I'll always keep you safe, even from them, if I have to."

After I had found Nadasdy out, we had never spoken of my family again. Nor anything really, until the press. We had remained odd prisoners of our vows. Nadasdy's prison was made of love. I knew that, but how could I forgive him, a man who opened the bodies of the women who lived under our roof? There were two men inside him: the impotent husband who loved his wife and the potent killer who loved above all the sight of blood. Perhaps it wasn't men and their ways that worried my waking hours, but the myths of men, the myth of absolute dominion over a passive earth. Perhaps all I needed to do was print some new ones. New earths, spinning about on the weight of ink.

"My lady, are you still with us?"

"Yes, of course."

"I thought you had floated away. Perhaps, if you have need, I should lend you my paddle so that you can steer your way back to us." More laughter.

"Much good would that do me. The tides will turn soon, and your tiny paddle will get washed away by the current that's coming."

He eyed me, all at once deadly.

"Pay attention, Bathory. The current is me."

I had had enough and called for Anna so she could lead me back through the corridors to our quarters, where I could finally lie down and rest. She took one look at my face and knew not to say a word as we wound our way back. As we passed under an arch that had been painted entirely in gold in the Ottoman style, she gasped the word, "Beautiful." I made a savage and disdainful sound.

"This place is just one expensive brothel," I said, "and it bleeds an entire Empire dry to foot its bill."

We returned to silence. When we were all but arrived at our quarters, I saw a young man leaning up in one of the palace window's hollows. He was dishevelled, even scruffy, but he carried himself nobly. His hair was long, and his cheeks were unshaved. He seemed nervous, biting his fingers and lips.

"Countess Bathory?"

I was suspicious of being recognised now and looked at Anna quickly as if to say, *Run and get help if he tries anything.*

"Yes?" I responded coolly.

"We've never met before, not even as children, but our families are deeply linked. Before long, I should like to come and visit you and talk. There's much to discuss."

"You can speak with my husband. Is it a matter of estates?"

"No, Countess. It's the Bathory in Cachtice that I need to speak with."

"What's your name? Who do you represent?"

"Bocksai, madam. And I represent myself."

"Come to me then after I have seen the Emperor, and we shall talk." I didn't know who he was or who he would become. I would pay in blood. We all would. Fate sneaks up on us in hallways, when we're distracted, tired and not really paying attention.

*

Space and time unfolded in four straight corners around me. I emerged holding a rectangular object in my hands. The rest of the room sketched itself into matter; a corridor ahead, a high ceiling, the clinking sound of wine glasses, a low murmuring sound of conversation. I held the sturdy printed rectangle right up to see it lest time take it away from me in a flash. *Undoing the Monsters: A Tale of Time.* As I did so, I could swear I heard the swish of an ancient dress covered in small jewels move around me. *"There's nothing in the world like the smell of new ink."* It was a whisper that came from within me. From Bathory, haunting me in my bones.

My book was published, and the prizes had started coming in. The professor, at first, was delighted. After all, it meant his 'great risk', as he called it, had paid off and more grant money was flowing into our department. But when the vice-chancellor came in to shake my hand personally, I noticed him blanch. *You're not meant to be too good. You're meant to be just good enough that we look all the better for supporting you.* The phrase spilled out from every gesture, every narrowing of the eyes. *Know your place.*

"Congratulations! Quite visionary. A very different notion of history. Not that we're really *that* progressive here," he laughed. "I'm sure a number of historians will be lining up to take their shots at you. After all, the entire discipline as it stands depends on linearity and chronology! It's also good to have a woman of your *background* finally gaining attention. Where are you from again? Originally, I mean?"

"Originally? Oh, I'm quite the mixed bag."

"Okay, don't tell me. But it's great to see someone here who ticks all the boxes. We all look the same, don't we?" And he gestured to a sea of whiteness, giggling nervously. "A different kind of... of face is," he circled his hand at the wrist, "well, it's refreshing, isn't it. Ah, I'm rambling. Nonetheless, we'll be expecting more good things from you. To your success." And he tapped my glass with his own.

We were in yet another dark, panelled reception room. I downed what was left in my glass in one gulp and went to collect myself another glass of prosecco so I could drown out the sound of all the comments that started out about the book but inevitably ended up with professors complimenting each other on how they'd supported something *a little different this time*. Professor Fuckwit (yes, I continued to honour Lucretia's request never to name him even in her absence) grabbed me by the elbow.

"A word."

It was menacing. I followed him to a little alcove.

"Don't get too *cocky*."

"I'm sorry?"

"You heard me. This is my department. It's great you've got the latest scholarly fashion working for you, but don't get ahead of yourself. For all this…" and he hit the top of the copy of my book that I was still holding with his knuckles "…you still don't understand how power works, do you?"

I started to walk off and he yanked me back hard. His eyes narrowed. He laid his other hand very heavily on my shoulder and then squeezed it, finding the soft place in between the bones to sink his fingers into. It was a warning, more severe than any of the others so far. I stared at him. Hunter and hunted, locked together. He bent his head to my ear. His breath was clammy and he spoke slowly.

"I see I'm going to have to teach you a lesson about power you'll never forget."

Chapter Ten

The hall fell to silence. The entire court bent down as if toppled by a sudden gust of wind. Rudolph, Holy Roman Emperor, walked quickly to his throne. Thurzo walked close behind him, as did a number of other nobles. Thurzo moved in long, slow strides. By contrast, the Emperor shuffled quickly, as if uncomfortable with being seen *between* places. When he reached his throne, however, an entirely different persona sat down. He snapped into action like a hawk making straight for its prey.

"And now we'll hear from Countess Nadasdy," he said.

I approached and curtseyed low.

"What, no boy's clothes? I'm almost disappointed. I thought we were to be offered a glimpse of the Siege of Eger. Will you not wrestle an Ottoman for us, then? No. Then tell me of the estates and the tribute you've brought me."

I listed off the taxes levied, meticulous in my presentation to the point of being entirely dull.

"Excellent," he said absently. Thurzo approached him from his position close by and whispered in his ear. "Ah yes. Our dear count has informed me that your husband will again be required by us soon. We're sending him home to you now from the Ottoman front. He's then to report to Thurzo immediately, who we have given our trust to in this matter. He has our new military orders and will relate them to Nadasdy."

Then out of nowhere he suddenly asked, "Erzabet, did you attend your cousin Andrew's funeral? It saddened me that he had to be dealt with. But you Bathorys are troublesome, no? Erdely is always a colourful place when the Bathorys are in power there."

"I'm sure you're right, Imperial Majesty. I've not been home for so long." And I curtseyed deeply.

The Emperor's eyes narrowed and with this gesture, I felt my world shrinking down to a point. I thought of Andrew slowly turning to soil, feeding the endless cycle of land and ambition for the throne with his flesh. He had given everything, even his bones, to achieve dominion of Erdely. In the end, it was the other way around. Erdely had consumed him. When Michael the Brave, the new self-proclaimed King of Erdely, had ordered Andrew's death, my other cousin Sigismund had fled too, vanishing in the arms of history lest he be called traitor to the Holy Roman Empire.

Andrew had been trained from birth to be a king – the natural king of the Bathorys in Erdely. His Catholicism granted him the opportunity to become a cardinal and he folded his church and his newly made country together like two hands that, no matter how hard he forced them together, never quite managed to touch in prayer. But then Michael the Brave had come and taken it all away. He had gathered Szekely fighters – the peasants and blacksmiths of Erdely – armed them and promised them the return of their stolen lands. *Always, the Szekelys, now fighting in Bathory wars, now fighting against Bathorys, and for what? For the return of their land?* They died fighting Andrew. The land, of course, was never returned to them. God himself wept in the churches and on roadside shrines. The faces of Erdely's brightly painted saints streamed with tears, or so legend went, and the land went the way of chaos again. Unrest. Blood. And still no unity between the great kingdoms. Rudolph – always there was Rudolph – laughed and returned to his brightly coloured animals and remained emperor over us all, presiding over all our tiny revolutions, keeping us captive to our ambition. To the idea of freedom.

But standing right there in court now, I thought it was more than that. Rudolph's power had transcended the possession of lands and castles or the politicking that had destroyed Andrew and Sigismund. He penetrated into words themselves. With only a sparing few, with only "*Did you go to your cousin's funeral?*" he had reduced my inner world to something small – the reverse of a star exploding across the sky. He used my own sadness against me, as if to say *I have done this. I am responsible. See how you all owe your life and death to me. Do what I say, Erzabet Bathory. Do your duty to me.*

"Nadasdy will join the new campaign against Michael in Erdely," Rudolph continued. "The region is always such a mess, not least because of you Bathorys and your perpetual misadventures. Luckily, I am here, Countess, to save it. Do accompany Thurzo and Basta back to your lands." The Emperor suddenly turned to me with a stare that froze my blood cold. I had no idea what he might say next. An invisible hand guided his every move, working behind the scenes, beckoning us towards life and death with its endless gestures that showed up in the things that bound us. It was an invisible hand that spelled death to all Bathorys.

"Can your husband only kill Ottomans, Countess Nadasdy, or do you think he is truly blind to who or what he ends?"

I was silent. I lowered my eyes. But then, despite my better judgement, I spoke.

"My husband Nadasdy can kill *anyone*."

He continued to stare into me in the way a lion might stare at a moth that crosses its light, deciding whether to claw at it or simply let it fly on its own perilous and unpredictable journey.

"Good. Then he will not mind bringing me Michael the Brave's Protestant head in a bag when he comes back from Erdely. I want it. I want Michael 'the Brave's' head. I want to see it with my own eyes. Nadasdy is fond of heads. And we are fond of relieving him of them."

I felt the warning run through my blood. I curtseyed again.

"I shall inform him of your desires, Imperial Majesty."

"Good. Michael the Brave's head in exchange for our favour. Do come again, Erzabet *Bathory*."

He used my family name rather than my married name, cutting me out of any remaining wisp of Nadasdy's protection in one quick motion, reminding me that I belonged to a family he had all but destroyed. And then he turned to other business. I felt my heart beating wildly, reached for my smelling salts and quietly slipped out of the room with Anna by my side.

Bocksai, still dishevelled, still ernest, was waiting for me in the corridor close to my quarters. He looked nervous and quickly took my hand, urging me towards a hollow. I nodded to Anna to stay close but not to raise the alarm.

"Speak plainly and quickly, sir. What do you want?"

He looked at me, exhaled in a devastated sigh, and proceeded to talk low and fast.

"Hungary is drowning in a sea of Hapsburgs. I have men all over Erdely. With your cousins, the rightful kings of Erdely, fleeing or beheaded, who can claim it? Erdely can't stand alone. But should the principalities of Erdely, Hungary and Wallachia stand together against the Emperor, we might find our prayers answered. You're a woman of honour – I know it. You're surrounded by powerful men who would tear your wealth from under you. Will Bathory stand and fight, even if she is a woman? Will Bathory save us all? *I* am a warrior, I don't need Nadasdy's steel in my ranks, but I also don't need to be on the wrong side of it. Dissuade your husband from war and join me in the name of freedom. Fight with me against unholy Roman rule with all the grace and all the guile your gender affords you."

He had a romantic way of talking, as if Erdely were the name of his favourite lover. Janus had said that men who spoke of war as if it were the same as love clearly understood neither. I'd heard of a brewing revolt in Erdely in whispers, but I hadn't expected its leader to be so earnest or to speak with such romantic passion. Nor did I expect him to corner me in Prague, right under the nose of Thurzo and the Emperor. It was bold. No wonder the Szekely people had fallen under Bocksai's spell. He was like a quarrelsome boy – though he looked anything but. He was rugged, with green eyes and black hair. And he looked at me now with all the depth and pleading his idealism afforded him. And with ambition.

I held my hands together, folding them at the point where my ribs came together and surveyed him for a moment.

"And you would do all this, with my money, I presume."

He looked a little embarrassed, as if we'd gone off track towards a destination he hadn't quite prepared for. I began to suspect that he'd anticipated I would swoon at all his fervour and flattery, losing the ability for plain speaking. His expression tightened a little and his eyes darted.

"How else will we buy the allegiance of men?" he asked finally, looking down at the floor.

"I've heard of your cause," I said.

"It's your cause too, Countess. Will your family have bled for nothing?"

"It's not my family I worry about, sir. The dead are already dead."

I hid a tremor that moved through me. Sigismund would hide in Poland. And Poland's king, my Uncle Stephen, would keep him safe. If only he had the good sense to stay hidden.

These days, the Emperor had a taste for Bathory blood. He would stop at nothing to keep his buffer states in eternal chaos. If we fought amongst ourselves, we would never unite. Our only common enemy were the Turks.

"Then worry about your people," Bocksai pressed. "Think of them. The Szekelys *are your people.*"

"Yes. *My* people..." I turned away, tapping one hand against the other. How could he presume me so enamoured of myself? Hadn't Mohacs taught us all to be a little more circumspect about our abilities? I was a countess. I had servants and peasants working my lands in scores, but I knew as well as anyone that I was no queen.

"What would you do for *my* people?" I lifted an eyebrow. "Would you rule them?"

"I would lead them to freedom."

"As selflessly as Moses himself, no doubt. Men, sir, lead with steel."

"And women capture hearts."

"My lord, the heart of Erdely has long been emptied. If you wish to capture it, first you need to fill it up. Then there'll be no need for my money."

I smiled my most winning smile and turned on my heel.

But something did, in fact, stir in my heart when he mentioned how the people of Erdely were suffering under the madness of the Holy Empire. So much blood. So much hatred and all in the name of warring Christianities. It had killed the Fabbris and thousands like them. Our women were raped and put to death. Our thoughts and prayers were bound up and pointed only in the direction of Rome. Our religions and our cultures were burned away. Life was stoppered up. No wonder the people of Erdely had lost their hearts. When blood flows only out of rather than towards the heart, how can it survive for too long?

When Anna and I returned to our quarters, I simply said, "Pack. We're leaving," and lay down on my belly on the bed. She came over to me and stroked my hair like she used to do before I was married. I could feel a small hole which had been growing for years inside my heart, grow a little bigger, as if a thumb had pushed into it, exhausting it of blood. It would keep pressing until nothing was left. It had begun the moment I had seen Nadasdy's vacant eyes in the heat of his murderous rage. But today it had grown bigger at the hands of Rudolph, and I realised that this was his true power – the ability to still a person's heart with a few words spoken from the position of empire. Death's face was unpredictable. It sat on a throne in Prague, played with exotic animals and extinguished lives.

*

The tawdry Christmas lights that had been hung around the research office's walls winked in the four o'clock light. When I emerged fully, they momentarily sped up, fizzing before settling down. In each of the spaces between the tiny bulbs, an anonymous decorator had lain greetings cards, their little, sparkling messages glittering from each frontispiece, hanging down over the wires like cats on a branch. It was a sweet gesture, and of course having been here before, I knew who'd done it.

Rachel was tall, blonde and had shoulders that hunched up towards her ears, an eternal gesture of anxious submission to the forces around her. She was, initially, an astonishing researcher, beloved by her students, but soon had been swept up by a man twice her age who happened also to be none other than the professor. She'd written one fantastic article on silence and then never written another word again. It was either a foreshadowing or a cry for help. Either way, what was done was done and she hadn't found a way to undo it. She 'helped out' with his research. She never finished her doctorate. Instead, she baked muffins, soothed tempers and retained a cheery disposition. One day, she came into the office with her long hair clipped short. She said they'd had a fight at home and called the change her 'revenge'. But to me it just looked like he had subdued even more of her wilder parts. *Here again, an emperor, a count, a lord profiting from the erasure of women.*

I'd been called in for an 'emergency meeting'. What could be so important that it couldn't wait? Rachel found me in the corridor and pointed to a closed door.

"He's in there." She smiled in the way I imagined robots in the future might.

When I opened it, the professor was sitting with a young colleague of mine, her legs wrapped around his under the desk in plain view. She giggled at me, narrowed her eyes, and without any preamble launched straight in with, "I'm taking over research here now and we've decided we want you to *rest*." She gave me a look of faux concern that wasn't meant to be interpreted in any other way than: *I've won. I've taken something you had no right to because you didn't play the game.*

"You should come for dinner with us both tonight," the professor said. "It'll relax you."

I rolled my eyes.

"There are ways of getting promoted in this profession, you know," she continued. Now they both giggled whilst looking me up and down. I'd have laughed out loud, but the air was more sinister than pathetic. Each word carried the promise of danger rolled up inside it. I felt that at any moment either of them might flip from childish and obvious to deranged. The air between them was poised and electric, but when they directed their attention on me, it was as if a hundred tiny magnets lost their charge, dropping everything they held to the floor. That's the strength of saying 'no'. You can feel it in the air.

The professor's jaw hardened. I sighed, exhausted with this particular part of time's replay. I knew what was coming.

"Oh? What profession is that?" I said. On my way out, Rachel ambushed me. She wasn't much older than I in linear time and was eternally clad in white jeans and frilly tops, which strangely made her look older rather than younger.

"If you know what's good for you, you'll put on something pretty and do whatever he says. And who knows, you might even enjoy it. Your pride will spell the end of your career, you know. We've all of us made sacrifices. Stop being so childish, Vera. This is how the world works. You'll get over it."

I felt sick. I knew that three years from now in linear time this woman would be the head of a women's empowerment programme.

I walked off, flicking my phone on and practically speed-dialling Lucretia.

"*Pronto?*"

"Lucretia, it's me – Vera."

"Oh, hi—" I cut her off

"Yeah, 'Cretia, I'm here again. I'm here at the moment before he… he—'"

"What?"

"Never mind."

I wanted to fight against time, but I couldn't. It was like trying to fly upwards by the force of will alone, taking on gravity.

"Vera, where are you?"

The phone screeches and scrambles and I'm sent ahead in time. It's only by a few days, but it's enough. *If only what comes now worked. If only he succeeded. It wouldn't get even worse. But it does. Because time wants me to know. Time wants me to get so sick of erasure that I'll risk everything.*

*

When Anna and the rest of the servants had finished packing, she told them to load the carriages.

"Good. Now I'll just have to wait. You can go ahead," I said.

"Why? What are you waiting for?" she asked, anxious and suspicious.

"Because I believe I am to be Thurzo and Basta's prisoner, for the journey home at least."

"My lady?"

"It's the Emperor's wish that I travel with them. I can only assume they'll send word when they're ready to depart."

But no word came. Instead, the following morning, a note was slipped under my door.

The Emperor requests your presence in the menagerie this evening.

You shall be escorted.

I lay on my bed all day, even though the sun streamed violently through the window, signalling the glory of Prague. When I threw up, Anna helped me, stroked my hair and told me stories of the south, from when she was a child. When evening finally came, I dressed in royal blue, wore pearls and scraped my hair into a vicious little bun, high on my head. I asked Anna to file my nails into sharp points. I painted my lips red and when a knock came at the door, I breathed in and opened it, ready for anything.

A beautiful young boy with angelic curls met me. He bowed deeply, wrapped my hand around his arm and requested that I follow him. He was so graceful and so elegant that I even wondered for a moment if he was entirely human. He led me through the endless corridors until we reached a large painted door. He turned the handle and opened it for me. There lay the most bizarre sight I had ever seen. Animals and humans everywhere. Spectacular creatures, all of them. They were like something out of an Italian painting. Music was playing and a young woman sang in such delightful and unusual tones that she almost restored me then and there. Some wore masks, others were draped in fine silks that had hand-drawn images of yet more animals, more menageries, until I wasn't sure if all of us in the room had become no more than imperial cloth, spinning in magical dances that stained us carelessly in wine.

I saw the Emperor drinking out of an elaborate golden cup. The cup had the same bizarre symbol I'd seen in the main hall of the court etched onto it. I wasn't quite sure where to place myself, but when I turned my head, I noticed Basta standing right next to me, a little too close for my liking.

"Countess, I believe we got off on the wrong foot." He kissed my hand and bowed his head. I remained silent and he stayed quiet next to me, turning to admire the singer. Eventually, he spoke again.

"Beautiful, isn't she? Perhaps you should request that the Emperor lend her to you? Sarvar won't know what hit it." He smiled to himself. "I understand you have opened a press there." It came out of nowhere.

"Yes, my lord. I have."

"Things of genius, aren't they? Those little machines have changed the world, like second emperors. Wouldn't you agree, Countess?"

"They certainly can produce pretty images."

"And the words too. I mean, the power to produce and distribute so many ideas across an empire, empires even. Imagine, you could send books from Rome to *Constantinople*."

"The Ottomans are suspicious of printing. They prefer to remain authentic to calligraphy."

"Oh, I didn't know that, Countess. It is surprising to me what you know." He appeared to survey the room, but in truth I felt him watching me, cataloguing my reactions to everything.

"The Ottomans have their own version of the Protestants, you know?"

I turned to look directly at him.

He continued. "Yes. They believe in Ali. They originate outside the Sultanate in Persia, but their word is spreading – largely from Tabriz and from Konya in Turkey. And with a little help from us and England." He winked. "God bless English adventurism! The Sultan really doesn't know what to do with them. He keeps some close to him. *Janissaries*. They also believe in this Ali. So brutal, all of them. They attack in droves, like rats piling one on top of the other, rushing to get onto the field."

He laughed and appeared for a moment to disappear into fantasy. I shuddered but not for the reason Basta might have thought. Mention of janissaries didn't strike me with fear; I simply realised how much I missed my old friend. Janus would have laughed out loud if I'd told him about this conversation. He would have called Basta an idiot and a brute, warning me at the same time that these were easy deceptions. Then he would have likened me to an oak leaf, or a cloud in the sky, and told me to watch for how these cleverer materials dealt with elemental Bastas of their own.

"See, Countess. Words are powerful. It's easy enough to shed blood on the battlefield, but to change a man's mind with a story, now," he paused and then emphasised each following word, "that's – real – power."

"Do you think that anything exists in the world outside of power?"

"Not in this court."

We both laughed together at this.

"I imagine power runs through everything. Like blood."

He looked very surprised for a moment. I had caught him off guard. He kissed my hand again.

"Then perhaps I should call you the Blood Countess."

I winced a little.

"You don't like the idea?"

"Of blood?"

"Of power."

I looked across the room. Thurzo was whispering into the ear of the Emperor, who in turn had his arm now draped over a young boy who couldn't have been more than ten.

"I like power well enough, my Lord Basta. And you?"

"Of course. Power and pleasure. Have you ever met the English queen, Countess?"

"No."

"In some ways, you remind me of her. Now *she* is a savage, in all the ways that power demands. Perhaps not in pleasure, but she understands how violence supports power. That she does! Apparently with you, it's the other way around. According to Thurzo, you fuck like an Ottoman. I find that interesting."

My jaw dropped. I had no idea and not much to compare it to.

"Now before you protest at me, Countess, think on this. You will either sink or swim. I know your type. You…" and he tapped the soft part at the centre of my rib cage with his fingers "…have an opportunity to change that here. You are either on the side of the Emperor or not. There's no such thing as real freedom in a principality, my lady. You're caught between the Emperor and the Sultan. You are caught. There's no escape. So, either sink or fight your destiny and rise." And instantly his countenance changed. "Ah, look, she's finished her song. Enough of the sublime, on to modernity."

He walked off towards the Emperor and his boy. Thurzo was standing close by. He was looking at me intently, throwing off the veil of rage that had obscured all parts of him earlier. It wasn't the desperate look of Nadasdy, who wanted only to be saved. It was the sort of look that implies nothing more than a pause in the action. I felt he was waiting to see whether I would finally capitulate to the plan laid out, that I marry and ally with him, handing my fortune over in the process, or whether he would have to have me killed. I realised that having no answer for him would be tantamount to an answer, and that answer would demand blood. Neither story fit me. I wasn't the victim, nor was I an aggressor. I fell outside of such day or night thinking. There was no appropriate story for me.

I remembered the bluebells in the field and how they had held our bodies up with their vibrant colours. I remembered the moment he'd also paused back then, had held my hand and sucked my finger and smiled so gently at me. I breathed in very deeply to steady myself and walked over to him. I knew what I was going to do was risky. I hadn't wanted anyone to find out. I hadn't wanted anyone to know or even suspect until I had decided what to do. I looked over his shoulder to the Emperor. The boy was almost completely naked now as many hands touched and squeezed at him disturbingly. I put my hand on Thurzo's shoulder. He remained rock solid, but I could sense his blood rushing and swirling inside his quickly beating heart.

"George, I'm pregnant."

He just stared for a while, blankly, not even at me but across the hall, as if his soul was in another part of the country and his body had yet to catch up with it. "George?" Still no response. I waited a few more heartbeats and then decided to turn about and leave. As I did so, he grabbed my wrist fast and sharp, like the jaws of a crocodile. Then he fixed his eyes on mine, their incomparable blue bearing into me, searching me out without seeing me, even though I stood right in front of him.

"Does Nadasdy know?"

"Why?"

"Answer me, Elizabet! Does Nadasdy know?"

I wrestled my arm from his grip and turned around fast, running to the door. He ran after me and grabbed me. A few courtiers laughed, but Thurzo didn't notice. All his attention was fixed on me.

"That's *my* child in there. I know it is. Tell me it's my child."

"What difference does it make, George? Your heart is set on ending me. I know it is. And that beast of a man you're mixed up with has just now threatened me. What will you do? Kill Nadasdy when he's on the field? Get rid of your wife, how did you put it – 'quietly' – and then marry me for my estates? How many times have you been widowed? Once? Now twice? How long do any of us have until you seduce and murder us? Who's next? The Emperor? How long does he have now that you've been in his bed?"

He slapped me hard in the face.

More laughter rippled across the room. An ibex crossed behind him and I noticed again just how many animals were roaming the room, their amber eyes blinking in a fragile tameness in the candlelight, and Basta amongst them, embracing the boy and the Emperor, staring at Thurzo and me.

"Ah, my favourite of all the pleasures," he shouted, "a lover's quarrel."

Thurzo was unaffected, as if Basta were merely a fly in his world and not the Emperor's executioner.

"You are playing with fire, Elizabet."

I laughed cynically. "What fire? Where? I'm already dead."

"Don't be so dramatic. I offered you what I thought you wanted." He paused and looked at me properly, taking me in for the first time since we had met again. "We're not all Nadasdy." He suddenly smiled at me. "We're going to have a baby." He grabbed my face with one hand, taking my chin and cheeks and squeezing them, pulling me to his lips. He kissed me roughly, still full of anger, then let me go.

"I'm tired, George. And I'm quite afraid of you." I slipped out from underneath his gaze and walked to the door gracefully, though my heart was in my mouth all the way.

The next morning, Anna led me to the carriage that waited for me. Thurzo and Basta hadn't come down yet, so I climbed in and waited for a good while. Usually, I would have left, returned to my rooms and then kept them waiting, but the carriage was quiet and cool, and I was less likely to be disturbed out here. I rested my head against the door frame and drifted off into sleep. I woke to Basta swinging himself into the carriage with Thurzo behind him. Thurzo sat next to me, leaving a good gap between us, as a child might. Basta sat opposite me.

"Ah, my lady. Did we keep you waiting long?"

"It's no trouble, my lord. I'm glad for the air."

"Yes, I'm sure. Last night was full of fire."

"I'm glad you both had an opportunity for some relaxation." I shuddered. "I found myself exhausted and had to retire."

"Pity."

For a long time, we sat in silence as the wheels turned beneath us. Thurzo continued to stare directly ahead of himself. I imagined he was piercing through the richly fabricked interior of the carriage into different possible futures, working his way through all of them, weighing up which would work out best in the end. An eternally long game that would stretch even past his own death. Basta, in contrast, looked out of the window, at me, at Thurzo, down at himself and then back around again, as if he had the mind of a butterfly rather than the razor-sharp one I now knew him to possess.

"Countess, tell me, how do you spend your days at Cachtice?"

"What do you mean, my lord?"

"At Sarvar, there is printing. At Varanno, there are festivals. What of Cachtice?"

"Cachtice is my home. I rest. As does Nadasdy. We rest together."

"I see. I should like to visit this Cachtice. Perhaps I might even bring a friend. With your permission, of course."

"Yes, dear Count," I said, annoyed and distracted with his prattling.

The carriage stopped abruptly. Thurzo and Basta immediately dropped to the floor. Thurzo then quickly pulled me down as a quiverful of arrows flew through the air.

"Arrows, not shots," said Basta.

Thurzo nodded, understanding something I didn't. Basta grabbed his sword and smiled.

"Time to kill some Hadjuks."

He kissed the flat part of the blade, took a brief look about the window and rolled out of the carriage. Thurzo did the same on the other side, opening the door and sliding down with more efficiency and less flair. I lay down on the floor of the carriage. Cries and howls filled my ears, but strangely, I couldn't feel a thing. The world had slowed to another pace, upturned, as if one wheel – my wheel – had been broken, leaving the others spinning fast in action as mine sputtered and flailed and came to an abrupt stop. I had always imagined the pace of death to be slow, even if its cause might be fast. I was becoming faint. Lifeless. And yet my mind fell into some kind of heightened awareness.

Now I can feel the floor of the carriage turning to snow. The wind picks up. I look about me and see that same unmistakable pool of blood that I'd seen those many years ago when I had been put on the blacksmith's throne and slid uncontrollably into the other world. My hair returns to the knotting lengths, falling on either side of my head. I am in puffy garments, made out of some kind of strange fibre, entirely unlike anything I've ever seen or felt. One knitted grey woollen glove lies a few feet off in the distance. The other covers my hand. I sit up and the world comes into view.

There are strange buildings that reach all the way into the sky, made of metal. They're the whitest things I have ever seen. The doors are almost all glass, with what looks like metal threads criss-crossed inside each pane. The handles to open the doors are straight, like teeth. Huge burning candles that aren't candles at all, but which give off the most intensely burning light, hang overhead in rows. My heart is beating so fast that it might break. Where am I?

I put my hands to my head. There's still blood there. I grab handfuls of snow and press it to where I can feel the burning of the wound. I touch my belly. But this isn't a woman's body growing a child. This is some strange reversal. It is a child's body with a woman buried deep inside it, caught somewhere on the ropes of time. I walk towards the strange white building, as if I'd been there before. I open the door, touching the lintel all the way around, though I don't know why. I go inside. I sit on the first step of an immense staircase for a while. Then I walk up it. It must have many, many more steps than my tower in Cachtice. Nonetheless, I start to climb.

I still feel faint, but I climb as if in a trance. When I reach a certain height, I know it's time to stop. I push at the heavyset door of glass and metal and walk down a long straight corridor. I can hear a dog barking behind one of the walls, but not the one I'm stood at. I suddenly have the impression that hundreds of people are inside this tower. Yet, I pick out the one correct door. I knock. It opens. A woman stares at me.

"What happened?"

"I need to get back home."

"Get inside. *Now.*"

I look at her, this utter stranger. I know I should know her. She is in a fury. I become frightened.

"I need to get back."

"Who did this to you?"

"I think I fell on the floor. I heard arrows, not shots."

She sighs sharply and matter-of-factly.

"Let's get you cleaned up."

And suddenly I'm returned to the carriage. There's blood. My blood. An arrow sticks out of me, just above my right breast.

"Angels, rocks, lights and stones, come to me!" and I pull it out, letting an involuntary scream escape. I can hear the sound of metal on metal. I sit up. On the other side of the carriage, at the open door, I see a lithe man with tall feathers protruding from his helmet. I'm so weak, but I manage to scramble to my feet, the remaining pulses of life rising, giving me strength lest I die again, this time as Bathory. Instead of trying to flee out from the other side of the carriage, I launch myself directly at the man. I howl at him. He throws me off him easily, but I have grappled the dagger at his waist away from him in the brief struggle. He bears down on me, and I slash downwards. He's shorter than I and I catch his face. He becomes a bear, a lion, a wolf – all three at once, and I become a creature from the underworld, a denizen of hell, unafraid, in the madness of the moment, of any earthly creature.

The dagger is welded to my hand with some ungodly fire. He has no sword anymore, only a bow, and I give him no time to recharge it. I throw myself at him again, shrieking and foaming. As the dagger goes up, I pause. I have become death itself. Only a moment ago, I was a child caught out of time and now I am death. I can't do this. He takes advantage of the pause to push me away from him. He grabs an arrow and hurls himself at me with the sharp end, intent on piercing my chest. I flip the blade I've stolen up in my hand and plunge it directly into his throat. He topples, sending me to the earth.

The world slows back down again. I feel him, this soldier, fallen on me and dying in my arms. It's the most terrifying thing I have ever experienced. He rattles slightly and then stops forever. Why can't I be in the snow now? Why does time torment me so much, taking me away when I'm alone but bringing me back to take the life of this plumed stranger and feel him extinguishing? To become, in this moment, a goddess of death. A murderer.

I become aware that Basta is standing over me. Thurzo joins him.

"At least we know now that she hasn't been intercepted by Bocksai yet," says Basta.

"Still, I shouldn't like to chance another brawl with his lackeys," replies Thurzo. "Good."

"Yes, a good day's work, I'd say," says Basta. "I wonder if I too should buy myself some Hadjuks. Might come in useful."

They heave the man off me and Thurzo wraps his cloak around my body. He lifts me to standing and half carries me to the unmanned carriage.

"Stay warm," he whispers as he does so, "there's a Thurzo to think about."

I blink. He lies me down across the seats. Rage floods in as I understand what's just happened to me. I whisper something inaudible and Thurzo leans down to me to hear. Now I bite *his* ear in bloody retribution.

"It's Nadasdy's. And he'll be a Bathory."

Chapter Eleven

Nadasdy looked up at me with those grey eyes of his. The wounds from his last skirmish were still bleeding a little and despite Anna's expert care, the stitching was rough, and he walked with tremendous pain. When I told him about my child, he had sunk into his chair, his hands searching wildly, unsuccessfully, for the right place to come to rest. I think he was trying not to cry. I knew I was delivering the kind of cruelty that fills men with the terror of witches, with the terror of just how powerful a woman can be to the inner landscape of a man. I stood my ground. I would accept whatever came next.

Nadasdy wasn't rageful. His whole body had a look of sadness about it, an empty church at the mass of sorrow. He simply wasn't there for a moment. After a while, he broke down the walls of the silence that had settled about us with a very slow, very gentle voicing.

"I fought Tartars this time. They have these... these green doublets. And I'm not sure what kind of steel they use, or how they make it, but it's strong. The first time you rip one of their stomachs, it's strange because the intestines spill out of the green and it's like… it's like…"

I knelt down to him, half in an attempt to quell whatever might follow, half in pity. He didn't move but neither did he push my hand away from his.

"I imagine it's like seeing the earth spill out. But instead of soil, it's the interior of a human body," I said.

He looked at me then, all grey tears and quiet.

"Francis, I can't imagine—"

"But you can. I know you of all people can. *Talto.*" He remained soft voiced, but he spoke the final word with such intensity, even reverence. The idea that I might have access to an alternative world filled him up even as the world he lived in tried to empty him out. In some ways, I felt he was speaking to me for the first time.

"Do you think I don't know?" he said.

"Don't know what?"

"Don't know what you do. Elizabet, I know everything you do. Did you think I didn't have you watched as you ran about… as you ran about with *him*?" He spat the word and became sad again. "I allowed it because… because I haven't been able to be your husband, and because I know how much you hate me for…" He swallowed, on the edge of a precipice. I could sense his vertigo. He was wondering whether taking this leap would bring him the redemption he sought or only more pain. I could hear him thinking, thinking, wishing, watching: can I do it? Can I do it? Can I even say it?

And then he did. For better or worse. The words came tumbling out of him.

"…For killing. For killing that woman. For getting carried away."

He started shaking and breathing so rapidly, unable to contain the weight of this sudden unstoppering. It was unnerving to see how honesty moved through his body. It poured from his wounds, mixing with the blood that wept quietly out of the stitches that held whole parts of him temporarily in place.

"There was one girl – another girl. Her father had brought her to me in exchange for – I don't know, Anna would take care of it all. I think it was some goats. And when she saw me, she blushed. She said how fortunate she was to help her family by being loved by a man so beautiful." He looked at me again.

"She thought I was beautiful, Elizabet. She thought I was going to be her lover."

Silent tears fell down my face. I was rooted to the spot. And then he continued.

"And I let her think it. I took her to one of my rooms. I dressed her up in Turkish clothes. I never tie them. I like to feel them fighting. And then I started to hit her until the blood came," he gestured, "from her body and over her skin. I started to get excited. I took my ring and heated it up and pushed it into her face, her arms, her back. She clawed at me. Like a bear. I put my hands around her throat and soon she expired. For a moment, I caught myself. I hated what I saw. But I couldn't help but feel this terrible excitement. For a moment, I was truly ecstatic. I felt divine, except this is not God's divinity. It's from the other power." Tears were lining both our faces, marking them momentarily with their salty trails. "On the battlefield, I'm honoured for it. Even the Turks call me their 'Black Bey'. But it's only the devil they're all honouring. All of them. All the empires."

As he spoke, I had taken leave of myself – of my senses – turning momentarily to see the child in the future, her chubby body lying on a bed marked danger; a woman blocking the doorway and a man with his hands pressed down upon her mouth until her little lungs felt they might burst. And I willed her to find a doorway in time, drawing one in the space around her even as I returned to *here, now*. Nadasdy had seen me disappear. Not in flesh, but in time. He was looking at me intently.

"I wish I could go where you go – to your other world. I

remember hearing stories from my mother's serving girl when I was a child. She used to tell me tales when I sat on her lap, of *taltos* with their magic horses that transported them between the worlds." He smiled for a moment. "I never thought I'd marry one." The sorrow returned. "I wish you could take me with you." He said it so quietly and so sincerely.

"No, you don't. I've come to realise it's no different. In all the worlds. We're still all bound by the same forces. The stories just play out anew, with small differences over and over. There's no escape."

He looked deeply saddened at this. Then after a moment, "There's no escape for me either. Every time I close my eyes, I have myself to contend with. When I open them, I'm on the battlefield. For me, there's no difference between the spaces. Does that make sense, Elizabet?"

"Yes." I nodded and he held my hand with such gentleness that I couldn't believe it was attached to the same man who was speaking. If there was a difference between spaces, it was here, now, in this tiny gesture.

"Tell me, where do you go?"

I didn't know how to answer this. I knew now that these were my memories, but that I was much larger than my own life. How could I explain that?

"When I've watched you, I've seen you sometimes sit so quietly. So still. For hours. I've seen it with my own eyes. And I don't know what's happening – I can't get inside there," and he tapped his head with his finger.

He had told me plainly that he believed himself animated by the devil. Could I tell him that I feared I was living across worlds? Could I tell him that in truth we were both simply the forces of time made material, the fleshly speech of our species' violent and deadly conversations.

He continued. "I think you're *listening*. Listening to something really quiet."

I stopped cold.

"Yes," I whispered. "Yes."

"But it's something deeper than anything in the air. What are you hearing, my angel?"

"I'm hearing time. And time has all things tightly packed into it. When it moves, whole worlds are created. Time is alive. It tells its own stories across us. Across our bodies."

He sat back and we were quiet for a long while together.

"Elizabet, I can't be this person anymore. I want to stop – I *have* stopped. But I want to stop in here." He pointed again to his forehead. I remembered Janus and all his strange stories about the heart being like a giant that can absorb anything, rolling all thoughts around in its alchemical blood until they come out anew.

"Maybe you need to stop it in here," I said to Nadasdy, and now I pointed. I pointed to his heart, just as Janus had those years ago when I was a girl frightened in the forest by the weight of the world's rage, when he had seemed to confuse the heart with the heavens, pointing at my chest whilst speaking of the stars. I supposed now that both revolved round and round, churning past, present and future inside their horizons. Perhaps a star and a heart weren't so different after all.

"How can I make myself right?" Nadasdy spoke desperately.

"I don't know."

His thoughts sharpened and his face concentrated in new lines that I hadn't seen before, as if he had begun to animate his body differently.

"I need to find a way." Then he sighed. "What if I fail?"

*

After I heard Nadasdy's story, or more precisely, after I'd remembered hearing Nadasdy speak his story to the Elizabet inside my bones as I wrote, I became hesitant to arrange all my relationships to life around the people I knew in it. They seemed so small. So full of tiny quarrels that led to unspeakable things playing out across the planet's surface until they dug in, penetrating even its crust. Humans seemed to me like large shadows cast by time, and because of this, we all lived in shadows, as shadows. We were all made of insubstantial darknesses that we spun on the loom of our bones into life stories. A patterned carpet unwoven only in the holy fire of deep forgetting.

I wanted to tell Nadasdy the story of time. I wanted to tell him to watch the crocuses in the fields and to understand that the root structures inside all things are more representative of a life than any short-term bloom. I wanted to tell him that this was no fatalism. That inside these roots and passages was where all the freedom he was hungry for lay. That we could bloom *differently* along any line in space or time. That choice is about making new differences. Tiny differences that go unnoticed by the large ignominious sword of history, which doesn't necessarily realise when it's being rewritten. But if I knew this, then so did Elizabet and she would tell him. She would tell him all the way back in the past and so I would have haunted myself in the future present.

*

The girl from the future felt so present to me these days, although I no longer saw her. I only saw myself, but I knew she inhabited the walls of my body, *as* my body. I stared down at my chest and arms. I saw my future not trapped in a wooden coffin, no doubt brought down by Thurzo and his machinations, but as her, in her. As Vera. Not even in my child, who would be born soon. My child's little future would be largely determined by how Nadasdy, Thurzo and I played our presents. It was the larger future I was thinking of. The great spine of time that was the real story that we fed with our tiny lives. I continued to survey my own body until my eyes came to rest on my wedding ring. I took it off and held it in my hands.

Nadasdy had gone off to war again to fulfil the Emperor's request.

"Now that I'm not eager to go, they'll kill me," he'd said as he was preparing to leave.

"I won't tell you to be brave, Francis. That's fool's advice. Just go. And come back." I took his hands in mine. I trembled slightly as if something moved through my body. Then I kissed them. His breath caught almost audibly in his chest. He smiled. It was a melting of years and years of compounded ice. I saw him momentarily *as* a field. It was rough and strewn with bodies, a boy pouring red liquid from a bowl ran across his own surfaces, his past living inside its own horizon. I could hear his mother praying across his hilly lines, whilst he, Nadasdy the boy, ran about her legs. She grabbed him and held him.

"One day, you will avenge all this. You will be the greatest warrior Hungary has ever known, or else you will die – we will all die – trying. Do you hear me, son?" The child nodded. The field trembled. It was already too full of blood. I imagined it then caking over with snow, with ice. Freezing everything childlike within him. And out of the ice, a terrible warrior. Nadasdy, the killer, the Black Bey of Hungary, carved into the shape of blinding rage.

And then he was staring at me with a smile that indicated something much bigger than relief.

"You're trembling, my love."

"I am, aren't I."

"Are you still afraid of me?"

"No."

"I hope it's just because…" he paused and looked at me with those pleading grey eyes of his "…you've forgiven me."

We became warm together in an instant, no longer mapping each other, fighting each other or hiding from each other.

"I wasn't listening properly, this time."

"Oh?"

"I think something in *me* just melted."

He was dressed in his riding armour, which was light and full of its own leathery sinews. It gave him the otherworldly appearance of something more-than-human, edging towards the divine, a second skin that betrayed his mortality. The horses were being saddled outside and there was a flurry all around us. But the world was slowing down. Instead of my heart racing, it was becoming rhythmic and gentle. He kept looking into me. Then ever so slowly he raised his right hand and laid his fingers *so carefully* on my cheek. He tilted my head upwards and smiled more deeply. I felt his lips open and linger at mine. I softened, removing the layers and layers of anger and hurt that had lain over me for so many years with him. His kiss grew into me. Then it grew in passion. I could feel fleeting moments of fear rush through him, as if he was working out the difference between violence and desire. He moved back and looked into me again.

He laughed at the first moments of discovering something wonderful and was immediately bashful of sharing it with me.

"Come back, so I can fall in love with you," I ventured.

"Yes, my Emperor," he said, and then did something I'd never seen him do, nor imagined him capable of. He winked at me.

Then he turned, sighed wearily, and left to meet Thurzo and Basta and the flock of mercenaries Michael the Brave had readied to kill him.

*

John had become uncharacteristically excited about something that he was eager for me to see. I always felt his attention to detail was threaded through with a private ecstasy. It was, perhaps, a way that he could transcend the bitter reality of our world, the loss of his fathers and the gaining of a new kind of ambivalent father in the shape of Nadasdy. I'd received his message to come urgently to Sarvar and arranged for a small retinue to accompany me from Cachtice. When Dorothea had suggested I not travel on account of my heavy pregnancy, I snorted at her. I had told no one about what had happened with Thurzo and Basta – how I had been laid out as bait to check my allegiances, to see whether I had been politicised by the warring internal forces of our time.

"My child has already lived through violence. A carriage ride will hardly agitate him further."

Dorothea surveilled me through her hooded eyes.

"How do you know God will bless you with a son?"

I stared her down.

"I couldn't care less. But a mother knows who she carries."

"I would be careful, madam, lest you sound too pagan."

"Nadasdy and I know the truth about our little one. You no longer have his ear. I've been patient with you up until now, Dorothea, but I would be careful, lest you start to sound like a revolutionary."

She 'humphed' at me, but I saw a moment of fear move through her body – a terrible grey fish that frantically swam around looking for an exit through her pores. What kind of nerve had I hit? I made a mental note to find out what Dorothea was hiding, to become the follower and watcher rather than let it stay the other way around.

When I arrived at Sarvar, I went straight to the press. John was so covered in ink that he'd taken on the appearance of a Spanish moor. I quickly looked up to check the roof, lest he had burnt yet another building in his pursuit of making Europe's finest bone-black.

"Countess! Look. Look what I found."

He rushed about until his hands found a scroll that curled about itself on one of his many tables. He presented it to me as if it were a holy relic and he a searcher and a wanderer, a true journeyman, like the Fabbris before him.

In every place the preachers shall preach and explain the gospel, each according to his understanding of it, and if the congregation like it, well; if not, no one shall compel them, but they shall keep the preachers whose doctrine they approve. Therefore, no one shall annoy or abuse the preachers on account of their religion, according to previous constitutions, or allow any to be imprisoned or be punished by removal of his post on account of his teaching, for faith is the gift of God, this comes from hearing, and hearing by the word of God.

Decree of the Parliament of Torda, Erdely, in the year of our Lord 1563

An act of hearing. I let the words circulate around me, writing themselves into me from the outside, permeating my flesh and fusing themselves deep. *An act of hearing.* The God for whom everyone fought so greatly was here mixed into the stories we told each other like a divine pigment that wrote out our beginnings and endings in crucibles of ink. I remembered the day I'd wanted to go mushroom picking with Janus before it had all been usurped by my marriage. How I'd thought of God not as some creature that demanded Turkish, Jewish and Christian blood to spill and feed the earth but as a mushroom – a mycelial being that webbed earth, star and flesh into consciousness. God was the fleshly ear we poured ourselves into with all our talk, and out of which we bore ourselves, in the trailing wisps of phantom speech, echoing ourselves into life, over and over again. Who could divert the course of this echo? Who could speak themselves *differently* inside the ear of God?

"My lady, do you see? It says it's legal to be whatever you want, to worship however you want."

And I was returned to the politicisation of God, to the creation of God out of listening into a king, a divine agent who had been responsible for so much blood. I looked over the document John showed me.

"Yes, this is how it is in Erdely. But they've long forgotten it."

I tousled his hair. He flinched but then grabbed my hand, boyish in his manner.

"I want to go to Erdely, my lady. I want to see what else they're printing."

I paused. "It's not safe, John. Even now, Nadasdy, Thurzo and Basta are at war in Erdely. For years, my cousin Sigismund was given the throne and each year, it seems, he abdicated and ran for his life. Then later Andrew was murdered for it. Michael has it now, and look how his days are numbered. No Bathory is safe there. No member of a Bathory household either."

"Then I'll go as Fabbri." After a moment: "It'll be nice to be known for who I am for once."

This cut me to the heart, but then I remembered that time had passed, and John was a young man now.

"And who is that, John?" I sighed.

"Madam, I *am* a Fabbri. I'm yours to command, but please understand, I print books, like my fathers did before me."

"You do so much more than that, John."

He looked at me with that strange adult gaze that I had first seen in the printshop in Venice. His face was maturing, but he was still a child to me. I couldn't in good conscience send him to his death in Erdely, no matter how progressive it was and no matter how much it seemed to mean to him. We were hated there. We had come in as conquerors, bled the Szekelys dry and now we were destroying their ideas, their religions, calling them 'Turk' and 'Jew' and 'heretic', seeking to erase their new syncretic faith that, as of yet, had no name. Surely, Erdely had become Mohacs displaced in time. It contained at least as much blood.

"Walking dead," Thurzo had said of the Szekelys when we'd been carrying on our affair – a thing that now felt long ago and yet was ultimately forever present, growing inside my body with me.

"Ask your husband." And he had smiled at some kind of secret knowledge that he would not make me privy to, no matter how I questioned him with my eyes. He must have always suspected Nadasdy's predilections.

"Just another bunch of heretic bastards to feed who then think they can make what they like out of God."

I remember thinking it strange that Thurzo would speak so crassly, but then perhaps he thought they had got what they deserved. Without *nobility*, Thurzo's world would fall apart, and yet, in some irony, he would never belong to the class he so greatly desired. He was wealthy and respected, but ultimately, his family's money came from copper, and the Holy Roman Emperor would never let him forget that.

"John, I can't send you to Erdely. You'll be killed. Do you understand? If not in the war, then by some faithless dagger in the night."

John nodded, but it didn't take any special intelligence to realise that he was already planning a new strategy. The very thing that made him such a good printer was the very thing that made him trouble: tenacity.

*

Maria-Christina, formerly married, unsuccessfully, to my cousin Sigismund, niece to the Emperor and the Princess Regent of Erdely now herself, had sent word a few days later that she would be visiting Cachtice soon and so I decided to return from Sarvar to make all the necessary arrangements. After Dorothea had packed my things, I asked her to call for John.

"When you send for John, ask him to bring me the Torda scroll," I said.

She returned, but produced neither John nor his scroll.

"I'm afraid he's gone, madam."

"What do you mean, gone?" I snapped.

"Vanished. Into thin air." She seemed secretly amused rather than stern.

"How does a boy vanish, Dorothea?"

She shrugged. Then ventured strangely, as if I were a child myself who just might believe anything, "Perhaps he has died and been buried in the churchyard. I know there was a funeral yesterday. A crime. They died in the woods. But the priest didn't get a look at the body. Could it have been our John, wandering about in the night?"

She looked at me testingly, as if daring me to believe in her scaremongering.

"What utter nonsense!"

She continued to look amused, so I slapped her hard in the face.

"John is my charge! He's more than a servant, he's my... my..."

"My lady's temper is strong today. Perhaps it's the pregnancy."

"Dorothea, if you have had a hand in John's—"

She interrupted me exasperatedly, suddenly bored with her own bizarre and vicious game.

"John's gone to Erdely."

I stared at her, open-mouthed.

"My lady, John can't stand by here and watch as Erdely rains blood under Catholic rule." She paused and seemed to steady herself. "None of us can. And John owes himself this, in the name of his father and the fathers who cared for him until..."

She looked at me curiously, wondering if I was a thing to be feared or a stupid creature to be chastised.

"Not a second passes when I don't imagine the suffering of the Fabbris, Dorothea! They offered me the closest thing I've known to friendship, artistry, goodness even. You were the one who betrayed them to Nadasdy! You, not I, came with soldiers to the printshop!"

Something happened to Dorothea then. She lost her steel composure, and her legs trembled a moment.

"I was trying to keep Nadasdy's eye away from our brothers and sisters in Erdely. I was trying to keep the Black Bey himself from our people hiding out here in Hungary! I am still trying to keep him from our girls."

Her eyes were two grey rivers; long, dry and hollowed out, but sad.

"So am I," I eventually said. "I'm… trying."

She looked at me, exasperated for a moment. Then she curtsied and left the room in haste before I had a chance to ask her anything further. I made to run after her but then clenched my abdomen as a horrendous pain gripped me and squeezed my body. I could hear Dorothea's steps running down the hall and then suddenly disappear, as if she had never been there in the first place.

I lay on the floor gasping for air as the pain flew through the inside of my body. I managed to calm my breathing. In between its currents, I found myself wondering why, if I had survived an arrow, news of John's disappearance would be the thing to break my pregnancy. Perhaps I was simply full of too many different kinds of sadness and my baby had decided already that the world was too harsh and too cruel to bother with. I couldn't fault that. Perhaps one day I would be able to unravel time's meanderings and roll myself back up into an idea, an unfinished moment of desire, cancelling out my existence as Elizabet, silencing the sounds I brought to help chorus the earth with.

All at once, the pain stopped. I feared that when I looked down there would be blood. But there wasn't. It was a momentary lapse. Nothing more. A reminder that, like John, I and my baby were both mortal and yet both, in our own incompleteness, so very alive. I needed to rest. If Maria-Christina wanted to leave court so badly, she could damn well come to me.

*

The pub was a reeling mass of people and sequins and strumming guitars. There was only one seat left – right next to the professor.

The women from before watched me as I stood there. One even sighed and said, "What are you waiting for? He's saved *you* a seat." The *'you'* was dripping with anger and jealousy, and I suddenly imagined I could hear the same voice hundreds of years in the past, a sound in a crowd of women all shouting for the death of a damnable witch. All dying to be seen to be on the right side of history. The professor snorted as I hesitated, looking around anxiously for another space anywhere but there. *You'll need to do more than that if you want to break away from me.* When I capitulated and sat down, thinking to myself, *To hell with it all! Good luck trying,* he turned to me.

"What can I get you to drink? You've worked so hard. Take some time off."

And he'd gone to the bar but before he returned with a large glass of white wine for me, another man sat down.

"I've heard about you. You're his favourite, the vampire girl, right? Not really sure what you do, but I *know* I'm going to like it. I have a position at my research centre waiting for you if you want it."

Under the table he suddenly grabbed onto my knee. I jerked it upwards instantly and he cried out as the back of his hand hit the underside of the table. The professor came back. "Ollie, leave her alone. You don't get to poach her – well, not *just* yet." 'Ollie' – whoever the hell he was – rubbed his hand and raised his eyebrows at me.

"Go and sort yourself out," the professor said to him. Then he turned and smiled serpentine at me as he got up, still rubbing his hand and mouthing a *'sorry'* at the professor but not to me.

"Here, get this down you."

Within moments, I went out for air. I knew something was very wrong and crossed the road before my legs appeared to multiply and then fail beneath me, grabbing onto the iron railings that lined the street, using them to pull my body along the empty pavement. My knees buckled as if made from dough.

"Come on," I whispered to my legs. "We've been here before. Time – it lives in the body," and I made it down the street with the last of my strength. I wasn't too far from my house. Luckily, the railings continued on, and I used them to track my way home now with no sensation below the waist and no sense of direction in my fast-extinguishing alertness.

"Stay awake. Stay awake."

It became my new mantra. I held on.

My thoughts flashed across snatches of all the possible endings to this moment. In all of them, my body appeared limp, cold, dead. A woman disappearing out of the world again and again and again. When terror hits the body, it usually goes rigid. But as my body was draining of what felt like life, instead, I oozed and slid and fell. I knew this sensation. I'd felt it before, time and time again. It was a lot like the first sensations of death. So I simply held on. It's hard to stay terrified when you're a time traveller. When you've died in the snow a thousand times already.

My legs seemed to be multiplying and fanning out, making them look like a denim spider. When I finally made it to the entranceway of my home, I threw myself at the door. It took several minutes of fumbling to get the house keys out of my pocket and even longer to find the endlessly shifting lock whilst leaning heavily on the door frame. The door opened and I fell down onto the stone floor of the corridor.

The streams of time were rushing around me. I could see Elizabet, Prague, Cachtice. Perhaps it was just the drug, but I couldn't work out whose memories were whose anymore or what sequence they ran in. I crawled along the floor and made it to the inner door, finally managing to open that too.

Just one more landscape, I thought to myself. *Just make it to your bed.*

Of course, it wasn't necessary. I was safe. But I needed to do it, to assert that I could defeat not just the drug and the strange, jealous and rageful professor that had gone to such lengths to bring me down, but the version of time itself that I had been living. I would not give into the shadow of death that perpetually hung about me, unwilling to be shaken off in all its permutations. Nor would I run from it. I would sail right into the centre of its eye.

I started to climb up the stairs on my hands and knees like it was the last mountain of my life. When I looked up, I saw the carpet had become covered in snow and instead of running from it to find a warmer place, to be away from the imaginary of the child who lay bleeding in the cold on account of the violence of our species, the child who was me in all the sideways versions of the events of my life that I lived *over and over again* in different permutations, I climbed towards it. I let out silent cries as the drug had left me out of possession of my own tongue.

Now all the parts of my body were shutting down one by one. I only had strength in my arms left, and even that was beginning to fade. I could feel the freezing snow on me, touching my skin and settling inside my hair like those little blinking lights I had seen in the office. Still, I kept climbing. I remembered what Janus had said, that the heart is like a black hole that absorbs everything, even the planets, which couldn't match its ability to expand out beyond thought.

And I made it to my bed upstairs. The snow disappeared and the plain beige carpet returned. I lifted myself up and fell, flat faced, down onto the mattress. I didn't wake up for thirty hours.

The following week, I had a meeting with him. He asked why I looked so pale, so drab and less my exuberant self and if it had been something to do with the Christmas party, or was I just depressed, a slow smile breaking over his face in case I didn't understand his meaning. *You can't even get drugged properly. What more do I have to do?* I stared at him, willing myself not to break his neck with my bare hands. But I couldn't accuse him.

Nobody had seen anything. That was the price of my escape. It would be hearsay.

So unfortunate you went through that. You should have said something. Are you sure you just didn't have too much to drink, my dear?

He continued smiling sweetly at me under the blinking fairy lights. "You still don't seem to understand how power works, my dear. You're just not getting it. How can you not be getting it?"

But in that moment, something occurred to the time traveller in me that made me genuinely laugh out loud. He had. He had taught me that lesson. *Over and over*. But not in the way he'd intended. I was powerful beyond his imagining. Through him, I had faced my eternal return to the moment of my death, this time as an adult, as a time traveller, as an ancient. And I had *survived it all*. All the tiny moments where I died inside a little more, the moments that time returned me over and over, until I had found another person to share time with. *A timewalker and a dreamwalker*. A friend. A teacher who had taught me to slow down time's violent erasures and enter into the spinning source of all our atomic whispers.

Elizabet also knew this kind of survival. She had written about it, towards the end of her life, in a little notebook of letters addressed to the Emperor, the pages of which she furtively sent rolled up inside accounts and registers and other such everyday things. It was her secret too. And so, consequently, it was also mine. Now it was my turn to do the same. To write her out of her prison, just as she would write me. Her book would never see the light of day. The letters would be destroyed before they could circulate, affecting new trajectories in the world. But we would change each other through our writings, in all the tiny and unnoticed parts of a life. And it would be enough to bring down our worlds and displace us both, finally, into the *elsewhere*.

Chapter Twelve

What a voice she had! Each time she slid from one note to the next, I could feel my body vibrate, as if my bones, my skin, my blood, was the sympathetic instrument that she played alongside her own. She'd come to stay here with the Emperor's niece, Maria-Christina. Beata was German by birth but had moved with Rudolph's court across Europe since she'd first been brought to sing for him as a child. It was rumoured he had lent her to the Sultan for a while and that the Sultan had immediately offered a small fortune for her, threatening to send back her head alone, if Rudolph refused. But I knew the power of stories by now, and whilst it may well have been true, it might also have not been quite as legend made it out. Nonetheless, it added to her mystique, and Beata was nothing if not mysterious.

Maria-Christina, on the other hand, was not. At first, I wondered if her childlike foolishness wasn't all an act, but after some time spent in her company, I realised that this was genuinely who she was. Some part of her simply hadn't grown up, and there were moments when I found myself not in the presence of the new regent of Erdely, but a girl who was no more than ten or eleven years old in her mind. Maria-Christina giggled and then cried with both amazing swiftness and predictable regularity across every conversation we had. To say she would be a marionette of her uncle, the Emperor, was an understatement, and I began to think that this would actually be how Rudolph would break the country. Erdely would fall to even more chaos if she were its official protector. Of course, he would appoint advisors, generals and spiritual officials to conduct the necessary affairs on Maria's behalf, but I could imagine that, even so, she would bring the same kind of destruction a toddler might bring to a room if left for a moment unsupervised.

But she was nothing if not sweet, and God knows we needed some sweetness at Sarvar. We had all grown too old here. We were ghosts of our original selves.

"Show me the press!" Maria-Christina begged, throwing herself at me.

"Give me a hug, sister! I like your strong arms. Don't hold back!"

Sometimes, she would put her hands over her ears and stand by the wall.

"There's too much sound in this hall! Bring Beata and ask her to sing over it whilst I keep my eyes shut, please. Oh please!"

I followed her every command to the letter. Not because she was a Hapsburg, but because she was oddly sincere and had such difficulty being in the world –even more than I did. I kept my eye on Maria-Christina out of concern for her fragile well-being. But I kept my eye also on Beata. Beata was trouble. It didn't take any special perception to realise it. She made the shape of every room she entered glow with her presence simply because she occupied no discernible shape of her own. I wondered if this was something that had begun in the womb. Her magical otherness was so angelic, so unlike the raw, meaty beauty of Hungary, that I could imagine she had not been born but had sprouted from some flat, painterly landscape hung on a palace wall. She invited fantasies. And she extracted a price for each one.

Dorothea was constantly furious with Beata, fixing all her vivid shrewishness on her, even rolling her eyes when she sang, which I was still incapable of doing no matter how uneasy I felt about her. Beata's eyes, by contrast, were everywhere. I could see her keeping mental notes on everything she saw.

"You've met your match," I said once to Dorothea, who had started to complain about 'this Hapsburg' at every opportunity.

Dorothea stared at me, the corners of her mouth souring down.

"In a way, she cancels you out, doesn't she? Do two spies cancel each other out if they're on opposite sides?"

"Does the Count know she's staying in his home?" was her response.

"I am the Count here, Dorothea. I am a Nadasdy."

"You are a Bathory, madam."

I could feel the war that had been paused since the day John left heating up again, but I was too tired out from the last stages of my pregnancy.

"Dorothea, what's the secret of all this animosity towards me?"

She paused. Then she looked at me dead straight in the eye. I could feel gravity unexpectedly change in the room. Everything became heavier, as if her stare had increased the pressure of the very stones that held us up high above ground.

"I am a Szekely." She said it proudly, as if announcing herself a witch at the foot of the stake, spitting in the eye of Calvin's god himself.

"What does that mean, Dorothea?"

"It means everything."

"No riddles. Just tell me plainly."

"You Hungarians have no idea. You walk about *on our land* like demigods. It's *our* land that you've stolen. You've made yourselves godly on the backs of our people. Then you sit there and say to me 'what does it mean?' and 'speak to me plainly'! Erdely is *ours*. I was born a countess myself once. Not like you. No, not like you at all. We have different ways. I see you, my lady. I see that you are, in your own way, trying to do the right thing."

She turned away, speaking to the wall as if looking at me would bring too many mixed emotions into play.

"It was your uncle who taught us to believe that land and birth were somehow mixed up together. Before the Bathorys, we lived as one community. *Bathorys* taught us to hate each other. Bathorys taught us that our lands were worth nothing. Bathorys made us poor, made us slaves, made us beg for the right to fight Bathory wars. And for what? Nadasdy has given us more money than any Hungarian to rebuild our lives – but even Nadasdy, he has a price to extract from us, doesn't he?"

She turned back to look at me.

"You know what I'm talking about, Countess! His price is the blood of our Szekely daughters. I ask you – Countess," and she practically spat the word, "was it truly worse at Mohacs? I still see blood every day. Was it all worth it?"

My eyes were wet, but I still kept her gaze.

"No, Dorothea. None of it is worth it. None of it is worth it."

The violence between us softened. It was as if the space between us, though not we ourselves, became something different – a level playing field across which we might meet as women together, away from the violence of nations.

"Don't you realise, Countess, that you've brought a Hapsburg spy into Nadasdy's house! We will all be dead soon."

"I'm keeping her close. Count Basta has already tried for my blood. And Thurzo, he isn't far behind."

Dorothea wrung her hands and paced.

"We might feed the singing Hapsburg little then."

"Little of what, Dorothea?"

She suddenly slumped her shoulders down and sighed, signalling that for a time she would speak to me without artifice.

"Didn't you know?" It was more a confession than a question. "John has started to print our book – our new Szekely religion. He's taken copies to Erdely. I smuggled him out through the tunnels below Cachtice."

"There are tunnels below Cachtice?" I was amazed.

"You know nothing, Countess. You've been so preoccupied with your lover and your strange wanderings about in the day and the night, with your books and your own little world. We are at the end of days. We are ready. Our sun and our moon will fly back over Erdely. Otherwise, we'll die. Small price to pay! We're already dead inside. This slavery must end. It must end!"

My breath caught in my chest.

"It was you! All along, it was you. You engraved my wedding ring. You found it in the snow and put it under my pillow. You're the mystery behind the sun and the moon."

Dorothea smiled.

"Not just I, madam. Everyone you see here at Cachtice. Even Anna is one of us."

"Anna? But she's from the south!"

Dorothea shook her head slowly from side to side. "Anna fled to the south when she was a child. She was put inside a coffin with a hammer and knife when she could barely hold either. Her father gave instruction to our allies hiding out there, but they had already been killed – burnt at the stake for practising the faith of our spiritual leader, Michael Servetus. She broke her way out of the coffin – it was said to contain plague. And she was reborn a southerner. But she found her way back to us after a lifetime. Anna is a Szekely. But she's more forgiving of you than I. She believes you have come to save us. She engraved the mystery into your ring so that you would find us. She says you wouldn't understand our story unless it was presented as a puzzle. And now here you are." She snorted. "But you're just a countess. What would you do for us? Nadasdy does more," she shook her head in disgust, "so we look the other way."

Underneath my own nose, all this time, a revolution had been brewing in the walls of Cachtice. A revolution that was now so full that it was spilling out over the sides. Dorothea was right. I had been so preoccupied with staying alive, and then with my press and my own inner world, that my eye had inadvertently slipped from the world around me. I would focus it back.

"No, Dorothea. Nadasdy won't harm another woman again. You have my word."

"The word of a Bathory!"

I eyed her and raised my chin slowly. "The word of *this* Bathory."

There was a moment of something different across Dorothea's face, a crack in the grey of her eternal sky.

"Will you get me a copy of the book, Dorothea? Leave it under my pillow tonight. I want to read more of this Servetus. You're under my charge, you all are. Szekelys, Hungarians, even Turks. If you're under my roof, you have my protection."

Dorothea's mouth went slack. She stared at me for a long while. Then she simply curtseyed and left the room. Later that night, when I retired, as requested, the book was there, and I trembled a little before opening it. Here it was and I knew what it spelled. The beginning. And the end.

*

The heart is a complex thing. It teaches us to love, to hate, to start wars. It teaches us to want things, things we might not want to want. Or perhaps it's the other way around – and it is the world that teaches the heart how to shape desire into a thing worth pursuing. Servetus' book was a plain mini-octavo, a tiny thing that could be easily spirited away into a pocket or under a sleeve. My printer's eye immediately recognised that this fact alone gave it the kind of revolutionary status everybody seemed to believe it deserved. If you wanted to possess something truly subversive, you didn't show it off, and you certainly didn't want it to be heavy, cumbersome, or overly beautiful. I smiled to myself. John would have found that hard – to print something so slyly ordinary. He was so in love with ink that the book that held it had to be nothing short of a work of art, its spine wrapped in gold, unaware of the meanings its lettering carried.

If a book is like a body, filled with stories, then Servetus' story carried something so extraordinary inside it that I actually gasped out loud. It was well into the dead time of night. Even the owls had stopped their eerie songs, giving the wind full rein to clear its otherworldly throat and take full possession the dark. Three-quarters of the way through the *Christianismi Restitutio* was a sudden and unexpected description of the workings of the heart.

Servetus had spent many years in a second identity, that of a humble doctor. He had rolled up his sleeves and healed the sick – rich or poor, Christian, Ottoman or Jew. He had studied the subtle movements of the humours. He had turned his gaze from the soul to the body and therein found that the organ of the heart functions not unlike the soul – it cleans the blood through breath. The lungs were the doorway through which the heart did the work of purification. Servetus had opened a body – a human one – and he had seen it.

I knew that the Mohammadan scholars had already seen this too. I had marvelled at Janus' stories about the body, its sinews and organs, each a tiny universe unto itself, connected together in magical ways, through tunnels, and tissues that pulsed. Stories that came from deep within the Muslim world. But to read it here, in the central node of a book that discussed not anatomy but the right of any human to discover that God resided within the revolutions of their very own hearts, was nothing short of a revelation. If God resided within and we undertook to do with

Him what the heart did for our blood, then we wouldn't need Catholic indulgences. We wouldn't need a priest to interpret for us the work of a Bible written only for well-versed scholars. We wouldn't be enslaved by a religion that resided either in Rome or in a palace in Prague. And that's why I gasped out loud in the dark. This book spelled out the end of the Holy Roman Empire itself if it was practised. No wonder they burned him. No wonder they destroyed every last copy of this book. Or so they thought.

I sat back in my bed, leaning my head against the ornate wood of the headboard. Its hard fibres and grains met the back of my skull through the rich, soft curls of my hair. This was once a tree, I thought. *A dead tree that's become no more than a relic standing at the forefront of all my nighttimes. What ghosts speak through its veins whilst I sleep? What incantations does it mutter in its atomic tongues?* The bed had been a wedding gift from some minor German lord at Rudolph's court. I turned around to inspect it, holding the candle I used to read by, hoping I didn't burn myself to a wisp in the process.

In the swirls and ornamental flourishes of the design, I searched out Nadasdy's crest, and when the candle illuminated it, in the dark shadows, I cursed Rudolph then and there. If Nadasdy's soul – if his subtle heart – had always contained an irreconcilable wound in it, then the Emperor had found it out early and pressed it until it had bruised his whole being. I'd glimpsed *Francis Nadasdy* in the corridor before he'd left, the man who had kissed me and winked at me before disappearing like a stain of ink into Rudolph's invention – the *Black Bey*; Tormentor of Ottomans. I put my index finger inside Servetus' book to mark the page I was on, and the candle back on the stand. I turned around to face the open doorway of my bedroom. Which man would return through it? Francis, or the Black Bey?

Chapter Thirteen

I heard the sound of Nadasdy's horses, wounded men and clanging armour like footsteps in my heart. The door to Cachtice opened and let him in. I had insisted on returning from Sarvar as soon as it was safe to after I had given birth, and Maria-Christina and Beata had, in turn, insisted on joining me, making it painfully obvious that they had been sent to keep a watchful eye on my every move. Consequently, Cachtice was awash with servants and visitors. I, on the other hand, spent most of the hours alone in my tower, looking into the face of my son. He was the most otherworldly being I'd ever encountered.

When Anastasia had been born, I had felt a kind of complicity with her. Her little hands like miniature versions of my own. But with my son, it was different. I imagined that he'd crawled down from inside one of Cachtice's tapestries and into my life, bringing all the softness of wool with him. His eyes blinked and squinted up at me and I watched as he went from seeing the world as a ball of moving lights to being able to recognise the outline of his mother. He often grasped my long fingers with his entire hand and squeezed, and it was at the same time for me the most real and unreal sensation. Although there was no trace of Nadasdy in him, he reminded me so much in this moment of our daughter.

The door at the foot of my tower was flung open. I heard heavy feet walking slowly and purposefully up the spiralling steps. Eventually, after what felt like an eternity, the door to the room opened and Nadasdy entered. His face was darkened from months of living in blood and mud, and it would take a good week of washing to restore it to its usual ivory glow. I instinctively held my son closer to me, staring intently at Nadasdy to see who he was today.

"Elizabet." He greeted me flatly.

I nodded at him.

He stood at the foot of the bed for a few heartbeats before prowling, like a slow, wild animal, around the bed and to my left side. His eyes were blank and each footstep he took sent a rattle of light armour through the room. He sat on the bed and looked at my child for a while. Then he looked at me. His eyes became less vacant with each passing second. I think he could smell my fear. So could the baby. He woke and immediately started howling. I put him instantly to my breast to quieten him. Nadasdy's jaw hardened into a sharp angle. He looked like a furious angel, strong as marble.

"Please," was all I said. Nadasdy had heard the word 'please' too often, I thought. I didn't ask it to remind him, nor to avenge the violence that had taken place in this, my very own, castle. I simply said it in the hope that he might see new life flowing under our roof, rather than pain and death. He took one glove off and extended his hand, brushing the length of my face with his finger and pushing a stray curl behind my ear. He seemed unable to touch the baby, who had stopped his eager sucking and now squinted up at me again.

"I don't know how to do this, Elizabet," said Nadasdy. He

put his finger on the baby's head, then, after a moment pulled it away.

He adjusted himself on the bed and looked blankly around, uncertain for a moment of where he was. When his eyes returned to me, he seemed as if he'd gone all the way to the battlefield and back in the few seconds his gaze had wandered.

"I fought alongside him this time. Thurzo, I mean. I think I might have even saved his life. Basta kept cawing at me like a cockerel."

He suddenly smiled to himself. "I avenged that, after the war," and he took my hand and mimicked pushing an imaginary dagger into its back. "The left hand, of course, my dear. He can still fight."

He immediately became uncomfortable with this action and wiped his face with his hands as if attempting to set himself right.

"As soon as we won against Michael the Brave," and he stressed the epithet with unexpected reverence, "Michael sued for peace and joined us against the Tartars. He was a good fighter. Clever too. Then later, in Michael's tent, Basta took his sword from where it lay in its sheath and cut his heels. He tried to run. Basta simply walked out after him and chopped him down. 'Sweet revenge for Erdely' is what he called it. Later, he informed the men that he had killed Michael when he caught him fleeing from the field. After we won and sent the Tartars back, we celebrated. Basta was eating meat off the bone like an animal, drinking and jesting with Thurzo, and I took the knife on the table and pinned his hand to the wood with it. 'Now who's the cuckold?' I said to him. 'You can't even keep your own hand away from me.' He screamed, like a piglet. But he left me alone after that."

Nadasdy sighed, as if releasing all the memories of the past couple of months in one go.

"It's a cowardly way to kill a man. I had no love for Michael, but in truth he did fight bravely. Perhaps Erdely would have been better off with him in it. We'll never know now."

"Francis…"

"Just – let me sit here with you… both of you."

He looked back at the baby and steadied his breathing. Then my son reached out and grabbed his finger with all of his. Nadasdy froze. I couldn't imagine what was going through his mind. He looked right at me and smiled, and a few silent tears of guilt and relief slid down my face. Nadasdy leant forward, careful of his armour, and kissed them, even as they dripped away.

"I want to be your husband, if you'll have me."

"I will."

"We'll have to think carefully about the baby. This could get very complicated."

I nodded.

"What do you call him?"

"I haven't yet."

"I think we should call him Michael. It seems fitting to me. I want to honour him."

And so Nadasdy named him. Michael outlived all of us – all our children; Anastasia and our other son, Paul, who would come to us later. In time, we would hide Michael away under the shroud of a different family, a different castle, far, far from Thurzo and Basta and Rudolph's reach. And for that reason alone, Michael would survive us all.

*

"Concentrate, Vera." Lucretia seemed agitated this morning, but she wouldn't say why.

I puffed my cheeks and exhaled so sharply that the tip of my nose went cold. We had practised the deep listening so often. The moments time had thrown me to places and events without

Lucretia, I practised it all the same. Slowing down time with my breathing, listening to the movements that crowded around inside the words people spoke, the way trees and birds moved in the sky, and the great and godlike turn of the earth beneath my feet.

Now whenever I read about Bathory, I read with my ears open. I listened to the spaces between the words, to the shake and buzz of the atoms that made up the paper and the ink. *Here, now,* Lucretia was beside me and getting just a little exasperated.

"Write to listen. Write it again. And really listen to the way you tell it."

I picked up my pencil, put it down, picked it up, put it down. But I was losing confidence with each attempt. Was it really possible to rewrite *any* story, let alone your own origin story? If time were a cosmic pencil that wrote us all into being, what would flow out of its carbon filings when it came to mine, mixing with the air and the blood inside my skin?

I shifted in my chair, downed half a glass of the red wine Lucretia had poured for us both and pulled out a copy of *The Blood Countess: The Life and Times of Elizabeth Bathory* from my bag.

"I don't know, 'Cretia. I just..." and I fanned my hands out. Don't know how to do this."

I flipped my finger and thumb along the white pages.

She stood up, paced about and then to my surprise took an entirely different approach.

"What do you remember about your death?"

"Not much." I blinked away the images that threatened to come in.

"Maybe that's the problem." She looked like she'd suddenly had an idea. It was like watching a giant black bird of prey swoop down on something hidden to everyone but her on the ground.

"Let me try something."

She lay on the floor next to me, slowing her breathing, and

then slowly lifted her palm to mine. I realised what she was trying to do and met her hand with my own.

For a few moments, she lay there, her breathing becoming slower and slower. I heard her heartbeat; its rhythm was quiet and long. And soon she was fast asleep. Time came for me not long after, as if it were in league with her, willing us to enact this strange kind of spell together. When it started to erase and redraw the world around me, it brought her with me. I could still feel her hand on mine, but it had become strangely ghostly, like the way a dream feels just before waking, only half real. I could hear Lucretia's voice: *Tell me, Vera, about the first time you died. Show it to me.*

Time responds. It brings us here, to the same place my death occurred. *Baby steps,* I think to myself. I can feel the moisture on my hair turning to tiny icicles across my scalp. The sensations drag and edge, but I remain staunchly upright. The wind has now taken one of my long curls, which has escaped the tight plaits that lie on either side of my head, and is pulling it about like a puppet string, trying ineptly to animate me according to its changing desires.

To begin with, I'd loved this strange landscape, littered with tower blocks and half-finished playgrounds that pushed their way up through the deep Nordic snows. I imagined the stories written into the land, stories of kings and long boats, of bearded men with axes thrashing their way across the sea in defiance of God, navigating via the stars. It captured my eight-year-old imagination. I had read about it on the back of a pamphlet entitled *Welcome to Stockholm!* – the one my mother had put in my growing hands before we'd arrived with nothing more than a suitcase between us to stay with family.

"It's complicated," was all she said whenever I asked why we were here. "We're here to stay with the family." She'd kept a few of the really expensive clothes and wore them proudly as we walked through the rough streets towards the apartment blocks where they housed the refugees who had come pouring into Sweden during the eighties to escape the war. When we'd first arrived, *everybody* stared at her designer sunglasses and at the way she carried herself in that fabulous coat.

Sure enough, it's not long before the passers-by spit and call me an animal. An old blue-eyed man looks at me and runs his fingers across his own throat in a slicing motion. He enjoys the sensation. He gives himself to it entirely. He wants me to get it, to feel all the harm behind it, even though I'm only eight years old. Time has brought me here so many times, but at the edge of my awareness *here, now,* I can feel Lucretia with me, watching everything around us in her dream. She gasps. But she doesn't wake up. She stays with me every step of the way.

The trees lining the way are tattooed in handmade posters with strange symbols littered over them, their black-lined waving arms spinning towards my sight like broken windmills hobbled at the elbow, whipping up the air to push me back to where I came from. Which side of the community you're on here is made clear by these hand-drawn swastikas. Everybody has a purpose and a position. The story's momentum has been written. If there are hunters then there must be an animal to hunt, something less than human, something other hiding right there, in plain sight, waiting to be captured. Until you've experienced true and murderous racism, it feels like fiction. In the moment of experience, you can move in seconds from the warm, gnawing hole of sorrow to the freezing tremors of *just surviving*. The internal landscape is never the same again.

Whiteness. The whiteness of snow. The whiteness of the sky in winter. The whiteness of the blanket I hid under to blot out the world in its winding terrors. The whiteness of my own skin growing lighter and lighter in the years after I first met my Angel of Death, as if, as part of the contract of staying alive, my colours burrowed deep, hiding my mixed geographies in my fleshy marrow, as far away from the surfaces of skin as possible. I am white enough, but with each passing day I become whiter and whiter – just in case I'm caught out and return to the moment the young man with those heavy boots tries to erase me from the face of the earth.

Lucretia watches as I abandon the snowman I'm making, waving at the oncoming stranger. She watches as he pulls me back and forth, throwing me to the ground. She watches as I make a run for it and find myself almost at the mouth of the huge metal door to the tower block that houses the refugees – my grandmother, my aunt and now my mother, a refugee from her marriage. Lucretia watches as he puts my head in the door and whacks once, twice. She watches as I escape back to the snow. She watches as he finds me there and stamps *over and over* again; head, face, sides. His boots aiming to crush me into snow itself as the sun slides to hide inside a pure and inevitable nighttime. She comes over to me when he goes. Her dreaming mind is wildly alive as I start to drift towards death. Her face is covered with tears. She pulls out a pen and puts its ghostly form in my dreaming hand.

Time lifts me away. It brings me straight back to her, to her colourful living room. But it's nearly two years later for her. She must have woken up from her dreamwalking to find me removed. Gone until God knows when in linear time. When I emerge fully, I can smell hot chocolate instead of wine and cigarettes. Her hair is a little greyer, but only with a couple of years' worth of that perfect seal-song colour.

"Here, have some of this." She hands me her warm chocolatey drink, a little ruffled at my sudden arrival on her sofa but not entirely shocked.

"What year is it?" I ask.

"2021."

"I've just come from the moment you *dreamwalked* with me to the moment of my death."

She pats my hand. It's full of sympathy.

"Good. Didn't I leave you something? I remember leaving you something. A pen?"

"Yes." I can feel it sharp in my shirt's breast pocket. I pull it out.

"Good. Let's write."

I smile. "If my memory serves me, I think there should be the perfect thing to write on somewhere on your bookshelf." I start searching for something specific. It's my own book, the one that will have come out by now, all on the history of Bathory. The one that will cause me so much trouble. I flip through the pages to the part where I'd already written about the deep snows outside Bathory's castle. About the wolves. About the women disappearing out of history violently at the hands of Francis Nadasdy.

Here, now, Lucretia and I write together. We write in the margins of the book, all around the printed text. At one point, when I pause to take a breath, my eyes blur and the texts seem to fold into each other until they become one great story, the same story told over and over again in different permutations: a woman disappearing from out of the world, over and over, through the cruelty of history. Disappearing from out of history itself. Only now, instead of following the line of time, I wind Bathory's story through mine. I wind it back to the final red mark I made with my body before time came unstuck.

The words flow from beyond me, from a place inside the spine of time – my time; our time. And it carries on flowing, *backwards, winding backwards*! It doesn't erase anything. It doesn't make all the things that once happened disappear as it reverses its usual flow. Instead, as it winds back, new things emerge, hidden things that bring a new voice from out of the shadow of events. A voice emerging from all the other voices that had looped around again and again in the same old pattern without respite. And I copy what I hear it say:

The blood on the snow turns from red to white. Each tiny flake is moving in reverse. Instead of the snow melting away in the bright sun, it's the heavy colour itself that disappears until it's only the sun that glistens on the white fields and not the hot, wet blood of a young girl. I put my hand to my mouth. My teeth are still in place. The tracks leading away from me walk themselves whole again, leaving no crunching trace of a murderous other. The back of my head no longer throbs. The tiles in the hallway of the white apartment block need no fervent cleaning from more spilled blood. The spirit of the girl hasn't fled upwards. It doesn't hover above the long white pathway that marks the parting of her black hair. It doesn't meet an Angel, nor glimpse the unfolding life of Bathory before even a word has been read. No one has shouted "Raus, Muslim." No heavily ringed fists or boots have made their way to my flesh. The pictures of swastikas drawn in stiff black lines in marker pen on white pages festooning the street do not flutter under their staples on the surrounding trees.

I blink. Under the sunlight, a teenager runs towards me. I think he wants to build a snowman with me. And he does! No more than that. No violence or murder fall across the field. We're simply two children playing together in a new imaginary of time. Not a hunter and hunted, locked in a story much larger than either of us. We roll the crisp white snow into a large ball. Then we roll another one together, a smaller one. He laughs at me as I'm too small myself to lift it up alone. We dig our fingers in to make a smiling face. He finds two small pebbles by digging deep into the snow, and neither get aimed or thrown at me. Instead, they become the small black eyes of our silent third; our laughing snowman that knows no harm. They see deep into a new future, a new meaning of the word 'snow' in all its felt sensations. The teenager laughs. The sun starts to set. He waves his hand at me and then walks off.

We never speak the same language, and yet, we've just rewritten a tiny portion of the world, a tiny moment that will never be the same again and so will imperceptibly change the world minute to minute. I see my Angel of Death in my mind's eye. *The her that is me across time. She smiles. The smile lasts lifetimes.* Now when I say the word 'snow', I really mean another word. Now the sparkling white material carries a new definition inside its playful symmetries. I haven't erased all the definitions of snow or all the marks it has made or ever will make. Snow can still murder. I've just added a new one here, now: Life.

*

About a week later, in the middle of the night, I heard a knock on my bedroom door. Nadasdy had disappeared again for a while. No one was sure where he'd gone. Anna assured me that he had not asked for any women, nor informed her of his plans. Anna had taken Michael with her and the nursemaid to give me a chance at some uninterrupted sleep. At first, I thought that something had happened to my son, and I rushed to open the door. But standing there instead was Nadasdy. He had a fistful of bright wildflowers in his hand, and he looked so very embarrassed.

"For you."

I took them from him appreciatively, laying their vibrant stalks on the nightstand and lighting more candles, until the room glowed yellow and gold. He didn't move from the doorway.

"Come in," I assured. He stepped inside hesitantly, as if he might have burnt to cinders had I not issued an invitation. He sat down on the bed, steadying himself by placing his arms firmly behind him, sinking his fists into the mattress. He looked down and waited, more tense and afraid than I had ever seen him. I climbed onto the bed next to him, my legs curled beneath me, and placed my hand on his chest, right above where his heart lay. He breathed deeply and looked right into me. I ran my fingers down the back of his neck and halfway along the length of his spine before circling back up his chest and over the gentle grooves that lay at the base of his throat. He smiled and laughed rather bashfully, his grey eyes turning pale green in the amber light.

"I don't know you like this, Elizabet."

"Nor do I."

He bit his lip and then, without looking at me, said, "I think you should do that again."

I explored with my fingers, touching him so very lightly until I could feel his skin responding in different ways, going cold in places and then warm, softening and then straightening at my touch, a wild mix of temperatures and contours. I unlaced his shirt slowly and he removed it from his body. I stroked his ivory skin with the backs of my fingers. I listened closely and I could hear the blood whirling inside him, erratic, allowing me to map which parts of his chest, his shoulders, his back were more sensitive, which parts shuddered expectantly as I encountered them, and which parts didn't. I varied the direction, intensity and pressure of my touch and soon came to understand where he was arid and where he already pulsed with lively desires.

He had a large cold scar that ran like a ribbon along his shoulder blades, marking the ghost of where a weapon had sought his death. I kissed the length of it, my lips and tongue working across the discolouration. He pulled me back towards him.

"Don't do that."

He reached into my hair and held my head in his hands – hands that grew warmer the longer he held me in them, as if life and touch were somehow entirely intertwined.

"You can't make it better. I don't want you to make it better."

I met his intense gaze and could feel my own desire coursing through me. I had never taken the time to realise just how beautiful he was. Looking at him now, I could see that he was utterly *breathtaking*.

"I want you to want me as I am."

"I do," I responded, surprised at how I could have lived with a man for so long and never really have seen him.

"You're being kind, Elizabet."

"No, I'm not."

His lips were plush and brooding and all I wanted in that moment was to feel them with my own and then with every part of my body.

"I will never hurt you, or any other woman. I want you, Elizabet, and you alone. Always."

He looked down and smiled again, all shy once more.

"I just might need a bit of practice first."

*

Beata was midway through her song. She had amassed quite a following in the castle. Even the servants lingered longer than usual in the dining hall when she animated it. Dorothea had whispered that I might want to receive a note from John that had just now come into her possession from Erdely. I stood and moved to the back of the hall, whereupon she passed the yellowish piece of paper to me. It was then I became aware of how closely Beata was watching me, even as she sang so expressively and with such seeming absorption. The note simply said, *Returning for supplies, J*, in fine calligraphic writing. I spirited it into a discreet pocket that lay in the thick folds of my dress and continued to listen.

Not long after, Nadasdy came into the hall and moved quietly to stand behind me. He surreptitiously took my hand, placed it softly behind my back and began gently rolling his thumb around my palm. The touch was so intimate that I must have blushed because Beata stared even more strongly then. This time, a flash of disquiet illuminated her girlish face. It was as quick as a sudden gust of wind, loosening blossoms from a branch. It signalled the coming of some kind of unwanted autumn. Perhaps Beata, young as she was, was wise enough to know that the arrival of love, even the smallest shiver of it in a land such as ours, could wipe out the Emperor's best-laid plans. Love was not a factor in the Empire. Love was dangerous. And Nadasdy should not have been afforded it – especially not him. Nadasdy was a sword that the Emperor pointed eastwards. And a sword does not love. A sword *cannot* love.

*

Nadasdy and I sat on the terrace overlooking the rough and beautiful contours of Hungary. He was drinking wine and I, sweet tea. Michael lay in an ornate cradle and was kicking his feet, engaged in some crazy horse ride across sheer slopes and winding pathways inside his blankets. A moth flew from the side of the cradle and onto my dress, eager and hungry for its warm array of fabrics. Nadasdy reached forward to brush it from me.

"No, let it be. We have an affinity, moths and I."

He sat back and smiled before snorting, not ill-intentionally, at me.

"Now moths as well? Is there anyone you don't take under your wing, my beloved?"

I blinked for a moment. This was the same man who had plunged a burning sword into a blacksmith's mouth. This was the same man who ordered the death of the Fabbris. It was the same man who had started to visit me with increasing frequency and passion at night, even in the day. It was the same man who had asked me urgently one night in the darkness whether I could help him devise a way to quit the field. There were so many Nadasdys, but I could sense that even he was now tired and desperate to unite them.

"Because moths understand forgiveness, my dear," I responded. "They understand that you need to burn away everything you know, everything marked into your body before such an act can really happen. Everything else is just vanity and nonsense."

He went shadowy for a moment.

"Francis, you have to forgive yourself, and the only way, I fear, you might do that is to make amends with the Szekelys. It won't bring a single woman back or restore them from whatever you did when you were prisoner of your own devil, but it's a start."

He looked angry for a moment, staring at me with rage, then took a deep breath, bowed his head and submerged himself in some thought or another. When he looked up, he was calm.

"I beat the devil out every day, Elizabet. What more can I do?"

"The devil *is* you, Francis. The devil was you then. Instead of beating some part of yourself, why don't you just start doing some good for those you've wronged?" I was getting exasperated with how self-centred he was, as if his eye was turning further inward, which would only result in him exiling himself from his own actions.

"You're not my mother, Elizabet."

"And you're not a child on the field anymore."

"No." He sat back and seemed to consider this for a long while.

"I can't go back. They'll come calling for me soon enough." He sighed and covered his eyes with his hand.

"Francis, tell me something. What is it to wage war? I've defended my life before…" He looked up sharply and I suddenly regretted my loose tongue. "…in a way, and I understand what it is to fight for your life. But to wage a war, to agree in some strange covenant to play out the desires of emperors, what is it that you must need to do to yourself, to your soul? I remember when I was a child, a thief had stolen from my father's castle. He was caught by the guards. They took the thief and bound him, then they cut open a horse's belly just enough to sew the man inside, his head protruding from out of it. Then the horse went mad and eventually both died in the square. I'm not sure I've ever recovered, Francis. My soul carries some kind of horror in it, a terror of kings and lords and the laws they make. To do what you've done and to be even capable of love," and I took his hand in mine and held it to my cheek, "surely that is some sign of an angel, not a devil animating you. Instead of beating out the devil daily and nightly, why not approach the angel that lives inside you? That's all I'm suggesting."

He fell into a silence outwardly, but internally something was humming, within him. It sounded like a mixture of revelation, excitement and rage all mixed up together in the course of his blood.

"I have done..." and he stretched each word until it became sonorous, "...*much* to forgive you, Elizabet." He glanced down at Michael to make sure I didn't miss his point.

"When you were sleeping with *him* right under my nose, did you stop to think what was animating *you*?"

I looked him dead in the eye. I could scarcely believe my ears, that he could be so utterly consumed with himself that he might mistake the murder of a woman for the same crime as infidelity within a loveless marriage. He saw my disbelief and began to blink a little, as if shaking off the memories from the edges of his lengthy lashes.

"It's not *at all* comparable, Francis. But yes. I have."

"Well?"

It was said half broodily, half disingenuously, like he was trying to inhabit his masculinity in a way that even he didn't believe in anymore.

"Terror. Isolation. Loneliness. Unmet desire. Naivety." I counted each one out on my fingers. "Is that good enough reason? Maybe not."

I paused and looked out over the horizon. "I'll pay for it. I know I will. We will both, but I'll bear the brunt of it. I fell into his hands like one of my little moths begging to be burnt. He and Basta have already done terrible things to me, Francis. And there's something in me, some part of me that knows that this is the smallest of deeds. There are others yet to come. I might have forced another man's son on you, but I've taken his away from him. Worse still, I've taken his ambitions, his truer desires for me, away – to be his wife, and eventually the cause of his happy widowhood. I would be in the grave and my fortunes in his pocket, and he would be closer to Rudolph's favour on account of these. I fear it's just a matter of time."

"Don't you think he loved you, even a little?"

I was surprised that this was his preoccupation but quickly remembered that Nadasdy was, in the most unusual and bizarre way, motivated by love – by a desire to find out, at least, what love was, to feel it and live it. To conquer the violence in him with it. I let out a quick and singular laugh. "Ha! Not at all."

"*I* love you. I always will. You," and his countenance changed entirely in a flash, "have ruined my destiny with all your talk of angels and forgiveness." He grabbed my arms and pulled me to his lap.

"My mother's going to *kill* you."

Then he started kissing me as if he didn't care a moment who might see us.

*

Together, we raced down the stone hallway. It had long passed midnight, but I had told Anna in no uncertain terms to let me know the minute John returned to Cachtice through the tunnels. Nadasdy was in my tower with me. He had fallen into a sweet and exhausted sleep, one foot sticking out past the mattress, held up by physics and thin air. With one hand, I lightly stroked his head on my chest, and with the other, I languidly played with a strand of my own hair. I had been laughing to myself that with all this loving my mind was becoming addled, and I'd better start to ration his visits lest I become unable to manage our household, let alone all our vast estates. A slow and quiet knock made its way across the room from the other side of the door, and I jumped up, waking Nadasdy. Anna held Michael in her arms and simply said, "He's back. Dorothea is with him in the grain store."

I kissed Michael on the head and bade Anna care for him a little longer. Nadasdy and I dressed quickly. I had two long, rough, hooded cloaks in one of my ready chests. I flung one at my husband and donned my own. He smiled as he put it on.

"If anyone sees me like this, all the rumours will be confirmed."

"What?" I asked absently, rushing to the door.

"That you've turned me into a woman."

"Don't be ridiculous, Francis. It's better that people raise an eyebrow and no more at two women heading to the storeroom in the cold dead of night than that they see the Black Bey accompanied by his *talto* wife!"

He laughed again, and we ran hand in hand down the winding staircase to hear news of Erdely from John.

At first, I only saw Dorothea. She threw her head over her shoulder when we entered. She appeared to be dragging a sack of flour.

"John?" I asked, concerned.

She motioned to the large, unmoving lump on the floor at her feet, a thing almost indistinguishable from the rough sacks that lay piled up in the corner. She lifted his head gently from out of the burlap that covered his body.

"He just passed out, my lady. He's lost a lot of blood."

"Get some paper from the print room, Dorothea," ordered Nadasdy.

I looked at him in disbelief. He caught my glance and before I could say anything, hastened, "This is *my* terrain, Elizabet. Dorothea, go quickly. And something to light it with."

I knelt down by John. It looked like someone had attended to a large wound that wrapped around his right side like the shadow of an ominous snake that clung to him. It wasn't healing well. Dorothea had brought some water and I used the hem of my dress to clean the wound, the fabric turning instantly into a rosette of cloth and blood.

"That'll need to be cauterised," said Nadasdy, "but it's a cruel way to wake a man." We sat in an alarmed silence until Dorothea came back with a small stack of paper. Nadasdy started tearing it into strips. He indicated for me to hold up John's near lifeless hand. He inserted the strips of paper between each finger.

"Hold his fingers steady and in place." Then he lit the paper. John came to immediately.

"You're home, boy. Now, I need to cauterise this, so drink some wine and breathe deeply." He got up and went over to the small, barely lit fire at the far end of the storehouse. He placed a poker in its centre and waited. He seemed deep in thought.

"John, here," and I held the tankard to his lips. He had the smallest amount.

"My lady," he whispered weakly. "Erdely, it's *amazing*." He was close to passing out again.

"Don't let him fall asleep," came Nadasdy's voice.

"John! Stay with us." I slapped him in the face.

Nadasdy came over. "Ready?"

John nodded. Then he screamed deafeningly, as if trying to wake up the whole of the Holy Roman Empire. I thought he was going to pass out again. But he simply went very quiet and very glassy, his entire countenance turning from solid and human into something translucent and breakable.

I looked at Nadasdy. He inspected the wound and laid a hand on John's forehead. He nodded at me in a way that indicated that John would be fine in time.

"Papa," John said, barely audible as he struggled through the pain that was clearly making him hallucinate. "Don't leave."

He grabbed Nadasdy's hand with unexpected force given his condition.

"It's all right, my boy. Sleep now and heal. I'll stay with you."

He moved down to the floor and made himself as comfortable as he could. "Dorothea, bring me some bread and wine and relight that damned fire. It's too cold. Elizabet, go and attend to Michael, I'll be fine here. Go."

I kissed my husband on the forehead and stroked my fingers across John's. A few hours later, I sneaked back to the cellar to check on both. Nadasdy was asleep next to John. They wound around each other like companion species who know all about animal and human worlds and how mixed up these are. Nadasdy was snoring a little and his chest rose and fell with the depth of his breathing. I noticed that lying upturned in a pyramid like a tiny fairy asleep on his contracting and expanding ribs was a small unremarkable-looking book, John's characteristic gold lettering across its spine, climbing and falling in space.

*

"You were right, madam, they really do curse the Bathory name in Erdely."

We were in the library, a small room at Cachtice that I had dedicated to the running of the business of our printing press. It was filled to the brim with ledgers of accounts, bills and extra copies amassed from the print runs that even now cascaded out of Sarvar. It was also tucked away from all the hustle and bustle that had descended since Maria-Christina and Beata's arrival. At first, Nadasdy had scolded me, telling me to house all things to do with printing at Sarvar and to keep our home separate from it all, but I found having a dedicated space at Cachtice meant I could spend more time here with Michael without losing sight of the business.

John, who was rapidly improving, was stuffing large pieces

of bread into his mouth whilst excitedly recounting stories of his expedition.

"The Jesuits have gained some power again and Servetus' work is being chased out, despite the fact that the Edict of Torda is still in place."

He pointed to his wound, which was healing well.

"A Szekely man who called himself David helped me escape them. He had several friends with him. I think they were in his pay, but I'm not sure. No one gave any names, but one was a soldier, I think from the East, and the other they simply referred to as 'the distributor'. The distributor wanted more copies and was smuggling me back to the border inside a cart filled two layers deep with the dead awaiting burial."

He shuddered a little and then winced, his hand instinctively going to agitate his wound. Nadasdy grabbed it and lay it back on the table.

"I don't really understand what happened," he continued, "but soon I was running. One of the Jesuits' soldiers was after me. David's soldier held the others at bay, howling like a creature of the damned and brandishing a curvy sword. The other soldier managed to cut me, but soon the Ottoman one, the Eastern soldier, came after us and sent him running to the woods with little more than a look. He fell to praying after that. Maybe he didn't really want to kill anyone, but it was still quite a scary thing to watch."

The hairs on the back of my neck and along my arms stood up. Everything in the room slowed down. John's words circled my earlobe before entering into my body, reaching the subtle ear that I imagined lay inside my heart and brought to life the small quiet world, the world that hummed and vibrated with its prescience. I could see Janus standing between John and Basta's soldiers. His dark hair and his thick neck. But he wouldn't turn around and so I couldn't see his face. I couldn't tell if it was really him. I blinked and returned my mind to the table.

"It's odd, my lord. David said they were helping Jews who weren't Jewish and Protestants who were neither Lutheran nor Calvinist. He said that more copies of Servetus' book would be very helpful for them and offered to pay me – us – well. Then he spoke about unity and said that unity, not trinity, was their religion. Does that make sense to you? Because the soldier prayed facing the East, and the Jewish distributor knew the Lord's Prayer like it was his mother's milk. Erdely is madness, my lady, and no one speaks straight, but always in riddles and poetry. Your cousins, Sigismund and Andrew, really *fucked* the place."

"John!" I exclaimed. "You might be my charge, but speak to me like that again and you'll be *very* sorry."

John looked at me and then nodded, still stuffing and swallowing bread and a good deal of air too. Nadasdy eyed him sternly and he soon lost his over-excitement.

"I'm sorry, my lady," he ventured after a rare moment of calm. I reached out my hand and gently pressed it to his, willing his heartbeat to slow just a little with the aid of touch. He had simply seen too much, too young and too often. It had quickened his brilliant mind and made him worldly, but now as a young man, his humours were all in a muddle.

"Accepted. So now that Maria-Christina is Princess Regent, what do they say of Hapsburg rule?"

"The Princess might be regent but Count Basta's the one ruling in the name of the Emperor. He has the Emperor's seal. Oh, and the soldiers, they're not normal soldiers, like the soldiers here. They have long plumes, feathers on their helmets."

"Hadjuks," said Nadasdy. "The Emperor must be desperate as well as out of pocket to sustain an army of them."

"The Szekelys want their land back. There was a moment, they say, when with Michael the Brave at the country's helm, they might have achieved it, but now..." He shook his head.

"And then there's Bocksai's claim to the throne. But they hate him almost as much as they hate Bathorys, if you'll pardon me, my lady. Bocksai executed most of the remaining Szekely men during what they call 'the Bloody Carnival.'"

He looked over at Nadasdy.

"My lord, I've heard of Mohacs, but I wonder if this 'carnival' wasn't their own sort of Mohacs."

The door had opened. "Mohacs, Mohacs, all I hear in Hungary is 'Mohacs'. Is it not Mohacs every day in Erdely?"

Dorothea had come into the room with more bread, cheese, wine and figs. Nadasdy glared at her. Perhaps Mohacs was his cross to bear as much as Andrew and Sigismund and all the Bathorys were mine. We both bore them all daily. "My lord, I believe she might be right," came John's speedy response. Dorothea curtseyed low.

"I meant no insult, my lord."

A silence fell as Nadasdy tapped the wooden tabletop and turned his head, surveying the library.

"Basta is ruling Erdely. I've watched him. I know how he thinks."

He ceased his tapping and a shadow of a thought that moved from doubt to certainty crossed his face.

"The Emperor has his eye on Royal Hungary." He turned back to me. "That means he's coming for our estates. It never turns out well – being the creditor of emperors. He's already got rid of Andrew and Balthasar Bathory, Michael the Brave and demoralised Sigismund Bathory enough to finally give up his failed attempts to rule Erdely by himself. Basta will consolidate Rudolph's position and sweep westwards into Hungary. Tell me, John, Dorothea, has he offered the Szekelys anything in terms of their lands if they swear allegiance?"

Dorothea looked down and then drew herself up to her full height.

"Yes, my lord. In terms of allegiance, I have been reliably informed that the lords of Erdely have been *incentivised*."

Nadasdy rose and paced around the room. His grey eyes were

sharp and wild, taking on a yellowish hue in Cachtice's light. He looked for all the world like a mountain wolf bending towards his prey, trapped in the body of a man – in the body of my husband.

"Do you know what I imagine?" He said it hesitantly at first, uncertain he wished to let us all in on his thoughts. He looked at me with those grey eyes of his and I smiled at him. He sparkled.

"I imagine that there's nothing more threatening to the Emperor than a reunited Hungary – than Erdely, Hungary and Wallachia fighting as one as we did before. Perhaps Rudolph is afraid that we may unite ourselves with the Sultan. A broken kingdom is easy to control. We're at the border, and our fissure, the crack that divided us after Mohacs, is our weakness.

"Rudolph, always Rudolph!" he continued, "he exploits that weakness. He bleeds Nadasdys and Bathorys dry. He takes advantage of our natural greed, setting Bathory against Bathory in Erdely until, with respect, my love, everyone winds up dead. Now that we know the anti-Trinitarian reformers who test the patience of even Calvinists have taken hold of the religious imagination of the Szekely people, Erdely takes a step even further away from Hapsburg rule.

"It appears to me that Erdely is the key. Erdely is the Emperor's weakness and so he sends his most dangerous dog to rule it. And Basta is a dog. He'll rip Erdely to shreds before grinding us all between his jaws."

He stopped pacing and came close to me, taking a chair and moving it so that when he sat again, he could take my hand. He pressed his forehead to it like a man at confession.

"Do you think, my love, that the angel inside me that you speak about might hide in Hungary, but rise in Erdely?"

Dorothea's head snapped towards us. John stopped his endless eating and fell into a kind of suspension. My blood ran cold in my body. I had imagined that Nadasdy might set aside more funds for the Szekelys, that we might help them rebuild their lives, heal their sick, not that he would ride in astride his warhorse to fight some deadly, unwinnable battle against Basta. Against the Emperor's interests. But Nadasdy was thinking like a general, a hero, a king. His solution would be more blood. Always, it came to blood in our land. Always. Blood.

"You once told me to kick you if you were ever tempted by the throne of Erdely, Francis. Now is that time."

His look hardened. Then something unexpected came to my mind as if written in another world, tearing the veils between its home and ours in a flash of inspiration. An inversion of everything that made Nadasdy who and what he was. I saw him in my mind's eye not covered in somebody's blood, but in ink.

"I'm thinking something else might be possible. Something even more radical than war," I said slowly.

"What could possibly be more radical than Nadasdy fighting *for* Erdely?" asked Dorothea slowly. She was looking at us both differently.

"I'm thinking about the power of a book."

A deep smile made its way slowly across Nadasdy's face as he understood my meaning. The flame behind his grey eyes flickered and he became excited, a rush filling him.

"Basta understands wars," he said. "He understands how to trick and cut his way across the Empire. I'm frightened of very little in this world but him. So, I've made him fear me and he has a scar on the back of his hand to remind him of it. But what Basta doesn't understand is something I've come to know through you, my darling. That a book can change a man's mind more deeply than blood."

"These are the world's new weapons. This is how we fight the Emperor," I replied. But the problem we have is that Basta *does* understand it. He understands all too well the power of printing. He's afraid of it too. He said as much to me in Prague," I responded. "We must be *very* careful if we're to outwit such a man."

"He may understand it, but he won't expect it from me," cut

in Nadasdy. "And to be so underestimated by men like him, this has, in a way, become my greatest strength."

He thought about it and paced about. When his eyes alighted on me, they danced.

"We'll fight a different kind of war for the Szekelys." A slow smile playfully crossed his face now. His features were dancing like small fires unused to feeling the warmth they give.

"We'll unite Royal Hungary once more, under the auspices of this." And he held up a little copy of the *Christianismi Restitutio* that had lain hidden inside his own pocket for God knows how long.

*

Third floor reading area. 3pm–5pm. Tuesday, 8th March, 2020

I put the slip of paper inside my pocket. I'm wearing my hair up and I'm in a black raincoat. I flip the collars up to make myself feel like a detective and check myself out in the glass reflection of one of the library's huge doors. *Not bad.* Then I start racing up the stairs like a wildwoman.

"Hello, again, even though I only just saw you!" I say to Lucretia, who's hunched over her books.

I pull out a chair, turn it around and lean up with my back to the desk next to her.

"Just now, I was back in the moment we 'first' met." I emphasise quotation marks around the word 'first' with my fingers. "Your hair is a *lot* greyer," I tease.

"I see."

She is wearing glasses and she also looks thinner than she did just a moment ago, which for her was a good number of years in the past.

She seems sad *here, now*. Preoccupied and gaunt. And I instantly regret my jovial entrance.

We stayed quiet for a little bit, just together in the snatched moment time had decided to give us. Then I said, "'Cretia, there's something I want to ask you. How come you've never asked me about… your future?"

The question hung in the air until she eventually looked up at me over the top of her reading glasses.

"Because I know what happens. I write books. I fight stupid intellectual battles. I refuse the attempts of jumped-up little professors. I practise listening. And one day I will die again. Case closed. Why are you wearing that coat like a detective?" And she tucked my collars down. It was quite maternal.

"Okay. Fine. Sounds like you've got everything figured out. The only deep mystery is… will you actually one day get a cat and stop talking about it?"

"Oh yes. I remember I really wanted one a few years ago, didn't I?"

"You wanted two. So want to go to the roof and do some…" I paused, waving my hand around a bit as if searching for the words "…weird listening stuff?" But she refused to be drawn into my playful teasing today.

"I've got work to finish. Why don't you go down and listen to the river?"

"Are you okay?"

She took off her glasses and rubbed her eyes.

"I'm just tired and I don't feel well."

"Hey." I looked deeply into her, touching her hand slightly.

She looked up at me with her dark eyes, trying not to ask me what I knew she wanted to.

"Hey. No. Not soon. And I will be with you every step of the way."

She understood me.

"I can't get rid of you, can I?"

"No, you can't. Sorry about that."

She grabbed my hand tightly and managed a quiet whisper.

"Thank you."

*

I emerge in time on a step and lose my balance falling down some stairs. I look around, disorientated. Black beams. Steep staircase. A receptionist cranes her neck from the vestibule below.

"Are you all right, sweetheart?"

I nod. She clicks her tongue and I know she thinks I'm either drunk or mad. Either way, she simply smiles patiently. The therapist's office is at the top of the ricketiest steps I've seen, and I wonder if they've been designed as a practice gauntlet for whatever mental hoops and obstacles the doc might want to make his clients jump through in the office. I've been here so many times. It's the moment I'm trying to convince myself I'm crazy and that help will come in the form of a small white pill. I try to guess why time has brought me *here, now*. What strange meanings were attached to the order of my disjointure? Did time act like a god, a great universal consciousness that blew me about with methodic precision? I doubted it. Why would time bend its body only to blow me about? I thought it had better things to do than concern itself with one human. *Time lives inside the body.* Perhaps it was my own tiny heart that moved me around like this. A tiny heart that was small but dreamt of seeing enormous things.

The office I arrived in was interminably beige, a colour that's anything but soothing.

"So, what's brought you here today, Miss…?"

I sat down, wondering if he heard me tumble.

"It's Doctor."

"Sorry?"

"Doctor. Not Miss."

He still looked a bit perplexed.

"Oh – yes. Of course. Can I call you Vera?"

I sat back in my chair, fumbled in my bag and removed a cigarette from its case. I didn't light it. I just turned it back and forth and back and forth.

"Call me whatever you like."

"I'd rather call you what you'd like to be known as."

"Call me Elizabet Bathory, then." My sarcasm was at an all-time high.

"O-kay."

If Doctor was going to ruffle him so, then why not go all in? Lean into the madness.

"Sorry. I'm just a little..." I glanced around at all the abstract art bursting out from the beige "...tense in here. Look, I'll get right to it. I feel a little... unstuck. And I thought maybe you could help me."

"'Unstuck'. What does that look like?"

Oh wow. This guy doesn't waste any time.

"I feel... like I'm never really in any moment for long. It's like... time is disjointed."

"Any sensations with that?"

"Not really."

"No lightheadedness? No disorientation?"

"Well, disorientation, sure. But it's *as if* I were trapped in a time loop. *As if* all the moments of my life were scattered on the floor, with no rhyme or reason. Out of order, in a sense. Broken. And that would be okay if I could change things, but I can't."

My eyes were glistening a little. I could feel the tears inside the corners. When they flowed, they'd hit the bright overhead light and send tiny glimmers across my vision. *How do you explain time travel to a therapist?*

"Have you ever heard of dissociation, *Doctor*?"

"Yes. And no, it's not that. I wish it was," I smiled hopefully at him, "but sadly, it's not."

"How can you be sure?"

I didn't know how to respond. I felt like anything I said would be like trying to fit the whole range of my experience, all the flights through time, into a neat and tidy tick-box, when in reality everything about my experience spilled over the edges.

How do you explain the idea that time is not and has never been linear to a therapist? A doctor? A clinician? His whole world was built on cause and effect, chemical cause and effect. The endless straight line of normalcy. But I had brought myself here. I'd needed to talk to someone, to see how the world, as it was, the modern world of linearity, might see someone like me. And I'd need to take myself home afterwards in a way that made sense.

"Because time is a nasty piece of work. It's like I can see the rafters and bolts of time being made and remade around me. It wasn't always like this. My first eight years ran forward." And I gestured a straight line with my hand cutting boldly forth in the space between us like an arrow.

"So what happened to change it?"

"I died, briefly."

"How?"

"I had a… bump on the head."

"Sounds like some bump."

"Yes, it was."

"So, you can see the workings of time? Must be difficult."

"Yeah. I just want time to flow forward. What do you think, can you help?"

"Do you want my help?"

It was a good question.

"What does *it look like*? Your help, I mean."

He noted my repetition of his words and smiled as if to say *this is going to be equal parts nightmare and equal parts fun.*

"Well, we can talk through the experience and, if it's necessary, I can prescribe you some anti-psychotics. But first things first."

"You have a pill to regulate time?"

"We've got pills for *everything*." He raised his eyebrows in a way that was cartoonish.

I could tell he was trying to mirror my humour to establish complicity. It was sweet, in a way. But it also felt a bit creepy. I wondered where *he* was in all this.

"What happens when you leave time?" he asked.

"I don't disappear, if that's what you're asking, or fly through a backstage corridor or anything like that. It's just, the world undoes itself and a new moment forms around me. It can be way in the future or far in the past."

"Oh wow. What does the future look like? Might be useful to know."

"It looks much like the past, but with more exciting tech."

"So maybe it's not a time problem at all but a history problem that you have."

I leant forward.

A history problem. A problem with my origin story.

"Doc, I think you just gave me what I needed to hear."

He smiled, but he also widened his eyes a tiny bit in a way that screamed *okay, we've got a right nutjob here.*

"So what do you do, I mean for money? To make ends meet."

"I'm a historian."

He laughed out loud. At first, I felt a little offended, but that was just the sting of pride.

"Sounds like the ultimate kind of wish fulfilment." He had a point.

"Uh-huh. I think if I set the record straight, maybe time will go back to being ordered and neat. Isn't that what justice is meant to do? Maybe there'll be a tiny space, a tiny crack in history, that'll permit me to live in it. You know, to be *part of it* rather than its prisoner."

"That sounds good to me."

When I left the office, I sauntered down to the river. The river reflected the sun as faithfully as it could, but the ripples across its surface disrupted its edges like static running down an old screen. Perhaps we were all, in some way or another, trying to sort out our *history problems.* I just lived mine in a way that was written large across my body. *Words and worlds, they're one*, I thought to myself. It's no secret that words have always been powerful.

Perhaps this is how all humans lived in the world – written through with tales and histories that lived inside one another. We storied the world with these patterns, creating heavens and hells beyond imagining, abandoning ourselves of our responsibility without even realising it. We were filled with powers we hadn't the first inkling of. *Listen! Look!* It was the way every ancient story began. And yet we hardly ever listened or looked. We hardly ever survived the arcs we made in time.

Now whenever I felt Elizabet around me, I was listening – listening deeply. I knew we were diffractions of one another, part of one great story stretching across time. I understood that to re-story her from out of the prison that history had made, I had to write her through myself. History had locked her up, made her into the shape of the *Blood Countess*. But this wasn't unique to her. It was something shared by all women in one way or another. So I kept rewriting her out of her prison, and she rewrote me out of mine, shifting all our histories subtly across time. She rewrote me in the letters she sent, in the books she printed, applying the legend *For the Future* to some copies, curling the letters on the page, in ink.

Soon, she would write of me directly, delivering her knowledge of our world now right to the Emperor in the hope that it might, in some tiny way, re-story him. We would all emerge differently in time *through* each other. When she scribed me, it would change, in tiny increments, the life I lived. When I scribed her, she would break the chains that made her, finding the other inside her, her own silent people across time. Would that we all could find our inner narrators, erasing our position in space in the past, present and future in an endless, brave momentum taking place in women's time.

Chapter Fourteen

Nadasdy, John, Anna, Dorothea and I had stayed up for the fourth night in a row, printing countless copies of the *Christianismi Restitutio*, which we stacked up along the back wall of a small hidden chamber directly behind the print room. We had returned to Sarvar briefly and Maria-Christina's retinue had left Cachtice at the same moment so she might visit another 'friend', which I took to mean 'report back to the Emperor'.

I insisted we not stay too long at Sarvar. I was eager to return to Cachtice, to Michael, and to a Hapsburg-free home. The books leant dangerously in their piles, threatening to topple over if we moved about too much. Nadasdy half smiled, half grimaced when he stood back to make an inventory of the amount completed. His eyes had become like the sea after a storm, burdened with a mix of greens and greys, stirred up by the racing of the invisible tides around him that were now taking shape and forcing him into history.

"I used to use this room to stash the swords and muskets I collected from each Ottoman battle I returned from," he said in a voice that sounded very far away. "I always thought it was important to have a working knowledge of the enemy's weapons. I would come in here and spend hours with them. Shining them. I never thought I'd see them replaced by books."

There was a large polished glass resting against a side wall that we'd moved out of the way when we first came in. It caught our reflections, making it appear that there were two of each of us; our own hazy doubles. The room had been otherwise empty. Nadasdy put his head down and seemed to disappear again for a moment. I didn't interrupt his reverie this time or ask him where these weapons had gone. I was learning to trust that Francis would come back to me on his own, in his own time, and in command of his own stories rather than at their mercy.

"How many books is that now, my lord?" John asked.

"Eight hundred."

"Enough to make a trip, I think."

I winced. "How do you suppose we'll manage to get eight hundred books across the border and into Erdely unnoticed?"

"Anna has an idea," Nadasdy said hurriedly. He was looking down and I caught a strong sense of fear and shame pouring off him.

"Oh?" I asked.

He blinked a few times. "It's one we've used before."

"Before?"

He was standing directly in front of the wall of books, surveying the breadth of leathery spines that were stacked all the way up to the ceiling. Anna leant at the open doorway behind him, half between the print room and half between the chamber. Neither could see the other, except in the polished glass, and yet I could almost hear the space between them become thick and full of shared shame.

Nobody answered.

"Before?" I demanded.

"Yes, my lady. But this time – this time–" Anna seemed unable to finish her sentence. She stammered and fumbled her words and Nadasdy grew at first red then pale, then almost ghostly.

Dorothea sighed exasperatedly.

"Enough. What they're trying to say is we think we can take the books to Cachtice, transfer them into coffins and send them through the tunnels. We can then transport them from there to the border on foot overnight. It certainly won't be an easy journey. But it's possible."

She paused, her eyes looking over the books, parsing each quadrant into rough estimations dictated by the volume of a coffin.

"We might even be able to justify repatriating the coffins as they are. God knows too many Szekelys from Erdely have died here already," she added, and though she looked down to her feet, I felt she would have preferred to stare directly into my husband's eyes. The room became a crucible of secrets, as if someone had fed all the air into the turning wheels of the press.

Nadasdy turned about and left in a hurry, pushing past Anna. John made to go after him, but I stayed him with my hand. Nadasdy needed to face himself alone. Although he and John had forged an incredible bond between them, if he fell into a rage, or a hot shame or a quick despair, he could be capable of anything.

"Let him be. He'll find you soon enough," I assured. I turned my attention back to the wall of books.

"Anna, do you think this will really work?" I asked.

"Countess, people are afraid of a coffin. They carry plague, death and the threat of the undead. And this is Hungary. The dead *are* everywhere, breeding unnatural fear. We'll simply say that some of the Erdely women here had fallen sick and we had no wish to alarm the public. People were always used to a few coffins leaving here in the night. This time, we'll tell them that the plague has struck again and more virulent, and that they should pray to God it doesn't spread. No one will want to inspect further, trust me."

"I'm not convinced."

It was Dorothea who crossed the chamber towards me with a ready answer. The rest fell silent and grave and distant, honouring lost ones as she spoke.

"Listen to me, my lady. All these wars we have – Hadjuk raids, Ottoman incursions, Tartars, even our own people fighting and killing each other, they have done something to us all. They've made us come to expect nothing from life perhaps *except* death. A full coffin crossing the square is as everyday as a man who comes to sell bread to the living. Our rebellion starts here, inside the symbol of death itself. It's fitting. And it *will* work."

I had no idea Dorothea had such poetic sensibilities. I remembered reading, an age ago – or so it felt – of the *ourobouros*, a magical symbol in one of the many prohibited books I had had John source for me. It showed a snake eating its own tail. If Dorothea had not seen this image with her own eyes, then some part of her had absorbed it from out of the air both she and the image shared. Or perhaps this was the way all things worked, and the first scratchings of the *ourobouros* had simply captured the truth of eternal return that we all already knew inside our bones.

I breathed out, as if for the first time in a while. "Out of death: new life. New stories."

All the air that had been pinched and held since Nadasdy's shame had come over him, suddenly returned, making the room light again. Anna and John came out of their silent mournings, returning to the present slowly.

"We could all do with some new stories," said Anna. "I was reborn from a coffin myself once. And Nadasdy, perhaps he can supplant his own deathly tales now."

John looked a little wryly at all of us. "You're all crazier than I thought!" he said. It broke the spell. Dorothea hit him on the back of the head in reprimand.

He laughed. It was infectious and for a moment we all forgot ourselves. I would remember that moment years later when everyone was gone. All the pain, all the revenge, all the blood. I would remember Anna, Dorothea and John's laughter in the print room, drifting out in tiny reverberations across rock, land and winds. Coming back to me years later in the laughter-like sounds of the crows and birds that would alight on the edges of my window. Haunting an empty Sarvar joyfully, inside a future I would never live to see.

Chapter Fifteen

"Don't go to Prague, Elizabet. It's a trap. I'm certain." Nadasdy's face was whiter than usual.

"I have to go, Francis. When Rudolph, Holy Roman Emperor, calls, you go. Like you," I joked, kissing him on the cheek as I rose, "he won't be denied."

He grabbed my hand to prevent me from leaving to find John and ask what was taking so long. The one good thing to come out of Maria-Christina's visit was that she had once let slip that Rudolph was pursuing a deep study of esotericism. It had, she said, 'become his sole obsession'. And he needed curing of it.

Rudolph had sent a private invitation. No reporting on taxes or lands. Just the 'company of the Countess Bathory'. I needed to go prepared; to enter into whatever story Rudolph was stuck on and remain two steps ahead.

"I'm coming with you, Elizabet. If they've found out what we're printing, I won't leave you to die alone there. There's only one way I'm leaving this world, and that's with a sword in my hand. And I'll be damned if I let you leave me first."

John came into the room with an armful of books and scrolls, rolled tightly and fastened with dark blue ribbons.

"Here's everything on alchemy, my lady. There's not much, but I can put my ear to the ground in Erdely, too. Maybe find out what's missing – what's not being written."

His wound had healed well. He was also filling out a little. John had never been tall and never would be, but he was becoming heavy-shouldered and solid, the very opposite of Nadasdy. Nadasdy had already led armies at the same age. It was a miracle both were still alive.

"I've decided to travel under a new assumed name," he announced to us proudly.

"Oh?" I asked. "Yes, that's probably a good idea. What name?"

"The Ironhead!"

Nadasdy and I both roared with laughter. John went bright red.

"What's wrong with it?"

"Nothing," said Nadasdy.

"Nothing," I chimed in. "Maybe make it a little less… memorable?"

"No. The Ironhead."

"What about 'Stephen'?" asked Nadasdy. "It's a common enough name in Erdely."

John went quiet and defiant.

"That's settled then. Stephen. Stephen Ironhead." Nadasdy smiled and winked at him as if to say, *Under all that muscle, you're still a boy*. John smiled eventually. Nadasdy's endless charm always won him over in the end.

We rolled the scant parchment material out onto the print table and piled the alchemical books in one corner. Nadasdy took an impressive-looking tome bound in vellum and lettered in gold and thumbed it, whilst I pored over the bizarre drawings and woodcuts that were unable to lie entirely flat, like bat's wings unfurled. One in particular caught my attention. It depicted a room with a chequered floor. At its centre lay a table with a host of musical instruments piled on top of it. It seemed like a first draft, something unfinished that would in time assume its real significance. Another page lay behind it with the same strange symbol I'd seen etched everywhere about the imperial court at Prague; the figure with the horizontal crescent moon moving through its head, crowning it with otherworldly power.

"Interesting," said Nadasdy after a while, shattering the intense silence we had created in our absorption.

"What have you found?"

He held the book in one hand and ran his fingers through his thick head of hair with the other. "I think it's by a battle surgeon. He suggests that instead of applying dung and feathers to a wound, you should just wash it and let nature heal the rest. I've been saying the same thing for ages, but everyone looks at me like I'm utterly insane."

He grunted in assent with whatever he was reading a few more times, flipped the book over in his hands to examine the binding and then turned it back upright to examine its frontispiece.

"Paracelsus. Definitely worth reading this one more fully."

I couldn't see what any of that had to do with alchemy, so I kept digging through the pages John had assembled.

"Look here, my love," Nadasdy said excitedly, "this Paracelsus also talks about a 'microcosmos', which sounds to me…" he paused and read a bit further "…like your 'tiny world' as you call it, the one you go into before you start *travelling*."

I went cold. All the hairs stood up on the back of my neck. Nadasdy came up behind me and planted a solid kiss on my shoulder, placing the open book in my hands. And then, without warning, it began – the travelling – called to life the moment Nadasdy spoke of it. I lost sense of this world and started to enter the other. The words on the page became large. Or perhaps

I had become small. I slipped through the bars and dots of ink. It wasn't as fine as John's bone-black ink, but I started to hear the faint ghosts of the animals whose bones had been ground once upon a time to create the smooth, silky lines of text.

The paper stood firm and straight as the trees that made it, and I walked along its surface. As I wound around the forest of letters, I began to feel a presence that wasn't my own. It was neither mine nor my angelic, deathly self, come to haunt me within the vision. For an infinitesimal moment, I caught a glimpse of the shadowy face peering out at me. Then I heard a clap and a roar like thunder. The golden horse made of light found its way to me and I clung on as we rushed through time. Just before I climbed atop its shining back, the face became clear: *Rudolph*!

*

I had never wanted to return to Prague. But this journey was entirely different to the previous one. Nadasdy sat with me. He held my hand firmly in his when I shuddered as the courtly spires came into view, elegant and bejewelled as fingers that aimed to grab at the frayed hem of God Himself. The carriage came to a stop. We had timed the journey poorly and the sun had not yet fully broken into morning when we arrived. The waters that had sparkled and blinded me before, like so many dancing mirrors, were now black and blue pools that slept deeply, undisturbed by our crossing.

We were shown to our quarters by drowsy attendants. No longer housed on the other side of the grand palace, we were positioned closer to the court's centre. The rooms were more ornate, the furnishings were finer, and the windows looked out over the most astonishing botanical gardens I could have imagined. I tapped my fan on the back of a golden armchair that was draped in silks from the other side of the world. I became something of a mechanical creature myself, tap-tapping my presence out in the room.

"What does Rudolph think we are?"

Nadasdy sat himself down on the bed in a manner far younger than that of his years, as if proximity to Rudolph reduced him in age, power and size.

"Rudolph's a collector," he said as he removed one boot and then the other, massaging his ankles and his calves as he spoke.

"He likes to find rare creatures and objects and display them in his *cabinet*. I think he thinks we're just such things."

"You, the great warrior of the East and I, the great warrior of the unseen?" I teased, opening and raising my arms hyperbolically, in the way I imagined a folkloric *talto* might.

"Let him believe. Let him believe." Nadasdy sighed. "I'm weary, Elizabet, of this captive life. I'm weary of Rudolph."

"I am too."

He looked around the room, his eyes settling on the astonishing image of a white crane that was drawn on the silk of the wall. He got up and started tracing the outline of the crane with his finger.

"Do you think that if you fell from the world's grasp, you would fall fast or slow?" he asked.

"Fast."

"And would you ever stop?"

"I wouldn't wish to. I'd wish to be blown far, far away from here."

"Far from me?" he asked, looking into me.

"I'd carry you with me."

"So I'd become small?" He returned to the bed. "A trinket in your hand?" He was half teasing, but also, in some way, half serious.

"No. I would carry you and you would carry me. Because we live inside each other's stories."

"You live in my heart, Elizabet." And he put his hand over his as he spoke.

"I think you're better at love than I, Francis."

He held his hand out and I joined him sitting on the edge of the bed.

"No, you just love all things equally. I love only you. The rest of the world can go hang. But which way do you think is better?"

"Neither. I think each person creates their own world. The laws of truth function differently inside each one of us."

"Hang on," he said. "No. No! There's only one truth. Otherwise, we'd be nothing more than pagans."

I paused, thinking this through.

"Why do all things always need to be one or the other? Can't God exist inside both, and all things in between them? I think it's a man who makes things one or the other. I imagine God inside the waves, and the veins that make up the trees, that make up bodies and blood. How do these things pray? How do they know God?"

"That's certainly pagan, Elizabet."

"I don't feel so. Take Rudolph. His desire for knowledge – if he truly desires alchemical secrets – is for mastery over a passive earth. My desire is different. I want love itself to absorb such godlike powers, such godlike divisions."

"That's not a world I can imagine."

"It's outside of kings and castles and courts. It's outside of the Holy Roman God. Yet maybe, just maybe it's not really *outside* of anything at all. I think we've all made the world very, very *complicated* in our endeavours. The universe is like a book. Its ink is made from the bones of every living thing."

At this, he started kissing my neck. Then he let me go, staring off into space. "Rudolph will have his way, but I won't surrender you without a fight."

"I don't feel it'll come to that, my love. I think Rudolph is playing in the other world and I reckon he wants me to help him pry into the secrets. So be it. Because, my dearest, there's nothing new to tell. Blood is still blood. Violence is still violence. Power is still power."

"And is love still love?"

I thought to myself across time, to myself as the girl in the wall. Did she love too, even after all the violence? Was Rudolph, or any thousand other Rudolphs in new faces, still in command, or had love managed to re-story power in her own tiny world, in the shape of her starling journey through time?

"Yes. Love is still love. Inside everything else."

"Well, thank God for that!"

My heart melted. Nadasdy the killer had disappeared even here, inside the court that had made him, used him, still used him. The blood remained spilled, however, and so justice would no doubt make a new story out of him. He would run into its arms as if returning to a new mother.

We wouldn't manage to save the Szekelys in Hungary, although their new religion would persist, spreading like heavenly wildfire as more and more copies of the book were circulated, read and committed to memory. As for us, we would inadvertently bring down so much death on our own house that the Szekelys, Hungarians and Turks, who still persisted in their hatred of us, would rejoice. But we would have already flown that house, in a way. The house made of bones. We would fly into the heart of these stories themselves. Faster and faster.

*

The professor kept looking down at the ground as I spoke in the arched auditorium, its stone beams and vaulted ceiling aping the grandeur of a church. I wasn't sure if he'd glimpsed it – glimpsed the way that I *thought* – and that that was what lay at the heart of his rage. Surely, it wasn't just what I wrote; it was *how* I wrote, *how* I moved through the world, *how* I thought about what it was to be human. It was everything I stood for and how my thinking, in turn, had ordered my world.

'Thesis' and 'antithesis', proposal and negation, can't account for the nature of wave fields. The world doesn't exist in bits, like atoms and empty space and nothing in between. And so, it's like... it's like it's the wrong kind of movement. The same is true for history.

As I said this, I also listened. I listened to hear what time was making of me, to hear what time had placed in the air around me. In return, the weight of the audience's words – their questions and thoughts – marched into my ear, forcing my body to enact a very slight swerve. One large dance that didn't care at all who was 'winning', who was 'right' or 'wrong', as long as we all moved together *here, now* in time.

Time itself would chew these moments all to dust. But the words would go on forever, puppeteering the generations that came after as well as those that came before. They would contain all of us, fold us all up together into the pages of a book. *And that's how it would all come to matter, in time.* The professor hated this. A young woman refusing to be bound into the right side of history that depended on *thesis and antithesis*. Zero and One and nothing in between. A young woman who didn't believe in history at all.

"This new work is *nonsense*. You cannot bend history to your version of it. End of story. I'm afraid I can't approve your request and will be withdrawing my support. You're welcome to go to anyone else, but as you know, my dear, *I* have the final say." He looked at me as if to say *If you'd only done what I asked, we'd be having a very different conversation. Your ideas, like your body, belong to me. When will you finally just surrender them both?* He opened his legs a little and leant back in his chair.

"Last chance. How important is it all to you?"

I went out into the hallway and stood with my back to the wall just to the side of his door, so he couldn't see me anymore, my head resting on the papery surfaces of the posters and flyers of all his previous projects. At first, my breathing was racing. I opened my palm and looked down at it. I called forth the image of a tiny moth, its wings flapping slowly as it sat on the ridge of my palm. It was a moth that came from deep in the past. Bathory's moth, which danced and died the night she first became a *talto*. I matched my breathing to each of those little wing beats. Then I did a few mental calculations.

I'd have to move again, sell the furniture and any other items to raise a little cash and find a way to publish around the professor's unofficial censorship. It wouldn't cost me my life, of course. But it would ruin me. I closed my eyes and felt the winds of time moving and scribing with all the grace of a thousand tiny moths, moving in the air about me in atomic flickers and beats. When I opened my eyes again, I was in the university café sat opposite the professor's wife, so I figured it mustn't have been the wind at all, but the intrusion of time, come to whisk me away.

"He wants to keep you close, so he can control you – control you through your work."

Rachel had finally said out loud what nobody would dare say directly. She sighed as she said it, banging her spoon frustratedly on the side of her cup before laying it aside, tired of explaining the alphabet of power as if to a small child. It was springtime and all the windows were propped open, letting the warm air rush in. She was chewing at nails that were already slung low across her fingertips.

"You should have just done what he wanted. Now you can forget about your research. And any position you go for anywhere else will be blocked. You need good references in this game, especially at this stage in your career. Universities are brutal. Like kingly courts. And you've pissed off a *major* lord. Why is it all so important to you? You could go *so far*. I'm actually a little jealous of what you *could do*. If you wanted it."

She looked at me as she chewed off another piece of her own finger. It was almost cannibalistic, and I wondered if she devoured herself so that he would have nothing left to take from her.

"I mean," she continued, "what makes you think you're better than any of the rest of us? We've all made sacrifices or turned a blind eye where perhaps we shouldn't have."

I stared at her, disbelieving at first, but then chastised myself for my own innocence. Of course this would be her response. She would do whatever he required of her so that she could be left to eat herself up in peace. I imagined it was part of the deal. I was just surprised by how matter-of-fact she was about it. I was broke, and Bathory would remain silenced.

All the same, I followed every avenue open to me, banging the drum about Bathory and history and justice like a small wind-up toy that had a finite amount of time left before its inner mechanics failed. Each person I went to nodded in sympathy, passed out clouds of tissues that signalled only crying was to be expected of me now, and then shrugged, destroying meeting notes and any evidence of my claims – even once in front of me; *I think these are unnecessary under the circumstances, don't you?* Before suggesting I seek help for what *must be such a difficult situation*. Over and over, brightly coloured leaflets for mental health support which I could find on the noticeboard outside were pointed out. *Welcome! We are gender and ethnicity sensitive! 5* service!*

"I told you," said Lucretia. "Not just libraries but people have been burned for less. It's not just that you won't surrender to him, in the bedroom, I mean. It's something else he wants from you, from everyone. These people, their power, it depends on you parroting *their thoughts, their whole way of thinking* from the position of your gender, your race, your sexuality. But, Vera, you want to introduce something new, a new way of thinking. It won't be easy. I'm not saying stop. For Christ's sake, I told you, keep going! But know what's at stake. They will try to take everything from you. Not just your work. But the thing that animates it. The 'you' that lives inside the shell of what you do. But don't worry. I'll be here. I'll be with you – with all the yous that live across time. I'll be beside you in your stories. Our lives are tiny. If you want to do it, go ahead."

"It's more than that and you know it, Lucretia. I need to do it."

"Do you think it will cure your time problem? When does the search for 'justice' destroy all justice?"

"You can't just change a story in your mind, on the quiet. That's not changing the story at all. And you know it. It has to be *breathed*. It has to be lived."

Time comes in again. Of course it would bring me *here, now*. I'm in a crowded pub near the main faculty building. The air is thick and tastes of salt. This time, I've bought my own drink and held onto it as if for dear life. The man I'm talking to works with the professor. He's come to 'reason with me'.

"What did you do to him?" he asks.

"Said 'no'." I shook my head and laughed. "What is it with you lot? What is it that you're all so scared of?"

"Vera, your work is good. Really good. But it's not his and it doesn't fit with what he's doing, and you won't do what he wants. How can you afford to be so stupid?" He taps the table with his knuckles. "Don't you get it? You, your work, everything you stand for, it's a wave we all see coming but no one wants to have to actually deal with. *Difference*. The end of one time and the start of another. Another *era*. Don't you see how threatening that is? These guys have been here for generations in one way or another. The professor, Mark, even me. And in you walk with your red lipstick and your legs and your dark skin and tell everyone that time as we know it, as we read it, as we write it, *doesn't exist anymore*. And you do it by rewriting the world's most notorious woman serial killer? What did you expect? Congratulations?"

"If I didn't know better, I'd think you were flirting with me." I say it to him kindly. But he takes the point.

"Fuck off, Vera," he says, laughingly. "You *cannot* be seen to be breaking away from him. It would undo his whole image. He wants you back, he just doesn't know how to get you onside. He needs you. For PR reasons. Don't be so naïve. You know, you *could* turn this to your advantage. Just give him a sign that you'll publish something a little less colourful this time. That you'll put all that passion towards something *more suitable, less... troubling.*"

"Ah, the voice of 'reason', come to find me in a pub somewhere."

He eyes me closely. I've always thought that when he squints, he looks like a little rodent scrambling inside the maze of cost and reward that we all call 'the university'.

"I see. You're not desperate enough yet. Don't worry. You will be."

And like a house of cards, the pub falls away and I'm back in my childhood bedroom, that large hand across my mouth, gasping for air. I'm certain of only one thing. This place is death. A lifetime of erasures and ghosts. I shut my eyes, let my body go limp and quiet and listen to the empty corridor. I listen to the story that hums inside the infinite number of atoms that come together to make *here, now*. And I hear *her* as if I were standing right there. She's in the courtyard at Cachtice. In front of her, Thurzo, a swathe of pearls about his chest. A flake of snow comes to settle on his shoulder. He doesn't know it, but the snow comes from far in the future. It comes from my world into his and he brushes it off. *I must be getting closer to it,* I think to myself. Time is collapsing all the stories faster now. Faster and faster.

And the lady has been accused of terrible crimes. We do not seek to put her witchcraft on trial but be assured the lady is damnable as we shall prove.

They think they've silenced her. But as happens with women the world over, her words have already taken shape across time, unseen, for now, through me. Through the spell she chanted at her trial, a spell that took root in her time only to flower in ours. I can hear her words as if my ear – the listening chamber of my heart – had finally grown large enough and tired enough to truly listen to the way she was writing me; casting a spell in time, a spell of history that I would write out hundreds of years in the future:

In the silence right here, right now, in your silence, dear reader – the silence that a book effects on the one who reads it, I'll tell my side of it all. I'll start as a girl, the first moment I arrived at Cachtice in my carriage. I'll tell my story to fold time; to be here and elsewhere, as if no time existed in between. I'll tell the story that lives inside what history has made of me. Maybe that's the power of a talto.

I was no longer prisoner of my own small stories. I could hear instead the prison of the larger story – the story of our species across time. Had nothing ever truly changed, in all the ages? Were we all still under the thumb of generations of Rudolphs who had taught us how to scribe our lives into patterns that only ever served an immortal crown? A crown that subjugated *everybody* under its weight – that silenced women and made men so violently afraid? What could possibly fight it? What, if anything, could such an empire fear? What did it shut away inside countless kinds of tower rooms across time?

Now my fingers fly across the computer. I no longer need Lucretia to cajole me to write and write it differently this time. My disordered world and the world of the book are folding in on each other. And all I can think is how beautiful it is. How these dancing moths all made of ink fly and flutter and flow out of me.

This kind of violence doesn't just attack the body – it attacks the heart. And so the arrow, not of time but of love, was perhaps the only thing left that could break violence itself in two, dissolving the endless gravity that kept it written in the bones, ruling from within. Love was something at the very heart of matter. Love, like writing, was a kind of technology. Elizabet had been certain at one point that my position in time – that what I shakily called the 'present day' – held some kind of secret knowledge that would answer her prayers, undoing all the dangers of her own moment. She believed that divine knowledge from the future could come to act as divine justice in her life, a thing that she might capture and print in a book. I had said that instead, I thought we were more like single starlings that formed part of a great flock of ancient stories; starlings who loved to fly. In my short lifetime, I was merely at the head, leading the story-flock towards some point in the sky. When the deeper currents of time changed, it would be her at the head, then another, then another as we moved in chaotic, ancestral patterns under the sheath of heaven. Without a single, heroic direction, all our efforts towards small justices were nothing more than lone, discarded feathers on the wind. Justice was deeper than we could know. It made worlds. Justice mattered.

As we listened deeply to the sound of ourselves at different points across time, we shared this knowledge. I could feel her laughing in her tower room, becoming more and more carefree despite her locked surroundings.

"Die, die in this love. Die to the din and the noise of the world. In the silence of love, you will find a spark of life." She said it to me like it was a lullaby, a story whose chemical compounds could be put together to make a medicine. Then she shook her head. "Little Wing, Little Wing. I pray we may both flutter light upon these eternal winds."

*

We had been called to dinner that evening. Rudolph had insisted we rest after our journey, sending word to us via a servant who did not suggest but, rather, seemed to require that we bathe first.

After indicating the way to the bathhouse, he left several small boxes with Anna and disappeared as if he'd never been there in the first place, a perfect shadow inside Rudolph's palace of lights. The castle rested in an uneasy silence. It felt oppressive and expectant at the same time, in the same way the ground under a hunter's trap lays still, anticipating its deadly mechanism.

Nadasdy lay still now, too. The water around him in the bathhouse trembled and rippled, making his body appear to lose its borders and boundaries. He hadn't removed his silver crucifix. It wasn't overly ornate or overbearing. It just lay there, submerged and lightly touching his chest, swimming above him, changing shape with the rest of him as the light bounced and diffracted through it. I had a sense that this would be one of the last times I would see him. I peeled off my underdress and jumped in, making my way quickly over to him, climbing on top of him and throwing my arms around his neck.

"What is it, my love?"

I didn't answer.

He held my head to his damp shoulder with one hand and put the rest of my body into a solid grip in the crook of his arm. My dark hair floated out over both of us, a large net that promised to do its best to hold us safe in the small shifting tides of the bathhouse.

He pulled my body away from him a little and stroked my cheek in that constant, gentle way he sometimes had when he was quiet.

"Come on, Elizabet. You're a Bathory! And I'm a Nadasdy. We'll survive this – whatever it is – together."

"I've only just found you – the 'you' you are now. I don't want to lose you."

"Elizabet, the one thing you learn when you're a soldier on the field is that we can't control death. We can only fight it. Death is cruel. It's brutal and arbitrary. The law of life isn't that different than the law of death. Both come and go. Both are violent. And both run according to their own time. You're the one with the strange relationship to time. You've seen the two worlds – this one and the *other* one. You're the one who tells me there's no real difference, that both are nothing more than moving shadows. I'll be with you for as long as I have. For as long as God decrees my fate in this world."

He laughed at my tears, but in a kindly sort of way. "Not so long ago, *in time*," he emphasised, "you couldn't wait for my death. I even thought you might have dispatched me yourself! Now look at you. You're even crying at the thought." He laughed and put his head back, looking up at the painted ceiling. He seemed so light. Little cherubs rolled around languidly in clouds, in the Italian style. The paint had flaked and cracked from years of rising steam, giving the cherubs long lines of worry, though they danced and sang together so playfully.

I wiped my tears and moved to the opposite wall, stretching my legs out to meet his feet with my own. The touch felt warm and fleshy. We looked at each other and smiled and I could almost hear our thoughts merging in the space between us: *We made this.*

*

The boxes the servant had brought from Rudolph were filled with jewels. There was a ruby brooch for me. It had two large rounded red stones, each the size of a child's eye, set in a circle of little diamonds that winked in the decaying light. Nadasdy received a belt buckle made into the shape of a lion's paw in gold. There were other small gifts too; silk handkerchiefs and several pairs of gloves. I marvelled at how odd these choices seemed for us but decided to pin my brooch on when we went for dinner. A sign of gratitude to our enigmatic and terrifying host.

Rudolph sat not at the head of the long, ornately carved table but in the middle. A group of noblemen sat around him, hanging on his every word, and he gestured as he spoke with them in a way that startlingly aped the last supper. I turned to Nadasdy. "Why have we been shown to dinner this late?"

He merely raised his eyebrows, shrugging and giving me a look that I interpreted to mean *just play along*. Rudolph entirely ignored us as we were seated on the opposite side of the table with a few other stray nobles, who looked as bemused as we were. We sat quietly, waiting to receive any sign of our emperor's intention. Then I noticed something odd. There was no food or wine on the table. It was empty of anything even vaguely ingestible. And yet dinner seemed to be in full swing, with metal plates and cutlery strewn around the table like a great feast was being had. The plates and cutlery were all still shining.

"Ah!" said Rudolph suddenly. Everybody fell silent and turned their eyes towards us. "The lovers have arrived."

He spoke incredibly quietly, only audible on account of the fact that the room had gone entirely silent. I noticed Nadasdy lay his arm on the table with a heavy clunk that was just polite enough to go unchecked but also at the same time loud and powerful enough to suggest that he would be prepared to fight his way out of here, if necessary.

"The Black Bey," announced Rudolph. And he gestured proudly as if he were showing off a trinket. "More the Black *Sevgili*." Rudolph spoke the Ottoman word for lover.

I knew this word because when Janus had been teaching me the ways of his inner religion, as he called it, it had come up time and time again. His god was not in heaven but inside the vein in his neck. He called Him his Beloved. And himself, he called *Sevgili*. I wondered at the time how God could exist inside the neck. When I asked him, he had laughed.

"Not just in the neck, Little Wing. In the veins that run inside the *atoms*, connecting us from land to stars."

He explained the word atom, which he said had been first spoken by the Roman called Lucretius more than a thousand years before. Then he'd dug underneath a fallen tree in the forest to show me its strange spindly roots grasping the earth, hanging on for dear life.

"There!" he'd said. "There is my Beloved."

Later, I developed a more complicated sense of what he was saying, bringing him mushrooms and spiders' webs and all manner of things I considered could be his god too. He discarded some and held onto others. Then he took my right hand and placed it over my heart in the way I'd noticed he often did himself.

"Here, Little Wing. Here."

Nadasdy didn't bat an eyelid at *Sevgili*, even though Rudolph stared into him with his vulture-eyes.

"Well?" demanded Rudolph.

"I'm sorry, Imperial Majesty, but I don't speak Turkish."

Rudolph sucked his cheeks and seemed to be contemplating Nadasdy right down to *his* atoms. Eventually, he sat back.

"I need you back against the Tartars."

Nadasdy tensed imperceptibly. I only noticed it because I had become so accustomed to the subtle shifts and tremors of his body that I could almost hear his muscles and sinews gathering momentum.

"Unless you want to hang up your armour and spend time with your *family*?"

Nadasdy still didn't move or even breathe, it seemed.

Then Rudolph smiled broadly, revealing his teeth, and gestured to us both, "Eat, eat! You must be hungry after your travels."

I was utterly confused.

"I said eat!" He seemed to shapeshift, going from vulture to lion as he spoke.

Nadasdy broke his silence and eyed Rudolph.

"My Imperial Lord, my wife the Countess and I thank you for your hospitality."

"But still you don't eat," replied Rudolph, relentless.

He nodded and immediately one of the nobles sat down on my right. He faced me directly with his body and simply laid a gentle hand on my arm, raising it from my lap and resting it on the table. He covered a good quantity of the flesh of my forearm with his huge palm and smiled.

Nadasdy picked up the metal fork beside him, spun it about in his fingers, eyed the Emperor with a slow, strange smile on his face and stabbed at the metal plate so that it rang out in the silence. Then he licked the empty fork and threw it on the plate, belching and exclaiming, "Turkish food!"

Rudolph burst out laughing and the sound was swiftly followed by the rest of the courtly company.

"Now we drink," Rudolph said. He nodded to somewhere just behind us, and I could hear the doors to the hall opening up. He started to talk in that quiet, low voice of his to the man next to him. I didn't recognise the man, but I could see he was Rudolph's new favourite. When I looked back at Nadasdy chatting coarsely with those around him, I noticed his hands were ever so slightly shaking.

The night wore on. I was the only woman there. No one spoke to me, neither the guests nor the servants who finally brought in food and drink. Nadasdy was busy placating the lords around us with what I assumed was military small talk. Rudolph was whispering furtively with the man next to him. They were of one mind on everything, taking turns to nod at one another. When I was certain I had become almost completely invisible to everyone, I put my hand over my heart. I heard my own rhythmic *thump, thump, thump.* It gave me comfort to hear myself counting out time – my own time and nobody else's. The noises around me blurred into one. When, for a moment, Nadasdy was spared the direct chatter around him, I reached out my hand to touch his.

"No!" interjected Rudolph out of nowhere, pouncing like a

tiger on this tiniest of gestures. "You are not to touch. I need Bathory pure. I *require* it."

"Majesty?" I asked.

He instantly flew into a rage, wine spilling over his bejewelled cup, his eyes white and black with anger.

"Control your wife, Nadasdy. She's talking to me."

"Elizabet…" He held his hand over mine but didn't touch me.

I was so confused and terrified that I stared, first at Nadasdy then at Rudolph. Rudolph lowered his eyes and his voice. When he looked back at me, the rage had disappeared, but his eyes hadn't changed. The white of them shone and the black became two pools, daring me, willing me, to fall in. He spoke evenly again, and again I had to strain to hear him.

"Bathory, I've often wondered what to do with you. It's been easy enough to deal with Bathorys before. You're all so damned greedy and ambitious. But you…" he trailed off "… *Elizabet* Bathory… Do you know what Basta says of you? He calls you the Blood Countess. Do you want to drink my blood, Blood Countess? Do you want to see if it'll make you become *divine*?"

"No, I do not."

"Ah, she's speaking to me again."

Now I found the quiet in his voice menacing. I would rather the rage, I thought. It makes him easier to appease.

"I don't need your tongue for what I have in mind, *talto*. Although it will be easier to keep it wagging rather than wait for your womanly hands to write the messages I want you to divine for me!"

And he turned his wrists around and around playfully as if writing slowly in the air, receiving the nervous, approving laughter of his acolytes once more.

"My Imperial Lord?" This time, it was Nadasdy who questioned him.

"Don't concern yourself, Bey. I won't touch your wife, but neither will you. The *papyri* stipulate it."

The man next to Rudolph nodded in scholarly assent when the Emperor looked at him.

"Now, enough of all this… this nonsense. I need Bathory to do the travelling that she's so famous for. I order her to do it for *me*."

"Her travelling?" asked Nadasdy, disingenuously.

"Does she not swoon? Does she not come to? Do you not both giggle and cry…" he mock-rubbed at his eyes with his dainty fists "…like children and speak, when you think no one's listening, about 'the other world'?

"My lark has listened and sung of everything to me. You know my lark, Nadasdy. You know her well. The scars on her back sing too, you know." He sniggered and then immediately bit the air between his teeth. "Don't fret, I will lend you her again whilst I take Elizabet. Perhaps she will return you to yourself. You've become dull, Nadasdy. Very, very dull. And besides, I need you back fighting Tartars. I need the Bey. I need him. Not you." He flicked his hand dismissively, waving him away as if he were no more than an irritating child.

"Now, Bathory. Are you ready to scribe for me? I have the divining chamber all set up. We have an Emerald Table and everything! Oh, you've never seen such magnificence."

His entire countenance had changed once more. Now he was an excited boy who couldn't wait to show off his toys to us all. He seemed to squirm in his seat with delight. This was his most frightening mode. If I were a fly, I thought, this would be the moment before he pulled my wings off.

Amidst his noise and madness, I noticed one small detail. One thing that Rudolph didn't seem to know. He'd said nothing at all of the press, of the coffins, or the tunnels under Cachtice. Had Beata not known, or had she omitted to tell him? I held the thought close to me. It was the only thing that kept the thin veil between me and my absolute terror in place.

*

The stone steps spiralled downwards, and I could tell from the echoes of our feet, searching their way upwards, that we had gone deep underground. I'd been blindfolded, but it seemed that this was more a part of some ritual than it was about keeping the location of the room secret. It had been easy enough to count the few corridors and turns from the dining hall we'd been sat in only moments ago. A door creaked open in the silence. I was left standing by a wall. The smell of incense and candlewax filled the room quickly.

I heard the unmistakable swish of cloth. The Emperor was being undressed and then dressed again in something that sounded more like silk than the leather and velvet he had been wearing previously. I heard him take a few steps, ascending from the floor, perhaps to a platform. Then he sat down abruptly, silks crumpling beneath him. There was one last creak that suggested a wooden chest opening, some fumbling, and then the crack of metal on stone as a great pole or staff was crashed down. Whatever madness was about to happen was now in session.

A hand wrapped around my arm and led me deeper into the room. The voice of Rudolph's advisor rang out loud and clear. "Bow before Hermes Trismegistus, daughter of the moon. Bow before your eternal sun." I was utterly bemused, and it was only when a foot kicked the back of my knee that I realised that the 'daughter of the moon' was me and not one of Rudolph's objects or animals. Two pairs of hands grabbed my arms. I could hear the sound of metal leaving a casing. If I hadn't known that Rudolph wanted me alive, this would be the moment that a dagger would have entered my chest.

But it wasn't. Instead, a third pair of hands ripped at my dress with the short blade. Some inner part of me, some devil-may-care Elizabet, wanted to laugh out loud at the scene that followed, but I bit my lip. The man ripping the dress hadn't accounted for the fact that I was well encased within it; that whalebone and layers of stiff satin resist the intrusion of barely sharp ritual steel. What had started as something pompous and ceremonial soon gave way to grunts and exasperation. He simply couldn't work out how to rip the dress off me.

Eventually, the man put the dagger down, stood behind me and started unlacing the corset with great difficulty. His fingers must have been fat, less than dexterous and unused to the finery of contemporary ladies' garments. When he'd managed to undo all the ribbons, the corset didn't fall away. I knew this was because it was also fastened by an unseen panel at the front which hooked around to the velvet ribbon that travelled up my bust and lay in a taut circle around my neck. He pulled at the corset again from behind and I nearly fell flat on my back. I reached around, slapped his hand and undid the rest of the front myself. I then laid the slightly torn corset down in front of me, stood up and started unfastening the skirt. As it fell, I could almost hear the disappointment fill the room. I now needed to undo all the linen undergarments whilst blindfolded on a stone floor that was so lacking in grip it must have been gleaming with polish. It became clear to everybody present that this would both take time and be an inelegant exercise.

"Enough!" shouted Rudolph. I could hear faint murmuring and gathered he must have been receiving advice from his favourite, who hovered beside him like an adhesive waiting to find a free surface.

He finally spoke. "Take the daughter of the moon outside, let her undress herself in the light. Then bring her back in here with her eyes re-covered."

A lantern was taken from off its stand, the men led me out, shut the door behind me, unblindfolded me and then watched me as I sat on the second lowest step to remove the rest of my clothes. I was re-blindfolded, but badly, and could see the space just in front of me. Then I was taken back into the room and the ritual began all over again.

Something cold and wet was daubed in sweeping motions across my chest and my forearms and I instantly recognised the texture and the smell. I was being written on with ink! I managed to squint down to see what was on my chest – a word that was not meant for my eyes but for those standing in front of me, and so it appeared upside down as I strained to read it from this angle. I surreptitiously sucked in and then puffed out my belly to see the full sweep of the letters from top to bottom: *R-E-B-I-S*.

I calmed my breathing and tried to recall where I'd seen this word before. Then I remembered. It was in one of the books John had brought to Nadasdy and I, just before we had set out for Prague. 'Rebis', from *Res – Bina*, meaning 'the two in one'. Suddenly a kind of sadness replaced the fear since Rudolph had first summoned us to him. I felt I'd become like paper in Rudolph's hands; my body, something to be written on and distributed amongst his peculiar company, but at the same time a thing that I was unable to see or read myself. I was not 'two in one' here. I was zero. I was being written out of myself and into Rudolph's strange ritual, letter by letter.

I smelled the ink again and straightaway the word 'solve' was written on my left arm and 'coagule' on my right – 'dissolve' and 'coagulate'; two alchemical actions through which the material world was transformed, or so they promised. When they scribed the word 'fix' on my chest over my heart, the matter was settled. My heart would be taken from me; not my physical heart – not now at least – but my subtle heart, the heart of my desires. I would be fixed. I would love what the Emperor wanted me to love. I would beat to the rhythm Rudolph wanted me to beat to. I would be written into the shape of the collector of secrets.

Perhaps a scribe is a nothing. A zero sum that is cancelled out the moment the story is told. The more Rudolph took his place as the 'sun', the more he erased his 'moon'.

"How do you manage to live so lightly, here?" I remembered asking Janus.

"Because I'm invisible. And invisibility can be the greatest power available to a man – or a woman," he'd answered.

"How can being invisible be good? It's like being a ghost."

"Exactly, Little Wing. No one can hang a ghost."

Standing naked now and written over with Rudolph's alchemical symbols, I was anything but invisible to the company gathered, and yet, by virtue of the blindfold, my own body had been rendered invisible to me. Also, I couldn't see how *they* saw me; I could only imagine it. All the terror. All the unknowing. I felt that in an odd way they were trapped under the very same spell they were trying to effect on me. For all my fleshly exposure, they couldn't see me – see that I was spreading Servetus' heresy about the heart and the divinity of humans without the church or emperor. They couldn't see a woman as a revolutionary and a reformer. They could only see their own writing, emblazoned on my body; a living incantation. We were both trapped in the meat we provided for each other's stories. But whereas I ultimately knew of their game, they had no idea, just yet at least, of mine.

Chapter Sixteen

Nadasdy had managed to get a note to me via Anna's hands. Rudolph had stationed a servant with us, a young woman called Gerda, who was almost entirely silent. She sat by the door and did little else, occasionally shifting from right to left in her chair to keep the blood flowing in her veins. Anna had started to hum a folk tune I recognised from Cachtice, rhythmically patting the side of her dress, which I knew contained a discreet pocket. Once I noticed, I feigned a shortness of breath and she ran over to me to loosen my corset, slipping the note from her pocket to mine in a movement that suggested she had been doing this kind of transfer all her life. Anna was born not for deceit but for revolution. There's a difference between them.

I could find no time to open the note until later that night when I lay in my bed. I had spirited its papery surfaces inside a Bible so stiff that it had clearly never been opened. I was reading it when Gerda surprised me. It was only now, last few candles guttering as the day drew to a close, that I'd managed to find a single unobserved moment to turn its ornately designed pages.

My dearest, I must know that you are safe. Get word to me however you can. I'm occupying the same room we were shown to when we first arrived but have no clue where you are. I will find you.

Yours in love, F.

I closed the book and held it to my heart.

"My lady is religious," said Gerda loudly, out of nowhere. Her sudden move to speech would have shocked even the dead.

"My religion is the religion of love," was all I responded cryptically.

Gerda looked sad for a moment and then resumed shifting and squirming in her sentinel position.

"Gerda, why don't you take a blanket from my bed if you're going to keep watch of me all night in that old chair. I can practically hear your bones bruising against the wood."

She looked at me suspiciously. She didn't move. I sat up and took the topmost woollen layer off my bed. I bunched it up into a ball and threw it over to her. Anna, who was in a makeshift bed next to me, laughed. Gerda snatched at it, smelled it, as if to detect whether there was some kind of poison lacing its fibres, and then wrapped it around herself. Then she sighed and looked at me for a good long while, becoming sad again. She was so young and round and healthy; I couldn't help but imagine that she would rather have been with a lover in a garden somewhere.

"I won't fall asleep, my lady," she said curtly. "Please don't try to slip out."

"Nor you, Gerda," I responded with a half-smile and a wink. She blushed. It wasn't long before she was snoring.

Several hours later, I heard sounds in the corridor. The night had become thick, and I could hear everything that stirred in the corridor. My breath stopped in my chest. Footsteps! A tall man in a black cloak, hood up, craned his head around the door and surveyed the sleeping bodies, sprawled as if on butchers' slabs. "Come, *talto*."

Gerda awoke. The man put his finger to his lips. "Shh… the Emperor has called. Fetch my lady's cloak."

Gerda leapt up from the chair and threw herself around the room, looking for it in the dark. Anna passed it to me, and I slipped under his robed arm and out of the door. I followed the man silently as he strode ahead. When we turned down an empty corridor, he swivelled me against a shadowy enclave and kissed me urgently. I wasn't surprised.

"Very ritualistic," I teased.

He felt my face with his hands, my neck, my shoulders and finally my fingers, as if inspecting them.

"Are you all right?"

"Yes. Nothing so far, save for some bizarre rituals. I don't think Rudolph means to harm me in any way, not yet at least."

Nadasdy exhaled and buried his lips in my neck and curls.

"Good. But be careful. Rudolph's like this. One minute you'll be his idol and the next he'll cut your throat. Are you writing these messages he wants?"

"No. It's strange. No messages nor even a whisper that I should *do* anything at all. I can hardly see, as I'm perpetually under a blindfold. They just keep muttering and writing on me and moving me around and not much else."

Nadasdy swallowed and eyed me with concern.

"I've been reading about their *papyri*. I asked Rudolph for access to his library, in a roundabout way, and he granted it to me. I stacked up a pile of books on Greek and Roman warfare and asked a servant to grant me access to all the classical texts. I found something. Not much, mind, but a reference to a ritual to bind spirits and demons. I'm worried, Elizabet. Very worried."

"What did the rituals require?" I asked, my veins flooding with fear.

"I didn't find much, but from the 'magician' – hair and nails." He'd gone white. "All of them."

He looked around quickly and then kissed both my hands.

"I don't know how to get us out of here just yet, but I will, Elizabet. I will get us out of here."

"I'm working on it, too," I said. "What does Rudolph desire, above all? If I can create a message that sets him on a course to his desire, perhaps he'll leave us be."

"I'll try and find out, my love. I'll keep in contact via Anna."

He made to kiss me, but a door opened and large, heavy boots, whose spurs clinked on the stone floor, made us pause. We hid inside the wall's arched integument as the man passed, hardly daring to breathe. Once he was gone, Nadasdy tried to move, but I held him close. His weight against mine made me feel strangely safe, even if only for a moment.

"We *will* be gone from here soon. I promise you," he whispered.

"I know. I believe you. But to what?" I asked. He stopped and I regretted the question as all the urgency and bluster drained away from him. He looked at me like a child might, caught in a perplexing question that was beyond him.

"Just… away from this," came his response.

I nodded and we searched each other's eyes. What kind of escape could keep us away from Rudolph's reach, in the end?

*

I'm standing at the open panel. *Nothing.* No note. No location. This is strange, and it doesn't bode well. Newness is not always a good thing. It can foreshadow something bad brewing on an undisclosed horizon. The ceiling starts to fall towards me, and the floor lifts me up. This time, my removal feels violent. The panels around me stretch out and then fold in like a giant concertina seeking to crush me.

"Don't you dare take me there, time! Don't you dare!" My words are powerless.

This time, it's not the snow. Time unfolds in straight rectangular arcs and I'm in a tiny office. The office is up a flight of stairs behind a bookcase in the library. I'm holding onto the door handle. I can feel its cold rattling as I emerge, shaking it and pulling at it in a frantic attempt to free myself from the nightmarish jaws of the trap that closes around me. I've been locked in there for an hour.

Footsteps sound out on the other side, heralding the arrival of my captors. 'Ollie' and the professor are on the other side of the door. I can see them through the small opening that lets a sliver of light in. A tiny window made of thick glass. The door opens.

"I told you not to get too cocky," the professor says. I make a run for the door, but they block my escape.

Ollie grabs me around the waist and the professor stands in the door frame.

"You can kick up a fuss all you like, but no one will ever believe you," Ollie says in my ear. "Now just pipe down a second and for God's sake *get the message*. How can you not be getting the message?"

The professor looks over his shoulder into the space that opens up behind him. Then he looks back. "You're very diverting. But it's time to stop now."

My body starts to shake and my eyes flutter in and out of time. I find myself between worlds, resisting a fall *here, now,* into a magnolia corridor.

Devastation isn't all it's cracked up to be. It's actually quite dull after a while. They don't always emphasise that. But then so many stories are often about how devastation happens or how you get out of it. They don't focus on the in-between bit. The bit that lasts years. The bit that stretches out like a long magnolia hallway with no end. Waiting. Watching. Locked up.

Whenever they take me and lock me inside their home, I always end up sitting by the front door at the end of the corridor that goes on and on, winding out in what appears to be a huge expanse to my child-sized body. I sit there because it feels like the safest part of the house. Like a waiting room that's only ever going to be temporary, never meant to be lived in. My small body can't reach the handle of the heavy front door. I try dragging a chair to it, fumbling and fussing the handle that's still above me. *They* come back into the corridor to see what all the racket is and promptly burst out laughing. This is how they teach my parents 'a fucking lesson'. This is how I pay for violences that were never mine.

"Go on then. We won't stop you leaving. Just open the door." More laughter.

I look at them both, the man and the woman, batting my childish eyelids slowly. Nothing. Then I know it will be hours before the door opens again. Each time one of them picks up my kicking body and lies me down on the couch, the tall man puts his huge hand over my mouth, over and over, so I 'settle down'. It looks like settling to him, but to me the lack of air is a sign that I know I am close to death *again*. Close to meeting my angel.

There's no defeating this kind of foe. I would defeat them later, from the inside out. I would defeat them when I came to live outside of time. They of course might be none the wiser, continuing on in their lives years after. It would be an inner atomic defeat – one that lives inside the cells pulsing rhythmic. Only I would be free of both of them. And they wouldn't *matter* anymore. Perhaps they would disappear altogether like a tree in a forest with no onlookers. Who knows how the universe works? Who knows how justice comes to *matter* in the hands of time?

But *here, now*, in this early pocket of time, trapped inside the never-ending expanse of the corridor, I look back to the front door. The handle twists and turns. It has buttons and locks. The woman inside me who lived years across time could have been able to open it. But to my child's brain, it is as mind-boggling as a Rubik's cube. I slide to the floor and cry. I never try it again. As an adult, whenever I was offered a jigsaw puzzle or some other impenetrable game, I'd blink my long lashes, mutter some thanks and hope that time wouldn't come and redraw the world around me, sending me back to the corridor.

I got given an actual Rubik's cube once, on my thirtieth birthday. A 'throw-back' gift along with neon plastic earrings and a card with some Kate Bush lyrics scrawled inside. Early in the morning, when everyone had left the party or was asleep on the living-room floor in a tangle, I went out into the garden and set it on fire, putting my hand on my heart and singing quietly like I'd just slain a monster.

And that's what I mean when I say devastation is boring. It lives inside the unnoticed things. It looks like a long magnolia corridor that you sit inside of whilst other people decide on your fate. Everyone these days remembers how colourful the eighties were. I just remember them as magnolia walls and brown ashtrays and his huge oxygen-defeating hands.

Here, now, as a young child, I sit back in that corridor again. I imagine myself throwing colour all over the magnolia expanse. I draw a beautiful sunset all over it in my mind's eye – blue and orange and yellow – all burning, bright colours. I commit each quadrant of colour to memory like a mandala, until eventually, I forget the lock and the other difficult bits – like when they would lift my body up and throw it around different rooms, playing *Ziggy Stardust* on full volume on repeat.

When I crawl back to my sentinel position in the hallway, waiting and knowing nothing will come, I can see the whole imagined sunset pretty much unchanged. I add little painted flourishes – a bird, a tower, a woman at the window also just waiting. Just watching. I focus in on her. I hear her singing quietly, then whispering gently to me, "Little Wing… Little Wing… We are both Little Wings…"

And I look at her beautiful antique face and smile. "Here it is. Here it is. I found it. I found the sky."

*

My fingers are moving across a keyboard again. I read out loud as I write, awash in the white and blue light of the screen, its glow brighter than flame, calling me to its pulsing and peculiar world.

Gravity. It lies at the centre of all space and time. Without gravity, nothing makes sense. With its incredible force, it pulls us to the earth and makes meanings out of nothing. Who in their right mind would try to intervene? It might be possible to tell new stories and hope that one day their quantum resonances might travel far enough into the brain to make us do something differently this time. But nothing really changes unless the descent to earth itself – the gravity of it all – is re-storied. You can tell as many stories as you like, hoping that just by thinking things anew you can change the world. But it means precious little unless it bonds to the tiny structures that make worlds. Unless the force that pulls you in, pulls you in differently, re-storying itself in the process through you and all your stories.

The words were taking shape on the bright screen in front of me. Not one letter at a time, but randomly. A curve of an 's' here, the straight back of a 't', the doorways of the 'o's pushing open. Language moves. *Language is alive!* Like time itself. It also lived in the body.

"It has to be done differently," I whispered to myself. All the patterns that arced out when time folded its divine fist, bringing origin stories back to it; these were the traces of how time and all its stories met with gravity, their trajectories sliding through the spaces between time's fingers even as they crunched down.

The fold, the crunch, the mark, they disordered time to human eyes, but in truth – in the tiny world hidden deep inside each of us – these were the things that scribed out the world as we knew it. *Time lives inside the body*, I said, and felt it circulate around my tongue, waking up something that had laid dormant within me, forging a deep knowing, a spell of sorts that brought me to life, lodging like a seed inside my belly.

All the locked rooms are gone – hers and mine. I click back on the keyboard and bring up an image of Bathory. Her portrait emerges. One of the last images to survive the fire they made after she died that burned away all the traces of her that fell outside the story. I know I can't save Bathory from the marks and folds that made her. The marks that appeared as Thurzo – the self-styled little emperor of his own growing kingdom, or in the form of Rudolph, whose fist was even now, in another part of time, crushing the world down around her in his ritual chamber. But perhaps Bathory could rewrite her world through me. Through my listening fingers. Was it selfish to hope that listening deeply to her, inside the ear of time, would provide a wise new structure, not just for her but for us all? For me. For the child in the snow and all the others that fell from time in violent ways. Another piece of women's knowledge, that when linked to all the other silent stories of women fighting *against all odds* to restructure the forces that bound us beneath our emperors, would help us create a new kind of gravity? Who alive could challenge gravity and survive?

I look down at my own hands as everything changes around me again. I breathe and *pause* – *I just pause* and there I am, in the world between life and death again, *here, now*. I can see a doorway made of pure light. Then I see my Angel of Death, and a little further in the blackness, punctured only by a few twinkling and revolving points of light, I see her – Bathory the woman. Bathory the radical. The printer. The revolutionary.

I breathe in and move towards her, tracing the beginnings of a circle with my footsteps. She mirrors my pace, and we orbit each other, moving in and out of time, shifting with each step from her castle wall, her place in the world, to mine. The curve we tread changes us back and forth and back and forth between worlds. At times, I am the ghost in hers, a particle that couldn't be seen but could be felt. Then she in mine. Our story becomes one story seen one way through the past and another way through the future until it doesn't matter anymore which is which. Except it *matters* so much. It creates the many worlds we live in and out of at each moment.

At the centre of our orbit stands our Angel of Death: our fulcrum. We spiral around her – the 'she' that isn't a 'she' but is somehow *originary,* beyond genders and at the same time the ending of all things. She isn't distinct from us. We, all three of us, are shifting points, an entanglement larger than ourselves.

"It's you!" I call out into the void that sucks in all the light. "Always you! You're the force that binds us! *You're* the story of gravity, not Rudolph, not any man or emperor, but an angel." The angel disappears and Bathory and I instantly collapse into one another. Like a homecoming. We're carried towards one another on an enormous wave brought about by our angel's absence who, in her disappearance, is no longer acting like a fold between the paperlike surfaces that keep us separate. Bathory and I reach for each other in this space, and as we're about to touch, a strange kind of magnetism overwhelms us both. It flings us apart all of a sudden to what feels like the furthest points of the universe. The further apart we are flung, the larger the universe grows, as if we hold a great tape measure between us which, as it is pulled out, gives shape and form and meaning to the world. Unfolded, we story the world. *Gravity* has many meanings. Inside it, all the heaviness, all the colour, all the light.

I'm flung back to the present. And quickly, I know where I've landed, so I also know at what point in her life Bathory has landed. The circle that diffracts our stories in space and in time speaks of the end of illusions. It speaks of love, *only love.* This is going to hurt. *This is going to be painful,* I think to myself. This is going to be a lesson to burn the powdery half-waking heart into a diamond. To teach it the substance of love and letting go. To teach it about flight, forging a path towards a new wise knowledge. Time wants to devour these stories. So, I'll place a little doorway around Bathory so she'll know how to deal with what Time has in store for her *here, now*. I'll fold the stories down together to find a new, lively word haunting its edges and use it to fashion an opening that leads in and beyond. Crossing worlds, from *talto* to *talto*. Then I'll whisper the word across time to Elizabet: *love. Only love.*

Rewrite your origin story never meant *imagine the world otherwise*. It meant circling inside the windmill, grinding the grist and the wheat and all the things that life brings to completion *just a little differently this time*. Until the stories led out of darkness and into the streaming dance of photons inside all things. Across all time.

*

I can still hear the word ricocheting as time sends me somewhere again. *Love. Only love...* And I know where I'm going now. I ready myself, half sad, half expectant, like looking at a photograph of one long lost to time, knowing it will wake up, stretch, and move out of its frozen two dimensions.

The first time I fell in love, it felt like heaven had reached down, sneaking off from its rightful position holding suns and stars and giant planets up in the sky to kiss me shyly on the forehead. My body felt *full* and light at the same time. Everything I'd known up until then, all the death, all the hurt, all the pain went away in a flash. I remembered thinking that God had decided to reward me for getting through it all, even at my tender age. That the reason for all my flights in time, the reason even for my untimely first death, had been to prepare me for the magnitude of falling in love. To appreciate it fully. If the world was so full of disaster, then this was divine compensation. This was what it was all about. And I had finally been given it. Not the postcard version of love. The version tourists of the heart give to one another. The love that washes the wound it inflicts, stinging like a salve, cracking you in places you never knew you had in you. The innocent tumult of your *first love.*

I felt it every time he picked up a paintbrush. Every time he hummed out of tune. Every time he held a brightly coloured ball aloft, saying, "Watch this" and flinging it with two others into the air in arcs that dizzied my mind like multicoloured butterflies that resisted gravity; eventually falling, just as we did together, to the ground. Every time he moved towards me, daring to kiss me, although it was forever an unspoken forbidden.

"I love you."

"I love you too."

The words are never enough. The stolen touches are never enough.

He keeps winning prizes for his paintings, and all the journalists want a piece of him. They're like dogs or sharks or vultures, out to catch him, whatever terrain he navigates. And he is a master of disguise. Part-boy, part-camouflage. A little bit of everything because that's how he survives. It wouldn't be appropriate for me to love an older boy. And besides, who knows where I'll be in time? Who knows where this unexpected early fame will take him? There aren't any warning signs. No suggestions that he might be hastening towards death's teeth. But my heart races and clatters inside my chest with tremors of knowing. It's a strange knowing – the knowing that death is advancing on the soul of your beloved. A satellite that orbits death's gravity, sending messages into space, hoping, waiting, *dying for* a response. He moved from virtual to actual and back again every day, in an endless haunting of what it is to be human. I was just too far away to hear him.

"What are you afraid of?" he asks.

"Nothing. Nothing at all," I lie as we walk through the fields, the bluebells swaying amidst a wealth of wildflowers that signal early summer. He wears a leather jacket, even in this heat, tentatively swinging an arm around my waist and then breathing in, anticipating retaliation. I don't. I just look at him questioningly. He responds – as he always does – with something totally unexpected.

"Let me tell you how I see you. I see you as a lion, pawing at life as if... as if you were... going to eat it!" And he lunges at me, making childlike roaring noises, bringing me down into his arms, becoming bold, a rush of pent-up desire cascading through him and reaching me in this sudden burst of intimacy. This sudden revelation of skin against skin.

"When I'm with you," he elongates the word *you*, crawling his fingers up my legs as he does so, "I am always amazed by what you say, by what you do, by how you make me feel. There. That's it. How's that?"

"Pretty good!" I laugh bashfully. The sun is in my eyes, and I blink to scatter the light. I still see his image, his beautiful face interspersed with the yellow-white rays of June. I fuse him with the sun then and there, unaware that each year, I will revolve around this snatched moment, that took place in a field, when no one else was looking; the opposite of death. Of his death to come.

"I have to go back to London."

"I know."

Six months later, I would be back there too. I would go to great lengths to seek him out slyly, evading the prying eyes of those that would forbid us. I would be just in time to find him. In a way. Just not in time enough. Standing beneath his window, I imagine the moment he decides to end it all, looking about his room with no place else to go. No place else that's safe, at least. All the tiny pills the doctor had given him would have vanished, leaving only the broken and erupted shells of discarded blister packs lying around his table.

So instead, he would have decided to roll up a huge joint, licking the paper between his fingers to seal it shut and burning the endpoint just enough. He would have inhaled deeply and stared at his most recent canvas, *The Three Graces*, all *fallen* from grace. The statues were painted broken, looking for all the world like they had been hit by an immortal hammer. A new kind of decision is come to. A broken and tired decision.

"Come, my boy, come out here to me." It would be the voice of his mother, always his mother; she who was forever calling him back home to her ghostly arms in the sky. Winding him back to her originary gasp – the first sound she made when she found out she was pregnant with *him* – her baby boy. He would have opened the window at this sound; to the sound of *she*. All the *shes* in the world, they all reach out to him...

And he ribbons his body out towards them, falling like fleece into their embrace. He never lands, though he's pierced by metal spikes below, clutching to the inside of his body like a second spine that now grows out from the first. But he never really lands. *Not really*. He defies gravity. He simply climbs higher and higher into her imaginary arms where all wrongs are righted. His Angel of Death in the sky smiles and wraps him in her warm embrace. The blood drains into the cracks of the paving stones, finding a new kind of flesh to inhabit. Later, it's washed clean with a power jet. There's no word for a horror like this. The sky, the atoms, the sounds fill the rim of the heavens with their angelic chatter.

And he would pick up the phone... I keep writing it pleadingly in my notebook, but gravity insists on pulling him downwards, from all his despairing, to the unforgiving street below.

Not in my arms, not in my life, but up there – up there is the place his soul seeks to call home. I let him fly up. I will keep the gravity and leave him the air. That's the only gift of love I have left to give. Take it, my love. Take it and go.

There are some things you just can't rewrite, no matter how hard you try.

The blindfold is removed. I stand in the stone circular room of Rudolph's design. I can just make out two hands on either side of my face, the cloth blindfold between them, slack in the middle, creating a moving swerve as the man who removes it stands back, smiling. His features become clear. It's Rudolph, smiling that sickly-sweet smile of his.

"Where did *you* go?" He emphasised the 'you' and I could feel him filling up with a mixture of jealousy and approval.

"I—"

He waved his hand as if to dismiss my words. "Fetch the Countess some water." A serving man soon came towards me with a plain goblet.

"No!" At first, Rudolph shouted it then almost immediately he regained his composure. He followed swiftly with a soft and gentle, "No, no. Bring it to me." The man hesitated then instantly took the cup to Rudolph, bowing his head and retreating cautiously.

Rudolph took the goblet and emptied the water into his own. The figure I had seen everywhere – the man-like image with the upturned crescent through its brow – shone out through the gold. Rudolph slunk back over to me. He put his hand around the back of my head, his fingers sliding across my skull like four live ribbons with which he pulled me towards him until our foreheads nearly touched.

"Drink, my little bird."

I eyed him, shuddering at his epithet. It was too close to the one Janus had given me and I wouldn't have his image sullied by fusing it, even in the smallest of ways, with the man before me now. He tipped the goblet towards my lips, and I drank a few gulps down. Rudolph smiled again, tender, and gentle as a snake crossing the grass. He lifted his own chin and surveyed me, then he suddenly let go of my head, uncertain of what to do with himself. He soon seemed to settle on an idea, though. He swirled the remaining water in the goblet, let a small trickle of spittle fall into it and swirled it again.

"Drink."

I wrinkled my nose and he laughed but didn't desist for a moment. I drank down the rest of the water. He beckoned the serving man back, passed him the goblet and when it had been spirited away, turned his gaze on me with a deadly seriousness.

"Now you can tell me where you went."

What kind of man needs to be inside a woman's body before he is capable of listening to a word she says? I smiled to myself. *This kind of man.*

"I went to the stars, my Imperial lord. I saw a great abundance of them."

"And then?"

"Then?"

"What did they say to you? What did they reveal?"

I paused. What could I say to him? How could I explain that the Angel of Death and my strange otherworldly counterpart were navigating a deep swerve that existed in the heart of all things, that brought the world into being *here, now.*

How could I explain that in a way that would be meaningful to anyone else? What could I tell him about the forces that bound us to the planet and how they functioned across time? The truth would be stranger and more outlandish than anything I might dream up. More importantly, the truth wouldn't satisfy him. My revolt had begun with Servetus' book, but now I could feel it taking me to the stars. Perhaps this was the place the real revolution would begin. Right here. Writing Rudolph out of the tiny world. Unthreading him from out of the world's story.

"They said… they said that a great force is coming your way. And that you must be prepared."

He looked annoyed. "That plan is well underway, Countess. Next time, try harder."

He went across the room to where his advisor stood. The advisor whispered in Rudolph's ear. He became excited, looking at me. He nodded to the man and then gestured he should speak.

"Go on. Get on with it."

The man crossed the floor. He was wearing long robes, black and purple, and was almost as pompous as he. He stood in front of me.

"I am Khunrath. You may bow."

"I'm sorry, my lord, but I only bow to the Emperor."

At first, his face wore an expression of utter confusion, but within a few moments it contorted into a look of pure hatred. *Ah, I thought to myself. Another man who wishes he were emperor.* I looked pointedly to Rudolph. He nodded, satisfied apparently with my show of devotion. I curtseyed low and Khunrath relaxed his jaws just enough to acknowledge my deference.

"My lord."

"I feel you are not telling everything that is revealed. But no matter, Countess. I think you're ready for us now. That you travel between worlds is not in dispute, not to me," and he looked back at Rudolph, giving one sharp and solemn nod. "I don't mind what world you go to. What we need is for you to bring back one of its demons so we can put it to use here, in this world."

"But I see no demons, my lord!"

"Silence!" screamed Rudolph. "A great master is speaking to you, and you don't have the wit to mind it."

I bowed my head again. Khunrath came close to me and laid one long finger on my shoulder. He pushed a little with its tip, signalling that I should kneel to him. When I had reached the floor, he bent down and whispered in my ear. "You *will* go, and you *will* find me a demon."

He stood upright and paced a little, scratching his chin in a performance of thought that was so hollow, so empty of any substance, that I couldn't bear to watch and so looked down to the floor silently instead.

"I will call one for you. You travel, *I* will call," he finally said.

I was dismissed and returned to my room. No one was there, save Nadasdy. He opened his arms, and I flew into them. He was the only thing that felt real to me, even in all his past murderous darkness and all his present light. I remembered Janus once telling me in the forests of Cachtice, in what seemed ten lifetimes ago, "Nadasdy is Adam."

"What?" I'd said, thinking he'd gone momentarily skittish again.

"He's Adam, the Adam of the Garden. He will fail in his heart and only ever long for the Great Return."

Then his fingers produced a couple of sweet dates from out of his pocket. He offered one to me and I ate it up, careful not to crack my teeth on the stone inside. It tasted delicious.

"You… you of course are his Eve." He pointed at me. "You will lead him both in and beyond. But mind that both parts of him really want to return. The garden of the heart and the garden of the world are always in competition. Nadasdy is split right down the middle."

Now in Francis' arms, I thought about it. I hadn't set out to save him, only at first to find a way to tolerate him. Then, it had turned to love. He had been right in the bathhouse. If he hadn't loved me and transformed my thoughts on him, I would have killed him. I would have eventually killed him in cold blood to save everyone who would be lost, and so I would have damned myself.

"My beloved, John has sent word. He needs me in Erdely. I've asked Rudolph to give you back to me."

He went and sat down in the sturdy chair Gerda had been occupying each night before. I wondered for a moment where she had gone.

"And?" I asked, not daring to hope.

"He says he'll think about it."

"Not likely. I think they're just getting started." I sighed. "Go,

Francis. Go and take care of John and Michael and the books. I don't want anyone else to die. We've put far too much in motion to let it all go to hell now."

He knew it was true. He'd known since he first received the note, no doubt. But he had come to me first. And for that I felt grateful.

"I pray we'll see each other again in this world."

"I've killed so many and spoken the words you've just said to me so many times." He covered the bottom of his forehead and eyes with his hand, shielding me from the beginning of tears – mine as well as his. "But I can't hear you say them now. Not to me."

He got up off the chair and knelt down, putting his head on my belly.

"I had hoped we might have a son one day, our own son."

"We still might."

"Yes."

I knelt down too, and our eyes met. He grabbed my chin, cupping my face in his hands.

"I have never loved before, and I will never love after."

"My love, my husband, my lord, don't say that. Say rather that you do love and that you'll always love."

He smiled at me like a child.

"I do."

*

Beata came to meet me and take me from my room to the ritual chamber. Her angular face and ash-blonde hair gave her the appearance of a sylph. If I peered really closely, I thought to myself, I might have even been able to see through her near-translucent skin and into her bones. What stories would they tell?

"Beata, where's Gerda?" I asked.

She stayed silent for the longest time. Then, just before I lost my patience with her, she started to speak. "Didn't you hear? Nadasdy got rid of her." Her eyes narrowed and she looked at me strangely, her head cocked to one side in a petty pretence of innocence.

"What are you implying?"

"I think you know what I'm implying. But it did feel good to see the Bey again. The Emperor has so missed him."

I waved my hand about as if brushing away an imaginary cobweb close to her face.

"You're not fooling anyone, Beata."

"I'm not the one doing the fooling."

It wasn't that I had unquestioning faith in Nadasdy; it was that he had simply become someone else. The 'Bey' - a figment of the Ottoman imagination in the first place - had given way to Francis who now begrudged a sword rather than flew to it. It would break my heart to truly believe he had gone back to his violent ways, but I still thought it would take more than a couple of weeks away from his wife to recreate Beata's version of him. He lived differently inside himself - inside his new stories.

"Beata. Has Nadasdy ever *hurt* you?"

She snorted at me.

"Tell me."

Then very calmly she started to tell me of how, several years ago, when she was still just a child, Rudolph had sent her to Nadasdy's room as a reward after a particularly bloody victory, when he was visiting court. She stopped in the hallway.

"You don't believe me? Hold up your candle, madam."

And she unbuttoned her corset right there in the draughty corridor. She looked at me languidly as it fell away. I saw her small breasts covered in marks.

"Look," she instructed, but all softness and sweetness in tone. And I saw long lines - scars - each one ending midway down her rib cage in Nadasdy's seal. The brands were like little kisses of ownership that had left their unkind marks on her.

"Now tell me who's being foolish."

I gasped softly and helped her to dress again.

"I know what Nadasdy has done. He will pay, in his own way, but he's not frightened of that. He will make amends."

"Twice foolish, Countess. This mark..." and she wriggled out of my grasp and pointed to a fresh scab, one running down her back, consistent with the tip of a small blade pressed a little more lightly than the others "...this mark was made not two nights ago. Shall I show you the others? Damn your 'Francis' to the hell he comes from and damn your blindness. Gerda was not so lucky, but then Gerda isn't beloved of the Emperor."

My heart slowed down, as if daring not to react, diving deep into a slow freezing. Had Nadasdy simply duped me these years? Did he play the lover with me and sadist with others? It would have to be some spectacular farce, some illusion cast not just over me and those around us, but one that he cast over himself. Perhaps I had been foolish. Perhaps it is possible to change one's story but never erase it. Had I simply added a new Nadasdy to the universe we lived in, and when one Nadasdy lived, the other one merely lay dormant, ghostly, until I and all my wishful perception exited the room and they exchanged places once again?

We arrived at the ritual room all at once, as if no time had elapsed since Beata's revelation.

"Have fun, Countess. Hopefully, we won't need to create a coffin to carry you across the border in." She smiled at me, knocked on the door in front of us and spirited herself away.

The door opened and I could see the Emerald Table Rudolph had boasted of before. It was the centrepiece of the room. Marks had been made all around the floor and walls in white chalk. I'd already blurred some of them with the arrival of my feet. At least these marks could be unmade. *Beata.* I caught myself for a moment, wishing for all the world that I was made of chalk. That I could live in a world where a giant cloth might rub away everything I had lived up until that point – including my own body, its surfaces appearing in and out of the world like magic.

"Come, Daughter of the Moon," said Khunrath. I wearily stepped forward.

Rudolph was dressed in a wild outfit, silks and satins and colours and symbols. "Ah, Countess. I hear you have lost your Francis." He smiled that sickly-sweet smile of his. "He's gone back, I believe, to assist Basta in Erdely, before moving on to the Tartar wars. He bids you a fond farewell, but if I know the Bey, he'll soon be back in Cachtice playing house with you, all alive and well again."

I remembered Janus' words, about Nadasdy being Adam, and I Eve, and how the heart could absorb anything, even a whole planet.

You don't know what the truth is, I thought to myself. *Don't let anyone ever convince you of anything.*

I blinked and the image of Thurzo biting into me and drawing blood from my earlobe came crashing into my mind, just as I had summoned up the sweet moment that Francis had pressed his thumb into my palm and whispered how he loved me into the very same ear. I stumbled a little as I walked towards the Emerald Table. The room had gone heavy, its air filling with incense. My head swam. My heart was pounding so forcefully that I could barely hear a thing above it. I fainted and, right before Khunrath caught me, I flew off into the other world.

But instead of arriving in the future of my present time, I found myself inside the Angel's arms. She held me firmly in her grasp. Warm. I looked down at my body. I was the future child again. My body was in what I now know was called a *snowsuit*. We had collapsed into each other, the two versions of 'I' that orbit one another across time. This was the moment where we

– where I – had died. The moment I'd floated up to the Angel at the end of the longest, brightest tunnel.

"You have lived all this and so much more," said the Angel.

I saw her as an angel, but I knew she was the part of me that was neither past nor future but somehow eternal; the part of me that was gravity itself, the centrifugal force that condensed me each moment, each *time,* into matter; into me.

"Do you remember when you looked after your mother when she came back from the war?" And I remembered the woman in bed I needed to reach up on tiptoes to kiss and the woman waiting for her husband to return from Mohacs, in the same instant.

"Do you remember when your true love died?" And I saw Nadasdy disappearing back into the Bey in the same moment that I saw the beautiful painter dead on the railings under the window of his apartment in the rain, disappearing into the pavement, the image inerasable.

"These are *all* your memories, Little Wing. Look," and she opened my palm with hers, resting the two on top of each other.

Out of the lines, as if growing from the markings of my fates, I could see the little doorways again, like I did before, when this story first started, on the day I died and returned. The doorways flashed up, tiny universes lying in the palm of our united hands.

"You live inside two of these at the same time, Little Wing, across time. I am an infinite number. When you rewrite the story this entanglement creates, you will die to it. Life and death are never separate; they pulse inside one another."

It was like one of Janus' paradoxes, and I wondered if he had sat before the same angel himself and then laid the pathways in my mind for such strange knowledges to find the way to me now.

"I choose the girl who died. I choose to die as her in some far-flung part of time."

"Then it will come to pass. But not just yet, Little Wing. You have more of this story to unravel first."

And I returned. Khunrath was holding me up on the floor in his arms like an Italian marble of the Virgin Mother and her Lord. I must have been heavy for him because I could feel his arms shaking as he clutched me. When I started to come around, he held my chin between his thumb and forefinger. He lifted my head up and I went from slumped to standing like a precious puppet.

"Come, Daughter of the Moon. It's time." He led me to the Emerald Table. A red length of silk was stretched out straight between Rudolph's hands, just enough for me to see some markings on it. It smelt strange, like dried blood. Khunrath pulled my right arm straight from the elbow and stood directly next to me, on my right. He raised his left arm, so the two of us touched from elbow to wrist. Rudolph bound our arms together. It reminded me of an Orthodox wedding. Only no one had asked me if I accepted.

"You are bound together, here and forever. You are one body. One gender. One thought."

Khunrath took a deep breath and nodded, and all at once a metal instrument appeared in Rudolph's hand. He stretched one of my fingers out and without warning dug the sharp part of the rod into my nail and yanked.

Flashes. White, cold thunder inside the skin. This isn't pain. This is beyond pain. I howled and nearly bit my own tongue off. And still he kept yanking. The huge attendant held me firmly in place. Rudolph stretched another finger out and repeated the process. My head lolled. Passing out with pain does not necessarily stop the pain. It was a strange state to be in. It was as if I had disappeared and the *only* thing left was pain itself. As I did so, I saw Nadasdy's face. His smile. The last time we were in bed together. Then, as I came to and Rudolph yanked again, I saw him in my mind's eye branding Beata. I saw a golden horse galloping away. I saw the boot of an angry young man kicking my head in the future, smearing my blood against the falling whiteness.

I saw Janus in the forests of Cachtice, passing me a handful of moss, from which I sucked moisture. I saw Thurzo, standing by the hearth and turning to look at me for the first time. I saw the golden cup and its stick-figure etching. I saw the man place his hand over my face as I struggled for breath. I saw my mother's smile – all my mothers, since the beginning of time. I saw into the centre of the sky, above the clouds. There was a strange absent space, and I knew it must be the heart of a dead star. I was pulled towards its light. As I fell in, I heard Janus' voice and saw him faintly, part of an incomplete drawing, the architectures of his being only half made; indeterminate. He spoke very softly, as if from far away: "Here, Little Wing, here," and he tapped on my chest, in the place just over my heart.

I fell and gasped loudly as I was flung back heavily to the present moment. I opened my eyes and blinked. Then, as the pain subsided a fraction, I saw Rudolph. I saw him becoming small, tiny, until he disappeared entirely from view, desperate to fuse himself to the atoms of the world. Then I was free from the man holding me back and I fell to the floor, dragging Khunrath with me. The binding was undone. The huge man picked me up like a sack of flour and the next thing I knew I was in my bed.

I thought I was alone. But through the haze of my unfocusing eyes I could see a figure. At first, I thought it was Nadasdy and I flinched and cried out. Then I realised it was Anna. Her face was wet with tears. I could feel a fever coming over me. I started to sweat. My throat felt swollen and watery. I blacked out and didn't wake up for days. Apparently, Anna never left my side.

*

When I finally woke up, I cursed the fact I was still here in Rudolph's palace. Why couldn't the angelic part of me grant me the smallest amount of mercy? And not to float in the in-between world or the tiny world, but to vanish entirely! To cancel myself out of the hum of the universe. I knew now that the death of one life was a simple question of scale, and that I would, in some way, go on living in my ancestors before me and in future generations to come, flocking across the earth, breathing and breeding the same old stories. In the birds and the stones, a great vibrational buzz, a distributed 'me' in an infinite array of doubles.

But a human is still a human. A lifetime is a life, at once linked to everything else and its own original. A particle arises and both it and its immutable double each cross an entire universe in search of one another. The horizon calls, and they smash together, cancelling each other out in their desire to become one.

It was the same with my husband, with the two parts of him that lived the same life, though he lived this in his own violent and peculiar way.

When I had come to and questioned her until my lungs, my breath, my heart gave up with exhaustion, Anna said that whilst it was possible that Nadasdy may well have continued his dark violence unsuspected, she knew for a fact that the books – that our *revolution* – were reaching the Szekelys. She doubted that this was all some plot of Rudolph's. John had written that Nadasdy had joined him and that they were evading Basta's spies, carefully sowing the seeds of a new world that would eventually bring him and Rudolph's reign down.

These are dark times and one can only hope, he had written.

I sat up. A thought struck me, and I related it to her.

"If Basta is removed, that means the Lords of Erdely and the Lords of Hungary can unite, just as Nadasdy had suggested before we started this adventure. They may even bring in our cousins in Wallachia. One united kingdom in the East. Free from both the Emperor and the Sultan."

"If Bocksai is made king of a united Hungary, he'll have secured the blessing of the Sultan," she replied, and rubbed her fingers together to suggest money.

I thought back to the odd, urgent man who had lain in wait and greeted me in the hallway the last time I had been at court. He had promised he would come calling and that he needed a Bathory. Now I realised there could only be one reason for that, since all the Bathory men had been murdered or executed, save Sigismund, who lived out his days in hiding, waiting for an assassin in the night. I was the remaining heir, and Bocksai knew it. But Nadasdy must have got to Bocksai first and convinced him that a military Nadasdy-Bocksai alliance would be the only way to win a war against a man like Basta. Claims and thrones would have to wait until after. I burst into tears again.

"Elizabet, what is it?"

"Nadasdy will fight alongside Bocksai, unite the region and then, when neither man gives up his claim, one will have to die. And Nadasdy will kill him. He told me to kick him if he ever made for the throne of Erdely. But this isn't the throne of Erdely under Rudolph. This is *a united Hungarian kingdom*. This is what one would marry a Bathory for."

I covered my eyes with my hands and wept through the gaps my bandaged fingers made. I sobbed from my belly. When there were no more tears left in me, I sobbed dry and bitter.

"Why would he go to all that effort to make me love him?"

Anna bit her lower lip. She had cried with me and held my head and kissed the bandages that were a mix of salt and blood.

"Perhaps he came to know you and feared you might just rid the world of him. Perhaps, after Thurzo," she was discreet, but I took her meaning, "he worried that Bocksai would come after you next." But she suddenly shook her head, seeming unsatisfied with her own suggestion. "*Or* more likely, my child, because for all his politicking and war-making, he also loves, in his own way. I believe it. I believe that in his strange way, Nadasdy loves you deeply. You're valuable to him, for sure, but perhaps you grant him something he desires just for himself: to be someone else, even for a few hours a day. A soldier, a king, a scholar *and a lover*."

"And the rest of the time…" I let the words vibrate in the air, becoming as much a question as a statement.

"The rest of the time, he is the Bey, *everywhere*, but with you."

"This is madness." I started to feel sick. Not in my belly. That would come later. The air around me became sick, as if Nadasdy's last touch still lingered and inside it I could now hear all the rooms and all the girls and all their terror.

"When I was with Thurzo, there was a time that he took me to Nadasdy's room. He told me that he could never love me as I would wish him to, but that in his own way he would. And I hated him for it. I hated that he might see me as a throne, a kingdom, a wellspring of power that he might tap and bring to fruition. But in that moment at least he was honest.

"Thurzo only ever sees himself in the future. He moulds future versions of himself along a straight line that traces destiny like a path across a mountain range. Nadasdy is all versions together. Nadasdy – now he loved me as I would wish to be loved. He made me feel part of our union, part of a circle that completed us both as much as it might complete a revolution, a new world, a new hope. And I believed him. I believed that together we could re-story our landscape."

"You can. You will. Just you, Elizabet. Just you. And I will help you."

"It's the deep pull downwards," I said, smoothing my blankets. "That's what needs re-storying. You can re-story ideas, but what happens when they meet the requirements of the flesh? The requirements of one breathing human being facing another? Ask Servetus. Where is his burnt-out heart now? Basta's Transylvania?"

"Where, my lady?"

I frowned, not recognising the word that had come out of my mouth either. It must have been *her* word for it across time.

I laughed bitterly to myself. Even Erdely itself already no longer existed. The girl who lived inside me – who signalled that neither past nor future existed but merely fluctuated and ruptured within us like tiny boxes stacked one inside another without walls – she knew no 'Erdely'. And so Erdely had already fallen. Not Basta, nor Nadasdy nor Thurzo, nor I, could ever carve something out of time and fix it in space. Except in our own stories. Except in the atoms that reached out in the hope of something that could become more-than-human. More than the man-made divine. Except when we reached out to the person right in front of us to say nothing more than: *this* is where we meet. *This is where we have always been meeting.*

*

I moved through the doorway and into the ritual room.

"Countess! How are you feeling?" Rudolph was in his ridiculous attire. He'd even found a hat and a staff with two spiralling lines circling around the central part of the staff. I remained silent. "Now, now, don't be sulky. We're making history here. We're changing the world together."

"Perhaps it's hubris to try and change the world."

He snorted a little and arranged his folds.

"Without change, what are we? Just animals in a menagerie. But we, Countess, we are human and so we are divinely obligated to create change. Surely you know that."

"What kind of change, Imperial Majesty, are you looking to create?"

"The kind that can't be undone by a sword. My brother is brewing up quite the little storm. And the Church think I am possessed by the devil. But such is the script that follows great knowledge, great change."

"What do you want from me today, Imperial Majesty?"

"Why, to go on the incredible journey with you!"

Khunrath, never further than two feet from Rudolph, chimed in.

"And to harness the power of a demon."

"Come then. Let's go and find a 'demon,'" I said, incredulously.

Rudolph smiled like a proud father, moved by success.

"See, I told you she would be pliable, eventually."

Khunrath eyed me suspiciously.

I walked to the Emerald Table. Its marks were obscured by an array of bizarre objects. A dead falcon that had been mummified and which lay on a piece of cloth that contained the remnants of my nails, a piece of paper with symbols drawn across it, and a bowl with what smelt like a mix of milk and honey. Individually, each looked sad and out of place, but together they seemed to vibrate with life.

"There's one more thing." Khunrath held up a large pair of scissors. "Don't be alarmed." He cut a strand of his own hair and lay it on the cloth with my nails and then gestured that he was about to relieve me of all of mine.

"Why don't you add your own nails to the pile too? Why just your hair?"

He shut his jaw fast and ground his teeth a little.

"Silence! Come here and turn."

I turned around and heard the sweep and high-pitched squeak of the scissors as my hair left my head and landed, for the most part, on the cloth.

"No tears?" asked Rudolph. "Hmm. I thought women were attached to their hair. Never mind."

My nail-less fingers throbbed with the urge to form a fist and punch him in the throat.

"Now. Travel."

It was my turn to snort. "I told you, it doesn't work like that."

"Make it."

We stood for hours. Nothing happened. Khunrath and Rudolph muttered in their half-Greek, half-made-up language. As I felt the chill of night continue into the dampness of dawn. I kept yawning and shifting my weight from foot to foot. My calves were close to shouting out in protest.

"Come on," I eventually said. "Please." I'm talking to Khunrath and Rudolph, but some deeper part of me is listening too.

"No! Not you," I said inaudibly to Vera in my mind's eye. But as the dawn started announcing itself in temperatures and moistures that shifted the subtle air pressures around me, I couldn't help but get drawn in closer and closer to the tiny world. The candles threw a warm, hypnotic light across my face and I thought of Nadasdy lighting dozens of candles before leading me to my bed bashfully like he did at the beginning of our romance. I could hear the sound of my heart closing. The flames flickered and danced and became large. Khunrath moved over beside me.

And there I am all at once, standing somewhere inside the towering yellow-gold fire. Except it's not fire but a large wave that takes me up. A wave made not out of water but of pure light, and I'm thrown about as if drowning inside it, a dry sea made out of nothing but brightness.

I can hear Khunrath's voice. I know that I'm at the same time inside the tiny world and in the large world of Rudolph's ritual chamber. His voice trembles and shakes about me and I squeeze my eyes shut.

"Oh, demon of the hidden realm, show yourself," he says. "Show your mighty self. I come to you in this form, in the shape of this woman, but we are one. I call you and bind you to me, in the name of the Holy Roman Emperor."

I see my future self – my scribe, my author – Vera in the other world. She's behind a flat rectangular shape that streams with a flickering blue light. The light changes colour and shape. I can still hear the faint sounds of her world and I jolt up abruptly. The rectangle is emitting noise and words and I hear my own name:

"*The Countess Bathory was deemed the world's first female serial killer...*"

I start, but I don't come out of the reverie all the way. Instead, I'm inside the blackness of the void. The Angel and the girl are there. I fall into their orbit, and we circle again. I smile at them. I feel like we're children together, playing together, circling each other with hands outstretched across time.

I would prefer to stay here, away from Rudolph and Nadasdy. Away even from Cachtice, from my son, Michael, and my daughter, Anna. Vera smiles back, and I know she has the same desire. We're pulled together fast again, but this time, instead of collapsing and then being blown apart, it's only me who collapses on the floor. I stand up, dizzy and confused. My arms are marked with words that have emerged from inside my flesh. Strange markings that have come from my bones make my stories manifest in crosses and lines over my skin. Khunrath smiles a yellow toothy smile and Rudolph trips over his gown. Sat on the Emerald Table. Shadowy and not quite real, Vera.

"I bind you, demon. I bind you to Rudolph the Second, Emperor of the West."

Chapter Seventeen

At first, I simply thought I'd wandered into a strange waking dream. Perhaps the books I'd been reading in the library had all folded together into one; the contours of their unknowable long-gone landscapes taking me with them into the dream world that surrounded me now. Or perhaps it had always been this way, and my world – the world of the twenty-first century – had been Bathory's dream and I was merely part of a story she was writing about the future. Now it was time to wake up. *Wake up, Elizabet!*

As I sat on the Emerald Table, I recognised only one thing in my surroundings: her face. Elizabet's face. Remembered from so many obscurely shared moments. From the walls and the floors and the archways. From inside my television set, which had been the last thing I had seen before landing *here, now*. Only a moment ago, we'd been dancing together inside a pocket of spacetime, and I had tried to walk forward towards her. But each straightly positioned step had led me in a curve that prohibited touch, until our Angel of Death had clicked her multi-worlded fingers and disappeared, drawing us together with such force that rather than just touch, we folded into one another.

Elizabet called it 'the deep pull downward', but I knew now that our dance was gravitational and that we were both tracing out the same question through the painful shapes made by our very different lives: What happens when the tiny world and the large world meet together? How does the tiny world reshape everything we know in time? There's no answer to this, except to live it. To be it. To recognise that this is what we're made of. It's no dream to do the deep kind of listening that Bathory and I both do. That listening is more real than anything else in the world.

When I emerged from out of the darkness and onto the Emerald Table, the two men standing in the small stone room went white as sea foam, one muttering protective charms and curses and biddings, the other remaining motionless, but not afraid. The Emperor had all the manner of a still cat. Waiting. Studying. Surveying. I felt him mapping every particle of my shifting being as if I fulfilled some need inside him that was taking shape even as he looked at me sitting on the deep green surface of the Table.

Rudolph himself appeared translucent to me, an unstable form finding itself slowly. It was the same with everybody in the room. They were present, but not reachable or fleshly. More like the hum of static when it clears momentarily to reveal shapes and forms and sounds. And yet the table still held me up and when I climbed down off it, so did the floor. It wasn't the same as standing up on the ground in my world. Each surface *repelled* me. It knew I didn't quite belong but at the same time kept me bound to it with all the magnetics of magic – a science that simply surpassed our understandings.

I had read about Rudolph before in my own world, gazing at his portrait, sensing him with all my abilities. But this meeting was unlike anything I'd ever known. It was ungodly. Unnatural.

He had conjured me here. He hadn't dreamt me in the way Lucretia had crossed worlds – mine and Bathory's. He had *conjured me out of Elizabet*, as if the cells of her body, her place in time and space, were a fundamental access point, a bridge between my world and hers across the streams of time.

If Elizabet was a ghost that forever haunted me in my cells, then the same was true of me. I haunted Bathory *in her bones*, in her blood, in the fibres of her being. Rudolph had guessed it. Rudolph had sensed it every time someone referred to her as a *talto*; traveller across worlds. A *talto* never disappears or vanishes from sight. *Taltos* went within. Therefore, in a way, they brought the otherworld to them. They travelled to the furthest edge of the universe – inside their own bones.

Rudolph had devised a mechanism by which to experience the secret that Bathory held deep. To turn her inside out. Not satisfied with dominion over Europe, he wanted to penetrate into the deep mysteries that held the inner worlds of his subjects together. He would have power over the atomic. Even over the felt sense of the world that lives inside each one of us. Rudolph: emperor not just of land but of souls. Holy Roman Emperor.

He extended his hand towards me, palm out. Then he flipped it over, exposing a dynastic ring, curling his hand into a claw. It hung suspended in the air, as if it always had and always would, even after his empire had long died. It's a strange thing to be asked to pay homage to history. I could see the ring, flickering and grainy from my shadowy state. It exerted a symbolic force over me, as if the jewel within it didn't come from out of the earth but from a place that was deeper. A place fiery and full of noise. I paused. I had tools of my own. I knew how to distill stories.

How do you bind a ghost, really? How do you wrap up the ghostly trace of somebody's future and silence the particular spiral dance it creates on its own? Rudolph's trappings weren't made out of rope or metal. They were made out of thoughts and languages and from the ripping of Elizabet's fingers into tiny pieces, of birds from the sky, of the fields made into cotton cloth, of the forests that lives inside paper, of all the things out of which Elizabet's world was constructed. These are the real tools of an emperor. Emperors fashion their prisons out of flesh and thought. And we walk our lives through them, through a system of hungry doors that lead nowhere, going round and round.

"What *are* you?" he asked.

I wanted to run. To shut the book on this dark world I had been compelled to fall into. But each time I tried to stray too far, he would twist the bindings tighter around the bird on the table and I would fall – not in the way a human falls but in the way static appears to fall if you follow a single dot with your eyes. When I looked up, I was at Elizabet's feet. She was looking at me in a mix of wonder and horror. It can't be an easy thing to see your innermost secret, the budding story of your future, no matter how raw, caught and revealed to the world around you. Bound. Ready to be made use of by a mad emperor. Elizabet drew so much of her strength from the hidden world she lived in. It was something we both shared – a mechanism for living inside places to which we had only ever half belonged, rewriting them from the inside out. Rudolph would have it. He would have this secret power. He would possess all the stories, writing himself into each one.

I looked up at Elizabet standing there in all her passion and desire, so entirely different in every way to the stories about her in my time, that would snatch her and bind her, in turn, into the shape of the *Blood Countess*. I also knew that this was a fate that would, in a thousand differing ways, be shared by all women. It was more than a history of silencing – it was a history of erasure, a history that would only become traceable in time by virtue of the hole it left. She heard this. She heard me *think* it. Her sparkling eyes filled with tears before becoming absorbed into her skin, disappearing out of sight but continuing onward to become the salt inside her body. She wanted to reach out and protect me from the smooth, ugly hands of those who had captured me, willing me to *go back! Go back! You don't belong here!* But I remained bound by the power of the table and the strange ritual Rudolph had devised.

"Tell me what *it* is," he commanded Elizabet, breaking the intense silence that had fallen over the room.

Just silence.

Rudolph became angry. At first, Khunrath muttered the word '*azoth*' several times over. Whatever it meant ,it was a hollow incantation. It did nothing, no matter how many times he repeated it. When he finally gave up, he held a dagger to her throat, suggesting that if she didn't do his bidding and communicate with me in a way *he* could understand, he would cut the knowledge out of her, "So help you, God." Still, she remained silent, her jaw straight and clamped down. I knew this wasn't some stubbornness on her part. All I could hear was the sound of her curious heart breaking. A fissure was appearing inside her that nothing would heal. I listened closely. This was greater than her loss of Nadasdy. It was deeper. It was the sound of a woman being crushed not just by love's inevitable bruising but by the weight of the forces around her. Her *talto's* heart, which had always been in some secret way free, was cracking open along the red seam that held it together. Then gravity had flown in, scattering her secret powers from the other world, forcing them to the ground. Forcing them towards Rudolph.

Nadasdy may have captured and broken her with his inevitable betrayal, but it was the Emperor who had caught her future and set it up on a table alongside his other trinkets. I willed her to fight it. I whispered to her – not in words, but in mind, in intent:

I am writing you. I am writing you even now. Your future lies not in the hands of this emperor. It exceeds his boundaries. Even my words, you exceed them too. Your story is already inside my bones and the bones of generations of other women who, like you, are greater than one single life.

Elizabet's tears dried on her pale cheeks as she looked at me. A secret holds a secret even when it gets captured and paraded about. Even when it's used like a weapon. Who knows the meaning of the secret 'I' that lives inside the shell of 'me'?

"You are a man of the past, Emperor," she replied. "You understand nothing of the future. You would be the fleshly king of time? Time will *eat* you."

At first, Rudolph flinched at the force of her words, which came from somewhere deep and immovable within her. He became like a cat, retreating only to attack more ferociously. The room was electric, charged by the forces of imperial rage. The white of Rudolph's eyes seemed to engulf the pupils, and two foamy wisps of spit collected at the corners of his mouth. Then he unfurled. It was like watching a river break. Bathory was the source and destination of all his inhuman force. She didn't buckle or break. She simply stood straight, eyeing him. I half expected her to die then and there but Khunrath lunged forward and grabbed him before he was able to reach her. "My Imperial Lord, if you kill the Countess, this demon might disappear with her!" he shrieked.

Rudolph pounced. But instead of ending Bathory's life then and there, he swung around. That Khunrath could be more in awe of a demon than God's anointed ruler was too much for him. He grabbed the ritual dagger that was still in Khunrath's hand. Then he threw him instantly into the wall behind him where he landed with a thud. He put one hand around the magician's throat and with the other started to beat his face again and again with the dagger's ornate handle. It was an ugly sound. The cloths and wrappings that Khunrath was shrouded in muffled some of it, but otherwise his shrieks and cries were terrifying. Rudolph grabbed at a long swathe of silk and stuffed it inside his mouth. Each time Khunrath tried to draw breath he made a noise like a broken animal. He then turned the dagger around and plunged it with an almost inhuman force straight into the arm Khunrath had grabbed him with. He stabbed over and over in bloody retribution until a blot of red that formed across the whiter parts of his robes spread out, across and down, affecting a transfusion of sorts, feeding the silk with his blood. With each stab, the Emperor shouted, "You *promised!*" and "*Make her listen!* and "*I am your Emperor!*"

I had seen Nadasdy through Elizabet's memories, plunging the sword into the giant blacksmith. I had seen how every day she lived in a world made of unhinged violences. In my own life I had seen and felt the heavy hand of death punching me over and over again until I had floated up to meet my Angel of Death. I had experienced violence through the eyes of a child and as an adult. But I had never seen anything like this. It wouldn't be the worst to come. Bathory would see things that would turn her blood to ice and make her doubt whether any of us were still *human* anymore.

Khunrath passed out, sliding to the floor, and Rudolph became quiet as fast as he had raged, though he breathed heavily. When he turned around, his face and neck were spattered in blood. He wiped his face with the back of his hand, like a distracted child at dinner.

"We've all seen time eat flesh, Bathory," he said softly, "but you've found a way to capture its shape inside you. You have transcended time. I can only imagine it. I can't stem its flow. I can't control its wishes. I can only sit back and watch it pass. Time has made me weak. Time, not death, is the rebellion that threatens me."

He wiped his chin with his arm again, becoming calmer, though he appeared nothing less than bloody and hellish, a creature from a more ancient part of the world. Bathory had slid to the floor, her legs weakened from what she had witnessed. Rudolph crossed over to her, lowered himself and took her head in his hands. He put his forehead against hers and then brushed it with his lips. "My dear," he said softly, as if suddenly speaking to a beloved daughter, "when Khunrath comes back to his senses, I'll have him find a way to compel your demon to speak. If it doesn't, I will tear your flesh from your body." He rose. "Freedom isn't found in silence, my lady. In our empire, freedom resides in the will to stay alive. Just that. No more. No less. *I* would have freedom. I would have it at any cost. I will die soon, or be brought to death by my brother, Matthias. Would you stand between your Emperor and his wish?" He put his hands behind his back and looked Elizabet over as if surveying a treasure, calm and even as the surface of the sea after a squall. Then he turned to the shifting, shadowy space I occupied.

"Truly, it is a miracle of time. Speak to it, Bathory. Do it for me."

Elizabet opened her eyes slowly. They were unfocused and heady. She rose almost blindly, wrapping her arms around herself. She was exhausted.

"My Emperor, all I know is that this *demon*, as you call her, is the ghost of my future. I can tell you nothing more than this: in time, a man is still a man. An emperor is still an emperor."

She looked at Khunrath who was now passing in and out of consciousness repeating, "*Azoth, azoth.*"

"Blood is still blood."

This kind of knowledge served Rudolph no purpose. Yet it made worlds. I knew that if he learnt to harness the power of the tiny world, he would truly become death's agent. He wouldn't make worlds; he would destroy them. Rudolph sighed, exhausted now too, and climbed his dais to his great stone throne. He took a sip of wine from the cup beside it and gestured to Bathory to do the same. She shook her head. He looked at me then; to the space I *occupied*.

"It's such a bizarre thing that I would have finally possessed what I wanted and yet be unable to hear its stories. What would it tell me? Speak to me, Countess. I am willing to listen. To truly listen. Tell me about this ghost of the future."

Bathory looked at me, not at him. Then she spoke quietly. "She is me, part of me. And I am part of her. We know the same things. We feel the same things. She's my shadow across time. I've seen her world. It's faster and louder, but I tell you, Emperor, power is still power. What men do with it – it's all the same. Always the same."

He sighed again before muttering to himself, barely audible, "Catholics, Lutherans, Calvinists, Turks, Jews and Pagans. And everyone is out for someone's blood. Did I do right for the Empire? I have *tried*." He seemed exasperated, for a moment almost pleading with some part of himself that he rarely allowed room to breathe.

"Tell your demon that I don't seek rule of the flesh. I have ruled the whole Christian world! What I want is deeper. I *will* have dominion over time. I *will* be at the centre. Let my brother, Matthias, come for me. Let him think he can rule the world. Let him have the headache of Catholics and Protestants and border wars! I'm bored with the earth. I'm bored with pleasure and pain. I have paid for it all in advance with my soul. Tell this demon. Tell it I will reward it with whatever it needs if it will sow me into its supernatural world. Matthias may rule over the land, but each leaf, each grain of sand and soil, each droplet of water will whisper *Rudolph*."

It became clear to Bathory in that moment that Rudolph wasn't that different from any other human being. He, too, was crushed by the crown of empire. He, too, knew that it was the crown and its stories that ruled, not him – not really. And he also wanted to displace it; to revolt. To cheat death. The crown itself kept him anchored to a world that had made him into the shape of an emperor. But he would be king *all by himself*. As if he could make himself *the only man alive* who possessed all of time inside his body. To shrink time into the size and shape of human ambition rather than dissolve into its vastness. Over and over, this story remained the same and we all oriented ourselves towards the pull of its open, chattering mouth. *Immortality...*

I had an idea then. "*Time lives inside the body. Come over to me,*" I whispered to Elizabet silently, willing her across time in this space *now*. She moved towards my position, bringing all the momentum of her world towards me. I lifted my hand, and she did the same. For a moment, we were of one mind. The magnetic resistance that held us in our separate places died down. Something about the Emerald Table and all the strange rituals that had brought me out of Bathory's future, her writer, her echo hundreds of years from now, allowed for a new kind of meeting. Origin and echo folded. We reached *through* each other, into the in-between world.

"Angel of Death," we whispered. Calling her to us together.

*

The room went dark. The Angel appeared, standing between the two of us again. She put one hand on my chest and one on Bathory's then she drew us together with a clap that was like thunder.

When I opened my eyes, I saw Bathory in front of me. The sun was warm on our faces, and we lay in what looked like tall grasses and flowers that moved like waves on the ocean, the breeze penetrating the spaces in between each vibrant stalk. But instead of being made of the fibres of plants and leaves, each blade pulsed and hummed, and each flower's head held within it a tiny spinning world that tremored electric. This was no ordinary 'field'. We were in the liveliest part of the in-between world. We were somewhere *life-giving*. I reached out and held Bathory's hand. It was also warm and soft, and pulsing. It felt like touching something or someone for the first time – as if we had never really touched anything ever before, just played with pressures and sensations that aped at *touch*. Our fingers travelled across each other's faces in a reunion of two people who had never met before because they had been inside each other all along.

"This can't be, it cannot be!" we both whispered.

The Angel of Death's voice came shuddering through both of us, reaching us in a space beyond the ear. "Listen to me, Little Wing. When you pass behind the veil of space and time, all decoherences fall away. You have found a story that lives deep inside yourself, scored into you by time, running forwards and backwards in an endless loop. A story about power, knowledge and violence in the human world, a surface of differing intensities that live inside the body and make the world. You can stay here now as part of this field, forever united as one being *inside the story*, or you can go back into the world of separations. The world where stories are written down. It's your choice, but once you separate, you will never again become unstuck. You will return to the finite world of cause and effect. The rip in front of your past will be sealed, and the rip behind your future will also be sealed. You will exist inside each other as echoes, as memories, but you will never again pass through the veil between worlds. You have found out what it is to be *exhumed* of your own individual stories and enter into a far deeper one. You have drawn an emperor to you, just as he has drawn you towards him. You have stood up inside the timeless fiction that makes us human. Now it is time to return to *time. Linear time.*"

I looked down. The writing returned momentarily to my skin as it had with Elizabet's, showing me the history I was written into. The history of women I wanted to rewrite *here, now*, with such urgency. She drew an otherworldly finger across the markings, moving from mine to Bathory's as if reading Braille, one story across our two bodies. She smiled at me. I sensed the world around us, the strange, pulsing field fading. Each blade of grass humming with its many worlds started to become blurred, filling with static until everything became one ancient hum travelling through space; through the stars.

"*Write me well,*" Elizabet whispered, and she blew me a kiss before she too dissolved into the void.

Chapter Eighteen

The shadowy girl from the future had disappeared. But I remained. I felt a calm inside myself, the likes of which I had never known. In her disappearance, I had reclaimed a part of myself. A vital and necessary part. Rudolph jumped to his feet.

"What have you done?"

All he had seen was the shadow touch my hand and then disappear into me, as if I had swallowed her whole.

"Your empire will never end," I said quickly from my position in the room, lest he kill me in cold blood right there. My words seemed to echo through the stone, catching and trembling like a caught flame made sonic. Rudolph's head snapped to attention. So, I continued.

"Your crown is sown into the land, forwards and backwards in time. It's just how the world works. It's the only way we know how to be human. We make heads for crowns, Majesty, passing ourselves down from generation to generation through the stories of men who seek to rule. You are that story. You are Rudolph, Holy Roman Emperor. You will persist forever in the memory of the living. You will live atomic, always, inside the flesh of the earth."

"And my dominion?"

"It just might be an eternal story. But a *real* one. One that lasts forever in the world. I will write it all down for you, Imperial Majesty. I'll write everything I know in my bones about the future. And I will send you everything about time's desires. Everything I know about its secret kingdom that lives inside ours. Everything that comes from the future to us *here, now*."

*

When I returned, I was thrown straight into linear time. I no longer moved across time in the strange pulse of now here, now there, now then. Cause and effect returned. And, at first, I felt nauseous in my belly. And I felt powerful beyond imagining. I still knew all the major events of my life to come. But small changes became large swathes of difference. Death couldn't be averted. In fact, now death had a strange kind of consequence to it. And so the moment it entered my life, I found a new way to stay with it. To stay with all the stories that came and went as we passed along on the back of the arrow of time.

2022. Her black hair was all gone, revealing the delicate shape of her skull as she lay in the hospital bed. She was singing under her breath. Sometimes, I could hear the words she sang. Sometimes, they fell away to one indistinct hum. She looked up at me.

"I look pale as death."

The metal rail running along the side made it look like she was in a boat tethered to a harbour. I had to lean over it to hear her.

I had gone to her when she'd first been diagnosed. I went back to her house as soon as the text message buzzed up: *Come now. Urgent.* In this moment, the brightly coloured geraniums on the window sill changed the light in the house form its habitual green to multicoloured, and two cats that lay on the ground curled up around her feet. Manuscripts and half-finished books in Latin still lay strewn about, including a new one of her own called *When the Fires Come: Myths about the Burning of the Great Library*. She sat down in her huge, overly embroidered chair, a half-finished needlework lying on its arm. It had a few letters that looked to be forming some Latin inscription; D-E-N-...

"Someone will have to take the cats when I... go." She stroked one around the pointed little ears and under the chin.

"I'll take them, 'Cretia."

"I'm not too worried about dying. I'll go back to the sea we all came from. Back to the wave-pattern. I hope I disturb it a little."

"Oh, I think you'll be around a good while yet, disturbing everything on land."

"Sweet. Too sweet. Did he kill you yet? That fuckwit?"

"I'm still here, aren't I? "

Just. 2022 and still hanging on. My silencing by the powers that be was still a fresh wound.

"I thought you wouldn't last five minutes, but you're still here. Academia is a brutal game."

"Under the elbow patches, a multitude of hard sins?"

"*Real* sins. Too real. I tell everybody to leave it by the door. My ears have heard too much already." And she pressed her blotchy white and pink hands to either side of her head. I imagined she could hear her own blood echoing inside her in the same way you can hear the movements of the sea inside a shell.

"My classroom, like myself, lives on the periphery. *They* take what surplus they can. They can make what they want out of me. I don't care. The rest of the time, well, we pay for the pleasure of living in one way or another, don't we? Life taxes *heavily*."

At the hospital *here, now,* I took her hand. She was on so much medication that I'm not even sure she knew it was me beside her.

She slipped into a hallucination, saying only the word *denarius*: 'coins' in Latin. It was plain that in her imagination I had now taken shape as the ferryman, ready to take payment from over her worldly eyes to allow her passage across the planes of life and death; to invite her to the underworld. As soon as myth and reality folded together like this, I knew she was ready to die and that I'd be the last to see her. She would leave her small stories soon and enter into the bigger one. *Pandora.* Her origin story; the myth that spoke through her. I would be her ferryman, her witness. I would sail her from one part of the ocean so that she could take new form inside another.

It was bone cancer. Everybody was shocked. Only Lucretia and I had known.

A few months back in linear time, she had said, "If we don't die one way, then we just die another."

Now in the hospital bed she had become small and her features more pointed.

"No coins, Lucretia. Not just yet."

She tried to wet her lips a little and started coming back to the present.

The thin white hospital blanket between us was becoming damp and I realised I was crying.

She made a sound that was close to laughter.

"You're so predictable, for all your talk about time. You can't let go of anything. Same, same, same. I'm leaving now. You'll be fine. You probably come here a lot."

"No more, Lucretia. I'm cured of time. In a way."

I used to think that my crumpled-up experience of linearity was the very opposite of predictable. But when she said it, *here, now*, I realised that she was right. So very *predictable.* Disordered time still means nothing but living the same old stories over and over, displacing them into the future, displacing them into the past. *So very predictable.* The Angel of Death had told me that I would never again visit the in-between world or fly across times again. That I would live back inside the world of cause and effect. And so this would be the first time I truly experienced loss, would truly feel the loss of Lucretia's final exit from this world. And it was strange because whilst I mourned her for the first time, I also felt strangely at peace. I had learnt from the disordered crumpling of cause and effect that death wasn't an end but always a sonorous continuation. Her resonance, the chord she made in a galaxy of sound, would echo forever, moving from grave, to soil, to voice, to psalm, onwards, forever unfolding the universe.

Lucretia's bones were rising and falling. They were the source of her trouble. But *here, now,* with her, I felt as she did, calm. Not eternally fighting death, trying to impose order and meaning to a disordered existence, battling in a heroic struggle against the forces around us. Even now – staring Lucretia's death in the face *with her* – I had come to accept that inside all the deaths that surrounded us, something else lived. Another angel woven into the story of space and time, as strong as the Angel of Death and as beautiful: The Angel of *Life*.

"I'm here with you, Lucretia. I always have been here."

I wiped my face discreetly and took her hand. More deaths would follow hers, and more deaths had passed. But so had *life*. It wasn't just death that inhabited the snow outside that refugee block, but shimmering liveliness as well. This time, no erasures came for me. This time, I simply sat and remembered. I remembered a fresh flake lying right in front of my eyes, settling on the ground. It absorbed the blood, like so many others. When the wind blew again, it flew upwards on its own magical journey. Life and death folding together, utterly inseparable, playing out an entangled erotic dance that extinguished the self in spirals of time.

Lucretia's wide-open eyes were staring at me. And I realised I had become *her* snowflake, momentarily now. Snow on the sea she was plunging into. Instead of *cancer*, now, I remembered the word *friendship*. Later, I wrote it down, crossing out the word cancer. Not to try to erase it. How could anyone erase it? Just to find inside the cancer the one thing it didn't kill, couldn't kill, would never kill. To find the friendship that remained. *These are the tools of the time traveller*, I thought to myself.

Somewhere deep in the past, ink dries on a freshly printed page. The last word is *hopehely*, the Hungarian word for snow. Bathory rolls it up, seals it in wax and sends it to the Emperor. She's older. Her hands are a little wrinkled. She tucks her own small notebook into a drawer. She smiles. Just that. A small slow light appears around her, though all the other lights have gone out.

*

I saw Cachtice in the distance and was filled with the same sensations I remember being filled with when I was a child. The moment I first laid eyes on it and felt blinded by its bitter and abrasive light. Nadasdy was absent from it all over again, just as he had been back then. I said nothing to Anna the whole journey back. I barely ate. I thought only of the girl and how, with her gone from me, I felt somehow emptier. Although she had done the unthinkable and managed to release us both from the dark underground chamber of Rudolph's mad and esoteric desires, I still felt somehow trapped by it.

I looked to my broken fingertips. The nails were beginning to grow back slowly and each day their hard, new surfaces bit into my skin. They were sharp reminders that an emperor's desire can mark a body. Was Nadasdy's desire not pointed in the same direction? Were Rudolph and Nadasdy just polished glasses set opposite each other now, reflecting each other in an infinity that curved outwards, and bent all our lives?

"We're home," Anna said when the carriage pulled up outside the castle's gates. I thought I had cried every tear in me, but still fresh ones emerged. "Come, Countess. Let's use those tears to create our own new world."

I spoke for the first time in a long while. "I'm tired of creating worlds."

"What else can we do?"

She had a point.

"You are the Countess Bathory. A whole undiscovered nation of people – of women hidden in service – are looking to you to set them out of their chains. If you give up now, then Rudolph has won. Get out of this carriage. Then gather yourself, get to Sarvar and print more copies. Roll up your sleeves and get to work."

"I can't do this alone."

"Who said anything about alone? You've got me, and Dorothea, and an army of Szekely women right here, ready to come to you and print. We need to send word out. We should get the Szekely women scattered across this part of Hungary to come and help. Leave it to Dorothea and me. Rudolph has released you. It's time to get on with what we've started."

I knew that if I walked into my tower room, I wouldn't leave it for weeks, if not months. So, I asked Anna to bring me a bowl for washing, some bread, cheese and wine and deliver them straight to the room where we stored the books. When she returned with the items, she found me clearing space against the long side of the wall. My fingers had bled a little, but I ignored them and kept shifting the volumes out of the way.

"Here. Here is where we should set up the press."

I had spent enough time with John and Nadasdy at the print room in Sarvar to know what we needed.

"Sarvar has become too obvious. Let's print the *Christianismi Restitutio* right here. The press we build should be simple. I imagine it'll be trial and error at first. And we'll have to source the parts discreetly and work out how to assemble them ourselves."

Anna nodded. She set the steaming bowl of water for me to wash on the table and held her hands out, beckoning me to pause and come to her. She dipped a cloth into the bowl and gently washed my face and the exposed parts of my hands. The water was fragrant, and her touch, which replaced mine as I had lost my dexterity for now, was kind and restorative.

"Are you baptising me, Anna?" I asked slyly. She laughed.

"Yes, my dear Countess."

"Some baptism!"

"It'll have to do."

*

The first few parts for the press arrived not long after, and Dorothea, Anna and I were struggling to put them together.

"Your drawings are inaccurate, my lady," Dorothea huffed.

"Then, tell me, how should it be done, Dorothea?"

"Like this," and rather than slot the pieces together, she picked up a huge hammer and nailed the bottommost part directly into the wooden frame. She moved around it with the kind of no-nonsense skill I had come to love her for, and though half of me expected the skeleton of the structure to fall apart, it held fast.

It took all three of us to hoist up the huge, heavy rollers. Dorothea had found two willing helpers, and when the second roller fell out of my barely healed hands, it nearly crushed one of their feet. The girl, who couldn't have been more than fifteen, shrieked as if attacked by a wolf.

"Quick! Take her outside and call for the physician!" I shouted. Dorothea and the other serving girl helped her out and Anna and I quickly covered our somewhat misshapen press with one of Nadasdy's tapestries. We ran outside, locking the door behind us.

When the physician came, he asked Anna how it had

happened. At first, she went silent, then she simply said, "She fell."

"No fall could have caused this, woman. Speak the truth."

Anna eyed him. I sensed some history between them. The fact that she couldn't look at me at all but wriggled her gaze out of mine suggested that it had something to do with Nadasdy.

"The truth is, it doesn't matter how it happened," said Dorothea, "all that matters, is that you fix it."

He eyed Dorothea and then me suspiciously.

"Countess?"

"Do your job. Then send her back to me."

"As you wish, my lady."

A few weeks later, I stopped lifting and shifting and building all together. Anna brought me a chair to sit in to supervise the rest of the assemblage. I was pregnant again. As my child grew, so did the press, and I knew that the two – my baby and my printing – would somehow be bound up together. It wasn't an easy pregnancy. I was far sicklier than I had been with Michael. I grew very pale and weak. I had never been dark, but my skin became so light that I feared I might look white as bone itself. Perhaps Prague had taken its toll on my body and when Rudolph had all but exorcised the girl in time from out of my experience, he had taken something vital and precious from me.

I was halfway through my term when a letter finally arrived from my husband.

I am well, my lady. All is unfolding as it should. We have seen many battles already and nearly been discovered several times, but John is proving quite adept at this game! Our friends are willing to join the fight and I have united with your old friend – the one you met at Prague those years ago. I think it's best he and I serve together in our cause. He knows everything and is agreed upon our plan, God willing, to forge a strong Hungarian alliance.

I have been informed that Rudolph has let you go and that you have returned to Cachtice. I have also been informed that you are carrying our child! I cannot begin to tell you the joy this brings me, to know that not only have you returned home but that you are bringing my baby into the world soon. I pray God will grant me the ability to see him soon. I fear this dual campaign of swords and words will take me longer than I hoped to resolve. I am fighting a formidable enemy. Wish me well, my love. If you wish me well, I know that I can defeat him.

Yours in love, F.

The letter felt heavy in my hands, even though it was on the lightest paper. Nadasdy was growing bold in his thinly veiled descriptions, I thought. It was barely cryptic. He had united with Bocksai, as I had guessed. It was clear that Basta now knew of Nadasdy's betrayal, but it seemed unlikely that they had clashed swords. But even if everything was known and Basta was merely biding his time, this letter could have fallen into anyone's hands. It was unlike my husband to be so careless with our plans. For a moment, I even doubted it was his, but the style of the prose and the letters that carried it were Nadasdy's through and through.

"Who delivered this?" I asked Dorothea.

"An altar boy for our church in the village in the final instance. Before that, I can't say."

I read and reread it almost a hundred times over throughout the day, my heart beating fast at times, then slower at others, as if churning Nadasdy around inside its lively walls.

The fact that it had taken him nearly five months to write to me suggested that, on top of all the difficulty he must be having in keeping himself hidden in Erdely, he was in fact avoiding me. Nadasdy could get a message out from the middle of a battlefield if he wanted to. He was nothing if not resourceful, and that meant he must have suspected I had found him out again. I closed my eyes and imagined his heartbeat. As soon as I heard its unmistakable rhythm and cadence in my mind, I listened deeper. I could almost feel his guilt pouring through his veins, hissing inside him like sulphur.

I couldn't leave a letter like that lying around for prying eyes. I pushed myself up out of the chair and went to the tall candlestick at the side of the room. My hands shook a little and I caressed the page as if it were the last trace of Francis' body. Then I put the letter into the flame. When the fire licked my fingertips, I dropped it to the stone floor and watched it burning itself out in a final eroticism, before disappearing into ash. I returned to the chair and sat back. I felt myself become cold as ice. Anna saw me shiver, took off her woollen shawl and wrapped me in it. There are some kinds of cold nothing can reach.

*

The press looked like some monstrous creature. It was cobbled together with parts that were sometimes too big, sometimes too small, all made of different wood and colours. There had been more than one accident in trying to build it and make it run. One girl had hit her own hand with a hammer so hard that she had broken it. Another had cut herself deeply trying to put the metal pieces together. But I, on the other hand, couldn't feel a thing. I sent them, dutifully, one by one, to Erzi, who had healing knowledge. If that didn't work then I sent them to the physician. I did this dispassionately, and soon even Anna reprimanded me for my apparent callousness. "She's deeply changed," I heard her whisper once to Dorothea. "I fear she may never come back."

"She will. For now she's carrying that monster's child. What do you expect?" Dorothea had retorted.

One evening, Anna sent for dinner to be brought down to us. Dorothea sat by me and, unusually for her, took my hand in hers.

"Countess, I know your pregnancy is deeply upon you, but we need you to be present here with us. I'm not sure this press is going to run. I don't fully know what happened to you in Prague, but whatever it is you still have a duty here."

"I know that what's happening in my own lands is wrong. But don't you dare come to me and call it my duty. It's care that motivates me. Not duty. I have a duty to no one."

She stared at me coldly.

"Then perhaps it's better to say that *I* have a duty to keep you alive and active in this fight."

"Agreed." I rose from my chair and rested my hands on the small of my back. "None of us set upon this path lightly and none of us can exit it lightly."

She nodded in silent reply.

"The turning wheel is set wrongly on this side. Give me some paper and something to draw with."

*

Nadasdy arrived as the first print run was completed, and I imagined that he sensed that things were moving beyond his control at Cachtice. He had brought John with him. Again, I heard his heavy steps wind up to my tower, and again I was in bed expecting a child in my arms at any moment. Only this time my trepidation wasn't that he was coming to kill me with his bare hands. This time, I simply feared that one glance from his grey eyes would bring me to the point of an internal kind of destruction. The door opened and his head emerged around the wooden casement first, like a child might enter. I closed my eyes. I could hear him padding in.

He didn't sit down. He stayed standing beside me. The air pressure changed in the room, becoming heavier and heavier with shame. We stayed in silence for a while. I breathed in and could smell his body. The sweat, the almost-cinnamon of his skin mixed with wood smoke, a smell that endlessly emanated from him, from years and years of sitting by open fires on enemy lines. I flickered my eyes open. But I couldn't look at him.

He sat and took my hand, which remained cold despite his attempts to warm it by rubbing it between both of his. "Elizabet. Elizabet, look at me."

"I can't."

"Elizabet, I'm the same man you loved."

"No. That's the only thing I'm certain that you're not. But no matter now. All things come to an end. I was a fool. But I did love. And I loved *you*."

He shook his head.

"You don't know the first thing about love, Elizabet." He said this quietly, without hatred or rage. He was simply sad. "I loved you so much that I became someone else for you. I erased myself, *for you*. Because I knew that you would never, could never, love me for who I was. I created the Nadasdy you wished me to be. I studied him and made him. How much more could anyone ever give?"

"But it was a lie, Francis. You're still the brutal killer. I saw the brands under Beata's breasts and the fresh wounds running down her back. And Gerda?"

"I didn't kill Gerda," he said quickly, interrupting me.

"But what, you hurt her so badly she had to flee?"

"I took her back to her family and gave them a king's ransom in gold. This is who Francis Nadasdy is, Elizabet. But so is your Francis. Both are real. I am *both*."

"One belongs to the Emperor, to the Ottomans and to Ursula, your mother. And the other?"

"Belongs to you. Utterly. And to John and to the Szekelys. I think that a united Hungary will probably require the blood of both of me."

"Then which Francis belongs to Francis?" I asked. I still couldn't look at him. He very cautiously reached out a finger and turned my chin upwards to force me to see him.

"There is no Francis."

"Then there's no one there to love."

He moved to kiss me, but my lips remained dead as ash. He pulled away, searching my face for some vestige of desire, some tremble or flicker, an opening for love. Then he nodded once and sat back.

"Can you imagine for a moment what it's like to know that your wife, that the one you love, has never and will never love you for yourself? Who has betrayed who, Elizabet? I was happy to take what I could, take only what I knew you could offer to me freely and willingly. But I had to get it right, so right. It's no crime to change for the one you love."

"That's not love, Francis. And it's not change. It's lies. Lies and deceit."

"You want the impossible from me. This is who I am! Who's the liar? You talk about love, and you can't even love the person in front of you. You need a soldier to be a hero. You need a husband to be a king. Who could live up to your fine ideals? I will protect and love you with every breath I have!"

"Then you'll go out and beat another woman to the point of death to satisfy your desires."

"It's not desire, not like that. I *desire* only you. It's… an addiction. I've told you before, I can't stop. But you kept refusing to listen. So, I made something different. For you. To satisfy *you*."

I thought about it, remembering Vera across time and how violence was sown into her life like an eternal seed that had grown from generations before her – that had even grown from me, from my stories that hung in the air untold centuries before her. She had been right in Prague. The Empire would never end. Violence was sown into the land, making matter out of us. Just as Nadasdy had made himself into two, living and breathing through both of them – through both of *him*. Violence made its own doubles across time. The way we touch, the way we speak, these are the things that bring us moment by moment into the flesh. These are the things that pull us towards each other in endless cycles of togetherness.

"I want the real thing, Francis. I want to be made into flesh day by day by love, not by violence, not by some imperial dominion."

"It's not possible. We're all marked by the world we live in."

"Yes! Yes, it is! It is possible. It is possible to love *wholly*."

His eyes welled up with tears. It was as if the clouds inside him gave up their silver linings and now poured downwards with rain.

"I've given everything I can." He looked at me, almost pleading. "Isn't it enough for you?" We looked into each other. I shook my head and bit my lip to stop the tears.

"All right, my love. You will hurtle to death with your ideals, but as long as I draw breath, I will try and stop it from finding you."

*

The day our son decided to come into the world, he announced himself with the most ungodly pain I could have imagined. It wasn't the kind of pain I had experienced in Prague. That pain travelled in an instant from the outside to within. Our son, who I called Paul, ripped and clawed and punched his way out of me.

"The baby keeps turning," said Erzi, the wildwoman who had terrified me when I'd first arrived at Cachtice as a child.

She sang and chanted to try to coax him to remain the right way for birth. When a foot emerged first, she went ashen. The process was unbearable. Different hands entered my body as his limbs tried unsuccessfully to get out. Eventually, my shrieks became so disturbing that Nadasdy himself ran in with an iron bar from the hearth and told me to bite down on it. The bed was soaked through with blood, and Anna, Dorothea, Erzi and Nadasdy hovered around me like faces mourning silently over a grave. I passed out. But when I came to, a tiny boy lay on my chest, grey and oily as a seal. And bloody. So very bloody. But alive. Just.

"Our witch-sister is strong," Erzi said

I looked at her with an almost drugged kind of gratitude.

"Thank you. Thank you, Erzi." I murmured it and she wiped my brow down.

"Drink this. It'll bring your strength back. But first it will make you sleep."

When I woke up, Nadasdy was sat in the little chair I had always had in my tower room. He was holding our son in his arms, wrapped in a clean white sheet. His face was pure and ecstatic.

"What shall we call him?"

"Paul. Call him Paul."

"He's *amazing*." Nadasdy was entirely absorbed.

"Give him to me."

"Yes, my love, in a bit. In a bit."

*

"What a mess, Countess!" said John. He was naturally very unhappy with the shape of the thing that he refused to call a 'press'.

I walked with a cane for a while after the birth, which I found great for gesturing with. I tapped it three times on the floor to get John's attention and then leant on it with both arms.

"No doubt, John, but it has worked. Here – look." All the pages were stacked up and well ordered, ready for binding. The text on each page lay upwards and downwards in alternating systems, so that each one could be folded and cut into sections and finally sewn in to make the binding. I imagined my husband was this way, folding his personas together into tight coherences that allowed the world to read him and make sense of him according to which order he had set himself in that day.

"Right," said John, and he ran his hand through his hair in a gesture identical to Nadasdy's. "Let me teach you all how to bind *properly.*"

Dorothea and Anna had canvassed well and soon more than fifty young women had arrived at Cachtice's gate. I set a programme for them so that they could alternate between printing in the print room under John's instruction and learning to read with me in small groups of ten at a time throughout the day. I had a strange gift for teaching them. It had something to do with listening. I could hear their brows wrinkling in confusion before their expressions changed, or their heartbeats racing as the marks on the pages started to make sense to them. They read aloud to each other and puzzled out sentences and their meanings in small groups together. I had taken my own abilities to read for granted for so long that rediscovering the excitement of doing something so bold and so dangerous as reading, through them, rediscovering the courage of being a woman who could and would read, was revelatory all over again.

They brought laughter back to Cachtice, these brave, young Szekely women. They ran down corridors two or three at a time. They found boys to stare and wink at. Once, I caught two kissing each other in front of an excited and at the same time terrified young blacksmith. I dismissed them with angry shouts, but as soon as they fled from me, I started to laugh. I had hoped that one might catch John's eye, but he appeared to remain faithful only to the press. His obsessive hands caressed only the inky shapes of type. He scolded his students when they were clumsy or forgetful and, as usual, did not sleep either for service of Nadasdy, or of the print room and all its requirements. He reset the machine perfectly, and though it was nothing at all next to the beauty of the one that was now going unused at Sarvar, it began to function more smoothly.

Erstwhile, Nadasdy spent hours at a time with our son Paul. I imagined that a man so used by now to creating doubles would be charmed and delighted by having his own son to groom. Perhaps we were both engaged in this way. I, with my many

Szekely daughters and he with his only born son. It made me miss Michael and Anastasia. But I took comfort in knowing that Anastasia was long married, and Michael was safely hidden. Though neither of us had seen Thurzo for what felt like an age, his strange absence caused us both concern. It was safer for Michael to be hidden away, even from us, under a new name, in a new life. Francis and I were playing a dangerous game, no longer with each other but with the world.

The constant chatter and giggles of the girls filled the halls and walls. I loved it. It was the sound of life. But Francis hid away from it and soon I began to worry. "If you touch a hair on one of my girls' heads, I *will* kill you," I told him once when I came to his section of the castle to take Paul for a moment.

He looked at me momentarily with pure hatred.

"Some have already offered, Elizabet. And I've been the one to refuse."

"Francis, you've lost the privilege of ever being believed by me again. You've spoken with such wounded fervour before, and you've lied. I don't need an answer from you. I just need you to know. I will kill you."

He shrugged. I turned. He spoke quickly then.

"Elizabet—"

"What?"

"Never mind."

"What?"

"I wanted to ask if you might feed Paul here, if we might be together for a moment with our *son*. We've lost both the other children to distant parts of the country. To a husband for one and a new identity for the other. Just give me a moment – a moment, that's all."

"So you can play at being another Francis? All right. Sit with me then." He looked like he'd been slapped in the face, but he still came and sat close to me. He put his head down and was filled with a deep sadness.

After a while, I reached out and put my hand on his shoulder. He had become a little freckled in the summer sun and I could see the dappling running down his neck. It must be across his shoulders too, I thought. Some time ago, I would have counted the trailing freckles down his body, walking my fingers across the path they formed before kissing each one in gentle awe of him. I missed us. I missed this. I set the image of Beata firmly in my mind and took my hand away abruptly. *This was a lie.* He didn't move, but for a moment his eyes glazed over, and I felt him briefly leave the world. Becoming absent.

"Perhaps I should return to Erdely. I'll come up with a schedule so that you can send over more books, and we'll have a continuous running supply. There are more writers springing up. More texts you could print that we could use. Our mission has expanded beyond Servetus now. There's a whole religion that thrives underground in Erdely. But still more hearts to win." He looked up at me.

"I wish… I wish you could be at one with yourself, Francis. I wish with all my heart you could. I understand you can't. I've accepted it."

"But you can't accept me."

"I can't accept it. Addiction, or passion. Either way, Francis, you are a *sadist.* Your violence leads to death. No one in their right mind could."

He stayed silent for a while. He didn't have tears or sighs, or even a single wisp of emotion. This was Nadasdy's truth. He didn't know what to feel unless someone told him.

"Then I'll go. I'll leave you with our son."

The magnitude of what he said hit me. It opened a void at my feet, and I struggled with a moment of terror, as if I might fall in and never land.

"Francis?"

"Yes?"

"Would you hold me one last time as my Francis would?"

"Yes."

He came behind me and enveloped Paul and me in his long arms. He put his head on my shoulder and kissed me sweetly and gently on the neck. I wanted to melt down then and there. To stay in this snatched fantasy forever. He squeezed a little harder, as if trying to make an impression of us all along the inside of his strong arms. Then he got up and left.

*

Pastor Magyery cornered me after mass the Sunday after Nadasdy had left for Erdley.

"Countess, I must speak with you. I fear your erratic visitations to Sunday mass are having an effect on our growing congregation."

"How so, Pastor?"

"These women are barely Christian, my lady. I've seen them flaunting their ungodly ways around Cachtice. If you insist on bringing them here – for what purpose – to teach them, you say? – then teach them. Lead by example. Be the mother on earth that the Virgin is to us all in heaven."

"They're young, Pastor. They can't marry because there are no more Szekely men left. Their brothers and fathers have all died fighting our wars." I tapped him on the chest with my fan in gentle admonishment. "Have a little compassion for their moments of joy."

"I have no compassion for wantonness, madam. Why are they here?"

"Because I wish them to read."

"Reading is dangerous, my lady. It leads to chaos."

"The world is reading now."

"And look at it. Look at our world, Countess."

"I will come to mass every Sunday, Pastor."

"Good. Now, speaking of our growing congregation, I fear

our church is running short on funds. I need, of course, to make sure each soul is properly cared for."

"And the Virgin would have dispensed of her cash too, I suppose?"

He eyed me condescendingly.

"The Bathory coffers are hardly empty, my lady."

"How much are we talking, Pastor?"

*

About a month later, John sent a note. It was simply a location and a number. I gathered the girls together to print. We had nearly doubled in size as more and more Szekely mothers sent their daughters to me. The word had circulated that I was clothing and feeding all young women of Szekely origin and, given their poverty, households with unmarriageable daughters were clamouring to send them to me. The reading was a side note. No one, save the pastor, seemed to care really. *For now.*

I had a good quantity of fabric sent over from Venice and when they weren't at lessons or secretly printing for me, I kept them busy stitching and sewing their own dresses. I knew I was taking a gamble. How could you trust a young girl to keep something vitally secret? It would be like asking a flower to bloom less brightly or a rock to stand less tall as the waves of a river battered and washed it, attempting to wear it down before its time.

When Dorothea informed me that one of the girls had boasted in the village that her arms were now stronger than any boy's because she had wielded dabbers and turned wheels for months, I knew I had to make an example of her. I lined the girls up in the main hall and shut the doors.

"Esther, come here." She sombrely approached me. What have you been saying in the village about what we do here?"

"Nothing, my lady."

"That's not true, is it?"

"No. I'm sorry, my lady. It will never happen again."

"If my husband were here, he would beat you until you were sent home in a box. But fortunately for you, he's not."

My hands trembled and my whole body shook a little.

"Listen, all of you. If you speak of what we're doing in the print room, at any time, at any place outside its walls, you will be severely punished. Do you understand? *Severely.*"

I picked up a copy of our newest book, turned the spine to face out and hit her very hard across the face with it. I knew she had probably been beaten far worse at home, but I hoped that the threat and humiliation of it would be enough.

She teared up but did not cry.

"Do you understand me?"

"Yes," said Esther. I looked at the sea of faces around me questioningly. An untimely chorus of 'yesses' rose up and eventually faded away.

"Good. Now, let's get back to work. Dorothea, please take your group to the print room, Anna, yours to dressmaking. The rest of you are with me. Remember, if you speak of *any* printing in any way, at any time, I will punish you and turn you out into the cold."

The 'yesses' started again. They found their groups and left. As soon as they were out the door, the noise and chatter and giggling started up all over again, as if I had never spoken.

Not two nights on, Dorothea came to me. "We have a problem, my lady."

"What is it?"

"Agota and Mary are accusing a young blacksmith here."

"Of what?"

"They say he cornered them and threatened to reveal that they were printing books unless they slept with him. They're very distraught. I'm happy to deal with this in a way I see fit, if you'd like to leave it to me."

I wiped my face with my hands and sighed.

"What do you have in mind, Dorothea?"

"If it's true… just to scare him a little." Her words were delivered lightly, but there was something strange forming across her face, a half-finished shadow, menacing and bitter, an anaemic kind of devil crossing her, settling on her.

"Do it. We can't afford this in any way. There's too much at stake. Send Agota and Mary to me after dinner tonight."

The two girls came to me in the evening. I was sitting in our main reception area. "Tell me what happened."

"We were just talking together and he suddenly said he would reveal everything and we'd be beaten and turned out into the cold if we didn't… if we didn't…" They both started crying.

"I see."

"Please, please don't reject us, Countess. We know we'll never be married, but please don't hate us. Don't send us out to be captured by Turks or Hadjuks." They both fell to their knees before me.

"Give Dorothea the name of the boy. We will deal with this. I would advise that you stop kissing in front of them, too."

"It's our fault. We beg for mercy."

I sighed deeply. Perhaps in some future time this kind of talk would cease. Perhaps it never would.

"It's not your fault. Do you blame a fly for buzzing too close to a web? Do you tell water that flows by a mill to avoid the wheel? No. You must be aware of danger, sharpen your wits and play wisely, but when violence comes to you in this way, you must never believe it's your fault. He will try to give you his own shame, as if his acts weren't already burden enough to bear. Refuse to take it. But please, for the love of God, be careful *and don't talk about the press.*"

When I walked into church the following Sunday, I wore my finest, blackest gown. Pearls and rubies dripped from the neckline, falling down the corset in swirls like curling red tongues. It was a dress the girls had created in the English style, but I had chosen the black to represent my sobering attitude to the world. I had hoped that it would signal the same to our pastor and to the pious nobles who sometimes attended our small service and who were curious as to why so many women were suddenly under my charge. The church fell into silence as I walked in. I passed a boy as I walked up the aisle to take my seat at the front and balked. He was missing two fingers on his left hand, and the wound was clearly fresh. Dorothea's vengeance was brutal.

I feared I wouldn't be able to control any of the aggressive forces that were taking shape in our new community. They were the very forces I'd fought so hard to quell in my husband and they had risen up in *all* of us the moment he had left. How could we re-story the world if we couldn't even re-story the rules of our own castle? A shiver ran through me. A sense that I had better tame the winds that threatened to tear us down or face extinction. I took my place at the pew closest to the altar and turned to see who was present. Sat to my right, flanked by local nobles and minor lords, was the last person I expected: Thurzo.

He had aged. The lines on his face were deeper and longer than they had been before. After the interminable service was over, I turned and walked out without acknowledging him, returning home immediately. Not long after I had sat down at home with Anna, feeding Paul, who was now managing more solid foods, a serving girl knocked at the door.

"My lady, Count Thurzo is here to see you."

"Send him to the main reception hall. Make sure the fire is lit."

I looked at Anna.

"Be careful, my lady."

I nodded.

*

And there he was, standing there by the fire again just as he had the first time I'd met him. I marvelled at how these cycles kept turning, each time a little differently.

"My lady," he said in his deep, gravelly voice as I entered. And he inclined his head a little.

"My lord. What brings you to my *home*?" I said, stressing the intrusion.

He surveyed me with that long, cold look of his. Then he glanced around the room.

"I see little has changed and yet, the entire place feels so very different. That's down to you no doubt, my dear Countess."

I remained still and expressionless.

"I like the black." He extended his finger and waved it up and down in the air to signal the cloth on my body. "You wear it well."

I didn't respond. He smiled, almost approvingly, at my demeanour.

"Elizabet, I have news. I wanted…" he paused, and his expression changed, softening into a momentary veil of kindness, as if the smallest amount of life had entered into his otherwise piercing eyes "…I wanted to be the one to deliver it. I know we've had our… differences… but I want you to know that I am your friend now. Truly."

"What is it, George? What do you want from me now?"

He smiled paternally, a look of wolfish pity creeping across his face.

"My lady, there's no easy way to say this, but I have news from Basta, from Erdely. Francis Nadasdy is dying."

Chapter Nineteen

Thurzo was eyeing me to see how I reacted to the news that my husband now lay dying. I said nothing. At first, I found myself staring into his blue eyes, feeling the marks of loss and guilt inside me. I didn't want to receive this news from *him*, the man with whom I had broken Nadasdy. The man after whose defeat Nadasdy had decided to forge a new *Francis*, an ideal lover, an ideal hero. I quickly moved my gaze to a spot just over Thurzo's shoulder and was immediately lost inside one of Francis' tapestries. The weave was faded, as if it too were leaving the world, evaporating into nothing. There was a bold and terrifying warrior pictured at its centre. Under his sword and his horse's hooves were scattered men. A crown was embroidered into the scene, hovering just above the warrior's head. They didn't meet. And Francis would never be king of a united Hungary.

I tried to say the word 'how', but it caught in my throat, breaking the coherence of the 'h', the 'o' and the 'w' as one, into their separate, component parts. Thurzo understood my meaning, nonetheless.

"I'm not exactly sure. But I believe it's an injury to his spine, a small injury, but it's affected his legs and I'm afraid he's not long for this world."

Francis was shutting down. His limbs were refusing to obey him, and he was sickly and unable to eat or drink.

I remembered how he had spoken of Basta and how Basta had killed Michael the Brave by cutting his heels whilst he slept so that he couldn't run. It sounded like his work. It sounded sneaky and cowardly. A small tear in the fabric of the body that destroyed it from the inside out.

"He's not asking for you. But if I know Francis, he'll want you there." He surveyed me. Then he turned around, putting one hand behind his back whilst running the other along the fireplace. I knew it was a gesture to remind me of what had happened here in this very room a lifetime ago, the last time he had run his hand over the exact same spot, before running it along me. It was then I realised that George was really savouring the moment. His long game was paying off and the pieces were finally falling into place. He had finally rid himself of Nadasdy. The constant thorn to his pride was at last dissolving; broken and draining away in a bed somewhere in Sarvar.

His hatred was so virulent that it actually served to bring me back to the room for a moment. If Thurzo had anticipated that this would sharpen rather than dull me, he would have spoken differently. He would have presented himself differently. A very small part of me smiled. It would have been the part of me inhabited by the girl across time, by Vera, if Rudolph hadn't taken her from me. Perhaps she could still hear me somewhere. Perhaps she would write it down. She would have known immediately that the reason that I smiled was because after all this time, Thurzo still continued to misjudge me. It was his one weakness. And I would use it against him.

"Thank you for bringing this to my attention," I said in a way that made him raise his eyebrows in surprise. "My lord, if you're hungry, feel free to stay and I'll have something brought to you. I, however, will retire. It's been a long day and church always exhausts me."

"I can't believe my lady is such a sinner," he quickly responded.

"No, it's Pastor Magyery. He's expensive to run."

"I see. I should like to stay if I may. Perhaps we might ride to Sarvar together in the morning."

"Perhaps."

I floated out, the silk of my hem gliding over the stones silently.

When I reached the bottom of the winding stairs at the base of my tower, I stopped. My stomach had turned when Thurzo had given me the news, and I still felt nauseous, though I'd used all my strength to steel myself in front of him. I steadied myself against the wall and started breathing heavily. It was as if Francis was trying to come out of my belly through the pathways in my lungs. I took the staircase one step at a time. The journey became a gauntlet. Each time I put my foot down, a flash of different images of our life together spun before my eyes. By the time I reached the top, just outside my door, only one remained: the moment he had arrived at this very spot, wildflowers in hand, after Michael had been born. I found myself lingering right there, as if willing myself to go back in time, feeling for whispered traces of him. If I could peel back a layer of reality, wind back the events that unfolded over the years, he would be standing *here*, in this exact spot.

I pushed the door. Anna was standing by the bed.

"Well? What did he have to say?" She cut into my wished-for reality like a knife, and the illusion of him being just here, just then, fell away as if she had dug him out from me.

I collapsed, knees on the stone floor, my face sinking into the mattress of the bed. Then I sobbed. Anna understood immediately. She tried to put her hand on my shoulder, but I slapped her away and looked at her with pure rage. So, she just stood there. She must have stood for an hour.

I stayed up all night and before first light broke, I told Anna to ready my horse and assemble a small contingency of guards to escort me to Sarvar. Anna, who had seen to Thurzo's comfortable consignment to guest quarters, assured me that he was still sleeping and that he'd wake to an apologetic servant who would inform him that I'd already left. She insisted on coming with me, not in words, but simply by saddling up her own horse and following. We rode without stopping. I would not rest. The minute Sarvar appeared on the horizon, I kicked the exhausted stallion faster. I ran ahead of everybody else and sent a reign of terror through the vestibules and corridors of the castle shouting, "Where is he? Where is Francis?"

Eventually, I found him. A priest stood by his bed with a box full of papers; some rolled and already sealed in Francis' unmistakable waxproof. Others lay waiting, in a heap, huddled together in anticipation of the touch of his burning ring. When I entered, his head lolled over in my direction, falling at an angle on the pillow, which made him look like he was a boy again, all curls and eyelashes.

"You shouldn't have come."

"Of course I came, Francis."

"No. I wanted… I wanted you to remember me as you'd have liked, as the hero. This is going to be ugly, Elizabet. Really ugly."

I moved and knelt by him, so our heads were close.

"I can stomach ugly, Francis. I'm a Bathory, remember?"

He stretched his lips and I realised this was an involuntary smile. His eyes danced for a second.

"Read to me, my love. Read to me about the heart."

"I'll do better than that." I put my hand to his forehead and leant close to him. I knew what Francis wanted. I had always known what Francis had wanted, even if I had lied to myself about what it was and how every day with him, I had inadvertently given him his wish. I whispered, occasionally catching his feverish white ear with my lips as I spoke.

"One day, a princess walked alone in the wood. She saw a prince: a man. He had grey eyes. He was tall, and beautiful. He told her he was not a prince but a terrible monster, a creature risen from straight out of hell. She laughed at him. 'I know,' she said. 'I fetched you from out of the devil's grip. Don't you remember? Don't you remember the shape and sound of hell?'

'No,' he said, 'I've no memory of that at all now.'

'Then how do you know you're from hell?' she asked him.

'Because they told me,' he said. 'Because they all told me. Because they keep telling me.'

'I'd stick to what you remember,' said the princess. 'And I'll only ever remember enough to want to forget.'"

Francis' mouth stretched into a long, curved line again. His eyes went in and out of focus.

"It's a good story," he said, as if each word required his lips to push back a mountain for him to be heard.

"Elizabet, there are – papers," and he gestured with a heavy hand.

"Yes, I'll see to it."

"No. *I've* seen to it all, for you. They will try to take *everything*. Put the money into something no one will – expect. Not the press…" he began to trail off as he nodded his head from side to side.

"I'll finish it. I'll finish what we started."

"It doesn't matter, my love. It's just games. We all play them. Make yourself… happy. Find your true love."

"You're my true love. There's only you, Francis."

"No. No, no." He tried to emphasise it, but the words simply escaped from him like the smallest traces of smoke, vanishing instantly.

"I'm just a story, Elizabet. A story created for you. You're the one who's alive now. I want you to have… *everything*."

"I love you, Francis."

I bent over him and kissed him, but he was already cold.

*

Death leaves marks too. It's not just life and the living that burn memory into the flesh, creating worlds, bringing matter into shape. Death does it too. I imagined the moments after Nadasdy's death would have disordered time momentarily for Elizabet.

I imagined Elizabet sitting by the bed, even though now I could no longer visit her in her walls and archways or in the in-between world. I saw her walking out of the room that held Francis' body and arriving at the print room in Sarvar without any recollection of how she got there. I saw her look down at her bandaged arm without any memory of how it had happened that a huge gash lay below the bindings. I saw her turning the wheels of the press by herself without any paper between them.

Anna would come in to find the room littered with scattered pages that barely held the impressions made by type. Elizabet would be sitting on the floor like a child, although, somehow, the space she occupied would appear in a way vacant. The type would be scattered and the ink she used would be dripping onto the floor. Having given up on trying to do the impossible and print all by herself, she would have simply picked up the iron blocks and dipped them straight into the ink, pressing them by hand onto the page like a medieval monk. The beautiful *F* that John had designed was the only letter pressed hard. The *R*, the *A*, the *N*, the *C* would be increasingly faint. The *I* and *S* would be shadows of their form, no more than indications. In this moment, Elizabet would not be able to narrate herself. Grief does that. In turn, she would not be able to narrate Francis for him, as she had done from the beginning of their union. Her ability to mark him down, to help him create himself, had been bitten out of her temporarily. This was the strange mark that death made. It marked her out of herself. History would try to flood in, precisely at this moment. History likes to take advantage. It is an opportunist, through and through.

"My lady, Thurzo is here," Anna said. Elizabet looked blankly at her, as if she couldn't hear a word, although time was now marching on.

"I'll tell him you're sick."

No response. But Elizabet tried to stand, shakily, and go to the hidden part of the room – the room within the room – where Francis had stored the *Christianismi Restitutio*. As she entered, she sighed, making the first audible sign of life. She pulled a few copies of the book down and several more fell. She lay down, put one under her head in place of a pillow and held another in both hands over her chest. Then she blanked out. I could almost hear her whispering into me. *Tell it how it happened. Tell it how I narrate it to you now. This part is important.*

When she came to, she heard shuffling. Then she heard something that tugged at a deep memory inside her. Clang! Clang! Rhythmic. Slow. Geometric. She fluttered her eyes open. He had moved to sit on a chair that he had pulled up close to the remaining copies of the books stacked up by the wall. In his hands, he held a fresh one. He was reading, utterly engaged. When she moved her head to the side to take in his shape, he looked up, put his thumb inside the book to mark the page and smiled paternally. He blew his cheeks out, scratched his left temple and cocked his head to one side.

"Well, well, my dear Elizabet. Here we are."

*

When I came to and saw Thurzo sitting there, my heart leapt into my mouth. I rose slowly. He, in turn, jumped to his feet and in a matter of moments found a chair to place below my unsteady body.

"Here, Elizabet. You're a little weak, I see. Please." Then he sat himself back down slowly. I didn't know what to say.

He surveyed me in silence. I could almost feel his body becoming strong and stiff with power. He looked back to the book, turned it upside down and placed it so that it formed a small pyramid on his left thigh.

I still said nothing. I knew he was waiting to see which road I would go down – placating, conspiratorial, contrite, or defensive. I wouldn't give him the pleasure. He would have to reveal himself to me first. I barely even blinked. The moment stretched out between us. One thing united Thurzo and me. We were both as stubborn as each other. Eventually, he smiled again. Then he spoke in a way that took me entirely by surprise: "*Got you!*"

I remained silent. He seemed to be suppressing a range of emotions. He was excitable. But he kept it close. As he looked at me, I sensed he was seeing so much more than a woman.

"Elizabet, you can still come out of this. I'm offering you a chance."

Still nothing.

He sat back and tapped the spine of the book repeatedly.

"Am I really so terrible?" As he said it, a look of playful malice crept across him.

"This is the world we live in. Listen to me. Now, we both know how Francis died. Be assured, Basta and I *will* come after you. We will take everything you have," he leant forward and spoke without once moving his eyes from mine, "and, Elizabet, I don't just mean the property. I mean your children. And I mean your girls. For God's sake, have a little self-respect. Have a little care for those you claim to love."

Still, I said nothing. He rubbed his chin.

"How about this? I'll let you keep the press. I think Calvinism has a future. You can print those texts if you want. And you can keep your collaborators and friends around you. It's quite a world we can build together. You have my word. No one here will be harmed. Could you have really ever said the same about Francis?"

The blue grew deeper the longer he looked at me. In my half-dazed state, I focused so much on that piercing blueness he carried inside each glance that it wasn't long before it engulfed me and I clutched onto his black pupils as if they might provide me with a raft, a way to swim out of the expanse of his reach.

"Elizabet, can you hear me?"

"Yes."

"Good, then it's settled. I'll need some time to… tie up some loose ends. We can be married after we've both mourned, perhaps next year. I'll adopt Paul and, of course, *our* own son." He stood up, put the book inside his tunic and adjusted his clothes.

"Better get rid of the rest of these. Here. I'll give you some time to say goodbye to Francis' work." He moved to one of the candlesticks and placed it closer to me.

"Shut the inner door firmly once it's all alight. Otherwise, this beautiful press of yours will likely get damaged. It's really quite something, isn't it?" He put his hand on my shoulder and looked down at me. His grip was vice-like.

Once he was gone, I threw the unlit candlestick at the wall. "I never agreed!" I screamed at the walls. "I will *never* agree!"

*

Anna came into my room holding a few different dresses. I had nothing at Sarvar appropriate for mourning save the black dress I had arrived in, which was now falling apart at the seams on account of my break-neck ride to Sarvar from Cachtice. She lay the dresses on the bed. They were from my younger years with Francis and looked gaudy and frivolous now.

"My lady, Thurzo won't leave, and I don't know how to get rid of him. I've told him you're unwell and in mourning, but he simply responds that that's precisely the reason he's here. He says Nadasdy has publicly charged him with your protection."

I looked at her in disbelief, but I didn't say anything.

"Maybe Nadasdy was trying to protect you. Thurzo could hardly bring you to harm in the wake of his funeral if Nadasdy had made him responsible for your care."

I looked blankly to the window casement. I imagined a shadow-part of me walking out of my body, reaching up to the stone edges and flying far, far away from out of it, back to my in-between world. I blinked and returned to the real world. To what was meant to be real in this sad place with no place to fly to.

"I don't have it in me to play this game right now."

"As always, my lady, I'll tell you the same thing. You have to. This *is* the time. It's now or never. If you let the forces around you carry you up in your grief, you will betray everything you are – everything you've fought for. Now or never."

I stood up to meet her words, but all the power was draining out of my legs and I faltered like a new foal, all angles and bends in the knees.

"Anna, you'll need to get me my cane, or make another one again. Right now, I'm going to need all the help I can get."

"Yes, my lady. At once." And she rushed out. I looked at the early evening light. The sky was brilliant in its golds and reds. I searched the long, bright strands that latticed across it for glimpses of Nadasdy, for some small sign that part of him was still watching over me.

Even in all his violence and despair, he had still been my husband. Perhaps my golden horse would arrive, and we would go careening through the worlds together. I tried to focus on the light, the pulsing stars in the still blue and yellow part of the sky, but the wind had picked up and the clouds were starting to move so rapidly that I began to feel dizzy.

Instead, I looked down at my hands, trying to see my skin shifting subtly even as I did so; stretching, growing, shedding itself with each gentle move of a finger or a knuckle. Still nothing. All the gates to the tiny world had closed. Perhaps I was no longer a *talto* and would never see the tiny world again. Perhaps Rudolph and I had changed each other forever. I returned my gaze to the view from Sarvar. There are some losses that you never recover from, and it was all too possible that between Rudolph, Thurzo and Nadasdy, I had become broken in more places than I knew.

My mind wandered to Paul and to the last moment Francis had held us in his arms before leaving for Erdely. He would soon hear stories of his father; of Nadasdy the war hero. Then, as time went on, the tapestries would start flooding in. Nadasdy would be stamped out in wool and thread and silk. No one would ever know that Thurzo and Basta were responsible for his death. He would be Hungary's great war hero and both of them would praise him and tell the world that a great man had been lost. The reason for his death would remain a mystery. It would be a strange chance occurrence. It would be the will of God. His death would be as much a lie as his life. But for Paul and his sister, Anna, the lie might just be the thing that would save them. They would be allowed to live as the son of the Black Bey, scourge of the Ottomans, the man beloved by all of Hungary, rather than as the children of a traitor. Michael would be forgotten, eaten by the very obscurity that would save him.

Anna returned with a cane. It was a straight piece of wood with a nondescript silver tip and round ball for a handle. God knows who she had taken it from. I imagined it suited an immense old man. It was sturdy and acted as a sober counterbalance to the frivolous dresses. She laced me into the green and blue one with painted flowers adorning its skirt. She had patched up the breaks in my ruby necklace and attached what was left of it around my neck. I almost laughed as I leant on the cane. I must have looked like a mottled doll, an Italian harlequin pieced together from bits of the past.

"Thurzo is waiting for you in the dining hall."

The hall was lit by three fires, and I noticed Thurzo sweating almost imperceptibly under his thick black finery.

"You look a little warm, George," I said as Anna pulled the chair out and helped me settle in. I rested the cane on the arm of the chair but didn't let go of it.

Thurzo inclined his head in a respectful greeting. He gestured to the servants to bring some wine.

"It's nice to share a table with you, Elizabet. I can't remember the last time we did this. I wish it was under better circumstances, of course. But in time, you'll look forward to these moments, I promise you. I can be charming too, you know. And we've…" he paused, nodded at the servant who had poured the wine now and took a sip "…so much history together. I'm sure we can make a good go of this."

"George, last I looked, you were still in *my* house. I won't suffer this. You threatened me not a few hours ago. Now you want to play the gallant gentleman. You always were nothing more than a thug, hiding behind all your airs and borrowed finery."

He ignored the comment.

"Power is a funny thing, Elizabet. You look tired. Perhaps" he turned to the servants "perhaps the lady should retire and take supper in her room."

My head snapped in their direction.

"If you take one step towards me, I'll have each one of you whipped." The threat was more for George's benefit. They were for the most part loyal, and since the moment in Cachtice, when I had hit the girl with Servetus' book to set an example, I had sworn to stop the violence in my houses; in myself. There had to be another way. Not one of them moved a muscle in a show of strong support for their Countess.

Thurzo quietly laughed as he turned his head to the side, angling it down in the same way he did when anger was brewing.

He looked around the room for a bit as if he was making a mental inventory of everything that met his eyes. Then he looked to me. His voice came even and quiet. It had a kind of hospitality to it, like warm rope wrapped around the mast of a ship in the sun. I realised he was being *patient* with me.

"When will you finally admit that you've lost, Elizabet? You've done your little dance and it's been very… engaging. And you've had some wonderful victories, my dear. Wonderful. You have it in you to make life very exciting. I understand Francis' penchant for you. I really do. But even you have to admit, now, in the cold light of day, with Francis gone, it's time to be circumspect. Be clever. Be smart. Please. If you won't do it for yourself, for your children, or for your dear girls at Cachtice, do it for me. *I will look after you.* I will. I promise. I can be very generous."

I wanted to reach across the table and stab my fork into the back of his hand.

"Let's say I agree…"

"You have agreed."

"I don't know what's given you that impression, George. You simply asked if I'd heard you. I had. Agreement is what's under discussion here, so don't get ahead of yourself and start *planning*."

"Fighting still? Okay, Elizabet. It strikes me that you need to be made aware of all the facts. Surprising, for a woman of your *capabilities*, but there we are.

"One: Basta had imperial permission to dispose of Nadasdy. Bocksai will be easy to defeat now, so your Erdelian rebellion won't last the month. Two: no one will speak of Nadasdy's treachery and so, for now, yours and Nadasdy's son is safe. One word to the lords at court, however, and I can't vouch for who might try to curry favour with the Emperor by bringing Paul Nadasdy's head to him in a bag. Three: Hadjuks are looting this region as are Tartars, and no doubt, with the Bey in his grave, the Turks will be on their way here soon. They've probably already started out. Without protection, you and your army of young women will be taken, raped and killed, or captured to please the Ottoman army. Not a nice end for those poor Szekely girls." He took another sip of wine, half shrugged and sat back in his chair. "It's simple mathematics, Elizabet. Nothing more."

It was quite a picture he had painted. But he had only tied up all our everyday fears into a neat and precise ball. I remained unmoved.

"These are, indeed, the times we live in. With so many forces of death around us, how do you think we survive? How do *you* survive, George? I mean really. How do you live every day? Do you wake up every morning and plan each step you take before the evening?" I smiled at him, genuinely enquiring. "Really, I'm curious."

He looked very uncomfortable, caught off guard again. Then he laughed, raised his glass at me, laughed again, put his fingers to his lips and blew me a kiss.

"You will come around, Elizabet. At the end of the day, you're blessed with enough good common sense."

*

I pick up my pencil and my little black notebook, remembering that Bathory had been famous for carrying her own small notebook around with her. I tut and hum to myself. What was in *that* notebook? Then I smile. I put my pencil into a small sharpener and twist it around and around until the point is nothing less than a charcoal needle. I think of Rudolph, of Nadasdy and Thurzo. I think of the Szekely women and the books, of Anna and Dorothea and John. Of Michael, his sister, Anna, and of the little child that Bathory has growing inside her. Her child with Nadasdy.

I push the sharp pencil into my arm. When I draw enough blood to coat the silver-black end, I start to write my first sentence. I think of her – of Bathory. This is the closest I can come to her now. To know she is always echoing inside me. I'd lived across my own life, burrowing into all my deathly trajectories to reclaim the pearls of *knowing* from inside the shells of each singular experience. Then when I met Lucretia, my endless world had changed. Friendship had changed it. It had brought small pockets of difference to rest inside the void that I made with my deathly 'life'.

Here, now, in this endless present, words taste new in my mouth; feel new as I write them. I don't write about *Erzabet Bathori*. I write about the girl across time, sat in her tower room with her pots of paint-becoming-sky, and the woman she grew to be. Not the legend. Not the myth – the myths made by men. I don't write to save her, or save myself, or save anyone. I write simply to listen. I write to hear a *new* story about a woman who had lived a revolutionary life in a time that allowed for nothing but the erasure of any kind of knowledge that didn't fit with the empire. I write her life through the life of the woman I could have been had I not died in the snow all those years ago. The woman we all were, all the legacies wrapped into a story whose shadows we played in and out of every day. Every time we walked out and met the world.

I breathe in and out. *Slowly, slowly.* I can see her as a young child, right at the moment it all begins. I see her running away from the carriage, her mother racing to catch her and put her in it. The carriage looms. She tries to refuse, but history won't let her. She closes her eyes and prays, "Skies, stones, waters and trees, whatever you draw your secret breath from, draw it for a moment for me. Do not let my heart close up," and she imagines a world far larger than anything she has ever known inside her chest. A tiny world living inside the normal world that she can't bear to be all alone in. A tiny world that is somehow, at the same time, far, far bigger than the skies that cover the earth.

And so, I write it down: *She squeezes her eyes shut to make the world disappear...* And the words hang in the air around her image, folding past and future into a pulsing resonance that one day someone will call *a spell. A spell living inside history, waiting to be uttered.*

*

All the leaves had fallen from the trees outside the church. They had become brown and broken, sending their powdery bodies across the pathway to its door at the faintest touch of wind. I had come to see Pastor Magyery. Dorothea's stunt with the young blacksmith hadn't sent the message of warning she had hoped for. Instead, it had started a small war. The blacksmiths, or some faction of them at any rate, had laid waste to Agota and Mary in my absence. Their bodies had been found outside Cachtice's walls. No more laughter stirred in the halls and walls, and the roads towards and away from the villages below were empty of the giggles, pranks and seductions of the Szekely girls.

"Countess, I understand you want to arrange a burial."

"Yes."

"And how, may I ask, did the girls come to die?"

I thought about it. What could I say?

"Plague."

"Plague?"

"Yes."

I thought of their bodies. Dorothea had laid them out for me to see how they had been brutalised. They had been burnt with blacksmiths' tools. Flesh had been torn from them and they had been left out overnight. It was, at some terrifying moments, hard to tell which of the wounds might have been made by humans and which wounds had been made by the other wildernesses that prowled around outside the castle at night.

"Yes. I've already prepared and sealed their coffins. Please see to it that they receive all the correct rites."

The pastor looked at me suspiciously.

"Of course, my lady. On another note, I have written a eulogy for our dearly departed Count to be spoken at church this Sunday."

"Thank you."

"Such a good Christian man."

"Indeed."

"We already all miss his good Christian ways and his patronage of our church."

"And you can expect to see the same patronage continue." I made to turn back to my castle.

"On that note, my lady. What with the Szekelys' wild natures, I should like to propose tutoring them in good Protestant behaviour. Perhaps you might like me to teach them how to better pray for God's mercy in these times of… plague."

"We shall all attend the funeral. You can pray then."

When I returned to my tower, I slid into my bed, grateful for its warmth. I took one of the many pillows, turned it sideways and clutched onto it for dear life. I slept the whole day and night and woke late in the morning. Having no time for grief was exhausting. Nadasdy was still coming out of my body. At times, I felt I could almost see his shadow in the room and at others, that I could feel his touch. When I mentioned this to Anna, she told me it was common amongst the recently bereaved.

"I only mourn one Nadasdy," I said abruptly to her, but she understood my meaning. "The other Nadasdy is still everywhere."

"When I feel more kindly towards him," she said, "I wonder if it must have been hard for him to carry all our violence, to be the symbol for what exists everywhere."

"And yet he will be loved. He has died *loved*. I will die unloved."

"That's not true, my lady. I love you. John loves you. The Szekelys will mourn you with love."

"I suppose it's not important. When we die, we die, loved or not. I just need to know that it has in some small way been worth it. All the pain. Has it been worth it?" I caught myself and considered whether this was simply a displacement of Rudolph's desire to persist, to persist in power throughout the ages.

"My lady, you were born into these times. And you can do only what you can. Day by day. The rest is empty. The rest is dust."

"Day by day…" A little warmth returned to my belly as I repeated her words and I put my hands across it, feeling its warm curves. My heartbeat thudded inside my body, circulating my blood in a wild circle. I remembered Janus talking about those giants in the sky of his, the ones that drew in all the light through their godlike mouths. I saw them eating all the stories, all the sounds on earth that floated up to the heavens, a great feast of information that would never be lost. Perhaps each story would become godlike the moment it passed into the giants' horizons, fusing with its new surroundings and going on to fashion new worlds in places we couldn't imagine existed, outside of time, outside of space. What of Nadasdy's stories? Would both of 'him' be on their way towards those gods now? Would *both* Nadasdys be eaten? Or would one be sacrifice enough, leaving the other to hover, timelessly, in the sky?

Doubles are a strange thing. Where was mine now? Since I'd lost my double across time, perhaps it was now the moment to create one in the present. A formidable and beautiful countess offering all my world – all the horror, all the sorrow, all the joy, all the love – into those giant mouths. A final sacrifice. *And so it would be done.* I got up without the cane. The edges of the room seemed further away, as if the space around me had enlarged all by itself, even in the blink of an eye. I looked out to the light in the sky again. Its gateways into the otherworld remained closed.

But it also seemed larger. Its colours were deeper, stretching out to an infinity that no longer seemed to run away from me but that now *contained* me too, catching me in its hands, making me an indelible part of its incredible journey of shadow and sound.

"The next time Thurzo comes, I'll be ready. I'll be waiting. Now, what to do with these blacksmiths? If the forces of violence are everywhere, if I'm to die and my lands and my children taken, if this history is *inevitable,* then perhaps it's time to admit that this is the story of this journey. Since the very first moment I arrived here at Cachtice. You're right, Anna. I won't stall any longer. And I will not capitulate. My time here on earth has already been set by all the tiny choices I've made every single day in the face of all the beauty and all the terror brought by the world we live in. So be it. Let them come. Let them all come. I'll be right here. And I will fight."

And, of course, Thurzo did come back. Even sooner than I had expected. He came back that Sunday for Nadasdy's funeral. Most surprisingly of all, he brought along his wife; his Elizabet. She was remarkably tall and yet so meek. Her shoulders were drawn in and a web of lace crossed over them as if she were aiming to create a thin protective net across all the space she took up with her body. I had seen her before over the years, but knowing that right at this moment Thurzo was readying her murder in anticipation of wedding me and claiming my fortune made me all the more impatient to talk with her. *I simply could not watch another woman die.*

He came up to me, *clang! clang! clang!* He took my hand, uninvited, in one of his and with the other extended his index finger to push the black glove I wore away. Then he kissed the bare skin above my knuckle.

"Countess Bathory, I'm so sorry for your loss. Where is your daughter? Where is Anna Nadasdy? Surely, she should be here for her father's burial." I wrenched my hand back. Anastasia had been forbidden to see me by her husband, even though we saw so little of one other anyway. Since the opening of the school, he had proclaimed me a bad influence to anyone who'd listen to him. She had written once to me, curtly. I could hear her husband's voice echoing across the paper her words arrived on. They would hold a private vigil at home.

Thurzo smiled as I turned away quickly to hide any expression that might give away my hurt. Then he pressed on. Persistent in his cruelty.

"My lady – wait. Unfortunately, Count Basta couldn't be here today. He has much to attend to in Erdely, as you might imagine. Apparently, there's a young man who goes by the name 'Stephen Ironhead' who's touting your name around. He buys himself shelter on Bathory credit and runs about leaving a trail of bodies in his wake. What's more, the town of Udvarhely has been inundated with coffins, and the people all whisper 'Stephen Ironhead.' Basta will, of course, put a stop to it. He's a Papist after all and will not tolerate whatever in the world this man is up to. I just thought you should know." His paternal smile returned. It made me feel sick. "But enough of politics. We're here to mourn Francis. Basta sends you a fond greeting. In fact, he asked me to deliver this." It was a small piece of paper, handwritten, its letters curling and swirling around with all the pomposity I'd have expected of Basta's hand.

My condolences to the Blood Countess.

The moment my eyes left the page, I felt a rage burn inside me. It was like nothing I'd ever experienced before. But I knew I couldn't scream here. I couldn't roar with the terrible primal sound that brewed inside me. It took all my will, all my shaky determination, to stop it pouring out of me. But I held onto it. This would be the rage that would get me through my grief. It would provide the inner knowing that would lead me through the forest Nadasdy's death had left me stranded in, through the worlds of Thurzo and the blacksmiths, through my hands that would never fully heal from Rudolph's strange and violent ritual, through Basta's eternal threats. I thought to the girl across time, to Vera. I imagined her response: *Listen to your bones and remember this rage. This rage is good. It will keep you alive and when it's gone, when the rage has turned to dust, either way, you will be able to empty yourself of this world, either in body or in spirit.*

I must have looked at Thurzo differently then because he took an involuntary step backwards. The space around my head felt as if it had ignited, sending streams of invisible fire racing down me, crossing at my feet and working their way back up.

"You play small, George. I know you think you play large. But it's small. It's all *so* small."

He looked at me quizzically, as if I had spoken in another language, but he kept his distance.

"Countess," he said, as he inclined his head. He looked up at me again and then moved back to the collection of nobles that milled about like a pack of agitated dogs sensing mealtime is approaching. Thurzo caught his wife's eye and jerked his head quickly to the side in a manner that meant 'come here'. She dutifully raced over to him. He put his arm around her waist, and she melted like butter left out in an unexpected sun.

*

I hadn't expected to like Thurzo's wife, Elizabet. I had imagined that years and years of being married to a man so cold and empty, full only of ambition, which is a quality determined by what one never has, must have bent her out of all shape. But it wasn't quite like that. Elizabet Thurzo was beaten down. But she wasn't stupid. In fact, she was very clever. She was a master of living well inside the flat world that Thurzo allowed her. She was all about horizons. She feared the sky, not for its distance but for its height, and so always sat with her back to the window.

At the funeral feast, she remained static, sitting beside her husband. She barely ate, and when she did, if Thurzo wasn't engaged in talking with those around him, he'd look sharply at her. She wouldn't look at him but would almost seem to sense his attention. Then she'd daintily put her fork down as if it had never been raised to her lips in the first place. Thurzo would put his arm on the back of her chair and sweep his eyes across the room like an impressive vulture. When he was re-engaged in discussion again, she would spirit a new mouthful up and swallow imperceptibly.

Unexpectedly, her eyes met mine. I knew in an instant that she was well aware of what Thurzo might be hatching. She had the quiet look of a small animal that waits until the coast is clear before storming across the land to find shelter elsewhere. I marvelled at her. I imagined that rather than submit through a lack of wisdom and a fear of reprimand, she submitted because she could make it all very much worth her while. She had desire in her. But it wasn't desire of the body. It was a desire of the mind.

Whether she had always been this way or whether it was a result of having been married to Thurzo was debatable. In the end, I found her very much like him. But whilst he soared, exerting pressure on the world outwards, pushing himself further and further to extend his boundaries, she scuttled. She exerted an inward, secretive pressure that started within herself, folding everything down, becoming so intolerable as a force that she somehow convinced everything else to fly away from her. She used this in tandem with him, I imagined, to expand their worlds together. It had a perfect kind of symmetry to it. He'd always described her as a 'sweet thing', but I found her anything but.

When she came to pay her respects, I asked her to linger. She seemed surprised, in that flat way of hers.

"Countess Thurzo, I've never had the opportunity to speak with you properly before."

She said nothing. She just drew me into that pressured force that she used on everyone to keep them at a safe distance.

"You must stay with me for a time."

"I can't, my lady."

"Come. Surely you won't refuse a grieving widow."

"I'm sorry you have lost your husband. But I must attend to mine, now more than ever." She raised her chin and looked at me down the length of her nose.

"Yes," I said. "I believe they call it do or die. I want you to know that you have my full support, if you ever find you need it."

She giggled like a harp brushed by the wind. Not tuneful, but random and full of sound.

"I'd rather you didn't, my lady. I have it all under control."

"As you wish."

She curtseyed to me, deeply, then said quietly as she rose, "You're the one in danger, Countess. Your pride obscures it from you." And she walked away to stand with her back to the hall's many window casements.

I appreciated her candour. I knew that I was on a trajectory that was leading directly to my extinction. I also knew now that the Thurzos, both George and his wife, would somehow prevail. Their expanding world of ambition and avarice marked this new entrepreneurial age we were heading into at the dawn of the seventeenth century. I had seen the future through the eyes of my double across time. It looked like Thurzo.

He came regularly to our church after that. He watched me each time for the duration of Pastor Magyery's service, a wild animal stalking his prey *carefully*. On the fourth week, he walked up behind me and whispered in my ear.

"Last chance, Elizabet." He took a few paces in a tight half-circle around me and then turned, bending down to kiss my hand. When he lifted his head to meet my eyes with his, their unmistakable ambitious hue matched the sky around him as if he had coloured the whole of my world with his gaze. "Last chance." He lingered. But I said nothing. Nothing at all.

Chapter Twenty

The war between Bocksai and Basta raged across Erdely. With Nadasdy gone, without all of the Bey's ferocity pointed towards becoming king of a united Hungary, the battles had gone from carefully crafted skirmishes to chaos and waste. Bocksai couldn't control the Hadjuks and without Nadasdy, who if nothing else had always paid the Szekelys handsomely, those who remained in the fight now doubted their surviving leader's loyalty. Erdely turned once again into a carnival of blood. This time, at the epicentre of its turning wheels, was Basta. Basta threw death at Bocksai, and Bocksai in turn covered the land in bones and eyes and severed heads. A wild mess of religious fervour; God's own festival of flesh.

The fighting spilled over Erdely's borders into my part of Hungary. I had written to Bocksai, pledging him to honour my husband's sacrifice by protecting my people and my lands in exchange for continued patronage. At first, it worked. Hadjuks would stage a looting to keep us all credibly abused in the eyes of my neighbours, but in truth, it was no more than a theatrical tithing, a taxation through which I continued to finance the revolution my husband and I had started. And no one would die. '*No blood to be spilled on Bathory lands.*' It was a promissory note that Bocksai had sent me, and I kept it sewn inside one of my gloves. Whenever I left my rooms, I wore them until the embroidered black fingers became dull and frayed. When members of my household began to remark on the discrepancy between my finery and my tattered gloves, I quoted sentimental value, muttering something about 'Nadasdy's favourite'.

The girls continued to print. I continued to send coffins out through the tunnels. John continued to evade Basta, returning from time to time to update me on the progress of our sustained efforts to keep him from re-appropriating Erdely for the Pope. The dream of a united Hungary had never been mine. I let Bocksai fight for it now. I only wanted to help the Szekelys – to help them keep their Servetus and all his talk of the heart from being consumed by the dark forces of the Holy Roman Empire. It was a personal passion made out of duty for the women around me who were invisible in this war. I wanted to preserve their stories. I wanted to preserve the beating heart inside them.

Thurzo, of course, played both sides and won. I wouldn't be so lucky. Between financing Bocksai and printing the books, of which John organised the free distribution, I found myself for the first time worrying about money. I remembered Nadasdy's words on his deathbed.

"Invest the money. Not in the press…"

"How can I, when everywhere I am watched?" I'd asked Anna and John one night.

"I don't know, Countess, but do it in a way that no one will expect. Do it with something the likes of Thurzo and Basta won't understand," said John, running his hands through his hair in a way that made me almost jump, as if I'd seen Nadasdy's ghost flash through him.

"That's how to keep hold of your fortune. Keep it out of Hungary."

I thought about it for several days. When a way became clear to me, I laughed out loud for the first time in what felt like years. I laughed so sharply and automatically that the bones of my corset strained against themselves, stretching and cracking like a deep-sea monster waking from a long sleep.

Later that night, I gathered the girls together in the main hall. I shut all the doors. John patrolled around to make sure no wandering ears were listening through the cracks in the lintels.

"We have a new agenda to add to the printing work you've been doing," I announced. "I'm proud of you all. You're a credit to the Szekely name, to the nation that will one day, again, be yours. Szekelys are cut from a different cloth from the rest of Hungary. You are brave, bright and strong. It's Szekely women who will keep Erdely alive – who *have* kept Erdely alive. As for our own fight, our own part in this eternal war, we will continue in our printing of your Servetus. But the times dictate new plans, new routes, new pastures to plough to keep us all alive and fed. In service of that, half of you..." The girls looked around, all at once anxious, some clutching to each other, forming quick alliances to demonstrate who they felt they could not be parted from. I nodded and quelled the rumbling with my gloved hand.

"...Half of you will go over the border to Italy. John will go with you. He knows Italy well. It was his home, before... before *now*." I looked down, my words catching in my throat. Perhaps the danger I was facing now had started then, the moment I brought John back with me to teach us all the magic of print. I had known it was going to be the defining moment of my life, even back then. I just didn't know how much blood would be spilled on account of it.

"John will organise meetings with Jewish and converso cloth traders. You'll be smuggled out of here and set up as *Italian dressmakers*."

I didn't tell them that I of course would, in effect, be purchasing from my own household. I would keep some, and eventually sell bit by bit parts of my immense bejewelled wardrobe to nobles across Europe and even into Turkey when news of its decadence and elegance reached the ears of bored wives from all the corners of the Empire. I would gift garments and precious stones in exchange for favours, powers and passage.

I didn't tell anyone, save Anna and Dorothea, that this would be how the Bathory fortune would cycle around, kept safe in the hands of a bunch of Szekely girls and *women's things*. Let the Hungarian nobility pick off pieces of my wealth day by day. When whatever remained was bled dry, a small silkhouse in Italy powered by Jewish traders and Szekely women would provide wealth enough to keep us all going – if we lived that long. A huge portion of the Bathory fortune would go into frills and tiaras and whalebone corsets – places neither Thurzo nor Basta or any other nobleman would think to look.

Dorothea, Anna and I split the Szekely girls into two factions based on their talents in either print or seamstressing, arranging a secret meal for them all during which they could say their farewells.

"If you join in this fight, you *cannot* speak to your family of it. You must die to the world you've known up until now." I raised my glass and toasted them all. The girls nodded solemnly.

"What choice do we have, Countess?" spoke Marta as the others all drank. "As for me, my family are all dead."

"You'll be transported to Italy inside coffins, two in each one and only four at most at a time. It will be a gruelling journey, I won't lie. But you'll be safe. And you'll be cared for in Italy."

I paused to let the magnitude of what I'd said fall on each of them. They would possess *their own money* as dressmakers, and they would have one eternal client: me.

"Each month, you'll send me a new wardrobe. Spare no expense. Spare no talent." Silence fell, before Marta spoke up.

"Spare no talent!" She cajoled the girls to her left and right until they began to follow suit, crying it out, taking possession of the phrase and turning it into a battle cry, a motto that made sense to them, one which made them feel closer and connected to one another and to our long task ahead.

Fear and excitement tore through the room. The two emotions rippled out between the stones and wood that held the room together, breaking into one another until neither was entirely discernible from the other.

I set my cup down and bade them all eat. The girls chattered and ate and dreamt out loud of their new lives. My lips had gone a dark purple from the wine.

*

"I've come to check up on you, my lady," said Thurzo. "I notice that Hadjuks have raided several of your properties, *properly* this time." He stressed the word 'properly' to suggest that he had unmasked my continuing patronage, Bocksai, in exchange for protection. I ignored the comment and looked at him, wide-eyed and browbeaten, a spotted rabbit racing between shrubs in an effort to stay alive; just vulnerable enough to keep him talking. We were stood in the main courtyard, a few paces away from the central gate. It was no place for receiving visitors, but I didn't want him to get too comfortable in my castle.

"I understand you're paying your neighbour, Betthyany, handsomely for *his* protection. He's no more than a boy, but I suppose Nadasdy was not much more than his age when he was spearing the Ottomans."

"I thank you for your concern, Count Thurzo, but like *everybody* in Hungary these days, I'm surviving. Day by day."

He hmm'd at me, watching me cycle through the different masks I had come to wear in his presence.

"Survival is difficult these days," he said, eventually. He looked genuinely tired and browbeaten himself, taking it upon himself to find a seat on a bench propped by the outer wall of one of the turrets. He settled himself onto it with a sigh.

"Would that Nadasdy were still here. At least the Hadjuks and Tartars would be less of a distraction."

"Well, trust you and Basta to have created that particular mess."

Thurzo raised his eyebrows high, becoming quick and animated again. He looked down to his boots, brushing dust from them, suppressed something – a smile? A frown? I couldn't quite tell – before his searching eyes snapped upwards, his head following more slowly, turtlelike.

"So, you're no longer in mourning. Direct is good, Elizabet. And we seem to be past pleasantries." He looked around at the inhospitable reception to make a point. "Thank God for it. You only need to ask me, and I will protect you. What can Betthyany do, really? You worry I'm after your fortune? Where was Betthyany when your estate in the north was taken, conscripted even, by that idiot – what was his name?"

"I won it back."

"Yes, but the point remains."

I didn't feel that the point remained at all. I had fought a greedy noble and I had prevailed, even in these times. Unmarried. Even without a sword. And for all her avarice, at least Elizabet Thurzo still lived.

George looked around. "It seems quieter," he said, changing the subject. "Where are all your girls?"

"Between the raids and the plague, there are less and less of them every day."

"I've been getting reports, Elizabet. I suppose I should get down to the matter at hand. Some of your girls' families are calling for answers."

"In these times? When every estate across the region is suffering violence and death at the hands of so many different enemies?"

"I suppose that if you offer to be mother to all, you take on a special and saintly glow, my dear. Woe betide if you should fall from the pedestal you've set yourself up on."

"I'm fairly sure that I fell from that perch a long time ago, George."

I absent-mindedly stroked the tips of my fingers through my frayed gloves. Bocksai's promise was becoming less and less meaningful the more he lost control of the Hadjuks and Szekelys, but I still wore his protection note with me every day. Each fresh looting lowered the price I paid him, and he knew it. Still, at this rate, it wouldn't be long before I lost the little that remained in the Bathory coffers. I took comfort in the fact that the girls were set up in Italy. Perhaps it was time I started to wear the costly clothing I was buying from myself. An idiot widow who squanders her huge fortune on frocks and frills during wartime is no doubt safer than a woman of means, power and potential.

Thurzo looked at me, daring me to protest as he made an inventory of my body. I didn't lower my eyes as I had when I was a child. I simply stared at him, unblinking. He laughed. "I don't know which Elizabet I prefer."

"I would prefer the one you married, George."

"No. Not that. I mean the woman you have become or the woman you were. Both Elizabets have their own special enchantments. Which reminds me, how is your son?"

Michael is safe, I thought to myself. *You will never find him.*

"Paul is well."

"I've given it some thought, and I should like to send you – him – a present of sorts. These are harsh times, vicious, in fact, but your son should not be denied an education. Surely you of all people would agree. It would be my honour to provide him with Hungary's finest tutor. I've engaged one. Master Imre. He should be here within the week." Thurzo rose. "Accept it, Elizabet. I may be all sorts of things, but I'm not a monster." He gave me a half-smile that was quite winning. "Well, not always."

He offered a polite nod in lieu of a bow and went over to the stable to collect his horse.

Imre arrived the following week. He was a man who, I imagined, had made a career out of being aloof. Perhaps he had confused it with wisdom. He was almost as hawkish as Thurzo – almost. They came together. I had Anna bring Paul down, who clutched to her skirt and wouldn't be shaken off until Imre produced a tiny wooden horse from his pocket to tempt him with. Paul ran over to him then in an instant and snatched the little creature up. I noticed it was painted gold, its otherworldly mane tossed in the wind, caught in the act of galloping by the artisan; a carved miniature, frozen and precise.

As soon as the two were engaged, Thurzo turned to me, all at once grave.

"My Elizabet is growing weak. They say she might have a sickness. I fear she won't make the winter. I know what it's like to raise a child without a mother and I do fear for Paul, my dear Countess."

"Fear not," I replied. "And let me loan her our doctor and our herbalist. Both have achieved wonders here at Cachtice."

"You're too kind."

"No. I'm a pragmatist."

I looked around at the quiet, empty castle, still as a graveyard, and sighed. "George, I'm getting tired of this. No doubt you are too. I will not accept your proposal. There are no threats and no favours you can tempt me with. You can't seduce me, and you can't terrify me. This is who I am, and this is where I live. I can offer you nothing."

"I see." He drew his chest and neck upright, exhaled and took on a different tone. It was administrative, nothing more, though it carried such malice, such bitterness under its even horizon.

"In that case, if we're being frank with each other, perhaps you should understand what comes next. Basta will come from Erdely. He will take up residence here for a short while." He let it hang in the air, a matter of fact-ness that promised nothing less than death. "And *I will not be able to protect you any longer.* You think I'm the enemy. I'm not. I'm your friend. I have always been your friend."

I looked at him, unmoved. He softened momentarily.

"Elizabet, you have taken my child from me, and you and Nadasdy took, for a good while, my dignity from me. What more do you want? What more could you possibly want from *me*? I'm a count, I'm a warrior, but I'm also the Emperor's Palatine. *I* control Hungary, and since Nadasdy's treachery, *I've* been the one who's been whispering in Basta's ear, telling him to stay in Erdely, away from Hungary, away from Cachtice, away from you. I will *not* be abused by you any longer. My wife is dying. All on her own, I might add. I've had nothing to do with it. You were always magnificent, but in this you're just being stubborn."

I looked at Paul, who was now climbing on Imre like a lost goat on a hillside. For a single moment, I wavered. I imagined my life as Countess Thurzo: I would keep the press secret for as long as possible at Cachtice by moving to Thurzo's estate, visiting only occasionally, leaving Dorothea in charge, bequeathing her Cachtice in everything but title so as not to arouse suspicion. Paul and I would live together for as long as Thurzo deemed my own life permissible. I could even find Michael. Thurzo would rule in the Emperor's name, and as long as I paid him and pleased him, he would allow me to live. He may well never even find out about all the money in Italy.

Thurzo saw my momentary suspension and decided to press his advantage, surreptitiously sliding his hand around my spine and reaching up to pinch the back of my neck sharply. It brought me back to reality instantly.

"George, I've learnt one thing over the years, which is that you can tell everything you need to know about a man by the way he touches you."

He looked like he'd been stung by a wasp.

"And you learnt this from Francis?" That look of pure hatred I'd seen in Nadasdy's bedroom and then in Prague a lifetime ago came back to him, as if he had traversed the years in an eyeblink. "Expect Basta. Expect him soon." *Clang! clang!* He walked away.

"In a strange kind of way, yes, I *did* learn that from Francis. And also from you," I whispered as he left. Imre looked up at me from where Paul had all but pinned him to the floor.

"Thurzo has always had your best interests at heart, my lady. Don't fret, I will tutor the son of Nadasdy… in any eventuality. Where are my quarters?"

*

I was still sending Rudolph secret handwritten pages about what I had seen of the future. I put them in and amongst the household taxes that were now always envoyed to him by soldiers instead of servants on account of the dangers of travelling overland. Each one was rolled up and made safe under the Bathory seal. In them, I tried to describe the strangeness of the world I had glimpsed. It was hard to capture the speed of things in words. Their world was so fast that it evaded the languages we had available to us.

Without any words for what I had seen, I compared the wonders I had glimpsed through her to lightning, rushing waters, racing horses, the odd, unchartable vectors that bees and flies took in the sky. But none of these came even close. I described the deep sense of isolation, disconnection and loss I had felt through the girl across time. I spoke of the portals that lit up in their hands and through which they could see across space, as if they had conquered the boundaries of distance itself, folding the world up into tiny rectangular suns they carried around in their pockets that were cool to the touch and radiated not yellow, but blue. I wrote about her writing about us. I wrote about how she saw our time, how primitive and stupid our tools and machines were, but how, in turn for all their speed, sound and light – light everywhere – they were no more evolved, no more intelligent, no more or less kind. To be human, it seemed, was to remain stuck in an endless loop, trapped inside the half-moon of a bow. Always aiming to shoot elsewhere. The pressure of *just being human* was never-ending. I wrote and wrote, filling notebook after notebook; ripping the pages out and sending them off each month to fulfil my promise.

Rudolph never responded. He never replied that he loved, hated, or even read the things I wrote. But I noticed one thing: I had stayed alive all this time. He could have, at any moment, ordered my head and seized my lands, but he didn't. A woman lives every day with the threat of her extinction by those who believe they allow her to continue. I knew this was still the case across time. I knew that women were still in a fight for their survival. That the war against women continued in full swing. Love me or die. Be my mother, angel, saviour, whore, child, and forgive me, always forgive me for what I do. As if women had special access to the role of Christ. As if women were in some way lucky to have the ability to suffer long and complain of the cruelty of the world less than men did.

I knew, as did the girl in the future, that men suffered. That their bodies were considered expendable by the crowns that ruled them and told them to fight – now for this, now for that. *Go and shoot until you get shot! Go and work until you bleed! When you return, you'll be taken care of, you'll be protected* and other such promises by an emperor that always forgot about them the minute they came home and left them to be taken care of by their *women*. Perhaps there was only one man in the world: the Emperor, who made every *body* else a little less than him, half man; quarter man; and so on, so that all men who lived as men feared the woman inside them as some kind of internal cannibal that kept them always at one remove from power.

Never hearing back from Rudolph, I began to sneak in a few additions. I wrote about Servetus. I wrote about how Janus had told me that in Ottoman stories the heart was the *only* thing that aimed the half-moon bow of our human experience elsewhere. I wrote about how the moment one aimed from the heart, the arrow of our species' story flew out of cause and effect, racing across a field of justice that no longer relied on either one of these to take root and germinate inside a lifetime, sowing itself into every experience. I wrote about all the other traditions of the heart, about the Jewish *sefirot* and the Spanish nun's *interior castle*. It wasn't long before my stories moved from tales of the future to become tales of the present. The two were, after all, no longer separable. Past, present and future. Each haunted the other, folded the other inside itself, pumping out stories inside the infinite rib cage we called the world.

I wrote until my fingers became sore. I wrote until we ran out of candles. And the girl across time, she wrote me too. She wrote about the heart of my struggles inside hers. In a way, I imagined us birthing each other out of our stories. Every day, I bore out my own mother, my own author. And I sent the pages to Rudolph to stay alive. I listened when I wrote. I listened to the words that hung in the air around me, accessing them like one might a secret letter that has only one destination: the heart. I knew what she was writing down. I heard her scribing me even as I walked, ate, sat, remembered.

If a man can't write himself safely into your world, if the languages are too strange, too dense, too unpredictable, too material, then what else can he do? Cause and effect set everything right side up. If you blur the boundaries between them, expect a shock! Expect turmoil. If you refuse to be protected, then expect the worst. Expect Basta.

I had sent my latest instalment to Rudolph, rolled inside an account of the losses I had incurred during the last Hadjuk raid and how it had had the unfortunate effect of lowering the amount in gold tax that accompanied the letter. The two pages folded across each other. If you read them together, the tale would be an uncanny one. It would speak of a kind of sadness that was copied across the two contexts. The differences between the stories pointed to where change was *possible*. To where differences silently nudged and stretched across the pages to create new forms of thinking, new stories, new life. Anna came in with Dorothea to bring me some more ink. She shut the door and once we had bolted the heavy oak from inside and removed ourselves to the furthermost corner of the room, they reeled off a whispered report in turn about the costs incurred by the books in Erdely on the one hand, and by the dresses in Italy on the other. The Bathory fortune was looking less covetable now, much to all our relief. A small dresshouse in Verona was doing very well, however.

"My lady, I still fear for your safety. Thurzo is in Erdely, and after your last refusal, I can't imagine anything good will follow him back from his visit. Perhaps you should leave. Anna and I can smuggle you and Paul out. Please. Please think about it. I can hold up the operation here."

"Dorothea, are you concerned for me? It feels like a few moments ago that I was trying to drug you in Italy so I could go and learn printcraft from the Fabbris – God rest their souls."

Dorothea managed a half-smile from out of her weathered mouth. It was a mouth that had held too many stories back, too much witness and testimony to the horrors the Szekelys had endured – she had endured – over a difficult lifetime. She always looked awkward when she smiled. I had come to love her for it.

I looked at her and Anna and felt a surge of protectiveness run through my body. The protectiveness turned without warning into a premonition, running its wildfire throughout me.

"It might be better for you all if I go. I've thought about it. I could gift some land to my daughter's husband in exchange for safety." I looked up from my papers, tapping the feathered end of my quill to my forehead before gesturing out with it. "On the other hand, with me gone, Cachtice, Sarvar and all my estates will more than likely be seized. Either way, I fear you are in danger. You could go together. You could go across the border to Erdely. I would suggest anywhere but there, but I know you. I know you both."

"We haven't come this far to give up now, Countess," said Dorothea. Anna nodded. "If death awaits, I will die a Szekely. I will die as someone who has first of all lived. Proudly."

Anna teared up and Dorothea simply stared at me.

"The Emperor and not Thurzo has stayed Basta's hand. I know it. Thurzo thinks me a simple girl at the end of it all. But I've had news from Betthyany that the Emperor's brother, Matthias, is calling for his reign to end. It won't come fast. Still, I fear something *is* coming. I feel it in my bones and I fear it."

"Perhaps we should start getting the girls out. One last print run. A large one. We can get them out in small groups at the most, two and three to a coffin. And we should send them not to Erdely but to Italy. Teach them how to pretend to be Catholic and get them out." Dorothea had clearly thought this through. It was a good idea and none too soon.

"Yes," I said. "Yes. Let's start tomorrow. If we wait, we die, *all* of us. Get them to Italy fast. Anna, who amongst them do you most trust?"

"Marta." She gave no explanation, but I had watched Marta and agreed immediately.

"Good, send her to me now."

"Yes, Countess."

Marta arrived at my tower-room door not long after the two older women had left. She was anxious, wringing her freshly inkstained hands and shifting her weight from foot to foot.

"Marta, please, sit."

She obeyed silently, but I could almost hear her mind racing, racing, wondering why she had been called in for a private audience with her Countess. She had the look of a terrified hare, making me the hunter and she the hunted each time she looked up at me.

"Take some wine."

She nodded and gulped down the cup I filled for her as if it would be her last. I had never realised before that I inspired such fear and awe in the girls. Perhaps they feared the Countess Bathory, not for who I was but for what I appeared to be: a woman fighting the world. A woman alone. A widow. Marked for death on account of her refusal to be anything other than who and what she was. No small thing. Not in our times.

"I'll be straight and to the point, my dear. The time has come to do one last print run of the *Christianismi Restitutio*. We are preparing to shut down the press. I want you to gather the girls and work through the upcoming nights if you must on one final print run. After that, I will be sending you all to Italy to join your Szekely sisters. I want you to lead them whilst I… whilst I… stay here to tie up loose ends. I'll send enough gold and jewels with you to keep you all well in the meantime. Esther is managing the operation in Italy. Join with her. Keep it all running." I took both her hands in mine. "I will follow you."

She searched my eyes.

"Promise me, my lady. Promise me. I didn't know what it was to be a person, to be alive, to be counted, until I started printing. Promise me you will join us and that we'll start up the press again after the trouble has passed."

Perhaps it was fear and love together, not just fear, that moved her and the girls. I looked her straight in the eye and lied.

*

The following night, the girls were occupied with printing. A thick silence fell across the horizon, as if the entire sky had become wool. I was in the main hall, papers spread across the dining table, hatching, on the one hand, plans for the dresshouse in Italy, and on the other, a good geographical point to dispense of the book-filled coffins in Erdely. I laughed at myself for a moment – at how macabre I had become. It all needed to come to an end now. It was time to get out for the sake of the girls. I'd gambled enough with my own life and the lives of my household. I couldn't bear to gamble away the lives of the Szekelys I had initially set out to save. The coffins would finally come to rest. Soon, Basta would arrive, and the thick wooden frames would be restored to their rightful purpose. But not tonight. Tonight, we would come as close as we could to finishing the final run. Then we would settle for escape.

Anna came into the hall, quietly holding what looked like swathes of cloth in her weathered hands. I nearly jumped out of my skin when she emerged at my side like an apparition flown in from between worlds. She gestured and I realised she was about to spread whatever she was holding on the table, atop all the papers. I moved aside and as she unfurled it, I realised it was a newly made dress.

"The girls have sent you something special from Italy. They want you to keep this one." The skin under her eyes was blotchy and she seemed moved. She had always been sentimental under those gruff, hard edges that marked her a southerner.

I came close and leant over it. At first sight, it was the most stunning silk dress I'd seen. It was deep red, like a fallen tulip in spring. The stitching was perfect. Blue sapphires were sewn into the bodice. As they caught the light, they flashed; a dozen incredible seas scattered across a map of blood.

"Look," said Anna, pointing to the skirt.

I lifted the outer layer. The girls had layered the underskirts so that they would rustle and then stand straight without a caged frame when the wearer moved about. As I lifted each layer, however, I noticed something unusual about them. I leant in closer and then gasped in amazement.

Each panel was covered in writing! They had printed excerpts of Servetus on each layer hidden under the red silk.

Anna flipped the dress and opened up the back of the stiff bodice. The part that would lie upon my skin was covered in a different text. I started to read. Across the ribs, hand copied, was the first text John had printed for Nadasdy and I all those years ago at Sarvar:

You shall have the power to denigrate into the lower forms of life and you shall have the power, out of your soul's judgement, to be reborn into higher forms, which are divine.

"The girls bid you to wear it, so you may keep them close to you. The silk hides you from the world, and the bodice keeps your secret, telling it quietly every day to your skin." A dress. A love letter. The whole story, worn silently to the world, though it spoke volumes.

I ran my fingers along it. Each touch fleshed out a little more the same primary sensation: *I will die in this dress. But at the same time, I will be reborn.* I had sent the girls out in coffins, and they had, without realising it, sent me a kind of coffin back. One made of silk. What a perfect circular exchange. The dress allowed me to animate the story of my life in a way that exceeded my flesh – the story that had imprisoned me inside the world I now lived in, *and* the story from which I had also, in my small way, escaped, becoming myself, Elizabet Bathory, leader of the Szekely women, conspirator of the Erdelian rebellion.

I slowly bent my body all the way down until I lay over it, smelling the fabric, sensing the writhing ghosts of silkworms, remembering my life with Nadasdy, the girls and their own fight to stay alive, to save their land through its stories, through Erdely's prophet and all his tales. I wept and wept into the fibres of that dress. When my eyes finally became dry, I lifted my head.

"Let it all be worth it," I said to Anna, my eyes black and half veiled from the world.

"It already has been worth it, Elizabet. It already has."

*

The first mistake was that one of the serving men, recognising the imperial seal flashed before them, had opened the gate. Basta rode straight in with nothing to stop him. In effect, we invited him in. The second mistake was that a few girls still remained. Thurzo rode in next. Master Imre came down to meet him, packed Paul onto a horse and rode off with him. *With my son.* I came running down from my tower room, dizzy from the winding descent. But I was too late. Paul was gone, and when I crossed to the main hall, I heard a scream that sounded like it came from the belly of the earth. When I came upon the hall, I realised it came from somewhere much closer and much more intimate. It came from the belly of Marta. Basta had cut her in two.

I had told myself that the sight of Nadasdy plunging the half-made sword into the blacksmith all those years ago would be something I would never recover from. It would be the one thing that would haunt my life forever. I was wrong. Seeing Marta severed under the ribs, lying there like broken meat, her inkstained hands curled downwards onto the slabs of stone floor at Cachtice, was irremovable. I screamed and screamed until Thurzo came up behind me and clamped his hand over my mouth. I bit into his hand, but it remained firm, as if he were made of stone.

"Open your eyes. Open your damned eyes, Elizabet!" he yelled. Then he whispered quietly, "You could have prevented this." Basta emerged from out of the shadows. He had been watching me closely. He pointed the tip of his sword downwards, letting drops of Marta's blood fall into the cracks on the floor, and leant casually on the hilt.

"You should have listened to your Giorgio, Countess. Now look what you've done."

Basta leant the sword carefully up against the shadowed part of the wall and then knelt down to the side of Marta's bleeding torso. He touched her face and chin with his hand and smiled at her, a father caressing his daughter lovingly on the day she comes of age. He pulled his dagger out from the sheath that hung at his belt and stabbed little points and pricks all over her until the more exposed half of her body – her head, her neck, her chest – was covered in tears and rips and cuts. The sound rapped like fists on the inside of my ears. My blood rose and pounded until the puncture sounds and my own blood were the only two things in all the world. When you see a horror like this, all things human leave the world. All things become empty – half here, half there. The senses become scattered, telling the world in distortions. You hear the sight of blood, and you smell nothing but the sound of iron.

When Basta came across her inkstained fingers, curled as if beseeching the silent stones for a way out, he held them and shook his head at me.

"What did you think? Did you think you could start a war with me?" He stared up at me from his position on the floor and said, "I think, for you, Countess, for you, it should be a slow one – death, I mean. I cannot kill you like I killed Michael the Brave, like I killed Nadasdy, like I will kill Bocksai. No. You, my lady, *you* fight dirty. And so you shall die dirty. You shall die a sneaky death. I will take your lands…" and he looked up to Thurzo, who nodded simply as if conducting no more than a simple transaction.

"…But I think I will also take your soul. You want to give Erdely a new soul? I think instead you yourself shall be made to take on the oldest of souls. It will hang over you forever. Nobody will speak your name for a hundred years, and when they do, they will call you something else," he laughed, "my dear Blood Countess." He turned back to Marta, opened her dead mouth and cut out her tongue. Then he threw the tongue on the floor beside the body. "Just in case," he said, looking at me with a smile. His eyes were blank and cold, though he laughed and leapt up like a youth in spring.

Thurzo stepped forward, threw himself down to the body and started to shout and shriek for aid. Basta removed himself quietly back into the shadows. In a few moments, clearly summoned beforehand, Pastor Magyery and his entourage of clerics came running into Cachtice Castle. When he found Thurzo, he merely pointed, aghast.

"Countess! Enough of your devilry! I cannot stand by a moment longer. You ruin the good name of Nadasdy. Vile, vile woman!"

Thurzo grabbed me by the arms and threw me down to the floor.

"I will deal with her, Pastor. The sermon this week should be nothing less than fire for this witch."

"Be careful, my lord. God himself alone knows the kind of spells and black magic she might cast over you."

"No, Pastor. No magic can corrupt the heart of a man absorbed in God. It isn't her magic at work here. She is simply a sick soul. She preys upon the weak – upon weak women and girls. She betrays her gender. And that is how she betrays God."

Pastor Magyery nodded, making the sign of the cross over Marta's mangled halves.

"Every one of your coffins adds another mortal sin to your roster of evils! Hundreds upon hundreds must have died here. Hell. Nothing less than hell for Countess Bathory!"

The pastor left. The castle went silent. Thurzo stood over me and just looked at me. He just looked at me. Nothing more. His eyes were cold, like Basta's. And where was Basta? No more in the shadows. He was running through the castle like a maniac, sword in hand, rounding up every last member of my household into the print room and the corridor that lay outside it.

*

For three weeks, Thurzo and Basta stayed in the castle. First, they hung Dorothea on a hook in the inner courtyard. It was snowing. Basta doused her in water and left her overnight until her lips went blue and paper-thin layers of ice formed across parts of her body. Then he brought me out and bade me look at her. She was barely alive. He skipped over to her like a child, stopping short of her body. Then slowly, ever so slowly, he leant in and then kissed her.

The kiss was so forceful that she swayed, right and then left, creating fresh tears in her back, letting more blood fall. He ran his hands along her wounds until his palms were slick and red. Then he came back over to me, stood in front of me and held me fast with one arm around my back. He smeared the blood over my face and lips. At first, I fought him. How I fought him! For Dorothea. He punched me a few times on the side of the head. Then I simply stood and let myself become his doll, limp and compliant and ready to be painted. He went back to Dorothea, perhaps to torment her, perhaps to smear more of her blood over me. She opened one eye, drew some strength from God knows where and spat in his face. I gasped. But what else could he do to her that he hadn't already? He laughed at her. That was all.

He returned to my side.

"Don't worry, Countess. I will bring her down soon. We need to hear from her. We need to hear from them all the terrible, terrible things that you've done."

He sniggered, wrinkling his nose in mirth like a rat. Then he returned me to my tower and locked me in. I ran to the window casement as the remaining girls were beaten, raped and hung until half-dead, in the courtyards, by the storerooms, everywhere. I forced my eyes to watch. *I did this. I thought they would only come for me, that I could get everyone out in time. I cannot deny them all witness.* Cachtice became the site of massacre. The screaming lasted so long and was so incessant that even the monks from the monastery across the way came to hurl their pots against the walls and shout for the devil-countess to desist her wicked ways. "Let us pray in peace!"

I screamed to them for help from out of my window, but they simply jeered and spat and called me the devil's whore.

A day, a week, or perhaps more passed. I had lost all sense of time. Basta came up to my room. He opened the door and tried to pull me out of it. When I refused to budge, holding my arms up across the open door frame, he kicked me hard, and I went tumbling down the stairs. *Please God, let me break my neck now. Let it be over. Let me fly back to the in-between world and then die. Please!*

But I didn't. I simply landed and was dragged the rest of the way, by the arms, hair, anything he could grab at. I was taken to the main reception hall. Thurzo sat at the table, like he had so many times when the guest of my husband, later, when he was my lover and not a few months ago, when he was my suitor. Anna was stretched out on the table, her body forming the shape of a human star.

"Tell us what you and the Countess have done. Where are the Szekely girls? Where are they!"

Anna said nothing. Thurzo slapped her again and again until the slaps became punches. Still, she remained quiet.

"Do you see now, Elizabet? Now do you see? Stupid, stubborn woman. Who did you think you were? Who did you think you were to say no to me, to take my child from me, to threaten my power here? Did you think yourself Nadasdy?" He tutted. "Tell me again, did my touch bother you? Did you learn all you could learn about me from it?" His voice was sardonic, a great grey and blue eel slicing through the waters at night.

I wept a single silent tear. He turned from me in disgust.

"*Now* you cry. Stupid, stupid *woman*. Watch what loyalty to you means. It's time to face reality." He looked towards Anna.

Basta crossed the hall to the table and sat down. He nodded

and one of my serving men shut the door quickly, so that only Anna, Thurzo, Basta and I remained in the room.

"Anna," Basta said quietly, "if you sign this, I will let you go. I promise. I will let you go." She shook her head in a no and looked at me, mouthing "*I'm sorry.*" What could she possibly be sorry for, this woman who had cared for me since I was still a child? This woman who I loved?

"Hmm. So loyal to your Countess. Now let me see how far this loyalty will last. Will it last as long as your flesh, I wonder?"

He picked up a knife that lay on the table close to where Thurzo had last taken a meal, all the way on the opposite side of the long dining table. He strolled back to where she lay and, without warning, thrust the carving knife into her flesh, tore a piece off her and then became darkly excited. I watched him as he ate it down, his head taking the shape of a fox to my eyes. Inside the shock, inside the *un*reality of what I witnessed, I found something of a voice.

"Sign it, Anna!" I shrieked.

She said yes immediately, but Basta wasn't done. He started to eat her until even Thurzo went white in the face and yelled for him to stop. I thought I saw a great golden moth fly from the gash he had made in Anna's body. I jumped on its back – part of me did. My body, which remained alive, turned cold as death and rooted itself into stillness, though I still breathed. My spirit, which was warm, flew to the great house in the sky and for a moment I lived in disjointure.

And Basta continued.

"Is this too much for your fine and noble sensibilities, dear, sweet Georgio?" Basta said quickly. "Remember me, Thurzo. Don't you ever cross me." And he nodded his head in my direction. "I own you. You are my boy, not the other way around. You are Palatine because I allow it. Rudolph's brother, Matthias, has him cornered now. The rules have changed once more. And Matthias likes what I can do for him. The likes of you and Bathorys, Nadasdys, Bocksais – you Hungarians all – you are nothing next to the force of holy Italy. Sectarianism will die. *That* is my holy rite. *That* is my communion. The Erdelyian heresy will die in Erdely, and Erdely itself will be torn up. Flesh of Christ in everyone? Christ inside the body and blood of all? Good! Very good. Then *I* will have my rite. I will have the sacred from out of you all." He cut and tore off one more piece of her, a finger this time, that made her howl and then fall silent.

Thurzo turned around and stifled vomit. Anna had passed out. But she would sign now. She would sign her confession. She would sign that she, Dorothea and I had been feasting off the Szekely girls, off disappeared noblewomen, off anyone who came to Cachtice with young female blood in their veins. And we had been doing it for years! We had got away with it for years and years! Few bodies had been found, save the one by Thurzo, when he had entered only a few weeks ago to put a stop to all the blood I was spilling. Why so few? Because we had simply eaten them up. And those we hadn't eaten or drained of blood, which we then bathed in to keep ourselves looking so young, had disappeared. Buried in coffins, two or three at a time. Lost – lost forever. The lost women of Hungary and Erdely, vanishing still under the darkness of Cachtice and its demonic countess.

*

I had tried to make something beautiful, a small corner of the world free of the stranglehold of all this human violence. I hadn't hoped to succeed. But I had hoped to create enough of an entrance point, enough of a crack inside the heart of an infinitely dark story to allow for something other to shine through; to arrive here, now, instead of displacing itself elsewhere, like a promise that would never be fulfilled. I knew I would be made to suffer for it, but I didn't realise just how much suffering would be exacted for all my dreaming until it arrived. It was the kind of suffering that takes generations to erase. It was the suffering that I knew the girl across time was still feeling, even now, hundreds of years in a future that was already taking place, that was already being scripted in every moment I lived out now; a history that lived inside her and women across the surface of the earth. My crime was to be a woman who exceeded her place in every way, spilling over, shifting between time and space and all the expectations of a body written into by emperors and other men.

Basta had made me realise that the body of any human was a mould that could be filled and unfilled, shaped and unshaped, by anyone with a sword and a divine right. Basta built humans. Basta created *man* in his image and cut the parts of women that did not conform to that image right out of them. We were all at one remove from power. Even Thurzo. Thurzo was in Basta's eyes *nothing more than a woman*. His Hungarian-ness made him less than holy and the holy was masculine. Only Rome's God was truly male. Everything else needed recrafting in its service.

I had finally sunk to the floor. From this vantage point I could see pools and rivulets made entirely out of Anna's blood. It travelled down the stones in the floor, along the cracks and other unseen places. In my half-conscious state I had the sense that these were the places where we could have lived as we had hoped. In the cracks and crevices and unseen places. But that hadn't been permitted for me, for anyone who could be at any moment *seen*.

I had lived across two states – the state of being alive, of being seen, and the state of being in between life and death, the state of the unseen. When Rudolph had taken the unseen from me with his Emerald Table, he had rendered me into something Basta could catch and remould. But I would be seen! I would have it that we all would be seen. How can any human be seen and be free? Perhaps it's not possible.

"The Sultan, now he *is* a man worth fighting, Thurzo. He may be king of animals, but I would prefer to fight a lion than a sectarian!" I could hear Basta continuing to talk. Thurzo remained silent and soon Basta became bored and agitated.

"Cat got your tongue, Georgio? Come, come. Don't fret. You will receive a good portion of Bathory's lands. You are *my* boy. You've fought well along with my army, and Matthias will know of it. Ah poor Georgio! He has a woman's stomach, in the end. I miss Nadasdy at times like these."

He sat down. "What does this *Elizabet* do to you? I cannot believe any person alive can be that good a fuck. She does something, no? Something to you. What does this Elizabet do that makes all these people flock to her and join her revolution, even when she runs straight to death?" He gestured to Thurzo, extending his finger and pointing up and down his body. "Maybe she makes you feel like you can be something you are not."

Thurzo eventually spoke quietly, but his voice was steel and ice. "Elizabet is about life. That's all. And that's why she doesn't fit. Look at her revolution, life from out of a coffin. Life from out of death."

"Then we must make her *all* about death. That's how we defeat her and any legacy she might have. We turn her into a harbinger of death. Not just a killer. No, it must be something much more than that. A reverse kind of hero. An antichrist. A dark angel. We need to pull down more than her body. We need to tear down her soul." He thought for a moment. Then he filled a cup with wine and nodded at Thurzo that if he wanted some, he should just help himself to it.

"I just realised something, Georgio." He drank and scratched his chin. "I've never fought a woman before. It's different."

Chapter Twenty-One

This time, there's no grand hall. No great box of wires and echoing expanse between chairs and a ceiling high overhead. The professor had seen to that. Not satisfied with one or two or even three attempts to humble me in the darkest ways he knew how, he had struck again. I had been relieved of my teaching; my research had been defunded. But at the same time, try as I might to find work elsewhere, he simply wouldn't let me go.

"I'm sorry, but I just had a call from your university, and it seems your references won't be coming through."

Or:

"I'm sorry but I just sought your references from your former employer and there's been a little problem."

Or:

"Thank you for your interest but we won't be taking this application further."

It lasted years. I had gone to everyone I could but, of course, no one had believed me. Or if they did, they turned their faces to the floor and went silent. A grand passivity that was tantamount to their belief in history: *you can't change the world, and this is how it works.* I had continued to write, eventually speaking online at student conferences across the world, navigating the strange new dawn of the information age with the same agility Bathory had of her new world of printing. And so, the professor had hit me inside my origin story, closing up as many avenues as he could for me to release the story of Bathory and challenge the idea that *history was built of cause and effect and so to avoid its violence, we must stay hidden.* I watched as more women went into the dark arms of his nondescript corner of the university and came out quieter, tamer, silenced. More and more told, *"No evidence, no recourse."* Living like this in linear time should have made me a bitter being. But I had learnt to listen to the deeper story. And I knew what I needed to do. *Just keep writing!* Lucretia had said to me. *Keep writing until time itself quietens down and listens.*

Here, now, I'm simply speaking into my computer. Faces flash up and flash away in little boxes running at first across and then down the side of my laptop screen. I haven't raced halfway across the planet inside an airplane with a wad of funding, jetting streams of white clouds behind me, sitting strapped in my seat far *above* the earth, looking down on the workings of the world; existing for a few hours in the gap created by mechanics that lift our bodies high even as the world below burns slowly.

This time, I've folded time and space by appearing live on a screen across several countries. Invited by a group of young scholars to give a talk, I speak to the endless flashing and rotating young faces that emerge momentarily; ghosts in the machine offering brief glimpses into synthetic lives in this orderly séance we've come to call the world. I unmute myself and the zeros and ones start to dance, partnering with my voice to create new atomic resonances inside every tiny person's home. I – like all of us – have become an atmosphere inside somebody else's house. Somebody else's story. Nothing more, but also nothing less. An atmosphere whose origin is blood and bone but whose body has become glass and circuitry.

I speak, and millions of humming, glowing parts inside all the computers networked together now buzz with the story I tell to faceless presences, numbers, codes. Here it is, I think. Here we all are. Coffins have become screens which an entire new population live *inside*. We smuggle ourselves halfway around the world in these coded coffins, finding new ways to resist the digital emperor we made out of the world. Ghosts, all of us. Ghosts with deep purpose who need to learn how to move inside this new body – this new world; to write it differently. I stare into the screen, catching a glimpse of a face here, a long limb poised to click there, a whole population of bright, young people who have shown up to listen to a story:

They always tell you to be true to life when you're writing. 'Be true to life' and 'write what you know'. Both are platitudes. But what about writing about something you don't know? Like what it feels like to be a woman unhampered by generation upon generation of rape and murder, and hatred and all the other things that have come to constitute our collected histories here, now. To be Bathory without an infinite array of Thurzos and Bastas, Nadasdys and Rudolphs looking to write her into the Blood Countess – to change her being, her ability to be part of her own history. How can I write that? How can you re-story something you've never known – never known in your bones? Our species knows all about power. Our species knows how bodies, whatever their constitution, are marked into position, trapped, like particles deciding where to be, when to be, how to be, this time. Material information, lighting up inside the urban pinball machine we call commerce, we call Empire.

In re-storying the world, perhaps she would not choose to reposition herself closer to power. She would not choose to be Elizabeth Regina or any other queen made under a crown. She would choose instead to be power itself rather than stand up inside it as a singular 'one'. Power caught and made like that exerts its gravity hard and fast, making us all slaves to its position in time and space, telling its story through us – even now. It is the very opposite of freedom. Perhaps she had chosen instead to dream us all inside a powerful uncertainty – powerful on account of its endless momentum.

Uncertainty has nothing to do with silence. It has nothing to do with fantasy either. Uncertainty leaves it up to the thoughts and marks born out of it to do the dirty work of separating our species out, to confine us inside an eternal measurability; an infinite sorting machine that teaches us each our place inside the world. Uncertainty flies, not away from measurement but inside it. Endless movement, breathing inside a fixed point. When uncertainty makes friends with momentum, it turns into a love affair. They birth new worlds. Uncountable worlds. Worlds that understand nothing of the fixing of time and space but everything about justice and everything about love. This kind of power acts to fold worlds together. It folds death down into ever-smaller pieces until only love remains.

Little signals arc on my screen: *reconnecting....* They flicker down for a moment and everybody watching *here, now,* becomes frozen. Trapped in their position. In my world, it's as if all momentum has been ripped from out of them, freezing them into static caricatures of themselves on the screen. Of course, this isn't real, I remind myself. They still go on living in their lives, unaware of how I see them, captured slices of time. At the lip of the world on my screen, all things have come to a stop. Time bends, and when my connection is restored for a split second, they all race and speed towards the present. *Time lives inside the body*, I think. *This body of zeros and ones glitching and exceeding itself is the body of our new world.*

*

At first, Thurzo simply put me under house arrest. It was all dealt with quietly, with the assistance of Pastor Magyery and the nobles of Hungary who found their fealty to Thurzo emboldened by the promise of more annexed land. Bathory land. He had killed Anna and Dorothea after they signed their confessions. I was not permitted to speak at my trial or at theirs on account of my devilry. My voice itself contained all the terrible powers of hell. And so, they reduced even my speech from being something dangerous in its reasoning powers to something more deadly and insidious. One single utterance, even the seed sound of a forming word, was a spell-caster. As if sound could vibrate in just such a way as to bring all the Christian men of court to their knees. If I uttered a word, I would instantly be put to death. A woman's voice itself is a weapon. It must be destroyed before it has even begun.

As I stood before Thurzo and the nobles brought to hear my case, one sad question hung over me: what of the girls? I didn't care for any of the condemnations they used to tar and feather me before God. But when their talk turned to the girls themselves, the victims of my so-called murderous cruelty, I waited for any information to slip from their tongues. Had they traced them to the dressmaking houses in Italy? When an answer came, it entered my soul like a warm fire, burning away some of the darknesses that had befallen me, allowing the smallest glimmer of hope to fly back into me and animate my body:

Who were they that Bathory had killed and where were they from? All questioned maintained that they did not know who they were or where the girls were from...

I breathed in joy, though my body remained stone so as not to reveal the inner prayers my atoms were singing even *here, now*. The remaining Szekely girls in Italy would be safe. They would *live*. They would continue to flourish, to even return one day to Erdely and love their God through the voice of Servetus, inside the walls of their lioness hearts.

When the sham trial was finally over, Thurzo brought new servants to Cachtice, which remained largely empty of visitors on account of the terror the *Blood Countess* inspired amongst most local landowners and their wives. It became no more than a staging post, a pit stop for Thurzo and his soldiers when they passed through. I had permission to wander most of the castle, but had an armed escort with me, except when in my tower. Still, I dressed each morning, wearing what the girls had made in silent honour of what we had all achieved. Denied speech, denied the written word, I spoke through my clothing. But no one except me was able to hear what each rustle meant.

Although I was allowed no books from the library, I still had several volumes hidden under my bed and inside my wardrobe and chests. How I wished I could get word out to John! I caressed the covers of some of the titles he had printed for me over the years as if they were talismans that might bring him to safety. I willed him to find his way to Italy from his last known position in Erdely.

When, instead, he emerged as a bearded serving man in Cachtice, bringing me herbal tea, I nearly spilled the damned thing all over myself. The armed guards noticed me but soon settled back into discussing something or other. John made to clear up and slipped a note under my plate as he did so. I spirited it into my dress and asked for permission to go to my room. As I did so, another serving man emerged at the doorway. He was dark and swathed in layers of cloth that fitted him awkwardly. He nodded at John and disappeared again before I got a look at him, but I already knew who he was, even after all these years. Once upstairs, I pulled out the note. It had simply two words scrawled hastily across it: *Be ready*. I held the note like a flower in both my hands, breathing in its scent. "I will," I whispered into it, kissing it before sending it up in flames with the candle beside my bed. Life had returned.

Two nights later, John emerged at my tower-room door. "Now," was all he said. I followed him down the spiralling steps. When we reached the doorway, I noticed someone in a cloak and hood. Her hair poked out of it, however, in a mass of wild directions. It was Erzi, the wildwoman, healer, midwife, madwoman. She silently traded places with me, passing me the bucket of piss and shit she was holding.

I followed John to the perimeter of the outer wall and tipped the bucket. It was a bright night, not pitch black, with a waxing moon overhead, filling its edges with pearl light. When we arrived at the gate, John muttered something about "getting the woman servant away from that damnable witch, even though she's as wrinkled as an ugly prune!" The guard laughed.

"No more girls at Cachtice anymore. Just that devil woman. I wish they posted me somewhere else."

We slipped out. The moon cast a strong light about, pearlising the grass and the shrubs and sending the silver birches into an otherworldly frenzy, standing like so many undead soldiers, watching our every move. When we arrived at the lip of the forest, I turned and threw my arms around John.

"Though I've born two boys, you are the only son I've ever had."

He smiled at me.

"I've lost three fathers, Countess. I'd be happy to be a mother's son."

"Anna… Dorothea…"

"I know," was all he said. "We're going to get you over to Italy. There's one more coffin waiting in the woods."

I let out a sound that was somewhere between a cry and a laugh and for all the world, I could have sworn the forest itself swallowed the sound up, eager to keep us quiet and safe. I hadn't been able to feel anything after witnessing all that Basta and Thurzo had done. It wasn't that I saw these things in my mind's eye; it was that my entire mind was blank. The golden moth I had seen emerging from out of Anna had taken me to a strange sky. A large purple cloud now lay over *everything*. There was nothing to see. Nothing to remember. Nothing to feel.

John pressed on quickly, lending me his hand so I could cross the fallen trees and white snow-capped roots and stubs that stuck out their muddy tongues to give an otherworldly voice to the hem of my dress. It rustled, whispering all of Servetus' secrets into the earth. The land around Cachtice would know them then, and whisper them back, in turn, through the fibres of the leaves and trees that watched over us through time. *The heart is a powerful thing.*

Ahead, in the distance, I saw a dark shape. It was a man, swathed in cloth, walking from the other side of the woods towards a coffin that lay directly between us. My own heart leapt. It beat wildly, like it hadn't beaten in years. With each step I took, I traversed a lifetime of pain, winding myself backwards in time to my original beloved like thread around a finger. When we reached the coffin, I stared at him. He was old now. Yet his face was somehow the same as it had always been. Only wilder and finally bearded, like an ancient myth of a man, at the same time human and savagely divine.

"No time for reunions," came John's voice. "Get in."

Janus smiled deeply at me, and John quickly lifted the lid of the coffin.

"I'll see you on the other side. In Italy," he said to me. "And I'll be with you. I'll be with you all the way."

He seemed solid and hopeful, just as he always had, his eyes dancing, always dancing. I felt *safe*. I put one foot and then the other into the open coffin. But when I lay down, something hard and solid met the small of my back. I leapt up in shock.

"What is it?" asked Janus.

I reached down and pulled out a leathery rectangular shape from inside the depths of the roughly made coffin. It was a copy of a Catholic Bible.

John took it, confused for a moment. Then all he said next was, "Run!"

We scattered in different directions. I ran until my feet were bruised, all the way across the forest. But at the break of dawn, I heard shots followed by arrows, as if all the technologies of war were after me in the same moment. Eventually, all I could see in front of me were small ignitions of fire that threw red light across the surfaces of the winter snow that lay around Cachtice, a promise of death, insubstantial, like a warning. I threw myself onto the ground to evade them. The noise stopped. The lights went out. I heard the crunch of snow underfoot. When I looked up, I saw only one thing: Basta. As if he had collapsed the entire landscape into his body. He was close. He lifted me up and held onto my forearms like a closed hunter's trap, unwilling to release no matter how hard I pulled against him. I was always pulling against the *Bastas* of this world. And they simply kept on coming. Throughout time. Across worlds.

"Ah, Countess. Did you not think I would find Stephen Ironhead one day? But what are you doing out of your castle? Searching out new prey, no doubt? I'm afraid all the women around here have fled."

I was returned by Basta to my tower. Each step back towards it was the colour and shape of death. The earth reached out its snow and mud claws to capture my feet when they made contact with it. The footprints I left – every one of them – were tiny internments. A hundred little destinies, lined up in the snow like fallen stars, all pointing now to the lightless tower.

"You are mine, Countess. You belong to me. I own you, body and soul. Rudolph is sick in bed. He will die soon. So, you no longer have what protection he afforded."

I simply looked ahead of myself, towards my destiny – the destiny I always knew was waiting for me. Cachtice, with all its strange light and racing skies.

"I'm curious, Countess," said Basta as we walked. "Rudolph could have killed you at any time. Any moment –" and he drew his free hand across his throat in lieu of finishing his sentence. "It would have been good for him to do it, too. He could have cancelled his debt long ago. So, again, Countess, why? You did not give him what you gave Georgio. And as for Nadasdy," he blew his cheeks out, "in honesty, we all thought you would be dead as soon as you produced an heir. What exactly did you do? This I am interested to know."

I said nothing. He had already taken everything from me. There were no threats, violences or terrors he could inflict on me that were any worse than what I had seen him do. It gave me a strange kind of power over him, as if I had turned the tables momentarily. He might rewrite my soul into his all the way across history, but he couldn't touch the real soul inside me – the soul I knew that somewhere in time, the girl in the wall was writing down through this spell called history. How I wished we could all find our own secret writers. Perhaps we could rewrite history entirely, and in that way and that way alone, we would change the world. We would change what lay inside our bones and so, what lay inside the body of the lived world.

Rudolph had wanted to understand *this*. My stories – the pages I covered in handwritten text about the future and how it was written by *us*, by we who lived *now* – these were the things Rudolph had kept me alive for. Not being able to use me as a source of power by which he might change his own rule, he kept me on as a scribe, as witness to what we were. All of us being fictioned in silence. Across time.

Basta replied to my silence *here, now* by simply nodding.

"Very well, Countess. Do not indulge me."

We reached Cachtice and, eventually, my tower. He led me all the way to my bed and sat me down on it like one might a child. Then he took a long look at me. The look surprised me. It wasn't a look of hate or rage, or even of victory. He was simply curious. That was all. Simply curious. He stood there for a while. Then he turned and called for the guard to bring some wood and nails. Cachtice was silent, except for the sound of a banging outside my door that sealed me shut inside.

*

At first, I panicked. But as morning rose, I set my chair by the window and counted the colours in the sky. There were so many! Each one fabricated its own expansive universe. When I concentrated my ear, I could hear the sky humming and buzzing along each one of them. They vibrated. When one layer of colour met with another, they blurred along each other's edges, both engaging in a playful construction of their borders, as if trying to build a house together awkwardly, along the boundaries of each other's lands. After about a week of listening in this way, I felt I had almost become sky. The light penetrated my tower room through the window casement. And I flew inside it.

The bread and water that was already up there when Basta nailed me into the room was long gone and I was delirious. I heard a commotion that brought me out of my prolonged reverie. I looked down to the courtyard. At first, the shapes of people were hard to distinguish. Everything was so heavy and fleshy, unlike the translucent, coloured light of the skies. But soon I recognised John. They had caught him and tied him up, and he was covered in a mixture of old and fresh blood. I could tell because the colour of his shirt was white wool mottled with dark browns and bright reds.

Pastor Magyery was questioning him.

"…And who… who ordered you to slaughter these women?" he shouted.

John looked up to my tower. I don't know if he saw me, but I hoped that he felt me. *Just confess what they want to hear,* I willed. *Tell them I am the killer they say I am. Save yourself from more pain.*

Something happened then that I couldn't hear. The pastor clapped his hands in delight, made the sign of the cross and produced something from his pocket. It was paper. John scribbled on it. Two men drove him to his knees. A huge man appeared behind him. He was all in black. When the blow came, it was heavy and final. A jet of blood bloomed, fountainous. Thurzo appeared then. He took the head of my John in one hand, holding it by the hair.

"The Countess' operation of terror has ended!" he shouted, and he jerked John's head upwards. Now he saw me. He looked directly up to my tower. For all my engagement with the light in the sky, I had become attuned to the movement of colour. I flung my head back in shock. The brown of John's dead eyes reached into me and buried me right there. I fell to the floor and pressed my palms and my face to the stone.

"My son is dead," I whispered into it. "My son is dead." Would that the tiny world inside the stones could hear me. It would understand that such a severance would annihilate anyone, breaking their atomic signatures until there was nothing left of them at all.

But Thurzo wasn't quite finished. A few days later, I awoke from sleep or reverie or parchedness – I could no longer tell which was which. The sound of the nails and wood being undone on the other side of the door was deafening to me. It was pushed open, and standing right there, in the very place that Nadasdy had once stood with wildflowers in his hand, was our son Paul. Master Imre stood behind him, one hand on his little shoulder, and Thurzo hovered behind, his face like that of an ancient ghost that longed to be present *everywhere*, at every intersection taking place across Hungary.

"Paul!" I bent down and threw my arms around him. But he recoiled.

"Here, here is the devil witch I told you about," said Master Imre.

"Mama?"

"Yes, my boy."

"Now tell me again what you told me you saw. Tell her."

"Mummy putting a girl in a box."

Thurzo spoke up. "That's enough for my ears."

"No, Paul, no! It's not like that."

"Mummy putting a girl in a box."

I shrieked to him from a place deep inside my belly as Master Imre took him away. It was from the same place I had birthed him, with all his kicking and turning and flailing limbs. But he was gone. Only Thurzo remained. He put some food and a bucketful of water on the ground. I threw myself to his feet and held onto his ankles. I kissed his shoes and begged him to at least let my son with Nadasdy know the truth. That no child should have both his parents turned into nothing more than the insubstantial shape of lies repeated over and over until no original trace remained.

Thurzo simply endured my protests.

"*I* was always your destiny, Elizabet. Always." He seemed to consider something, then looked back down at me.

"There's a part of me that thinks you only ever wanted to die. And yet, you've somehow outlived your entire household. I have it from the new emperor, Matthias, that you won't be put to death. You'll live out the rest of your days walled up in here. This tower, this castle, will be a beacon for hundreds of years. You will continue to inspire young women, Elizabet. But you will inspire them with nothing but terror."

I steadied myself at these words and went to the water bucket. Thurzo's cruelty always seemed to have the opposite effect that he desired on me. He was always sharpening my will. Perhaps that was our bond. Thurzo would always try to take more than was freely given, and I would always fight to stay alive. I took several long draughts of water, cupping my hands. I made him wait for my response. When I was refreshed, I turned around and rose to my full height.

"I'll tell you what I told the Emperor, '*boy*'." I used the word Basta had to remind him of the fact that even his power was limited, levelling him with my eyes. "You know nothing of the future. You're already dead."

I don't think it was the words that affected him. It wasn't that. It was something inside me that I suddenly realised he had always feared and that had grown strong from the first day I had met the girl from the future in the wall. From the moment Janus had taught me how to *travel*. He thought he would subdue it with sex. Then he thought he'd subdue it with power and death. But standing here right now, he realised that these things had all washed over me, like water drawn not from a well but from the depths of what it is to be human.

"You're bitter, George. You have little holding you together but the stitching in your jacket and years of compacted rivalries that have squashed you into your current shape." I exposed my neck to him, lifting my chin high. It was not seduction; it was acceptance. Not defeat. The very opposite of defeat. Victory inside a pointless defeat.

"You've taken everything you can from me. And still, you know deep inside yourself, inside the empty space in your chest, that I still possess *everything* I first came here with."

He gasped without wanting to, as if I had turned into a terrible tiger, out of place in this country and threatening to maul him. He took a step back and stumbled a little. Then he left. I never saw him again.

*

It seemed I had stayed alive in spite of everything that had happened to me. I had refused to die in the snow, and time had re-oriented itself continually around me. All the rage and violence in the world was not enough to drown me. It drowned in me, but it never consumed me. I remained larger than it. I had found the field of life, the endless wave-pattern that storied the shoreline into being. Sometimes, I wondered if I were sewn into with tiny, invisible magnets that kept inner darknesses at bay. Darknesses that continually broke across the borders of my life in the form of anger and beatings and rapes and druggings and tiny well-thought-out mental tortures enacted with such coldness and precision; all the rage of our species made flesh and bone.

But perhaps that's because Elizabet had taught me how to understand the power of stories and the inherent magnetism that lies inside each spoken tale. Not the stories that take you away from here, but stories that take you inside the here and now if you listen closely enough. If you listen *lovingly enough*. The stories of matter in all their dancing vibrations. Stories that help you to intervene in the endless displacement of violent realities enacted by humans; *now here, now then, now there*; cycling around with no place to go but across our planet over and over, flattening landscapes, raising others, sinking into oceans to be swallowed by fish and driven onto winds that are travelled on by birds.

Perhaps Bathory had written into my bones when she wrote to Rudolph of the future and what she had seen. Perhaps somewhere deep in the past, I was being rewritten into life. And, in turn, I knew that Elizabet had one more battle to fight before she found the inner home she had been circling since she had first left for Cachtice. I wrote it down. It was, in a way, the hardest battle of them all. It appeared to her in the shape of the Ottoman.

*

I was travelling on the deep, bruising rays of dusk. It was nothing like being a bird. It was like being the light itself. My fleshly body was vibrating ever so slightly. I could hear and taste the colours as they penetrated my skin, changing my hue and temperature from human to stellar. I felt that my bones, my hair, my muscles were light itself, compacted and sedimented into something that moved and breathed and felt pleasure and pain. Unlike light, however, I also felt what it was to love and mourn. At that moment, I came to know that this was what it was to be human. To be a mixture of flight and fall, eternal life and eternal death, circling across a horizon that *never stayed the same*. To be light and solid in the same second.

Thurzo had instructed the new servants to make my encasement in the tower more permanent. I had smelt the wet mud and stone as it was piled up on the outside of the door. When it was finished, they told me to simply open the door from the inside. I did. A little hatch had been placed in the new wall, as large as two handspans and no more than that, but long enough to pass a tray of food through. I was to use the bucket to shit in and simply throw it out of the window at will. If I hadn't known all my life how to fly on the light in the sky, to see the whole world and more in a few heartbeats, I would have surely gone mad. Then again, perhaps I had always been mad. Perhaps to be a *talto* is to have an intimate connection with the only kind of crazy that keeps you sane in this world.

When I wasn't revisiting the events of my life, travelling along the skeins of light that burst through the dying winter's clouds, or reading and rereading the books still in my room, I was trying to find a way back to Vera. There must be something I could do, anything, to unweave Rudolph's unwitting magic and bring her back to me. Something kept us apart. I feared it was like the angel had said, and that only death itself would bring us back together. But I also sensed that more had to be done first. Not just for me or for her, but for the angel that bound us. I chastised myself that it was pride alone to anticipate the needs and wants of the angelic. But something kept alight in the back of my mind across the days that soon turned winter to spring and back again. A thought like a candle flame that would not be blown out. It remained regardless of the passage of time across a body that had lost its freedom, begging the question: what more could possibly be done now?

I wasn't allowed ink or paper, but at the bottom of my wardrobe I found a long-dry bottle of John's bone-black. Over the course of a few days, I wetted it with the water they gave me for drinking and a little of my own blood to keep it thick. When I had enough useable ink, I tore a few pages of a spoiled, unfinished copy of Servetus that had been tossed in the cupboard after a botched print run. It had been rendered almost unreadable for all its smudges and stains and must have been lying there for a decade. From when Nadasdy and I had loved each other. I started to write in the margins. I wrote a letter – a note really – to our daughter. To Anna. A woman I hardly knew anymore, who had children of her own. Who had made herself safe in a life with her husband. A woman who had denounced her devil-mother, as any sane person would do under the circumstances of our times.

My dearest child. I know I have never been a mother to you, but you have always been a daughter to me. Please don't ask me to explain why that has been the case. There aren't words to describe it and I wouldn't burden you with any more history than you already have in you. I ask you to guard this letter until one day – one day when the world's soul is large enough to accept me. No small ask, I know!

There is only one place strong enough to withstand the violence of things. It's built to rotate us between the poles of good and evil and everything in between. It can be bruised and broken. It can be filled with fantasy and even sorrow. It can lead us all astray. It's the seat of all desire; the seat of all wonder; of all justice. Servetus knew it. The Ottomans knew it. There's not a book printed today that doesn't somewhere point to it, even if it remains absent from its pages, like the face of an angel, hidden, but alive, beating its wings inside the threads of the paper it's printed on.

I'm talking, my dear child, of the heart. If we want to survive on this earth, from generation to generation, if we want to save something of the human even though all our will seems bent towards our own erasure, it's this: the heart is the only doorway through which we might pass safely, from one place, from one time, to another. Every day, my daughter, every day make sure you pass, at least once, through this door. In the simplest acts, the smallest gestures. Pass through this doorway. It's the only way through.

In love, your mother

*

One morning in spring, I heard the customary rap on the hatch door and the whinge of the screws when it opened. A tray was passed through to me. I took it, but the hatch remained open. I bent down, a good distance away in case someone on the other side meant to do me harm with a sword or dagger. I saw a hazel and green-coloured eye. The eye retreated a pace or two back and then I saw its owner's face. Janus! He was still alive. He must not have been captured! He must have stayed away again all this time until it was safe to come back to me!

"Is it really you? After all this time…"

"Little Wing. My dear Little Wing." He reached his hand through the hatch, and I grabbed onto it. We stayed like that for a while, him holding my hand as if he held my entire body in his. I kissed his fingers and he mine. He was still as tender with me as he had been when we sat in the forest before my marriage to Nadasdy. He smiled and kissed them again, brushing the circles of my knuckles in little rounded caresses. Then we sat back on the floor on opposite sides of the hatch in the door and looked at each other through the rectangular opening it offered. Although age had weathered us both, he was still the same janissary that had saved me from the blacksmiths, taught me about the giants in the sky and the workings of the heart, how to sit with my legs folded underneath me and marvel every day at how the entire universe was only ever one breath away. He was still my Janus.

And in his presence, I became Little Wing again. Young and uncertain and full of curiosity for the world.

"How did you evade Basta's men?"

"You forget I'm a janissary. I simply climbed up a tall tree. When they were gone, I came down, ran, and climbed up another and then another. After several days, I reached the other side of the forest. The men had all gone. They thought I must have been taken by the cold. But I know how to keep warm in winter. I slow my breathing *right down*."

I laughed a little, although tears had come.

"You haven't changed. You still tell such stories to enchant me with."

He laughed too.

"Ah, Little Wing, why do you cry?"

It's impossible to express a lifetime of sorrow in one exhale. I rose and went over to the bedside table. I grabbed the letter I had written for my daughter and pressed it into his hands.

"Give this to my daughter. Find her and give it to her."

He nodded, spiriting it into his clothes.

"Where have you been these years – since the woods? Since John…" I couldn't finish my sentence.

"I returned to Erdely, but… Basta… Even the Sultan, it seems, cannot defeat him. Erdely is Catholic again. But some of Servetus still survives and will survive long into the future. You and John and Nadasdy made sure of that."

I shut my eyes as looking at him gave me the sensation of being crushed, but not from the outside in. From the inside out. I felt the weight of time inside my body. It left no atom untouched, unwritten, unmarked.

"Little Wing, don't cry. I'm not going anywhere. Only a Turk will serve you. All others fear to. I am that Turk. I will serve you here until the end."

The sound of his voice speaking still in my native tongue, as if I had returned home after all this time, was rich and warm and inviting. But it also stirred up something deep. Something I hadn't realised I had been carrying inside me for so long. A thought like a blade that had inched its way every day a tiny bit closer to the innermost part of my heart. It had been there all along, although I had only just become aware of it.

I opened my eyes. This time, I looked at him differently. He noticed instantly and drew grave.

"You left me. You left me to suffer it all. You could have taken me away from *all of it*. You could have saved me from being Bathory. How could you leave me that day at the smithy? How could you leave me knowing everything that had happened and everything that was waiting for me?" My voice had become loud. It scratched its way through the hatch towards his ear. But he didn't flinch. He simply listened.

"How could you *betray* me like that?"

*

When no one ever comes, when you realise there's no rescue and there never will be, there's only one thing to do, and that's to go inside the deep currents of yourself. It's only there that you can start to unravel all the stories about justice that the human world has been telling us to keep its borders safe. Safe from the dangerous uncertainty that has always been threaded through cause and effect. Justice is intimate. It is a lover that never leaves you, just as time never leaves the body but is constantly engaged in turning it into something else. Certain justice is all about power and measurement. How many bodies went to the gallows? How many cells filled with prisoners? How many fines were paid this week? And other games you can play with numbers. Uncertain justice is about love. Because how much justice is *just enough*?

I knew I would never be able to meet my killer. And so, I would never be able to exact justice. And it would be unlikely that I would be able to meet again those who had brutalised my body even before my first death. But I didn't succumb to the thought that *this is just the way the world works.* You don't have to have suffered these things to know what the world expects of you, how the world marks you into being. We know this because we still instinctively move to protect our daughters from the world more than we protect our sons. Be free, be bold, but don't go out into the street at dusk. Meanwhile, our younger brothers go out and play and come back late without explanation. The same fear isn't drummed into them. They have the reverse problem. They need to '*be a man*' about it all.

It would be too easy to say that I met my first death because nobody was there to stop it. Just as it would be too easy to say that it happened because that's the world – cruel and bitter and full of darkness. When death comes and you get to travel, even for a moment, along the borders of life and death, it muddles cause and effect. The world becomes *expanded*. Its frames no longer capture things in the same way. So, when I returned from death unexpectedly, confused and bleeding and uncertain how I had come to be upright, sitting at the base of the apartment block built to house outsiders – the poor, refugees, and anyone whose skin and hair was darker than the rest – I had trouble at first adjusting to the light.

It wasn't just because the light on the snow was so bright and powerful. It wasn't just because time had passed without me in it for a moment and the sky had turned from broad daylight to murky dusk with no colours in between. It wasn't because the in-between world had been so bright, or so dark, or both at the same time. It was because my eyes had looked on the expanded universe for a moment. I kept silent about what I had seen in death, until I wrote. Until I learnt to fold death into love inside all the stories.

*

My first memory takes place before any of the childhood intrusions threatened to stop my little life. Strangely, it's one I never revisited when I was falling through time. And so, I often wondered if it existed outside of my own timeline entirely. As if it never really happened in this world at all. There I am, aged three in the summer. The English countryside is so delicate and warm. I stare down and see a deliciously glistening stream at my feet. I dip my toes in – one foot, then the other. I giggle. A shining woman rises out of the water. The droplets that she shakes off her glitter, making her *for all the world* like an incredible fish. Pearl and silver and full of secrets. Her eyes are green and hazel, and I feel like I've seen these eyes before, a long, long time ago, in another life, sparkling like fallen stars. Astral. I turn to my parents. "Mummy, Daddy, look at the woman!" They absent-mindedly smile. They're not happy. I know this. I already feel older than them, as if my soul's eyes, knowing what is to come, have become accustomed to *writing out* their thoughts in the air around them both, in a language that only I understand with my child's mind.

I turn back. The woman walks across the water *as the water*. The waves move and shiver her into being, but her body reminds me of the warm white blankets in my cot in all its iridescent flowing. She plants a kiss on my forehead. The kiss is cold, a marker, a placeholder for another time when I will need to wake up and see the world – the world that *she* comes from. For the moment in time that I will die and choose to come back from death. So I will not be frightened when the river of blood from out of my body flows red, when I float up to meet another of her kind, the Angel of Death that is also me – me at the end and beginning of time.

I know instantly that it's her who, beneath the falling stars of heaven, imagines the ship-bearing seas into form; imagines the earth full of life even as she becomes the fruit of life itself, desiring nothing but our lips upon her body, giving all life;

giving each atom the power of nothing less than the sun. She is Venus. An angel. The Angel of Life.

All these floating gods. All these bright angels. All these lights in the sky. All these human and nonhuman ways of being in the world. Listen! Look!

I write it down as my computer glows brightly in the dark.

When the man screams at me, therefore, in the falling snow, *Go home! Raus! Raus!* his fists beating and boots kicking, I know that there's only one kind of justice that can undo this, and all the wrongs done to me even before this seductive pull towards death; even at this age, even as a child. It's the justice that exists in the expanded horizon, permeating all things, thoughts, and flesh.

How can locking up a childkiller, killing a childkiller, a rapist, a murderer or a demon-made-flesh ever deliver the kind of righting such a wrong requires – the wrongness of our species? And so, I went within. I went to the photons and electrons and all the gravitational matter that condenses and makes us human. I didn't seek justice from the outside world. I sought justice from the tiny world. In the space that sits right next to love and sometimes reaches over its tiny hand, so tentative and shy, to touch something much, much larger than the world we think we know.

*

"How could you *betray* me like that?" It hung in the air and punctured the space around us like a lung, killing our relationship until neither of us could breathe. His green and hazel eyes clouded for a moment.

"You could have stopped it all. You could have saved me. I was no more than a child. I was a young girl, full of fear and hope and all the little things that make us human. All you needed to do was turn around. Why didn't you turn around? Why didn't you rescue me from my life? Answer me!"

He had shut his eyes now and it enraged me, halting my access to the river of him.

"Open your eyes!" I commanded. It came from a place deep in the other world. A place that could no longer be reached, a ghost that longs to unite with its living beloved but remains trapped, forever, on the other side of a window that separates life and death. He didn't. And I told him that by not doing so, he was only failing me all over again.

But after a pause he did speak. He opened his eyes, and they were shining, starlike again. He stared into me, as if he were climbing down into my heart. I was enamoured and at the same time I felt an unexpected sharp sensation come through the hatch. But perhaps I had expected it all along. When it reached its destination, I gasped. But I was unafraid, even as the blood pooled on the stones below me.

"Here, Little Wing. I've given you traces all along but look now at the world around you. This is the beginning and the end."

I returned instantly to the tiny world. But this time there was no Angel of Death or girl in the wall. A huge black cavern opened up. Its jaws were made of rubies and sapphires and all around its edgeless perimeter, I could make out four gateways. Each gateway held smaller entrances inside it. They flashed around each other fast enough for me to realise that they were in effect all the same entrance displaced, forming at different points, not in time, but in something deeper than time or space. They were points that made up *life*, scattering it across the universe. They were the ascending and descending shades of reality that pull us all in and out of our own wise flesh.

Here I am, I thought. *I'm inside the mouth of one of Janus' giants in the sky.* I started falling and rushing as the giant swallowed me down. I was no smaller than a seed, a tiny point of light that would *appear* to go out, but instead of extinguishing, would throw itself across infinite planes of thought made matter.

I saw the girl sitting in her room with her lamp glowing strong. She wrote me down. The words on the surface of her square sun stormed across its own perimeter. I became the black and white flash that she made of me as her fingers raced. And I came to life again there and then. She *saw* me – not my body. Not like it had been at Rudolph's court. She saw me inside her words, inside her *bones*. In the same moment, I looked through the hatch to Janus. He smiled at me.

"I see," I said. "I understand." Then I smiled too, disappearing into the mirror of his eyes and he into mine as we both let a few tears fall. The tears merged together, right in between the two sides of the little hatch. The light was falling more powerfully than I had ever seen it at Cachtice.

"I did it," I said to Janus.

"Yes, Little Wing. You did. You did it." I looked down, but I was far away from the red that stained the floor in all its inevitability.

I turned my attention back to the girl across time.

"Come," I said, taking her by the hand in our in-between world. "Come. Finish the text. Unwrite it all. Then let's go. Let's go back to the field that made us."

I finish my sentence. I turn to her. We're back in the in-between world, with our angel.

"Come, Little Wing," she says. "Come, and be at peace."

We take hands, all three of us, rotating like a singular snowflake inside the fall that drags us up and down to eternal elsewheres.

Somewhere in time, a little girl wearing a snowsuit that's covered in blood smiles, shivers and breathes in all the beauty of the world,

for

one

    last

time.